About the Author

David Cliffe is a retired journalist who spent nearly five decades working on newspapers, magazines and public relations.

Born in North Staffordshire, he has a strong bond with Leek and the Moorlands, having lived in the town for many years. He is a former editor of several newspapers and magazines, including the *Leek Post & Times*. A local history enthusiast, David has a particular interest in Victorian and Edwardian photography.

The Buried Secret is his first work of fiction.

Also by David Cliffe

Fiction
Images of Revenge: Old Leek Mystery N°2
Tragedy strikes when a travelling theatre comes to Leek

Non-fiction
A Moorland Album: Leek, Cheadle and neighbouring villages in Edwardian times from the photographs of W.H. Nithsdale

Victorian Views: Leek & District's first photographers

For more information or to purchase any of the above titles email moorlandalbum@gmail.com

THE BURIED SECRET

DAVID CLIFFE

A TALE OF DEATH, DECEIT & DETECTION IN EDWARDIAN LEEK

First published November 2021

Copyright © David Cliffe, 2021

David Cliffe has asserted his right under the Copyright, Designs and Patents Act 1988 to be identified as author of this work.

All rights reserved. No part of this publication may be reproduced or transmitted in any form or by any means, electronic or mechanical, including photocopy, recording or any information storage and retrieval system, without permission from the author.

This book is a work of fiction. Names, characters, businesses, organisations, places and events are either the product of the author's imagination or are used fictitiously. Any resemblance to actual persons living or dead, events or locales is entirely coincidental.

ISBN 978-1-80068-318-1

Typeset and designed by David Cliffe, Leek, Staffs.
moorlandalbum@gmail.com

Published by Independent Publishing Network

Printed in the UK by Printondemand-Worldwide, Peterborough

A Word of Thanks

This book would not have been possible without encouragement and advice from my wife Delia and my friend David Butler.

David Cliffe, Leek, November 2021

CHAPTER ONE

October 1902

He clung ever-tighter to the handlebars, struggling to remain upright as wind and rain tore into him across the moor and his tyres fought for grip on the rough limestone of the lane.

Calf muscles burned with the effort, arms ached from wrestling the bicycle's fearful jolting as it bounced over unseen stones. His shirt was soaked and his sodden tweed trousers were heavier by the minute. But Nathaniel Blake kept his feet turning, standing out of the saddle to urge the hefty machine up each new incline. On each downward slope he clung on and kept pedalling, gaining momentum to help him climb the next rise. Then he was out of the saddle again, straining to turn the pedals once more.

Darkness was creeping across this bleak stretch of Staffordshire moorland as he made his hasty retreat from Flash, the hamlet that sat at the highest point on the road from the market town of Leek to Buxton, a route mapped by the Romans nearly two millennia before. Once away from the village, Blake was fully exposed to the elements, battered by a fierce wind coming from the east, flecked with ice-cold rain.

But neither the declining light, the weather nor the state of the road would slow his head-long dash for the safety of home. Blake paused in the shelter of an abandoned tollhouse. He fished his Vesta matches tin from a waistcoat pocket and, with trembling fingers, managed to light his paraffin lamp. The gleaming Lucas Silver King lamp had looked so impressive on the front of his bicycle, but in these conditions it was nigh-on useless, its faint glow giving little clue to the hazards ahead.

Though Flash was notorious for being fog-bound at almost any time of the year, this evening was mercifully free of mist. But the wind that whipped the fog away brought the rain clouds on at greater pace. Blake peered down the limestone-covered road as it snaked towards Leek, ten miles away. Although he was familiar with the road and its challenging contours, he also knew that a pothole, a wandering badger, or a stray ragged-fleeced sheep could spell disaster for a cyclist alone on a night like this.

His spectacles were rendered useless with rain and mud; his feet slipped on the rubber pedals; his fingers froze around the handlebar grips. How he wished he'd brought his cycle gauntlets. And not lost his jacket.

In the gloom Blake could sometimes make out an oil lamp glinting dimly in a farmhouse window, the ghostly shapes of sheep huddled for shelter beside stone walls, and roadside piles of limestone awaiting the road-mender. He screwed up his eyes, trying to see ahead, occasionally checking over his shoulder to see if he was still being followed. He prayed not.

After two, perhaps three more miles of open, wind-blasted moor – it seemed much further compared to the spring days when he'd ventured here before – he came upon the Royal Cottage. The rough-looking inn claimed to have offered respite to Bonnie Prince Charlie on his march into Derbyshire in 1745. Should he also choose its shelter? Smoke was being blown horizontally from its chimney top, so the fire in the tiny bar room must be lit. He could stop and revive himself with a jug-poured pint. It was tempting, but he dared not rest. He kept the pedals turning.

At last the road levelled off a little before it plunged from the edge of this bare granite plateau to the rolling farmland below. To Blake's right reared the silhouette of Ramshaw Rocks, blacker than the night itself. A heather-clad haven for ramblers on a fine day, it was a menacing and jagged ridge on a night such as this. Blake had no time to think about the rocks tonight though, his mind was on what lay ahead: descent of Cat Tor, the steepest hill in these parts. A leg breaker when cycling up, a heart stopper when hurtling down. He cursed not having a rear brake – the front one was of little use on the greasy rim and barely slowed his descent. He hung on grimly, trying to keep a steady course despite his increasing speed.

And then a bad night got worse. The front wheel jarred and twisted in an unseen pothole, the handlebars were wrenched from his grip and Blake was pitched off. Catapulted into a clump of sodden grass, he sprawled on the ground, the breath knocked out of him. After gently checking he could still move his limbs, his face showed renewed consternation. Struggling to his feet, he leaned over the stricken bicycle and wrestled open the straps of a boxy, leather case slung on the handlebars. Groping blindly, his fingers ran over the contraption strapped within, a compact folding camera he had bought only a month before.

"Thank goodness I chose new celluloid film instead of glass slides," he thought. The photographs he had taken in Flash were not his usual landscapes – they could turn out to be far more valuable and it was vital they survived this journey.

Blake stood motionless and listened for the sound of a horse approaching from the direction he'd come. He could hear nothing except the wind as it whipped through sparse trees and the distant banging of a barn door. He found no damage to the bicycle, except a permanently extinguished lamp, but decided to walk the remainder of Cat Tor's fierce slope. At the foot of the hill, he gingerly got back on the saddle, forcing his squelching leather boots to turn the pedals once more, and resumed the remaining four miles into Leek. Away from the high moors, the wind subsided, but it was still slow progress. At Solomon's Hollow, a deep cleft cut by a rushing stream a mile from town, he dismounted again and trudged through the dark until the road was less challenging for his aching legs.

The best part of two hours after fleeing Flash he reached home, a substantial three-storey terraced house not far from the centre of Leek. A gas lamp gave a pool of yellowish light along the street. Leaning his bicycle against the front wall, he closed trembling fingers on the brass doorknocker to summon the warmth, comfort and safety of his family. The door was snatched open and Edith Blake stood with hands on hips, inspecting her husband from head to muddy toe.

"Heavens Blake, where on earth have you been until now? You're soaking wet – where's your jacket? Your trousers are ripped! And are your spectacles bent?" She called him 'Blake' when she was annoyed and he had feared this reception. He often put work before his wife and family, but in recent weeks, he had been more preoccupied than ever.

"Needless to say, your supper has gone cold, and William and little Emily have gone to bed without seeing their father – yet again," Edith continued. "Oh, be careful with your filthy boots!" she protested as he barged through the door, clinging to his camera case.

Entering the tiled hallway, Blake knew now was not the time to explain what had gone on since he'd left the house after luncheon. "Edith dear, I'm sorry. It's a long story. Just get me a cup of tea, will you?" was all he could manage as he slipped off his boots and slumped into an armchair in front of the fire in the parlour. Weary from the adventures of the afternoon and his rain-lashed ride home, he gazed into the glowing coals.

"A long story, certainly, and how the hell did I get into it?" he thought.

Chapter Two

Four weeks earlier

"Are you sure this the right place?" Fifteen-year-old Cora, eldest child of the Blake family and assistant to photographer Nathaniel Blake, was standing in a field of buttercups, setting up the camera tripod.

Blake had established himself as a photographic artist when he moved to the mill town of Leek ten years earlier, relying largely on portraits of the local well-to-do. Now he felt at the dawn of a new era, a new century had begun and their new king, Edward VII, had been crowned. Blake had decided to pour his enthusiasm into recording the places, the people and events of this district on the Staffordshire edge of the Peak. The new craze for picture postcards was a chance for him to make some money, too.

Like most of her friends, Cora had started work at an early age and had helped her father to develop, print and frame his photographs for three years now. She channelled her artistic inclinations into the curls and swirls she drew on the borders some of the photographs and postcards. Secretly, she looked forward to the day when she would take charge of the camera herself and become Leek's first lady photographer – she had watched her father so many times she knew exactly what to do.

Slightly built and with her hair pulled into a ponytail, Cora looked probably younger than her years. But she had a serious manner and spent long hours reading in her bedroom. Blake could see some of his own traits in the girl, she was confident and inquisitive. She was shaping up to be a useful assistant, he thought with satisfaction.

Admittedly, the strong-willed Cora could be a little wearisome. She had been eight when Blake married her widowed mother, and the girl had not developed the sort of unquestioning obedience he had hoped for. As Cora grew older, it became clear she was prepared to take nothing at face value, be it his advice on her choice of reading, or her mother's views on young ladies wearing leggings astride a bicycle. But father and daughter worked well together – as long as she remembered who was in charge. Both Blake and his wife Edith were pleased Cora had agreed to attend occasional days at Miss Keates' Academy for Young Ladies, an old-fashioned dame school which was not quite as grand as its name suggested.

Cora naturally had something to say when the two of them had set out from the studio that Tuesday afternoon in the middle of August. "*How* far?" was her reaction when Blake told her she would need to carry the tripod for half an hour. "Are you sure we can't hire a trap? The carter's only around the corner and it will save us so much time."

But Blake's mind was made up. "No question of a trap. It would cost us three shillings at least. And it's such a beautiful afternoon. Think of it as a stroll into the country, not work. Come on, you will enjoy it."

Cora grudgingly agreed and the two of them had set off, the photographer carrying his gleaming hardwood and brass

Sanderson camera and a leather holdall containing the wooden frames which held his glass photographic plates. Cora took up the canvas bag of the wooden tripod, hauling it first on one arm, then the other. They lugged the equipment through cobbled streets lined with the terraced homes of workers in the town's silk mills. The sound of a child crying or a dog barking could be heard from the narrow passageways which led from the streets into cramped courtyards where many of the two-up two-down houses were to be found.

When they reached Abbey Green on the edge of town they were suddenly in the countryside, the River Churnet flowing lazily through lush fields. The moors and the rocky skyline known as the Roaches rose up grey-green in the distance. Huge trees swayed in the gentle breeze. Oak, beech and spruce had been planted in this valley centuries ago, bordering the river and either side of a straight track that led from the lane. Wood pigeons cooed amongst the branches. A peaceful setting, but it was not the rural idyll that had drawn Nathaniel Blake here that day. It was the ruins beside the track, the remains of an historic abbey.

Seven centuries earlier, a devout nobleman had chosen this place to found Dieulacres – its ancient name pronounced 'Dew-la-cress' – when he returned from the Third Crusade. The Cistercian monks who settled here led a simple life, but the Abbey's landholdings yielded great wealth. There were farms stretching for miles from the valley bottom to the rocky edge of the moors, water mills powered by the River Churnet, rents from numerous properties in the town itself and a salt mine over the border in Cheshire. The monks had even straightened the course of the river to relieve flooding and dug ponds for a reliable supply of fish for their refectory.

The estate provided sustenance for the monks and their many workers, and income to create an imposing complex of buildings and, according to local legend, furnish it with the finest artefacts.

But three centuries of peace and prosperity had come to a dramatic end when Henry VIII declared himself head of the English Church and set in train the Dissolution of monasteries, their wealth seized, their property dispersed. One October morning in 1538, labourers arrived to reduce Dieulacres to rubble.

The ruins still bore witness to that medieval splendour. Though the Abbey's roof had been ripped off and most of the walls demolished, the magnificence of its chancel was echoed in the remains of soaring gothic windows, their skeletal inner arches etching a tracery of stone against the sky. A procession of fluted columns, once massive, were now a fraction of their original height and covered in lichen. Grass grew where monks had walked on marble tiles to their prayers. In the distance, a footbridge made from three massive stone slabs, crossed the river marking the monks' ancient route into the town and the parish church on the top of the hill.

Visions of the ancient religious life came to Blake as he contemplated a jumbled collection of stone blocks, some carved, some elegantly curved. His reverie was interrupted as Cora brought him back to the job in hand. "Are you sure that these stones are worth photographing? I know that it's historic, but will anyone really want a picture of a ruin, and particularly such a ruinous one," she shouted across the field. He had given her the job of erecting the tripod and attaching the camera while he paced the site, checking light and shade, gauging the angle for his next artistic achievement.

"It isn't just the stones, my dear, it's what they represent." Blake struggled to sound patient. "Local folk have passed down stories about this place for generations. Just think of the history, the things that happened where we're standing."

Yes, history right here, he thought. Legend told of the cruelty by the monks in ancient times, equally harsh punishment of the

Cistercians during the Dissolution and hauntings amongst the Abbey ruins since. A headless skeleton had been dug up a year or two before. "Best not to mention that now," he thought.

"I've read that many of the monks lived off the fat of the land in those days." Cora barely took a breath. "Rich folk should share out their good fortune, don't you think? Look at those poor boys and girls who queue for the free stew in the Market Hall."

Why did Cora have so many opinions, Blake wondered as he walked across the field to where she stood beside the camera on its tripod. He decided to change the subject. "Let's see how the view looks from here," he said, slipping his spectacles on to the top of his head and ducking under the camera's black cloth hood. He checked the image on the ground glass screen at the back of the camera. It was never as sharp as the final photograph would be and, of course, it was upside down. But like many photographers, Blake considered that viewing an inverted image helped him concentrate on the picture's composition.

Muttering to himself, he sharpened the focus by adjusting the leather cloth bellows behind the lens. "No, that's not quite right," he said, "let's move a few feet so we can see more of that beautiful tree next to the stones."

Cora knew this was when her father gave way to his creative side and so she made no comment, simply stepping forward to help move the camera to a new position. The tripod legs adjusted for the sloping field, Blake once more began his squinting and humming, compressing the bellows a little and tightening brass knobs until he was completely satisfied. He knew from bitter experience that once the shutter was pressed it was too late to change anything.

Satisfied with the composition, Blake's hands moved with the deftness of a conjurer in a routine he had done a thousand times. Removing the focusing screen, he reached into the leather case by his feet to select a slim wooden frame which held two delicate glass plates. He slotted the frame into the camera, pulled out a panel to expose the plate and finally pressed the shutter. He wouldn't know the result until the negative was developed and the image printed onto paper. He extracted the plate-holder, flipped it over and re-inserted it before exposing the second plate. He then decided to try a different angle.

Cora had been gazing out across the riverside meadows – she could appreciate the beauty of this place, but wouldn't admit that to her father just yet. She helped to move the equipment so that the adjusting and focusing, the slotting and sliding could begin all over again. Two more exposures and they moved again, this time closer to the crumbling stonework.

But the next photograph was never taken. Blake was loading fresh glass plates into the camera when a scream pierced the afternoon peace.

"What was that?" cried Cora, visibly flinching and looking for danger one way and then another. Blake didn't have time to answer before the screams resumed, now more of a high pitched wail. As Blake stared across the field he spotted, to the right of the ruins, a grey-haired woman in a dirty white apron, running toward them with her arms raised.

"Help! Someone help me. It's my Amos. He's dead!" the woman shouted.

Blake dashed in her direction and, as they met near the stone columns, he was forced to grab the woman as she pitched forward in her panic.

"Dear lady, calm yourself. Whatever's going on?" he said.

"Amos. He's dead. Murdered," she groaned, clearly about to faint. She looked to be perhaps in her fifties, but the hard life of a farmer's wife meant she could be ten years younger. Judging by the blood on her apron, she had been in the middle of some farm chore, perhaps a newly-slaughtered chicken, he thought.

Cora caught up with them and looked uncertainly at the

groaning woman, clearly at a loss what to do. Blake glanced across to where the woman had come from, a low farmstead on the far side of the Abbey ruins.

"Cora, you stay here with this good lady while I go to look what's happened. It must be an accident," he said.

Cora nodded and put her arm round the woman's shoulders while her father walked purposefully towards the farm buildings. As he drew close he could see the farmhouse was built of stone, much of it expertly carved and crafted, doubtless scavenged from the abbey ruins generations ago. Even the arched entrance to the barn, standing across a rough yard, was decorated with what looked like the head of a saint, lovingly sculpted to adorn a more holy place than this.

Ignoring an old sheepdog that crouched growling beside the farmyard wall, Blake made straight for the farmhouse door which was wide open. He steeled himself against what he might find. A glance around the kitchen, lit by two small windows, revealed no one. "Hello, anyone there?" he called as he ventured further inside to inspect the tiny bedroom beyond. Still no sign of either the farmer or the trouble that had caused his wife to flee.

Returning outside, Blake stepped carefully across the muddy yard and approached the barn, its doors ajar. As his eyes adjusted to the shadowy interior he could make out the shape of a scarecrow which, surprisingly, stood in the middle of the straw-strewn space.

"What on earth's going on here?" he breathed, as he took a step further into the building. Puzzlement turned to stomach-churning horror when he realised that the 'scarecrow' was in fact the body of a man, bound by his arms to the rough timbers of a cattle stall. The man's head sagged, his face and head a battered and bloodied mess. His shirt ripped open to reveal slashes that had seeped blood down his breeches. There was no doubt he was dead.

Blake's mind whirled and his heart pounded as he took a step towards the lifeless figure. Then, hearing the woman's moans moving closer, he spun round and went back outside to see the distraught wife leaning heavily on Cora, the two of them about the enter the farmyard. Cora's dress was now streaked with mud – no it wasn't mud, he realised, but blood from the woman's apron. The farmer's blood.

"Cora, don't come any closer. Take this lady into the farmhouse and sit her down. If there's a kettle handy put it on the stove. And then I want you to go straight back to town," he said.

Cora looked towards the barn, obviously fearful what may confront her there. "What's happened father?" she asked, her voice wavering. "The lady says her husband's been murdered ..."

Blake cut her off, not wanting to go into details with the girl. "It looks like the farmer has been attacked. He's certainly dead. I want you to go home, but on the way I need you to call at the police station in Leonard Street and tell them to send someone down here straight away. I'm going to stay to see if I can help."

"What about the camera?"

"That's the least of our worries at the moment, my dear."

Inspector Albert Ramm was lifting his afternoon mug of tea to his lips, satisfied that his desk was neat and tidy and wondering if today, being a Tuesday, there would be meat and potato pie for supper. Like himself, Mrs Ramm kept to her routines. He took a swig, wiping the back of his hand across his luxuriant greying moustache. His equanimity was disturbed when Constable Knowles dashed down the corridor from the front desk and straight into the Inspector's office, without even his usual hesitant tap on the door.

"Sir. Young lady out front. Says there's been an accident at Abbey Green and we must go down right away," said Knowles, somewhat excited at the prospect of a reprieve from an afternoon of unbroken bookkeeping.

Though Leek was no bustling metropolis, its regular crop of market town misdemeanours were enough to warrant a force of eight officers headed by Ramm, who saw his elevation to the rank of inspector as the reward for years of dogged service. The town constabulary had recently relocated to an impressive new station, a source of pride for his officers on their daily foot patrols of the town. Admittedly, most of the incidents they had to deal with were either alcoholic – Leek was famed for the sheer number of its inns and alehouses – or agricultural – the local farming community was never short of neighbour disputes or missing livestock. Colleagues knew that Inspector Ramm was a stickler for paperwork, hence his rise through the ranks, they believed, rather than a talent for detection. This meant that Tuesdays in particular were a time for the checking, cross-referring and, if necessary, rewriting of notebooks in preparation for the town's weekly Magistrates Court the following day. Constable Knowles, whose handwriting was amongst the best in the station, was given much of the paperwork.

"Steady on Knowles. Let's see what this is about. Bring the young lady in." Ramm was a little less happy than Knowles to have his afternoon disturbed.

"And you are?" asked Ramm as Cora, looking more uncertain of herself than usual, was ushered in.

"Cora Blake. But that's not the thing. Something terrible has happened and the farmer's dead. You must go."

"And your address Miss Blake?" continued Ramm, taking up a pencil, apparently intent on proper procedure.

"What's that got to do with it?," she blurted out. "Oh, very well, 6 Moorside Terrace. My father's the photographer, and we were down at the Abbey ruins when a lady came out of the farm shouting about a murder or something," she went on, gaining in confidence. She stared at Ramm impatiently. "It's terribly urgent."

Ramm was suddenly alert. His back stiffened as he looked at the young woman with a stain down the front of her grey dress. He rose to his feet and made for the door, speaking as he did so. "Young lady, I will need to take a full statement from you in due course. Knowles! Get your helmet, we're going down to Abbey Green. You use the station bicycle and fetch mine from the shed. And don't forget your notebook."

Cora, left alone in the office, looked at the Inspector's empty chair for a few seconds, trying to calm herself, after the shock at the Abbey ruins, her breathless dash back to the town, and her first ever visit to a police station. Her eyes dropped to her lap and the blood now drying on her dress. She steeled herself, determined not to burst into tears before she reached home.

Blake sat opposite the distraught wife in the farmhouse. He had brewed tea in a dark brown pot, busying himself because he didn't want to face what was in the barn. The woman, whom he now knew to be Rosa Carter, sat beside the scrubbed kitchen table as she told him more of her horrific discovery.

"I was worried where Amos was. After his dinner he'd gone out to see to summat in the barn and I went down the meadow because the sheep been wanderin'," said Rosa, her voice barely above a whisper. "It took a bit longer than I expected and when I come back about an 'our later he was nowhere about. I left it a bit longer, then thought I'd better go and see where he was. I went to th' barn, and there, and there was Amos. I tried lifting him up, but it was no good..." Her story trailed off as she began to cry again.

Blake didn't know if he should go back out to the barn. Surely there was something he could do for the poor man, give him some dignity? But should he touch anything before the police arrived? Was the culprit still out in the fields somewhere? Should he have sent Cora out on her own?

The sound of bicycle tyres crunching along the track interrupted his thoughts. He went outside to find the burly, immaculately uniformed policeman he knew to be Inspector Ramm placing his bike against the farm wall. He was accompanied by a younger officer whose tense eyes were darting about the farmyard.

"Mr Blake, what's to do?" asked Ramm brusquely.

"It's the farmer, Amos Carter I believe his name is, he's in the barn. Dead. It's a fearful sight, I'm afraid."

"And the wife?"

"In the house. She found him. She's in a terrible state."

"Knowles, you go to Mrs Carter," ordered Ramm. "I'll see what we have in the barn. Mr Blake, will you come with me?" The photographer wondered if the policeman actually needed his assistance or just wanted to keep an eye on him until he was sure what had happened.

Ramm led the way into the shadowy barn and, as Blake had done earlier, took a moment to become accustomed to the gloom and take in the scene before him. "Good Lord, this is a grim business," he said, approaching the body. He gently put his finger under the dead man's chin to raise his head. Blake, hanging back, forced himself to follow the policeman's gaze as he looked into the man's battered face and then inspected Amos Carter's body, pulling the ripped shirt open to take a better look at his wounds.

"Looks like he's been in a hell of scrap – or something worse. He obviously made an enemy of someone," said Ramm, taking a deep sigh and opening his hands slightly, almost in exasperation. Turning to Blake he said: "Amos Carter was a good, God-fearing man. I've never known him to be in any trouble. You found him like this? Did you see anyone else?"

"We knew nothing until we heard Mrs Carter scream. I came in here and found him."

Apart from a hen scratching in the straw, there was silence in the barn as Blake and the Inspector, both deep in thought, contemplated Amos Carter. Though hardened from his years in the force, Ramm never ceased to be appalled by human capacity for cruelty, and this was as cruel as it got. He suspected that this was going to be a challenging affair to sort out.

The policeman resumed a business-like air. "Right, we must get to the bottom of this. Mr Blake, I will need to question Mrs Carter now and send for colleagues to help to move the body. In due course, I will require a full statement from yourself about what you were doing here and how you became involved this afternoon. For now though, you can go back to town and leave us to our work."

Then Ramm checked himself as if struck by an idea. "I take it that is your camera and such stuff out in the field?" he asked, tentatively. "Perhaps you could assist us by taking a photograph of what we have here in the barn? I know it is a little outside your usual field of work, should we say, but it may be useful for our investigation at some point."

Blake took a moment to reply as he pulled himself together. He was still sickened by his encounter with the corpse, but felt he now had a responsibility to the Carters to help clear up this hateful crime in which he'd unwittingly become involved.

"I'll fetch my camera and do my best, inspector. If the photograph's successful, I will bring a print round to the station first thing in the morning," he said. He was almost relieved to return to the familiar territory of work.

"Good. Thank you. We shall talk in the morning. Perhaps nine o'clock at the station?" And with that Ramm turned swiftly towards the farmhouse.

Blake carried his equipment to the barn, avoiding looking at the body too closely. He opened the barn doors wide to allow the slanting rays of the sun to penetrate the gloom and cast a golden glow over the interior. If it had not been for Amos Carter's body, it could have been a study in pastoral peace. As he went through his usual routines, hands moving automatically, he thought how a man could have been beaten to death while he and Cora were innocently photographing the Abbey ruins. Blake had always been squeamish about death – he could never bring himself to do the posed portraits of deceased relatives that had once been in fashion – so he steeled himself to concentrate on his task.

In the camera's inverted image, the dead man's position appeared even more grotesque, but Blake pressed on. He exposed two plates which he resolved to develop that evening. When he had finished, he glanced across the farmyard. Through the open door of the farmhouse he saw Mrs Carter, sitting straight-backed with her hands in her lap, speaking haltingly under the steady gaze of Inspector Ramm. Constable Knowles, with pencil and dog-eared notebook, was painstakingly recording all that she said.

The spring that had been in Blake's step when he and Cora had set out for Dieulacres Abbey had disappeared as he trudged along the track through the ruins, weighed down not only by his equipment, but by the experiences of the last two hours.

Joining the lane towards to town, his gaze was fixed on the distance, his mind flitting between the horrific scene in the barn, the woman's distress and Cora's shock. He didn't notice an unkempt figure lying in the long grass on the opposite side of the lane, leaning against a knapsack, alert eyes that watched the comings and goings at the tragic farm.

Chapter Three

Nathaniel Blake dropped off his camera and tripod at the studio and hurried home to find out how Cora was.

Edith, balancing infant Emily on her hip, met him in the hallway and was obviously agitated. She glanced up the staircase as she spoke. "Cora came home, started crying as soon as she was through the front door and then ran up to her room. She slammed the door and, when I went up, she told me to leave her alone." She searched her husband's face for an explanation. "What's going on? Have you two been arguing?"

"Edith it's far worse than that. Cora has had a terrible shock, in fact we both have. I'll tell you about it in a moment, but first I must see how she is."

Upstairs Nathaniel spoke gently at his daughter's door, knowing better than to barge into the bedroom. "Cora dear, I know this has been awful, but you did so well helping the farmer's wife and then fetching the police."

Silence within.

"Can I come in?"

A muffled response.

Nathaniel tentatively opened the door and saw the girl lying full-length, boots on, face into her pillow. She turned towards him, tear stains on her cheeks, eyes red. "What happened to the farmer?"

"It's probably best you don't know all the details, but it looks like he... died... in a fight... or something."

"While we were there, in the field?"

"I don't know when it happened. The police are going to investigate and they'll talk to me tomorrow."

"And to me. That policeman said he'd want to know what I saw. He was quite frightening at first. I didn't think he was going to take any notice of me."

Sitting on the edge of the bed, Nathaniel was about to hug her, but wondered whether she perhaps felt too grown up for such reassurance. Instead he leaned forward and placed his hand on her shoulder. "You've been really brave, my dear."

Edith, waiting in the kitchen at the end of the hall, was suitably shocked when Blake told her what had happened. "Murdered? And you let Cora walk home on her own?"

"I had no choice. I had to stay there with the wife, but someone had to tell the police. And I wanted Cora away from that farm."

"Nathaniel, I simply don't know what scrape you'll get that girl into next, or yourself, for that matter. I'd better go up to her," she said, handing the baby to her husband, "while you see what William is up to in the parlour."

Edith had not thought to ask how Nathaniel felt, however she reckoned that some time with his five-year-old son and his wooden toys would calm her husband's nerves.

After supper, which had seen more questions from Edith but near silence from Cora, Blake had made his way back across town to his studio to develop the photograph Inspector Ramm had asked for. Lit by the red glow of the darkroom's lamp, the horror of the barn reappeared as he swirled the glass negative in an enamel tray of chemicals. Once the negative was fixed he used another lamp to project the image onto a sheet of photographic paper.

He peered with renewed revulsion as the farmer's body took shape as he developed the print in a second chemical bath. Amos Carter's rope-bound figure was already etched in his memory, but the photograph gave him a new insight into the scene. Earlier he hadn't noticed just how topsy-turvy the rest of the barn was. Studying the still image Blake saw that nearly everything in the barn had been tipped over or thrown to one side. The drawers of a battered chest – used for tools perhaps – had been pulled out and emptied. An earthenware jug smashed. Straw appeared to have been scattered down from the loft.

Whoever had attacked the farmer had obviously been looking for something, he thought.

The sound of St Edward's Church clock striking nine drifted across Leek's rooftops as Blake hurried to the police station for his appointment with Inspector Ramm the following morning. Many townspeople had started their working day hours earlier, trooping into silk mills to begin a ten-hour shift of spinning, weaving or dyeing. Others had already collected skeins of silk to twist into thread in the shades, the long attic work rooms above their terraced houses.

The young constable on duty at the police station counter sprang to his feet when Blake announced his name, obviously forewarned to expect the photographer. Ramm looked up from a sheaf of papers when the visitor entered his office.

"Take a chair, Mr Blake."

As Ramm straightened the documents into a neat pile, Blake reached forward to place a brown envelope on the desk. Inside was the photograph taken in the barn at Abbey Green, a gruesome record of Amos Carter's death. Blake was still puzzled by the scene in the barn. "It looked a decided mess in there. Do you think someone had searched it?" he asked as he slid the photograph across to the Inspector.

Ramm studied the photograph closely for a long time. "Very good question, Mr Blake," he said slowly, "although it's usually me who asks such things."

Yesterday Ramm had been concentrating on the farmer's injuries and, to his regret, had barely focused on the state of the building. By the time he had finished with Rosa Carter it had grown dark in the barn, and the scene had been disturbed when his officers had untied the body before taking it by cart to the morgue at the Cottage Hospital.

"It mystifies me why Amos Carter should be attacked. He was a simple farmer. According to his wife he had no enemies and there had been no arguments with anyone. And what could he have had that was worth killing him for?" said Ramm. He appeared genuinely moved by the farmer's plight.

"But we'll get to the bottom of it," Ramm went on resolutely. "My guess is that it could have been a stranger passing through – there's a few rough sorts that walk the road from Macclesfield, looking for work hereabouts. Now, Mr Blake, just tell me how you became involved yesterday."

Ramm called in the constable from the front desk to take notes and Blake recounted the events after he and Cora had arrived at the Abbey ruins.

"So you didn't see anyone loitering about the farm or in the lane? Nothing struck you as odd before Mrs Carter started shouting? You heard nothing unusual?" Ramm posed a string of questions, but Blake's replies, much to his own disappointment, were all negative.

When the constable finally put down his pencil, the photographer felt he had offered little to the investigation. Ramm thanked him and said he would also need to talk to Cora later. Could they both come back at four o'clock?

The Inspector also had something else to ask Blake. For some time now he had been thinking that a photographic record of a crime might help in their investigations. He had already begun adding photographs of some local criminals to their files. Such pictures – mugshots they called them in the *The Police Gazette* – were becoming standard practice in some countries. Some forces were even measuring criminals' skulls. But Ramm's plan went further. He hoped that photographs of the scene might help them solve a crime, or convict a suspect.

"Let us have an invoice for your work Mr Blake, because I want this to be on a business footing." He paused. "If you agree, from now on I would like to call upon you to take other photographs that may assist our enquiries. Hopefully they will not all be as distressing as this one."

Blake blew out his cheeks as he considered the suggestion. One encounter with a crime scene had been disturbing enough, but on the other hand, the idea of getting involved in police work sparked his curiosity. As well as that, he now felt personally involved in the Carter case and wanted to help Inspector Ramm in any way he could.

"Yes, certainly I'm prepared to assist, if you feel it worthwhile."

As Blake left the police station, he wondered if he really knew what he was letting himself in for – the last 24 hours had shown just how unpredictable life could be.

The Inspector gathered his notes as he prepared to attend the post mortem due to take place at the hospital in half an hour. He would then call in at the Magistrates' Court to see how cases were progressing, although thankfully today's court list was of little consequence – the usual crop of drunks, straying animals and someone throwing stones at an inn window.

It was fortunate the workload was light because this Carter case was going to take some solving, he thought. Blake had obviously seen nothing, but things had happened at Abbey Green that none of them knew about yet. He would need to handle the whole affair very carefully if he was going to get to the truth.

Cora was relieved when her father had suggested she should start work a little later. Throughout the night she had been haunted by thoughts of what might have happened at the farm, so near to where they had stood. She went through the events of the afternoon in her head, going over what she had seen, trying to reconstruct her view over the ruins and the farm. Was someone there? Was something out of place? She knew that the police inspector was sure to call her to the station. What was she going to say?

After a later-than-usual breakfast during which her mother had cast her numerous worried looks, Cora made her way to the studio, her eyes sore following a sleepless night. Leek could be decidedly dull most of the time, she thought, but today was market day, the day when the town really came alive, and the streets were bustling. "How can all these people go about their business as normal when such a horrible thing has happened?" she wondered. But she knew the answer – unlike her, they didn't know about what had gone on at Abbey Green.

Passing the livestock market, which occupied a central area of town, Cora saw that local farmers were filling the pens with animals ready for the weekly sales to begin. Sheep had been herded from nearby farms or brought by cart, young pigs lifted by the back legs from horse-drawn traps, and cattle driven along the street forcing pedestrians to dodge out of the way. Herdsmen waved sticks or tree branches to urge their beasts along, shouting at their hindquarters. There was much coaxing and shoving and the occasional uncooperative calf was lifted off its feet. Above the plaintive sounds of the animals, she could hear snatches of the auctioneer's harsh voice calling up bids for an early entry in the sale ring.

Leek market day was a focus for country folk from across twenty miles or more of the moorlands and large numbers travelled here every Wednesday. Derby Street, the town's main thoroughfare, was lined with all manner of carts and traps which had brought market day customers, many of them farmers' wives armed with wicker baskets. The horses and ponies were now tethered in the yards of inns or a spare corner of the cattle market. The carts also brought quantities of eggs, butter, cheese, vegetables, poultry and game, direct from farms and smallholdings to be loaded onto stalls in the newly-built Market Hall. Here and there, a trader stuck to the old way of selling straight from his cart on the street, making rapid sales that they hoped the council market inspector wouldn't spot.

Reaching the far end of the street, Cora had to thread her way through an even greater swirl of activity as she entered the Market Place, crammed with rows of sturdy wooden stalls, each topped by a canvas awning that today would act as a sunshade rather than shelter from rain. The cobbled square was alive with haggling over all manner of goods – saucepans, umbrellas, bonnets, cloth, books, toffee, live rabbits, chickens. A hawker announced the wonders of his miracle medicine, newly arrived from America. Another waved sparkly trinkets to a group of housewives. A knife grinder was busy at his wheel, a cardsharp was shuffling his deck. A fishmonger rinsed his new stock in the waters of an ornate public fountain before placing the fish on his stall.

Cora's eyes were drawn to a brightly-costumed juggler and someone else performing a strange eastern dance, but then she passed a gaggle of beggars claiming a variety of afflictions and ill fortune. Some were missing an arm or leg. One wore a notice around his neck announcing "I am blind". Another, sitting on the pavement, held up an engraving of a grisly pit accident with one deformed hand and rattled a tin with the other. She couldn't help being touched the plight of these poor souls.

On the edge of this group, leaning against an inn wall with a battered hat at his feet, stood a rough looking fellow who stared straight at her as she walked past. Cora returned his look and saw not the usual expression of pleading, but a sense that somehow he recognised her.

"Miss," the man called. "Miss, can I have a word. Just wait a moment."

For one of the town's poorest, he was surprisingly well spoken. His accent was a little odd, certainly not local. Cora dropped her gaze, concentrated firmly on the paving stones in front of her and walked just a little faster.

Thankfully she was only yards away from a street called Sheepmarket where a bay-windowed shop bore the sign announcing *Nathaniel Blake, Photographic Artist. Portraits, Groups and Rural Vistas a Speciality.* She went through the small downstairs showroom where sample photographs, postcards and various frames were on display, and made her way up a staircase at the rear to the studio above. The door to the adjoining darkroom was closed and she guessed that her father was busy in there, processing negatives and prints.

"I'm glad you could face coming into work, after what happened yesterday," said Blake as he emerged, wiping his hands on a cloth and then hooking his wire-framed spectacles back over his ears. Dark curly hair ruffled and waistcoat undone, he seemed glad to get out of the cramped windowless darkroom, stuffy with chemical fumes.

"Having something to do will take my mind off things, father," Cora replied. "It's busy in town today, isn't it? And there are quite a lot of odd looking characters about. In the Market Place, by the Bird in Hand, there was a scruffy fellow who tried to stop me. I had to make haste to get past him."

"Don't worry, I'm sure you were perfectly safe," Blake reassured his daughter thinking that yesterday's events had probably made her more wary of strangers. "I'll go out and take a look, if you like."

With that he went downstairs. Outside the Bird in Hand he could see the line of beggars, but none more suspicious than usual, although a ragged-looking man of the road was ambling away from him down the street. Was that the one who had scared Cora?

Back at the studio, Blake tried to settle his daughter. "I didn't see anyone to worry about, my dear. The man was probably just begging. Certainly nothing to do with yesterday." Cora nodded meekly, but looked worried again when her father told her they were expected at the police station at four o'clock.

Blake checked his pocket watch and asked her to take up position by the counter in the shop as he had an important client arriving soon. Returning to the studio he began arranging a plush upholstered chair, drapes and the camera tripod ready for a portrait sitting. He was checking the camera and the photographic plates when he heard the familiar tinkle of the bell above the shop door, followed by the rustle of heavy silk. After hurriedly fastening his waistcoat and straightening his tie, he slipped on his jacket as he headed downstairs to greet the customer.

As befitting one of Leek's wealthiest and most respected residents, Mrs Elizabeth Heathcote had the bearing of a person who was used to having her every need met, her every command obeyed. Wife of a mill owner, daughter of a banker, dedicated churchgoer and staunchly teetotal, her patronage was important for the standing of any business in the town. If Mrs Heathcote chose Blake to take her portrait, then so would her acquaintances.

Hence he was anxious to please when he came under her austere gaze.

She was obviously taking the occasion seriously and had dressed with subdued resplendence. Her flowing gown was made out of many yards of heavy silk in the darkest blue, above which she wore a short, fitted black velvet jacket, edged with intricate black embroidery. Her face – sharp nose and chin, sallow skin, rather sad eyes – was ringed by the frilled ribbons which secured an elaborate bonnet decorated with black silk flowers. The style echoed the final years of the late Queen's reign, rather than the very latest fashion.

At Blake's invitation she made her way up to the studio, her skirt dragging on the wooden stairs. Blake almost stooped to support the mass of material like a pageboy, but thought better of it. After casting an appraising eye over the patterned carpet, heavy drapes and painted background cloth depicting a rural scene, she perched carefully on the edge of the button-back chair.

The large window, part-shaded by a calico blind, lit Mrs Heathcote and the intricate detail of her outfit to Blake's satisfaction, but he was anxious nothing should go wrong with this sitting. He took even more care than usual with his composition and focusing and could tell that his subject, though maintaining a frozen pose, was getting a little restive. Her expression seemed more stern than ever. After taking several images of Mrs Heathcote seated, he persuaded her to stand and place one arm decorously on the back of the chair in a pose he had used a hundred times. Though she did as he asked, he could tell her patience was draining away. She said nothing. He attempted conversation, but there was still silence from the woman.

"Well, Mrs Heathcote I believe that should take care of it," Blake announced as he emerged from beneath the cloth hood over his camera and removed the final glass plate. Her face seemed to relax a little. Blake realised that his sitter had perhaps been as nervous as he was. Had that steely expression had concealed an inner turmoil about having her photograph taken?

"I do hope it turns out well, Mr Heathcote has such high standards," she began to say in a cultured accent. Blake realised that these were the first words she'd uttered since arriving. She was about to say something else but halted abruptly as the door bell was heard from below, followed by the authoritative tones of the man himself, her husband Enoch Heathcote, as he spoke to Cora.

Elizabeth Heathcote stood up immediately, smoothed her skirt and headed downstairs to where her husband was towering over Cora. At least a foot taller than the girl, he was looking at her earnestly, apparently trying to engage her in conversation. His gaze moved from the girl as his wife stepped into the showroom.

"Elizabeth my dear, a successful portrait sitting?" he smiled. "The carriage is right outside so you won't need to trouble yourself with the crowds. We can go straight home."

Enoch Heathcote was a balding sixty-year-old with bristling side burns. Taller than average, he was quite powerfully built, but there was a noticeable paunch beneath his expensive frock coat. Broken red veins in his cheeks indicated that, despite his wife's beliefs, he probably enjoyed a glass of spirits as much as his food.

Turning to Blake, who had followed Mrs Heathcote down the stairs, he spoke with the confidence of a physically large man who had plenty of money. He not only owned a mill employing hundreds of people, but ran a significant part of the town itself through his membership of local councils and numerous public bodies. At least he liked to think he did.

"Mr Blake, I'm very pleased to make your acquaintance. My thanks for accommodating my wife this morning. I've heard very good things about your photography and I'm sure you will do us proud." A firm grasp as he shook the photographer's hand. Blake was impressed by the man's good natured greeting.

"Yes, a number of friends have praised your services," Heathcote continued. "In fact, I'd very much like to see more of your photographs some time. I say, what about coming round to the mill? I'd be happy to give you a tour. You may find it interesting." He fixed Blake with searching eyes.

This really was an excellent development, thought Blake. An influential friend such as this could do wonders for business, and he seemed a very pleasant fellow, too.

"I don't know what to say. I'd be delighted to visit. Could I bring a camera?"

"Of course, of course, and bring this young lady along, too, if she's interested," Heathcote replied, swivelling back to Cora, his eyes searching Cora's face for a response. She managed a slightly awkward nod. "If father wishes."

Silk-clad Mrs Heathcote started to rustle towards the door and Cora darted out from behind the counter to open it for her, resisting the urge to curtsy to the grand guest.

Heathcote meanwhile took Blake gently by the elbow, turned him to one side and drew a little closer to exchange a few more words. "I hear you were involved in this awful business down at the Abbey yesterday," he said.

"Well, in a way. It was quite a shock. But I'm surprised that you know about it."

"Oh, Inspector Ramm gave me some details. I've just seen him at the Magistrates Court. I'm Chairman of the Bench, you know, and on the Police Committee. The fellow feels it's his duty to keep me informed of what's going on."

"Ah... that explains it."

"Of course, I'm not one for tittle-tattle." Heathcote's tone was casual, apparently this was simply polite conversation. Then he went on. "So what did you see?"

Blake was rather taken aback, not least because he thought he was free of talking about the murder for a little while, even if the memories stayed with him..

"Well, I saw nothing of the crime, only its result. Mr Carter's wife found him in the barn. She was in terrible state."

"Nothing suspicious going on, no one lurking about?"

"No, not at all."

"And the wife, did she say much?"

Was Heathcote asking because he was a public-minded citizen, or was he simply curious, Blake wondered.

"She was just very upset. I'm only pleased that the police have it all in hand now," he replied, hoping to extricate himself from the interrogation.

"Yes, yes, of course, Ramm's a fine fellow. I'm sure he will get to the bottom of it." Heathcote paused, then apparently decided not to pursue the topic.

"So you'll come to see us at the Great Mill? What about next Tuesday, eleven o'clock? Ask for me at the desk and I'll show you round," he added.

With another firm handshake and a nod to Cora, Heathcote left, joining his wife who was already seated straight-backed in their open carriage outside in the street. A groom, dressed in immaculate grey livery, waited patiently at the reins.

"What an interesting character," said Blake, as the carriage moved off. "The wife's rather severe, but I think I'm going to like Mr Heathcote. And he could be a very useful person to know."

He had feared Heathcote would be officious, but Blake had actually found him quite friendly. The mill owner's praise for his photography and the offer of a visit to the mill had flattered Blake, even if he was a little put out by those questions about what had gone on at Abbey Green. Perhaps it would be a topic of conversation he would not be able to avoid from now on.

"I didn't like the way he looked at me. He seems rather

strange," said Cora.

Oh no, thought Blake. Now the girl's going to be suspicious of everyone. Perhaps yesterday's events had shaken her more deeply than he had realised.

"Please don't look like that, father." She had guessed what he was thinking. "Before you came down he was trying to be very friendly, but his mind seemed to be on something else. His eyes never stopped moving over me when he spoke."

"Cora, it's the first time we've met him! I thought Mr Heathcote seemed fine. He's a very highly respected person, you know. And very wealthy." But even Blake had felt unnerved by Heathcote's earnest gaze. As for Mrs Heathcote, she was much more difficult to fathom.

Cora sighed. She was not going to get any further with her opinions, so she decided to say nothing more.

After lunch – a slice of pie each from the baker's next door – the photographer said he needed to go to the railway station to collect an important parcel. Cora assured him that she could look after the shop.

"I shall be back in plenty of time for us to go to the police station. Remember, if you need to go out, lock the door behind you," said Blake, and set off to get his package. He had decided to invest in a new type of camera, a folding model, smaller and lighter than anything he had at present, much easier to use when he was out of the studio. Unfortunately, yesterday had dulled his excitement about the arrival of his new acquisition.

Alone in the shop, Cora began to dwell on yesterday's events and her planned visit to the police station. She resolved to make a better impression on the rather stern Inspector Ramm. Wondering if her father had developed the photographs from the previous day she went to look in the darkroom. After lighting the red-shaded lamp, she focused on a row of prints that Blake had hung up to dry before Mrs Heathcote arrived. Pictures of the Abbey ruins. She took them down one by one and studied them. Ancient stones, trees, grass, a glimpse of the river.

She tensed and looked closer at one photograph where she could see the corner of what she now knew to be the barn, just visible behind the remains of the Abbey. In the field next to it she could make out a figure apparently walking away. "How did I miss this yesterday?" she thought.

Perhaps this would give her something to tell the Inspector, after all. But was the photograph any use? The image of the person was so tiny. She realised she needed an enlargement. Right now. Spurred on by her discovery, Cora decided to take the matter into her own hands.

"I've seen father do this lots of times, I'm sure I can do it myself," she said to herself. After finding the correct glass negative from a stack in paper sleeves on the work bench, she set up the lamp and the wooden frame which Blake used to project an enlarged image onto a piece of photographic paper.

Printing the image, enlarged but still sharp, turned out to be far more fiddly than she had expected. Twice she adjusted the enlarging frame, shone the light through the negative and then sloshed the paper in a tray of developing chemicals, and twice it was a failure. One was too light, one was just a black mess. Chemicals spilled onto the bench. Sweat appeared on her brow.

Cora let out a frustrated cry. She couldn't do it after all. It was hopeless. She would have to wait for father to come back, or even until tomorrow. She took a deep breath to calm herself and started again. Mouth pursed in determination, she concentrated on the portion that showed the person in the field. This time, as the print emerged in its chemical bath, she saw that it was much clearer. She was eager to look even closer, but knew the print needed to dry off before she could handle it and take it to the police station.

While she waited for the print to dry she glanced over the rest of the photographs around the work bench, then picked up a folder. Inside were two prints and glass negatives. Cora choked back a cry. She now saw what her father had discovered in the barn. A horror beyond her imaginings of the previous night.

She felt she was going to faint. She needed some air. She must go outside, get away from the picture, from the farmer. Grabbing the photograph she had just printed, she dashed downstairs and out of the shop, spinning back at the last second to lock the door with her key. Then she ran, no thought to where she was headed.

Across town at Leek Railway Station, her father came upon the exodus that followed a busy market day, country folk waiting for trains to rural halts along the branch line. Platforms on both sides of the track were crowded with women swinging wicker baskets heavy with purchases or balancing packages wrapped in brown paper. Men manoeuvred rakes, spades and crates of chickens. Station porters dashed back and forth.

Just as Blake was making his way to the parcels office, the train from Manchester arrived in a cloud of smoke and steam, clanking to a halt. Market-weary, and occasionally beer-fuddled, folk surged towards the carriages just as the new arrivals stepped down onto the platform. He decided not to barge through the crowd and stood to one side, waiting and watching. He would often do this, stand and watch people, sometimes listening in to snatches of conversation.

His attention was drawn to a man who appeared from the maroon and cream painted carriage and then turned back inside the doorway to retrieve a highly polished leather case. The newcomer was quite a striking figure. Over six feet tall, he had a long face and small, well-trimmed moustache. He was immaculately turned out in a blue striped summer blazer, grey waistcoat, gold watch chain, high-collared white shirt and straw boater. His tightly-knotted green necktie looked to bear the insignia of some regiment or college.

The man's erect posture made him look even taller, he literally stood out above the crowd. His head jerked slightly as he looked first one way and then another, apparently getting his bearings at an unfamiliar destination. He strode over to the newspaper stand, where a surly young lad in a Smith & Son cap slouched against a display of newspapers, magazines, books, hog-skin tobacco pouches and traveller's knick-knacks. The newcomer made some enquiry and received directions accompanied by much pointing. He then walked purposefully past Blake towards the station forecourt and climbed into a waiting horse-drawn omnibus which took new arrivals to the town's main hotels.

Once mail bags had been unloaded, the guard had blown his whistle and the train had left the platform, Blake collected his precious parcel. Returning to the studio ten minutes later he was surprised to find the door locked. After letting himself in he went upstairs and saw the darkroom door open and the lamp lit. Inside, things had been disturbed and on the floor was one of the photographs he had taken in the barn. Horrified, he realised Cora must have seen it. Where was she? What state was she in? Glancing at his watch he thought she may have set off for the police station early and decided to go there himself.

Cora had fled in the opposite direction, head-down, barging her way through folk on the pavement. She found herself in front of St Edward's Church, opposite the market square. She went through the stone arch of its lych-gate, up the steps and flopped down on an iron bench near the church door. At least she was away from everyone else.

She was still clutching the photograph showing the figure walking away from the barn. She looked down at it. Was this the person who had killed the farmer and was responsible for what was on that hideous picture she had seen in the darkroom? And why had father photographed something so horrible? Her mind whirled. She wished they had never gone anywhere near the ruins yesterday.

She had no idea how long she slumped on the bench, but she jolted upright as bells in the church tower began to strike four. Four o'clock! She'd be late for Inspector Ramm! Cora dashed off in the direction of the police station several streets away. She was breathless as she ran through the main door to find her father standing beside the high counter with a worried look on his face.

"Cora, thank goodness you're all right. Why did you leave the shop? And what's that you've got there?" Blake was both relieved and perplexed to see his daughter, who was obviously agitated.

"I saw this photograph, and then I saw the other, the horrible one, and then ... I just ran."

Before they could say any more Inspector Ramm had appeared in the corridor. "Ah, Mr Blake, Miss Blake, I'm glad you're both here now. Please come into the office." His expression indicated that he had noted it was now nearly ten minutes past the hour. Once seated, he focused his full attention on Cora.

"Now Miss Blake, I know yesterday was very upsetting for you, but I need to find out if you saw anything that can help us." He was about the lead her through events as recounted by her father, when the young woman interrupted him.

"Excuse me Sir, but I've brought something to show you. It might be important." She held out the photograph, its edges now a little crumpled.

Ramm was surprised both by Cora's confident attitude and the fact that she was holding a picture different from the one he had seen that morning. Blake seemed equally startled and leaned forward to look at the photograph.

"Father took this at the ruins a little while before the lady came running out. I think that's the barn on the left and there's someone, I think it's a man, walking across the field."

"Is that one of those I printed this morning?" Blake asked his daughter.

"No, it's an enlargement I made this afternoon," she replied matter-of-factly. Blake's eyebrows went up. In his haste to prepare for Mrs Heathcote this morning he had obviously missed something important, but Cora hadn't. He realised he may have misjudged just what his young daughter was capable of.

By now Inspector Ramm had pulled a large magnifying glass from a drawer and was studying the photograph keenly. The figure walking away was still indistinct, perhaps a well-built man wearing what looked like a battered straw hat and carrying some sort of bag over his shoulder. He was walking towards the footbridge over the river.

"Well, this is very interesting," he said slowly, still looking intently at the photograph. "I don't know exactly where it takes us, but it's very useful to see it." He raised his eyes to Cora. "You're obviously a very sharp-eyed young lady."

After Cora had confirmed she had seen nothing else of importance, the Inspector told father and daughter they could leave.

Ramm looked again at a document on his desk, the medical officer's initial notes from that morning's post mortem. Amos Carter had been beaten about the face and head, but the cause of death was most likely trauma and blood loss arising from the injuries to his chest and abdomen. They didn't appear to be random slashes in the heat of a brawl. More like deliberate cuts made with a very sharp knife.

He looked again at the new photograph. Was this man the murderer, he wondered.

Chapter Four

It was seven o'clock on Saturday morning and there were few people around in the middle of Leek. Mill workers would not be on the streets until their half-day's shift ended at midday. Then the town would become much more lively, shops and inns filled with locals relieved at the end of their working week.

After looking each way along Market Street to check who was around, John Gibb turned down a narrow alley which ran at the side of the building where the town's weekly newspaper, the *Leek Lion*, was based. As a man of the road, he'd known for a long time that the alley was the place to find a supply of fresh clean newspaper. He used it to stuff his makeshift mattress, and, in winter, wrapped his feet in it for a little extra warmth within his battered boots. On the coldest nights, a layer of newspaper beneath his coat had probably kept him alive when he was sleeping rough on the moors or in an abandoned farm building.

But today Gibb wasn't looking for warmth. He knelt beside the piles of paper, scrap copies of the *Lion* placed in the alley late the previous night when printing of the new edition was complete.

Gibb reached into the pocket of his grimy overcoat and pulled out a knife. Sliding the razor sharp pointed blade from its black sheath, he cut through the string which secured the topmost bundle. For a proud Scotsman like Gibb, this knife, a dirk decorated in silver with a stag's head, was his most treasured possession.

He tossed a couple of poorly printed copies of the newspaper to one side, found one good enough to read and sat down on another pile of papers. Gibb was literate, unlike most of the vagrants he had met and he knew there were plenty of townsfolk who struggled with their letters and numbers. He was well educated but kept this mostly to himself. His eyes sped over the closely printed columns – most of it was irrelevant to a man like himself – until he spotted the item he was looking for. A report of Amos Carter's death earlier in the week. He read it twice and then set the newspaper aside and sat in thought.

"What's Inspector Ramm going to do about this?" he said to himself.

Gibb was accustomed to death. He'd killed men. Others had tried to kill him.

An hour later, seated at the kitchen table in Moorside Terrace, Nathaniel Blake was also studying the *Leek Lion*. The boy from Naylor's newsagents had delivered the newspaper bright and early and Blake had snatched it up while Edith was busy at the coal fired range preparing breakfast. As usual, she had been up early to light the range so the hotplate would be warm enough to cook on.

Blake, like most Edwardian men, was blissfully unconcerned about such domestic matters. His first task this morning was to read through the tightly-packed advertisements which filled the front page of the broadsheet *Lion*.

"St John's summer fete.... New season boots just in... The Queen steam laundry now open... Strong stable lad wanted.... Patent artificial teeth."

Blake scanned advertisements covering every facet of life in Leek until he saw the one he himself had placed. He was keen to make sure there were no printing mistakes.

> **LEEK TEMPERANCE HALL**
> Monday August 25th at 8 p.m.
> (Doors will open 30 minutes in advance).
>
> Mr. Nathaniel Blake's Descriptive Lantern
> Entertainment
>
> **"GLIMPSES OF OUR MOORLAND SPLENDOUR"**
>
> 120 illustrations, many of them prize winning.
> Interval entertainment by Mr. Ernest Rushton,
> violinist and comedian.
>
> *Part of the proceeds will go to our gallant men
> on their return home from The Cape.*

"That seems to be correct," said Blake.

Edith was apparently more concerned about the eggs she had put on to boil. She didn't share her husband's obsession with his coverage in the *Lion*. But for Nathaniel the lantern slide show was valuable publicity. Although he was giving some of the ticket money to local Boer War veterans, he expected to sell a few dozen postcards. He also rather liked showing off his pictures to an appreciative audience.

"Now, where's the news item that Finch said he was going to put in about the show?" Nathaniel continued. "And I suppose there will be something about Amos Carter." The photographer was on friendly terms with the newspaper's editor, FJ Finch, and had expected decent coverage for his lecture.

He stretched his arms wide to open the *Lion* – its four pages were printed on a single vast sheet of paper – to begin searching the news columns. There were dozens of reports set in type small enough to strain the eyes, the headlines barely any larger.

"*Local Intelligence*, this is where it will be," he said, locating the section for local news items. He read the headlines aloud. "Drunk and Disorderly at Longnor... Found in Possession of Blackbirds... St Edward's Church Bells to be Restored... The Price of Bread... Concert by the Volunteer Band. Hang on, here it is... Shocking Death at Abbey Green."

Edith turned from the egg pan and looked anxiously at her husband who was about the read out the whole item.

SHOCKING DEATH AT ABBEY GREEN. – A most disturbing event has come to our attention. On Tuesday last, Mr. Amos Carter of Dieulacres Cottage Farm, Abbey Green was found dead in suspicious circumstances. Mr. Carter was discovered in the barn where he had been gravely assaulted by person or persons unknown. Inspector Albert Ramm of Leek Constabulary informed the *Leek Lion* that it appeared the deceased's injuries had arisen from an argument which had gone badly wrong. The culprit may have been a complete stranger to the district, the Inspector suggested.

We understand that Mr. Nathaniel Blake, the Leek photographer, and Miss Cora Blake have been helping police with their enquiries. No arrests have been made and investigations were continuing as the *Leek Lion* went to press.

H.M. Coroner Mr. V.J. Mountford opened an inquest into the death yesterday (Friday) and the hearing was adjourned following an initial statement of the facts.

Mr. Carter was well known in local farming circles for his Ayrshire cattle and was a former member of St. Edward's Parish Church choir. He had farmed at Abbey Green for more than 30 years with his wife Rosa. The couple have no children.

Blake stared fixedly at the newspaper, then slammed it down on the table.

"That's awful. They've made it sound like you had something to do with the crime. And they've used Cora's name," said Edith.

"It's a great pity you got tangled up in the first place. You're always very quick to get involved with things, aren't you dear? I'm not happy about Cora getting mixed up this," she continued, picking up the newspaper to read the report for herself. "You're going to have to have a word with Finch about it."

"I'm going to go round to see Finch as soon as I've had breakfast," Blake replied, but he knew that there was no way to undo what had already been printed and what the town would be reading, and then talking about, that morning.

At that point young William came running into the room and little Emily, who had been sitting happily in her high chair, began to scream for something to eat. Cora came downstairs to join them at the table and both Nathaniel and Edith thought it wise not to bring up the subject of Abbey Green again. Blake folded the newspaper and put it to one side while the family ate breakfast together.

Half an hour later, Cora was at the sink washing the dishes when she announced that she planned to meet her friend Polly that afternoon. Blake, who was determined to visit the *Leek Lion* office, said he would be back home in time for the family to visit Pickwood Recreation Ground before lunch. The small park, which had children's swings and roundabout and had become very popular since a local worthy donated the land, was a short walk from the Blakes' house.

The *Leek Lion* office was located in a small former mill just off Derby Street, its many-paned ground floor windows covered in dust. It was a building of three storeys, each floor consisting of a single workroom. The flaking green entrance door led directly into the print room, its whitewashed walls spattered with various other colours, chiefly splashes of black and red. The air was thick with the smell of printer's ink. A young lad, armed with a rag, was laboriously wiping down the iron and brass hulk of the printing press standing in the middle of the room.

The previous evening this workshop had been filled with activity, dominated by the clank and hiss of the press. Tom, the machine minder, made constant checks on the print quality and adjusted the press's controls, while his young apprentice loaded fresh sheets of paper at one end and hauled away printed copies of the newspaper from the other. Bundles of the *Lion* had been sent out in hand carts to shops around the town late last night. More parcels had been dispatched to villages by horse-drawn cart and the local train first thing in the morning, spreading news of the Abbey Green murder far and wide in this corner of the Peak. Some townsfolk, anxious to read the paper before anyone else, had made a late-night visit to the print room door, slipping Tom a penny for a copy hot off the press.

Along one wall, shelves were loaded with numerous tins, the drips running from their lids revealing that they contained the treacle-like ink used on the printing press. Against the back wall, sheets of fresh newsprint paper were piled as high as a man. In the far right hand corner, a square hole had been cut into the ceiling to accommodate a rudimentary goods lift, iron chains hanging beside its vertical metal frame.

A lad of about ten years old barged in past Blake to collect a bagful of *Lions* to sell on the street and earn a few coppers for his trouble. "That's more people who will be reading about me," the photographer thought, as the lad ran out again.

Blake took to the staircase which led from the front corner of the room to the next floor. Here another print worker, Alfred, his brown overall liberally smeared with ink, was surrounded by high workbenches. Wooden trays were propped up on the bench tops, divided into numerous compartments, each filled with letters and numerals in varying sizes, all cast in lead. Below the bench tops were cabinets of wide shallow drawers, some of which were open to reveal thousands more pieces of metal and wooden type.

As the *Lion's* highly skilled compositor, Alfred would normally be busy typesetting the advertisements and columns of news, his tweezers flying back and forth to pick individual pieces of type and insert them into metal frames. He was now deep into his Saturday morning task of deconstructing the inky metal pages used to print this week's edition and which had returned from the press room via the lift. The air was filled with the smell of paraffin that soaked a rag Alfred was using to rub the ink off the face of the used type.

Taking a final flight of narrow stairs to the top floor, Blake reached the newsroom, where the *Lion's* editor FJ Finch sat behind a desk at the back of the room, partially obscured by a large, green enamelled typewriter. A younger man, Oliver, the *Lion's* junior reporter, sat at another desk, facing the wall. He pecked at his own battered typewriter with two fingers, stopping occasionally to consult a notebook scrawled with some sort of shorthand notes.

The room was so crammed that Blake worried for the strength of the uneven floorboards. Stacks of newspapers, bound by string at the spine, stood in the corners, edges frayed, the paper yellowing. These were the frequently-consulted files of back issues of the *Lion*. Behind Finch was a bookcase, its shelves groaning with numerous volumes, many of them leather-bound directories, dictionaries and reference books. Calendars, advertisements and assorted notes, both printed and handwritten, were pinned around the room.

Against one wall cardboard boxes were bulging with hundreds of new books were lined up. These were compendiums of local history, speeches by town worthies and poems by local vicars which Finch published as a sideline and, of course, publicised tenaciously in the *Lion*.

The two desks were covered with yet more paper. Official-looking documents, rival newspapers, notebooks, diaries, ledgers of advertisements, and finally piles of plain 'copy paper', the trimmed-down sheets onto which Finch and the reporter hammered out their stories one paragraph at a time. Typed reports, folded in half to keep the sheets together, were already beginning to stack up in wooden trays on both desks. There were also spikes on which the stories were thrust after being edited by Finch and returned to the news room from being typeset downstairs.

Finch rarely used his full name, Fellowes Jeremiah, preferring to be known by friends and colleagues simply as FJ. In his late forties, he had long thinning red hair which clashed with the green of his waistcoat. He rarely relaxed, unless intoxicated. His head and hands were constantly in motion, and his expression seemed to challenge anyone and anything that came before him. Hence he was immediately on the alert as the photographer appeared at the top of the staircase.

Facing the editor in his lair, Blake's eyes were drawn to the large poster which had been pinned to the wall deliberately behind Finch's left shoulder. "*THE LEEK LION, WE ROAR THE TRUTH*" it said in bold capitals, repeating the slogan which had appeared under the newspaper's masthead since Finch had founded the weekly twenty years earlier.

Blake snatched up a copy of the latest edition from the junior reporter's desk and waved it at Finch. Before he could say anything, the editor said smoothly: "What can I do for you old chap? The advertisement to your satisfaction, I take it?"

"Do not "old chap" me, Finch. This simply isn't good enough." Blake's anger had festered as he walked through the town. Now it boiled over. He crumpled the paper and virtually threw it at the editor's desk.

"Steady on, my dear fellow. Let's be sensible about this." Finch knew exactly why Blake had come to the office. Like the editor of any small town newspaper, he was used to being confronted by those whose names appeared in his pages, whether it was for good reason or ill.

"I know it's an important story, but this report on Amos Carter is just misleading. It's wrong. It might even be dangerous."

Blake was particularly concerned about Cora's name appearing in the newspaper. Thank goodness Ramm had not mentioned that his daughter had spotted someone in the photograph. However he was uncomfortable having an argument with the editor because he had hoped to get Finch to use his photographs occasionally. That was going to be a challenge, because until now the *Lion* had only ever printed two pictures – one was of the late Queen, and the other her son, the new King Edward.

"We were just going on what Inspector Ramm told us, weren't we Oliver?" The reporter, who Blake realised must be Finch's son on account of his red hair, nodded to his father, glanced nervously at Blake and then returned to his typing. "According to what he said, the farmer was in some sort of fight, died, and then you and your daughter found him," said Finch.

Blake sighed. "Firstly, you make it sound like Cora and myself were involved in some way, which we weren't. Secondly, you shouldn't have mentioned Cora at all. Thirdly, I'm sure it wasn't the usual sort of fight. This poor man looked like he had been tied up and tortured to death."

Finch, ever the news man, was suddenly more interested. He leaned towards Blake and gestured to the bentwood chair in front of his desk. "Here, sit down Nathaniel. Let's talk about it. You obviously know more about this affair than we do."

"That's what worries me, FJ. You go to press with half a story and, the next we know, the whole town is talking about Cora and myself being questioned about a murder. It's not fair. Neither is it the truth, as you call it." Blake pointed to the *Lion's* motto on the poster.

"I just printed what we picked up from Ramm. He was cagey,

as he usually is, but he gave no hint of it being anything other than some sort of fight. To be honest, he didn't appear to think it was particularly important," said Finch, and added soothingly: "I had to include your name because you're so well known in town, Nathaniel. It might even do you some good. Public-spirited citizen and all that."

Blake was doubly disturbed. First he had thought that Finch had let him down, but now he was more concerned that Inspector Ramm was going soft on the investigation. Was the murderer going to get away with it?

Finch, a master of smoothing his way out of trouble, continued: "I promise you, if we find out more and if the Inspector Ramm and his trusty team make some progress, we will follow it up next week. But I must be careful not to tread on Ramm's toes. What you say certainly casts a new light on things – can I quote you?"

"For the moment, just leave me – and Cora – out of it," said Blake.

Bidding Finch good-day, he headed back down the creaking staircase. He was uncertain what to do next. Should he steer clear of Ramm and let the police get on with the case? But he couldn't help being intrigued about what had happened. He wanted the truth to be uncovered.

Blake was calmer after a stroll to the recreation ground with Edith and the children had restored some normality to their family life. How pleasant to see Cora pushing William on the roundabout and Emily, squirming in her father's arms, trying to watch what her brother and sister were up to.

After luncheon, Blake left Edith at home – he was sure she had things to do – and set off on his bicycle to deliver copies of the portrait photographs to the Heathcote residence. The previous day he had printed a selection of photographs for Elizabeth Heathcote to approve and was anxious that she should see them as soon as possible and choose which to have reprinted.

The Heathcote mansion, Longview, was just out of town, rural enough to enjoy expansive grounds surrounded by countryside in all directions, but also close enough for a short carriage drive to Enoch Heathcote's business. It was about a quarter-mile beyond the lane leading to Abbey Green and as he passed the junction, Blake was reminded yet again of the grisly events he and Cora had become involved in earlier in the week.

Like any visitor to Longview, Blake was awestruck as he pedalled down the long drive beside a sweeping lawn large enough for the town sports day that the Heathcotes hosted every summer. The house itself was a squarish Georgian mansion which had been extended on both sides over the last century. It now presented a wide expanse of huge windows, ornate chimneys, a tower, a colonnaded entrance portico and, on the right hand wing, a vast conservatory which looked to be modelled on London's Crystal Palace. The driveway wound round to the left into a courtyard of stables, but Blake made straight for the front door, a suitably imposing oak-panelled construction easily nine feet high.

Pressing a brass button on the doorframe he heard a bell ring somewhere in the distant interior. No doubt the Heathcotes had all the latest electrical gadgets, he thought. He had time to straighten his jacket and take the envelope of photographs out of his shoulder bag before the door was opened by a young woman in servant's uniform.

"Is Mrs Heathcote in? I've brought some photographs for her to look at."

"Do you have an appointment Mr....?" The girl was obviously a little puzzled to see an unexpected visitor.

"Blake, Nathaniel Blake. The photographer. I met Mrs

Heathcote on Wednesday."

"I'll go and see if Madam is available." The servant closed the door, leaving Blake to wonder if he should have gone to the tradesman's entrance round the back. After a couple of minutes, the door reopened and the young woman announced that unfortunately 'Madam' would not be able to see him and he should leave the photographs. She held out her hand.

"If that's the case, is Mr Heathcote available perhaps?" he asked.

"No, Sir is at the Lodge today, sir."

"The Lodge?" This was the first time Blake had heard of the place.

The girl seemed surprised that he should be so ill-informed. "Yes sir, Heathcote Lodge up on the Roaches. Mr Enoch goes there when he's shooting the grouse. Today there's a whole lot of them up there. They won't be back until supper time."

After handing over the envelope, Blake retrieved his bicycle from behind a fir tree. He was disappointed not to have had chance to make a better impression on the austere Mrs Heathcote. As he set off down the drive he glanced back at the house. On the far right, among the palms in the conservatory, he could see a figure. He was sure it was Elizabeth Heathcote, standing watching him leave.

Heading back along the main road, on the spur of the moment he turned into Abbey Green Lane. His visit to the Heathcotes having been so brief, he had time to spare. Why not call upon Rosa Carter? Blake was genuinely concerned for her welfare and, after his conversation with Finch, he also wondered if the case was being handled properly. The truth was, he couldn't contain his curiosity.

Images of what he had found in the barn came back to Blake as he approached the farmstead and he was relieved to see Mrs Carter outside the house, so that he wouldn't have to go near the barn again. At first she looked warily at her approaching visitor and then, recognising him from the fateful day, she raised her hand.

"Mr Blake, isn't it? It's good of you to call round to see me." Sadness was etched into her features. She looked as if she had slept little and was obviously bone tired. "I was just going to sit down for a cup o' tea – will you join me? It's the least I can do after all you did on Tuesday."

"If it's not too much trouble, I'd be happy to sit with you for a few minutes. And let me say again how sorry I am at Mr Carter's death."

Once the two were in the kitchen and the kettle set on the stove, Rose took up the conversation again. "Yes, it's a mystery what happened to Amos. And it's been an awful shock to me – thirty odd years we'd been together and now I'm on my own, trying to cope with the farm."

"I'm sure you will have help when folk find out what's happened," said Blake, trying to give the widow a glimmer of reassurance. "In fact even Mr Heathcote was asking about you the other day."

"Well he would, wouldn't he?"

"How do you mean, Mrs Carter?"

"Well Mr Enoch's our landlord, isn't he? He owns everything in these whereabouts. He'll be wondering if I'll be paying the rent this Michaelmas now that poor Amos is gone."

Blake was surprised by this information. "Oh, I didn't realise..." he began, but Rosa, glad of someone to talk to, was now in full flow.

"Usually it's his man, Gamage, the steward, who sees to us. But Mr Enoch himself has been round here a few times these last weeks. I don't know what he wanted because he and Amos would go off somewhere and talk between themselves. Private like. That might have been what was worrying Amos."

"So he was worried about something?"

"Yes Mr Blake, my Amos was sorely troubled for weeks now, but I don't know why. I don't think it was the money, because we'd sold a couple of nice beasts just recently. He wouldn't tell me, though – kept it all bottled up, y'know."

"Has Mr Heathcote called round since Amos died?" Blake asked.

"No sign of him, thank goodness. But I had a stranger here yesterday, poking around. Never seen him before. Tall fellow, posh clothes, looked like he'd never seen cow muck in his life. He wanted to talk to me about the Abbey, he said, but I told him to clear off. I've got no time for strangers at the moment."

Picking up his mug of tea, Blake realised that there was much about Dieulacres Cottage Farm that he didn't know. No wonder Heathcote was so curious about what had gone on. And the stranger sounded distinctly like the man he had seen arriving at the station. What did he want down here?

Cora met her friend Polly in the teashop in St Edward Street that was run by Polly's father, Jabez Pickford. Because the place was reasonably quiet at that point, Jabez had allowed the two girls to sit at a small round table in one corner on the strict understanding that if it was needed for paying customers, they would have to move.

Polly had been Cora's pal since they had started school together as four-year-olds. For the last three years she had worked for her parents, doing needlework in her mother's millinery shop, and washing up and waiting on in the teashop next door. The family lived in rented rooms upstairs and the Pickfords, including Polly and several brothers and sisters, were rarely away from work. However, an hour off on Saturday was her special treat – providing the teashop wasn't heaving with customers – and the two friends caught up regularly to swap news and gossip.

"Has anything exciting happened to you this week? Have you heard about this murder?" asked Polly as they sat down, each with a china cup and saucer in front of them. Polly thought Cora's work for her photographer father was much more interesting than her own duties, but she apparently knew nothing of Cora's involvement in what was already becoming a big topic of conversation in the town.

Cora hardly knew where to begin. It took her a full ten minutes to tell what had happened at Abbey Green, her increasingly vivid account being punctuated by gasps from her friend. Polly then reached across to hold her friend's hand and look sympathetically into her face.

"It must have been horrible. I just don't know how I would have coped with that woman screaming, and then having to go to the police station."

"On Wednesday I had to go back to see the police again and go through it all with the inspector," Cora continued. She realised that her experiences, dreadful as they were, thrust her into an adult world very different from the girlish stuff she and Polly usually chatted about.

She had decided not to tell her friend about the awful photograph of the dead farmer. She'd had nightmares about that picture and didn't think she could actually talk about it without crying. Neither did she mention the other photograph of the figure walking from the barn. She was frightened of him – if it was a man – and thought the least she said, the better.

Changing the subject, Cora moved on to the Heathcotes and their visit to the studio. "They're both really odd and I especially didn't like Mr Heathcote. On Tuesday, father and I are going to the Great Mill – he's going to show us around, so I suppose I'll just have to put up with him."

"You're lucky, most people only go in there to do a day's

work," said Polly, whose younger sister Meg and several cousins had started to work at the Great Mill once they'd turned twelve.

"Oh yes, I forgot Meg was there. What does she say it's like?"

Polly's excitement over Cora's Abbey Green adventure had faded when the Heathcotes were mentioned. Somehow the atmosphere had changed.

"It's work, isn't it? Something we all have to do," she said bluntly.

Cora realised that she was lucky. While most of her classmates had gone into the mills, she herself had never had to do any real physical work, day in, day out.

"According to Meg, it all depends on who's above you. People order you about and it's hard at first when you make mistakes," Polly went on. "There's lots of girls there so you make friends, but not everyone's nice."

"Do they see much of Mr Heathcote?"

Polly glanced around the tearoom to check if anyone could overhear their conversation before leaning forward confidentially. "I shouldn't get too close to him when he shows you round the mill, if I were you. Meg and my cousins say that the youngest girls are a bit frightened of him. He has his favourites, you see – the ones he makes a fuss of, especially the little ones."

"So why's that frightening?" asked Cora, recalling her own unease when she met the mill owner.

"Ada, that's one of my cousins, says it's fine if you play along with him. He even buys some of them special things if they're nice to him. But if you're not, he can get nasty."

"What do you mean 'play along with him'?"

Polly realised she might have said too much. "Please don't tell anyone about this, Cora. Meg and my cousins could get into trouble. They might get the sack. And so could my uncles who work there."

"But it seems unfair. If he's such a bully, someone should stop him," said Cora. Her cheeks started to burn.

Polly had no intention of saying anything more about the Great Mill and the two friends moved on to happier topics, including Bostock & Wombwell's circus which was coming to town in a couple of weeks. Then Polly's older sister Annie, who also worked at the tearoom, came to tell her it was time to get back to the kitchen and the girls agreed to meet again in a week's time.

Cora thought about the Heathcotes and the Great Mill as she walked home. In the last few days she had discovered so much about the nastier side of life in Leek. She decided that she was going to keep a sharp look-out when she visited the mill the following week.

By Saturday evening, the news of Amos Carter's death had begun to spread across not only the town of Leek, but far into the countryside beyond.

In the village of Flash, high on the moors, items from that week's *Lion* were being read aloud at the bar of the New Inn. As was usual for a Saturday night, the inn was filled almost entirely with men – the only women present were the landlady behind the bar and her daughter collecting mugs. Judging by the state of their clothes and boots, customers had sought refreshment immediately after leaving their fields and cowsheds, or after returning from the quarries near Buxton where many local men worked. With a pint of ale in one hand, most also had a pipe or cigarette in the other, so the atmosphere in the low-ceilinged room was choked with tobacco smoke. All form of decoration had long since taken on an amber tint. A shelf of bottles behind the bar was covered in dust.

Isaak Nadin, who kept a smallholding on the edge of the village but seemed to spend most of his time in the New Inn, was performing his weekly task as news reader. It was an arrangement which not only spread the news amongst as many people as possible for the price of a single copy of the *Lion*, but also benefited those whose schooling had left them unfamiliar with the written word.

Nadin had the *Lion* folded twice so that its large pages were of a manageable size as he leaned on the bar, his pint of the sixpenny best within easy reach. He enjoyed the attention, declaiming from the *Lion* as if he had written the news stories and announcements himself. After each one, he would pause while the news and its relevance to the village were discussed amongst the huddles of pipe-smoking drinkers. Items of absolutely no interest to a hill farmer – cricket, ladies' garments, the Boer War – were omitted.

When he came to the story about Amos Carter, Nadin took a sharp intake of breath, an overture to the item's importance and signalling his own consternation at what he was about to announce. The words "*Shocking Death*" had stilled any conversation in the inn and the news was heard in silence. Once he had finished there was a general hubbub, for both Mr and Mrs Carter were well known in the area.

"Amos Carter dead? Poor devil!"

"Whatever happened, it couldn't be Carter's fault. He wouldn't 'urt a flea. An' Rosa's as a good a sort as you'll find."

"I only saw 'im at Leek Market last week. 'e sold a good looking beast down there. Mind you, 'e didn't 'ave much to say."

There was general agreement that it was a shocking affair and Amos Carter was a most unlikely victim. Some declared their intention to attend his funeral, once the date was known.

In one corner of the pub there was a notable absence of discussion on the subject. Four men were engaged in what seemed to be a serious game of rummy. Playing cards were being slapped on the table, pennies pushed forcibly back and forth between winners and losers. All four men were well built, obviously muscular beneath their dusty shirts, hard expressions on their scarred faces. They looked like quarrymen used to long hours pounding a chisel into rock or breaking stones.

When Nadin read out the story about Amos Carter, one of the four looked up at the man who was opposite him, Caleb Salt. If anything, Salt was in even better physical shape than the other three. The first man seemed about to speak, but Salt stared straight at him and gave the slightest shake of his head. They both turned their eyes back to their cards and said nothing. Soon afterwards, the four finished their game, supped up and strode out of the inn, nodding a curt farewell to a couple of men who were standing closest.

"Well, I would have thought that Caleb, of all people, would have something to say about what happened to Carter," said one of the drinkers. Others grunted their agreement. Their thoughts were interrupted as Isaak Nadin raised his voice as he started the next news item: *"Drunk and disorderly at Longnor."*

A dozen miles away in Leek at this hour, man of the road John Gibb was not in a position to enjoy the convivial atmosphere of a local inn. Few public houses would have welcomed him, and he wouldn't have wanted to visit those that did. Much as he preferred his own company and the peace of the countryside, he had decided to hang around the town for a while longer. He wanted to see how the affair with Amos Carter went with the police, and with that man and girl who had been at the farm.

Gibb had scavenged some food from a couple of the indoor market stalls which were closing for the day and a clergyman's wife, one of his regular supporters, had given him a mug of tea. He had one or two regular haunts where he knew he could get a decent night's sleep, undisturbed by town ruffians who liked to make fun of homeless folk, but tonight he felt the need for safer surroundings.

He started to make his way to the town workhouse. There he

could take shelter in the vagrants' ward which was comfortable enough, but unfortunately the master would charge him a fee for the night.

As he walked up the Ashbourne Road he weighed the options. He could pay a few pennies from his precious savings – he had earned a few shillings from doing odd jobs on farms – or hide his purse in the stones of the wall outside the workhouse. A lot of tramps did that so they could plead poverty and not pay the fee. But as he approached the imposing front of three-storey building he noticed a few local lads skulking in the shadows. They would search the boundary wall if they saw a tramp hide anything and then make off with the money. Gibb pushed open the workhouse door. He would pay the fee and keep his remaining coins and his meagre belongings safe in his pack for the night. Tomorrow he would see what a new day would bring.

Chapter Five

"Pay attention lads, this won't take long." Inspector Ramm called his team to order. This gathering of all eight officers – six constables, one sergeant, one inspector – had become a Monday morning routine at Leek police station since Ramm had taken charge five years earlier. He reckoned they were a good set of men and were largely well liked and respected by the townsfolk, except by those they escorted to the cells. But his resources were limited and he knew it was important to keep his team focused.

"Now, where are we?" he murmured, tracing his finger down the station ledger. "The usual weekend crop. A few drunks in Derby Street, neighbours in a disturbance at Warslow, a stray horse at Cheddleton.

"As you will all know, we have three miscreants in the cells. Looks like they were down from Manchester on a thieving expedition. Sgt Reynolds and Constable Baker detained them at Rudyard, complete with a bag of stolen items. Well done lads." A nod to the two successful officers.

"Knowles, when we've finished I want you to pop up to Mr Blake and get him down here to take pictures of those three. I want them adding to our records while we've got them under lock and key. Other stations might be looking for these three, so photographs could help them, too."

The Inspector sighed and looked around the seven officers. "And, of course, we've still got this affair at Abbey Green to sort out. We're still no wiser as to what happened, except that someone made a real mess of Amos Carter. For those of you who don't know the details, this was no ordinary fight – it looked like someone was torturing him. No sign of anything stolen from the house, not that the Carters had much worth stealing.

"I'm still hoping someone saw something. The photographer and his daughter were nearest, but they didn't know what was going on. I wonder if we need another word with Mrs Carter, she may know more than she's letting on. Amos was worried about something apparently, but she says she doesn't know who it could be in Blake's photograph, walking away from the barn."

He glanced down at some notes, then continued. "I can't believe this happened out of nowhere. Let's try to find out if Carter was involved in anything risky. I want a couple of you at the cattle market on Wednesday to speak to as many farmers as you can. Show them the photograph, although it's unlikely anyone will recognise the man." Ramm paused. "But we need to tread very carefully because the Chairman of the Magistrates is nosing around. Mr Heathcote is going to be on our backs if we don't sort this out to his liking. To make matters worse, he owns the Carters' farm which might be why he's taking a special interest in the whole affair."

Ramm brought the meeting to a close. He wished he had something positive to say about the Carter investigation. He had tried not to show his irritation about Heathcote. He knew Constabulary Rules & Regulations said all officers should show deference and respect to magistrates, but the man had even tackled him at church the previous day.

When the Inspector and Mrs Ramm had been to St Edward's Church on Sunday morning, the Heathcotes had occupied their prominent pew, having made their usual grand entrance when the church was almost full. Ramm disliked the way some churchgoers bowed and scraped to the wealthy couple. After the service, Ramm and his wife were standing outside the church door, about to exchange platitudes with the Vicar, when Enoch Heathcote appeared at his shoulder.

"Could I have a word Inspector?" he said quietly, drawing the officer to one side. "How are things progressing at Abbey Green?"

Ramm decided to be as vague as possible. "We are working on it, Sir. I'm sure you don't want us cutting any corners in a matter as serious as this."

"So, no idea who is to blame, then? No more witnesses? No motive?"

"No positive identification as yet, Mr Heathcote."

"Well, be sure to keep me informed, won't you, Inspector?"

Ramm was irritated at being pestered like this, especially on what he saw as his day off. It had been just the same at Wednesday's court when Heathcote had cornered him and asked what was going on. "Just let me get on with my job," Ramm had wanted to tell him, but of course he could do no such thing. Not if he wanted to keep on the right side of Enoch Heathcote, the magistrates and his superiors.

The Inspector had barely finished the Monday meeting when he faced more irritating questions, this time from FJ Finch. The newspaper editor had called at the station to make his regular check on incidents, accidents and arrests. He was familiar enough to be allowed to wander around the station almost at will. After quizzing the Sergeant at the front desk, Finch came down the corridor to see the Inspector.

"I gather the Abbey Green thing could be a lot more serious than we understood at first," said Finch. "According to Mr Blake..."

"Why, what's Blake been saying?" Ramm interrupted.

"Only that Amos Carter was tortured. Nathaniel seemed to think my report didn't give the full details. I assured him that you, Inspector, would be keen to keep the *Lion's* readers fully informed."

"Mr Finch, we're still investigating this matter. By the time you go to press, I'm sure we will have more to say on the matter." He brought the conversation to an end, but knew he would need to feed the *Lion* more information if he was to keep the case in the public eye.

As Finch was leaving the station, Blake arrived accompanied by Constable Knowles who was carrying the photographer's tripod. "What's this Nathaniel, helping with police enquiries again?" Finch joked.

"Nothing for you to get excited about," Blake replied. He still hadn't completely forgiven Finch for the way the Amos Carter report had been written.

Blake's visit to the police station was going to be different than his usual portrait sessions. These would be the first police mugshots he had taken, although he had seen examples in *Photography* magazine and knew what was expected. Plain background, one close-up picture facing the camera, another one taken from the side. He set up his camera in a room that had decent natural light and the three suspects were brought from the cells one by one under Sgt Reynolds' stern eye. Each of the surly trio stared dead-eyed at the camera for the straight-ahead shot, holding a slate on which Sgt Reynolds had written the man's name, the suspected crime and the date. One smirked as if the whole thing was a waste of time and all three had a general air of menace. Blake was glad to disappear under his black cloth hood while he took the pictures.

Once finished, he asked to see the Inspector. Ramm said he looked forward to seeing the results, there could be many more of these mugshots in the future.

"Pleased to be of service, Inspector. While I'm here, I thought I would ask about Amos Carter. Has there been any progress?"

Not someone else quizzing him about Carter, thought Ramm. "Mr Blake, I appreciate you and your daughter's help, but you must now leave us to pursue our enquiries," he said.

Blake realised the Inspector was not going to elaborate. That irked him. First the *Lion's* report, now Ramm was cutting him out. And he had been the one to call the police in the first place!

"I simply thought that..."

"I promise you, we will be in touch if we need any further assistance." Ramm's patience was getting thin and he was not going to say anything else.

Disappointed at being sidelined, Blake left the station, chewing over Ramm's "promise" to contact him. However neither man knew that they would be seeing each other soon enough, brought together by another suspicious death.

Walking back to the studio, he passed a figure he thought he had seen before. One of the regular town tramps. Grey beard and bushy eyebrows, long ragged coat even though it was a warm day, a pack on his back. "Was he the one who spoke to Cora?" Blake wondered.

"Excuse me, can I have a word?" Blake was still smarting about Ramm and was inclined to take it out on the tramp, tell him to steer clear of Cora. But the vagrant turned his back and walked away down a side street. With equipment in both hands, Blake decided not to pursue the man, but made up his mind to look out for him in future.

John Gibb was back on the streets of Leek after spending the previous night in an abandoned building on the edge of town. His stay at the workhouse had been cut short, the master telling him to move on after the trouble he had caused on Saturday night.

It had been the nightmares, again. Gibb had drifted off to sleep to the snores of his fellows in the vagrants' ward. He had woken up in the heat of Africa, faced by a madman waving a machete. His attacker had a wild expression and was screaming in a language Gibb couldn't understand. The man ran towards him. Then there was blood, the man's blood, as Gibb lunged at him with his rifle bayonet.

As his attacker fell, Gibb saw more men running his way. He was surrounded and terrified. He shouted for help, his own screams as wild as his assailants. His arms were flailing. And then he did wake up, in the workhouse this time, gripped by a cursing tramp who was trying to shake him out of his dream.

Gibb's mind was filled with memories like these. He'd had the same nightmare many times in the ten years he had been on the road. He realised he may never be free of his past. That was why he preferred to be on his own. But sometimes he couldn't help getting involved with others when he thought a wrong had been done. It didn't always turn out well, though.

That evening, Blake was pleased at the attendance for his lantern slide lecture at the Temperance Hall. Slide shows like this, where he would project as many as a hundred images during the course of an evening, were valuable publicity for his photography as well as a source of income. Appreciative murmurs greeted his scenes of Leek and the moorlands, his witty commentary even raised a few laughs. Although Cora had been to Miss Keates' Academy during the day, she was by his side this evening to hand him glass slides in the right order and to sell his postcards.

Concentrating on the screen, Blake had been unaware of who was in the darkened room around him, but this being Leek, he guessed most of the audience would know each other. However there was at least one stranger, a tall man who came forward as the photographer was packing away the acetylene projector at the end of the show.

"I would just like to say how interesting I found your presentation. It made a very pleasant diversion. What a picturesque area this is."

Blake turned to see he was being addressed by the tall well-dressed man he had spotted at the railway station the previous week. "That's very kind of you. Do we know each other?" Blake was curious to know more about the polite newcomer.

"No. I'm a visitor to the town. Crosbie Sneyd is the name. Dr Crosbie Sneyd." The voice was cultured, his words precise.

"You have family in Leek, perhaps? Or are you visiting on business?" Blake asked innocently.

"Research. Historical research actually."

"Local history? I may be able to help then, Mr, I mean Dr, Sneyd."

Sneyd was always happy to talk about himself and his passion for ancient things. He had been on his own for several days and welcomed this chance of conversation with someone who seemed reasonably intelligent. He gestured towards two empty seats. "Perhaps we could sit for a moment." Blake left Cora replacing the lantern slides in their wooden case and took a chair beside Sneyd.

"I have never been to Leek before, but over the last few months I've become rather fascinated with the area, or with one place in particular. Dieulacres Abbey." Blake was now sure this was the visitor that Rosa Carter had turned away from the farm.

"I'm a fellow of Jesus College, Oxford," Sneyd continued, absent-mindedly fingering his college tie, dark green with a trio of white stags. "I'm lucky enough to spend a lot of my time delving amongst our ancient documents. Many go back to when Queen Elizabeth founded the college, but some are much older. It's a treasure house for a medieval historian such as myself." Sneyd paused to give Blake a chance to digest the information and appreciate his learned visitor.

"We have hundreds of documents which were collected when Henry VIII ordered the Dissolution of the monasteries. Most of them are inventories, but in a bundle relating to Dieulacres Abbey I found something quite striking. It wasn't the usual list of properties, it was a personal letter written by the last abbot of Dieulacres, Abbot Whitney," he went on excitedly.

"I had certainly never seen it before and neither had our archivist. In fact I don't think anyone had ever noticed it was there. It was written in Latin, but that was no problem for me. I'm a Latin scholar you understand, so I translated it easily enough. The contents were quite remarkable. And that is what has brought me here, to look at the Abbey, or what's left of it."

Sneyd expected the photographer to press him for more details, but was disappointed because Blake's mind was on present day matters. He realised Sneyd's interest in the Abbey was a dusty document from years ago. The academic obviously had nothing to do with the tragedy at the farm.

"So have you been down to the Abbey ruins yet?" Blake asked, although he knew what the answer would be.

"Yes, I went and looked around the site a little. I would like to have spent more time there but the good woman at the farmhouse was not very welcoming."

"Well, Mrs Carter found her husband dead last week, so she is rather distressed at the moment."

"How unfortunate," Sneyd replied, but showed little interest in something that wasn't connected with his research. "I shall be staying at The George a little longer while I make more enquiries. I want to look at some of the old documents in the church vestry so I plan to contact the Vicar, Reverend Maitland is it? Monks from the Abbey sometimes worshipped at the church, you know. I was also hoping to see the landowner while I'm here, in case I can find out more about the site of the Abbey. I would like to do a proper survey."

"You want to see Mr Heathcote?"

"Yes, that's the fellow. I wrote to him a couple of months ago to tell him about my discovery, but heard nothing from him. A businessman I gather, so he's probably not bothered about historical matters such as this."

The conversation was brought to an end when the caretaker interrupted them to put the chairs away.

"I hope we see each again while I'm in town," said Sneyd as he strode out of the hall.

Blake mused on what Sneyd had told him. "Something else that Enoch Heathcote's involved in," he thought.

Cora was packing the last of the glass slides when she had overheard Heathcote's name mentioned. Her thoughts turned to the following day when she and her father would visit the Great Mill. She had been thinking over what Polly had told her about the mill girls. If there was more to it, her friend had dared not say. But tomorrow she might see for herself what it was like to work in the mill.

Chapter Six

Nathaniel Blake carried his new lightweight camera as he and Cora made their way to the Great Mill the following day, along a side street close to the town centre. It was not one mill, but several four-storey buildings, some adjacent to each other, two more facing across the street. Looming in the background was a huge chimney, its red brick stained black by soot, a cloud of smoke pouring from the top. Though separate buildings, the mills were linked by high wooden bridges and by passageways which had been tunnelled beneath the street. It created a vast complex of noisy workrooms, warehouses packed with raw materials and finished goods, and dark basements that held the steam engines which powered the machinery. Cora glanced up and saw a worker pushing a handcart loaded with boxes across one of the wooden walkways.

The two walked through the imposing main entrance, the words 'Heathcote & Company' carved in stone above the doorway. Near the door, a clerk was seated at a high desk encased by glass screens on three sides. When Blake introduced himself, the man said that "Mr Enoch" was expecting them and rose to show them the way. He led them to a grand oak staircase of the sort that was usually seen in a luxury hotel, and then up to the owner's office on the floor above.

Enoch Heathcote's domain was a double-height room with a polished parquet floor and high arched windows. The mill owner was seated at a large mahogany desk, its leather top holding numerous wooden document trays, a green-shaded reading lamp and a telephone, one of the first to be installed in the town. There was also a panel of brass switches which he used to summon the managers of far-off departments when needed. On the wall opposite the windows were a series of framed displays, each containing dozens of multi-coloured ribbons and braids and the various insignia of textile exhibitions.

As they were shown in, Heathcote laid down his fountain pen on a blotter and looked up. "Mr Blake, dear fellow, how very good of you to come to see us." He was as friendly as he had been the previous week, offering his hand to the photographer and then turning his attention to Cora. "And Miss Blake. Very nice to see you again."

Already the girl felt uneasy in the man's presence. She nodded, but said nothing.

"I hope you two have recovered from last week's, er, disturbance at Abbey Green. Bad show indeed. I don't suppose you have heard any more of it?" Blake was unsure whether the mill owner was about to interrogate him again or whether those searching eyes were how Heathcote looked all the time.

"Not really. I did go to see how Mrs Carter is faring. She told me that you knew them."

"Oh yes, of course, we own the farm – there are so many in our estate, you understand. I wouldn't say I know them personally. One can't afford to get too chummy with tenants." Heathcote waved his hand airily as if to deflect any doubts Blake may have had.

"Last night I met someone else who seemed very interested in the Abbey."

"Who would that be?" asked Heathcote, now fully focused on Blake.

"His name is Dr Crosbie Sneyd, he's an historian from Oxford. He appears fascinated with the Abbey ruins. Seems quite a clever chap. He's come to Leek to do more research."

"Has he now. Sneyd you say? Never heard of him, I'm afraid."

"That's odd, because he said he had written to you a while ago."

"Well, I certainly don't recall seeing anything from a Dr Sneyd. Now, shall we begin our little tour?"

For the next hour Enoch Heathcote, the proud owner, led his guests through an almost bewildering range of departments peopled by hundreds of employees. Heathcote & Company, he explained, was one of the country's leading names in the clothing industry. It supplied fashionable braids, ribbons and trimmings, as well as clothing labels, sewing threads and boot laces by the million. The Great Mill handled the complete manufacturing process, from dyeing raw silk in the latest colours, and then spinning and twisting it into threads, before finally weaving the thread into a huge number of different designs.

"Our little empire here at the Great Mill has brought together many of the trades that years ago were scattered across the town in different buildings. And we're still growing," said Heathcote proudly.

In the weaving shed, the mill owner opened the door onto a cacophony of noise produced by the huge powered looms crammed into the building. The machines were driven by numerous belts spinning from shafts running along the ceiling. Bobbins whirled as each loom drew together hundreds of threads to form colourfully patterned ribbon. Young lads and their male overseers stood amongst the machinery, some using sign language to communicate with each other because of the din. Many would be destined to lose their hearing in later life.

In another workshop, dozens of young women braid weavers

sat in rows, their feet working frantically at treadles which drove their individual looms. Heathcote strode down the room, voice raised above the clatter of the machines, as he explained what was going on. Cora, trailing behind the two men, saw their host casually brush his hand on the backs of one or two of the teenage workers bent over their work. Most of them, she noticed, stared fixedly at their looms as he passed.

After a brief visit to the dyeworks – a male-only environment where Cora almost choked on the steam and fumes rising from the copper vats – the guests saw woodworkers knee-deep in shavings as they made new bobbins on lathes. In another department, women were producing hundreds of pattern cards for use on the power looms.

They then entered one of the subways, its curved brick walls dimly-lit by gas mantles, and came out on the other side of the street in a building that produced all the company's cardboard boxes. Here, some of the mill's youngest workers, half-time girls barely 12 years old, were brushing dollops of paste onto strips of paper to seal the boxes.

Heathcote leaned over to one of the youngsters, grabbed her by both shoulders and peered into her face, laughing. "Nellie, isn't it? You're doing a fine job there, my girl. You're going to need a good bath tonight." The girl wasn't quite sure how to react to the big man and quickly went back to her pasting.

Blake had no background either in Leek or its silk industry and so was fascinated by the tour. His interest was drawn particularly to the different pieces of equipment, asking the speed of one, the capacity of another. In each department, he spent some minutes taking a photograph or two.

For Cora, on the other hand, it was the workers who drew her attention. She was shocked to see how hard the mill people were working and she especially noticed the young women of a similar age to herself. She tried to imagine their working lives – and what it must be like to have someone like Mr Heathcote prowling around.

The spooling room was another area crowded with the younger girls. Here mile upon mile of sewing thread was being wound onto small wooden spools and then labels attached. Once again, the mill owner praised his junior employees and gazed proudly over the busy scene. Cora hadn't seen the bully she had been expecting. Instead Heathcote was acting like a doting uncle.

Leaving the clatter of the looms behind, the visitors were given a brief tour of the offices where the accounts manager was keen to show off his department. Looking across the women seated at desks, Cora was sure she saw one or two glance warily in the mill owner's direction before swiftly turning back to their ledgers. The tour over, Heathcote assured Blake that Mrs Heathcote would be in touch about her portrait photographs. He himself had a business meeting to attend and must bid them farewell, he said.

The whistle signalling the end of the morning shift sounded as Nathaniel and Cora walked away. Minutes later the street outside the mill would be full of a bustling crowd as hundreds of workers took their lunch break. For the youngest girls and boys, this was the end of their half-day at work and they would be back at school in the afternoon.

"Well that was certainly interesting, don't you agree Cora?" said Blake as they made their way to the studio. "It's amazing what goes on inside those buildings. And the machinery, so modern."

"I still don't like Mr Heathcote. I've heard that he's not very kind to some of the girls," his daughter replied.

"Unkind? Surely not. You saw how he was today, he seemed to be really quite caring."

"That's it, he makes a fuss of some of them, but then he can turn nasty. That's what I've heard anyway."

"Well, as you've never worked in a place like that I don't think you appreciate what it's like to take orders from someone.

Sometimes young folk just have to do as they're told, as everyone else does."

Cora was exasperated. "Don't be patronising, father," she thought, "just give me credit for my own opinions." Struggling to keep her temper, she began to walk faster, putting a few paces between the two of them. In Derby Street she noticed a poster for a trade union demonstration being held in town the following Saturday. It was an appeal for female workers in the mills to join a union and defend their rights. "Perhaps that will help the girls in the Great Mill," she wondered. However she couldn't help being concerned about Heathcote.

Back home that evening, her mother handed her a folded note that had arrived earlier. Cora recognised that her name on the outside was in Polly's handwriting.

"Dear Cora. We're going roller skating on Friday night after work. Do you want to come? I expect some of our friends will be there, as well as our Meg and some of my cousins. We're going to meet up outside the rink in Salisbury Street at half past six. Polly"

Cora was more than happy to go skating. The rink was becoming very popular and she and her friends had been several times. She also realised that this could be her chance to ask some more questions about life in the Great Mill.

"Do you have everything under control?"

Elizabeth Heathcote focused her steely gaze on her husband, seated at the far end of the oak dining table in their mansion, Longview. They had just finished their evening meal, eaten in silence, as was their habit.

"Yes, yes, of course dear," Enoch Heathcote reassured her.

"Have you heard any more about this business at Abbey Green?"

"Inspector Ramm is under strict orders to keep me informed, and I'm sure I will see him at court tomorrow. According to what he said on Sunday, they are no further forward."

"And what about the mill? Are you behaving yourself?" There was no hint of levity in Elizabeth's tone.

"I'm sure I don't know what you mean by that, dear. As far as the business is concerned, things are going smoothly. Very smoothly indeed."

"You saw Blake today, didn't you? Did he have anything new to say?"

"He seemed to be surprised that the Carters were our tenants."

"We should have got them out of there years ago, but I expect the widow will give it up, soon enough."

"He also mentioned that historian fellow, Crosbie Sneyd. Would you believe it, he's arrived in Leek and been poking around. Apparently Blake met him last night at some event and Sneyd was blathering on about the Abbey."

Elizabeth's expression became even more stoney than usual. "Sneyd? That's a rather unfortunate coincidence," she said.

"He said he's staying at The George for a few days. But I'm sure there's absolutely nothing for you to be concerned about, my dear."

Enoch was growing weary of his wife's questions and at that moment just wanted a little peace. "If you will excuse me, I'm going to enjoy a cigar in the billiard room while I pot a few balls. I need to practise because Henry Aston's coming tomorrow night and I don't want to give him the satisfaction of beating me." He got up from the table and left the room.

Elizabeth was far from reassured. She knew all about her husband's philandering with young women and for a long time had taken steps behind his back to make sure that his dalliances would not damage their good name nor the business. That was one of the reasons she kept watch – from a safe distance – on what went on at the Great Mill and in the town, and then kept people quiet by whatever means she thought fit. Now there was this trouble at Abbey Green and she had little confidence in her husband's ability to keep abreast of developments.

Elizabeth left the dining table and settled into her armchair in the sitting room, reaching over to press a brass button on the wall beside the fireplace to summon Margaret Gamage, her paid companion. Wife of the Heathcotes' estate steward, Mrs Gamage was willing to meet her mistress's every wish. More importantly, she was Elizabeth's eyes and ears on the outside world, passing on titbits of gossip she heard in the town. She also quizzed, and bribed, various women who worked in the Great Mill. Within moments the companion appeared in the room. The gaunt fifty-year-old had an austere demeanour to match her mistress.

"Gamage, I have several things for you to do this evening. But first, is there anything to report from your… contacts? Nothing said about the Carters?"

"No, Madam. I saw Martha Bailey in town earlier, but she had little news from the mill." Mrs Gamage paused, considering whether her next information might unsettle her mistress. "There's a trade union demonstration at the weekend. Apparently they want to recruit more mill girls so that they can try to get better working conditions."

Elizabeth Heathcote snorted with disdain. "They can try if they like, but they won't get anywhere with us. Keep me informed anyway."

"Yes, Madam."

"Now, to this evening's tasks. There are one or two errands, for you to do, but first bring me a some writing paper and envelopes. You know the colours I like. I have some urgent letters to send." Elizabeth knew the efficiency of the GPO meant that a letter posted tonight would be delivered locally before midday tomorrow.

Tuesday evenings were usually quiet at the New Inn in the village of Flash. After tending to the thirsts of the regulars standing at the bar, landlady Gladys Sheldon had time to pop outside. On a muddy patch behind the pub were a couple of young pigs which she was fattening nicely on a daily diet of beer slops. It was time to coax them in the sty for the night. By Christmas there would be roast pork all round, she thought.

When she came back inside she saw that a new customer had arrived. Caleb Salt was sitting in his usual chair in the corner waiting for his ale to arrive. Gladys knew exactly what he would be drinking, sixpenny best from the brewery at Leek, and also knew that he didn't like to be kept waiting. In his early thirties, Salt was tall and broad-shouldered. In contrast to many villagers – who looked thin and beaten down by their hard life high on the moors – he was in the peak of health, physically strong, confident. That's why few people dared to cross him.

He nodded to Gladys when she placed the glass on the table in front of him. "Shame about poor Amos, weren't it?" she said.

Salt's grunted response revealed nothing. Bad things happened in life, why should he want to talk about it?

Gladys went back to the bar and Salt continued to study a scrap of paper bearing a column of names with numbers against each one. It was a list of boxers, for that's what Caleb Salt was, a bare-knuckle fighter. The paper was a list of possible opponents drawn from across several counties and the purse on offer for each match.

As well as its reputation as the highest village in the country, Flash had two other claims to fame. In olden days it had been a centre for the counterfeiting coins – flash money as it was called, hence the village's adopted name. Secondly, it was notorious for illegal boxing. This was where the boundaries of Staffordshire, Derbyshire and Cheshire met, and it was said that illegal activity could be moved across the border from one county to another to avoid the attentions of the police. Bare-knuckle bouts were organised in secret and held either inside a large barn or in an open arena out of sight from the road. Word of the boxing would circulate around local inns and the fights attracted large and raucous crowds. Substantial sums were often waged, though the gambling was just as illegal as the boxing match.

This was the brutal world which Caleb Salt had been born into. He'd known cruelty since he was a boy, brought up on the edge of poverty by a bruised mother and a brutal father who had used his fists at home as well as in the ring. One way or another Salt had survived and ultimately had himself gained notoriety, and a fair amount of money, from boxing.

His work swinging a sledgehammer in a local quarry kept his muscles in shape and he also did the occasional job for Enoch Heathcote. Villagers knew that he worked as a beater when the mill owner was shooting grouse on his moorland estate. The locals therefore registered no surprise when the Heathcote steward, Bernard Gamage, appeared at the pub door that night and made straight for Salt. Square-jawed with short cropped hair, Gamage was the man who did the tiresome and sometimes unpleasant tasks that kept Heathcote tenants in order and the estate running smoothly. He was the one who arranged the shooting parties and organised the casual labour needed for the day's sport.

"Evening Caleb. A message for you."

Salt looked up, apparently annoyed at being interrupted. Heathcote money had been useful to him, but he couldn't care less about Gamage and showed the steward little respect. Equally, the steward disliked a ruffian such as Salt and wasn't best pleased at having to ride out to Flash of an evening to act as messenger boy. He was in no mood to waste words.

"You're wanted tomorrow night. Orders to be given."

"What, at the Lodge?"

"No, you're to go to Longview. Back door, mind. Eight o'clock."

"Another shoot planned?"

"You'll find out tomorrow. Be sure to be there on time." With that, Gamage turned on his heal and walked outside to his horse, tethered near the inn door.

The locals at the bar pretended not to overhear the conversation, but when the steward left, two or three of them couldn't help exchanging looks. Few liked Gamage, who was less than sympathetic in his dealings with Heathcote's many tenants in the district. And most of them were wary of Salt, who they knew had a fierce temper.

Salt returned to his list – he had several bouts planned for the next few weeks and wanted to consider his likely opponents. He would be sure to go to Longview the following evening, but if his new plan went well, he could soon be free of Gamage and the Heathcotes for good. With enough money he could give up boxing and leave Flash for ever. A rare smile came on his lips.

Chapter Seven

Nathaniel Blake made an early start on the Friday three days later. This morning the bells were to be moved from the tower of St Edward's, the Old Church as townsfolk called it. The 200-year-old bells were being sent for re-tuning and Blake had been asked to photograph the occasion. By the time he had collected his portable camera and a satchel of photographic plates from the studio, it was half past seven when he arrived at the church. A group of people were clustered at the foot of the tower. Blake assumed they were looking at the first of the bells brought out of the belfry, but as he approached he sensed concern in their murmured conversation. He then saw what they were standing around – it was not a bell, but a body.

"Stand back please. There's nothing to be done." Police Constable Knowles was keeping order whilst waiting for his superior to arrive. The Vicar, Reverend Maitland, detached himself from the group as he saw Blake arrive and came towards the photographer. "A most terrible accident, Mr Blake. I'm afraid this is going to delay proceedings. In fact we may have to postpone moving the bells altogether."

"What on earth's happened?" asked Blake.

"It seems that someone may have fallen from the tower. The verger and myself found him when we came to the church about an hour ago. He's quite dead, the poor man."

"Was it one of the workmen moving the bells?" Blake asked.

"It's certainly not a workman. I just don't know how or when it could have happened. There was no bell ringing practice last night, of course, so I haven't been into church since yesterday afternoon," the Vicar replied. Though presumably accustomed to supporting his parishioners at times of death, he was obviously taken aback to discover a tragedy such as this at his own church and appeared remarkably flustered.

At that point the familiar figure of Inspector Ramm arrived and the knot of people, which included several church officials, drew apart so that the policeman could get closer to the body. Blake himself also drew a little nearer and saw the body of a man, face down on the paving slabs, his arms and his long legs spread wide. A dark shape – a pool of blood, now dried – encircled the man's head. To his horror, the photographer recognised the dead man's distinctive blue striped blazer. "No, surely it can't be Dr Sneyd," he thought.

Inspector Ramm bent down next to the body and then looked upwards, gauging the man's fall from the tower. He stood up, asked the bystanders to disperse and ordered Constable Knowles to stand watch over the body while he went inside the church. Blake, still trying to come to terms with the scene, had moved further along the church path when a familiar voice came from behind him.

"Well, this is not the story I was expecting to write this morning." Like Blake, FJ Finch had come to the Old Church to see the bells removed and had just arrived.

"So what's going on? Do we know who it is? When did it all happen?" Finch had already begun to write in his notebook. "And you're on the scene, once again Nathaniel." Seeing the photographer's shocked expression, he realised he should change his tone. "I'm sorry. Are you all right, Nathaniel?"

"I think I need to sit down," Blake managed to reply. But before he could make it to a nearby bench or say any more to the newspaper editor, Inspector Ramm came out of the church and walked purposefully towards the two men.

"Good morning Mr Blake, Mr Finch. A sorry affair. There was little chance for anyone who toppled from up there," he said, nodding at the tower.

"A nasty accident then, Inspector?" Finch was keen to nail the details for the *Leek Lion*.

"It looks to be. But please, Mr Finch, give us chance to sort things out before you put anything in the *Lion*." Ramm turned to the photographer. "I see you have your camera, Mr Blake. Could I ask you to take some photographs for us. Of the body and also from the tower, perhaps looking down on where this poor chap fell? It will be the usual arrangement, for police files you understand."

Blake pulled himself together and, with the constable's help, moved the onlookers away from the body. It was the very last thing he expected to be doing this morning, but Blake went about his task of photographing the tragic scene from a number of angles. He couldn't allow his personal turmoil to disrupt his professional duty to the police. Though the man's face was smashed when he hit the paving stones, Blake was now sure that the victim was Dr Sneyd.

Blake then went inside the church and made his way up a narrow staircase at the back to the belfry. He climbed a creaking ladder which led to a hatch opening onto the lead-covered roof of the tower. On any day but this he would have wanted to capture the views out over town roofs and the countryside beyond. Today however, he leaned over the ancient parapet with its crown of stone pinnacles and pointed his camera directly downwards to where the spread-eagled body lay fifty feet below. As he looked from the tower his mind was full of what must have been Dr Sneyd's last moments on this very same spot. Having clambered back down the ladder to the belfry he saw scuff marks on the floor. The thick layers of dust on the centuries-old wooden bell frames had also been disturbed. "Probably the workmen preparing to disconnect the bells," he thought.

Once outside, he could see the local undertaker, supervised by Inspector Ramm, was preparing to remove the body. Over to one side, Finch was jotting notes as he talked to Reverend Maitland. As Blake approached them he could hear that the Vicar was still distressed.

"It's one tragedy after another. To be honest, I am still coming to terms with what happened to poor Amos Carter," said the clergyman.

"So you knew Mr Carter?" asked Finch.

"Oh yes, I knew Amos quite well. Over the years he had been very active in the church and I know he was proud of being associated with both Dieulacres and St Edward's. Our church used to be part of the Abbey estate, you know. Centuries ago, the monks were responsible for rebuilding the church and would come to worship here. It's a hugely important part of our history." The Vicar seemed to be lost in thought, then he continued. "It was such a shock when Amos was… killed. I had been expecting to meet him, but unfortunately never got the chance."

"What, the day he died? That was a grim coincidence. On some church business was it?" It was obvious to Blake that the journalist was trying to extract information for his story despite his efforts to mask his curiosity.

"I don't know what it was about, more's the pity. Amos had sent me a note saying he had something important to discuss. It had troubled him to a long while and it was time to make a clean breast of it all, he said. But sadly I never found out what he wanted to say. I just wish I had been able to give him some help, some peace of mind. And now we have another tragedy... We must look to our faith for strength."

Shaking his head, the Vicar walked away to speak to his verger and Finch turned his attention to Blake. "The Vicar seems rather shocked by all this, but so do you, Nathaniel."

Blake's mind was in a whirl. He had been confronted by two deaths in a matter of days. Last week it was Amos Carter, now it was Dr Sneyd. Where would it all end? "I'm sure I knew him, the man who fell. In fact I was only talking to him on Monday evening," he said.

"Local fellow, was he?" Finch had his pencil at the ready.

"Not at all. His name was Crosbie Sneyd, he was an academic from Oxford University apparently. He told me he was here to find out about the Abbey ruins." Blake could see that Finch was immediately interested, and he knew the risks in being candid with a journalist. However, at this moment he felt the need to talk to someone.

"Let's sit on this bench while we catch our breath," Finch suggested. The two sat down and Blake told haltingly of meeting Dr Sneyd at the lantern slide show, the historian's discovery of an ancient Dieulacres document and him staying at The George.

"Well, I suppose you will have to tell the Inspector," said the editor, "but such historical matters may not be relevant to what's happened today. This ancient document does sound rather curious, though."

Ramm had left by now and Blake had no idea if the police would need his help in identifying the victim. The Inspector might tell him to leave the police to get on with their work, just as he had done on Monday.

"Do you think this has anything to do with Amos Carter? They were certainly both linked to the Abbey. Or am I jumping to conclusions?" Blake said, as much to himself as to Finch. Both men were curious to find out what had happened, although perhaps for different reasons. Blake felt a connection with the two victims, while Finch sensed that there was a good story in this. "Why don't we go across to The George, just to check things out?" Finch suggested.

Blake was uncertain about the idea at first, but, reassured by Finch, put his doubts to one side and the two crossed Church Street to The George Hotel opposite. Inside, a young woman was clearing away last night's debris from the bar and a couple of early drinkers look across from their pints. Finch, needless to say, knew hotel-keeper Jacob Watkins on first name terms, and told him a fanciful tale that they were returning items belonging to Dr Sneyd, who may or may not have had an accident. For the sake of keeping good relations with the *Lion*, Watkins seemed prepared to accept the story. He showed them to the top floor room which the historian had been using.

Blake noticed the bedroom window looked across to the church tower where the unfortunate academic had met his fate. He started to regret intruding and would have preferred to go straight out of the room again, but Finch was already looking around for anything of interest. The room was furnished with a bed, a chair and a nightstand on which sat Sneyd's straw boater. On the floor was a polished leather suitcase, its lid open to reveal a few items of clothing and a collection of papers.

Finch glanced round to make sure the door was closed and then reached down to pick up the bundle of papers. He spread them out on the bed.

"Do you really think we should be doing this?" asked Blake, becoming more uneasy by the minute.

"I think we could both find something of interest here. And if it eases your conscience, you can go and tell the Inspector when we leave. Now, let's look at these," Finch replied, examining the documents one after another.

Blake saw that one appeared much older than the rest and picked it up. It was a piece of thick yellowish paper that he presumed was vellum, curling at the top and bottom. A handwritten text in what looked like Latin began "*Hoc monasterium fuerit sanctifactio mea in multi annis....*" The sheet appeared to have been rolled up originally and Blake could see the remains of a red wax seal which had secured the scroll.

The next piece of paper he picked up was more recent and he guessed it was Sneyd's translation of the original letter. He read it through.

This Abbey has been our Sanctuary for many years. But now our time of peaceful devotion here is coming to an end. Our future is in the Lord's hands, but I fear that our beloved Abbey will be destroyed as have so many others in this time of tumult.

My Brothers and I have tried to live an honest and humble life in the service of God. It has not always been so and we give penance for the misdeeds of those who came before us. The lands that the Holy Brothers have tended for centuries are being torn from us. Tomorrow the stones of Dieulacres may come down, but I swear that our Holy Treasure will not be taken from here. We have vowed to protect the Abbey's most precious possession, our Golden Cross, which our Blessed Founder, Lord Ranulph, rescued from the Holy Land.

On this night we have wrapped the Cross in leather and buried it deep in the ground, beside our ever-flowing Churnet. It will rest within sight of the Abbey where it has graced our worship for so many generations. The place where it lies is marked with a cross. I pray that one day this most treasured Cross will be returned to a Holy Sanctuary. Until then, may it remain safe from the grasping hands of heathens.

Thomas Whitney
Abbot of Dieulacres
Tenth day of October, the year of our Lord 1538

Now Blake understood why Dr Sneyd had been so excited by his discovery in the archives at Oxford. A golden cross buried beside the Abbey? A relic from the Crusades?

"Have you seen this, FJ? I think it's the important one. It's Dr Sneyd's transcript of the ancient letter." Finch took the paper from him and read it quickly. "A couple of local history books did say something about treasures that were lost from the Abbey. Apparently the Abbot put up quite a fight to keep the Abbey and its property together. He made numerous appeals to Thomas Cromwell and his Commissioners. But I've never seen anything about relics being buried down there. What this says is extraordinary!" Finch's mind was working overtime, headlines already appearing for the articles he would one day write on the subject.

For Blake, the affair he had become involved in now seemed even more complicated. He rapidly leafed through the other papers, most of which appeared to be pages of Dr Sneyd's neatly-written notes. Then amongst them he found a smaller piece of blue notepaper, a letter written in a different hand.

St Edward's Vicarage, Leek
27th August
Dear Dr Sneyd,
I gather you are visiting our town to further your research into Dieulacres Abbey. Our church records contain some ancient documents which relate to the Abbey. I believe these may be of interest to you and I would be happy to show them to you.

Unfortunately I am very busy with church commitments this week, however I could meet you at St Edward's on Thursday evening, if that is convenient. I shall be in church from 8 p.m. onwards.

Yours sincerely,
G.W. Maitland, Vicar

He handed the letter to Finch, who was now writing in his notebook. "This doesn't make sense. Less than an hour ago Reverend Maitland told me he had not been near the church last night. But according to this letter he was going to have a meeting there with Dr Sneyd," Blake said. He was horrified. Sneyd had been invited to the church where he had met his death.

"It looks to me there are quite a few things that don't add up around here. Perhaps the Vicar was mistaken. I'm going to make a note of what the old document says, anyway." Finch paused to think. "Better still Nathaniel, perhaps you should take a photograph of the Abbot's letter and the translation. If nothing else, they're historically important and it would be good to make a record while we have them in our hands."

Blake unpacked his camera and photographic plates. "Let's move this chair closer to the window and I'll place the papers on the seat so they are in the best light. FJ, you will have to hold down the edges of the very old one to stop it from curling up."

After photographing Abbot Whitney's letter and Sneyd's translation, Blake was about to pack away the camera when he decided take a picture of the note from Reverend Maitland, too. That letter troubled him as much as the others and he thought it might be important.

Having the put the documents back in the suitcase, the two men left the hotel. Standing on the pavement outside, they agreed it was best to delay telling anyone of their visit to The George and Finch headed for the *Lion* office, already sketching out his report for the next day's newspaper. Blake went to his studio, keen to develop the photograph from the tower that Ramm had requested. When he delivered the print to the station he would tell the Inspector that he thought the dead man was Crosbie Sneyd.

John Gibb was taking a swig from the drinking fountain near the church gate when saw the two men leave The George just across the street. The tramp had spent the previous night in the churchyard, not amongst the gravestones but sheltered by the boundary wall. He had seen comings and goings at the church that evening before falling soundly asleep. He knew nothing of the accident until he woke up that morning to see a crowd outside the church and had retired to a safe distance at the far side of the graveyard. He was now looking along Church Street when he saw someone else he recognised go into The George. Like the photographer, Gibb felt he was being dragged into an affair against his wishes. He knew he had a choice: either to walk away, as he had done many times before, or to face up to his responsibilities. Sooner or later he was going to have to confront photographer Blake.

Inspector Ramm was satisfied with his morning's work. With the investigation into Carter's murder still proceeding, the last thing he wanted was another mystery on his hands and he had convinced himself that the tragic death at the Old Church was an accident. He had yet to find out all the details, but he could not see how or why foul play should be involved. It might even be suicide. He expected to have the matter wrapped up without need for a lengthy investigation, although to be safe he had asked the medical officer to carry out a post morten. As to Amos Carter's murder, things were less satisfactory. No farmer at the weekly market had been able to identify the man in the photograph and Mrs Carter had given them no further help.

Having finished his lunch of a beef sandwich, Ramm was about to begin writing his initial report on the Old Church incident when Nathaniel Blake arrived with a print of the photograph he had taken from the church tower. "I believe I may know who the unfortunate man was. I met him on Monday evening," said Blake as he handed the photograph to the Inspector.

"Dr Sneyd you mean? Yes, I think we've identified him,"

Inspector replied, looking at the photograph and shaking his head in dismay. Seeing the body pictured from the top of the tower brought home just how far the man had fallen. "The poor man had some calling cards in his jacket which gave his name and an address in Oxford. We managed to get through to the Oxford police station on our new telephone and ask if they could find a relative who could come to Leek to give us a positive identification. Not a pleasant trip for someone, but it has to be done.

"There was also a receipt from The George in his pocket, as well as a room key, and it turned out that Dr Sneyd was staying there. I sent a constable to look in his room."

The photographer was relieved to hear this. With luck, he would not have to reveal he too had visited the hotel that morning.

"Dr Sneyd told me he was in Leek to carry out some research into the Abbey and he intended to visit St Edward's," said Blake. "I expect your man found Dr Sneyd's papers in his room."

"Papers? No papers, I'm afraid. No documents of any kind. What makes you think there would be papers, Mr Blake?"

"Er, I'm only surmising, Inspector. I simply thought he would have brought some documents with him. Obviously I don't know if he did or not." Blake was taken aback that Sneyd's papers had not been found. He now needed to cover his tracks.

"I must admit it's rather strange that a learned man, such as you describe, would not have even a notebook with him. Perhaps he lost his papers at the church. Scattered to the wind when he fell. Certainly Mr Watkins, who keeps The George, said he'd seen no one else go to Dr Sneyd's room."

So Watkins had not revealed the visit he and Finch had made, thought Blake. Was he concealing the theft, too?

"Papers or not, this has all the makings of a tragic accident, Mr Blake. I think Dr Sneyd must have decided to visit the church and then climbed up to the tower. He was a stranger and so he could have misjudged the height of the parapet and fell over it – it is rather low and he was very tall fellow. Probably nothing more complicated than that."

Inspector Ramm seemed so satisfied with his explanation that Blake made a rash decision, just as he had done with Finch that morning. He decided not to tell of the documents he had seen in Dr Sneyd's room. How could he without admitting he had been to the hotel? He would keep it to himself, at least until he knew whether it was important to the investigation or not.

After leaving the police station, he hurried back to the church with his camera. The eight huge bells were now lined up on the path outside the church door. Soon they would be taken by horse and cart to the railway station and then by train to Croydon Bell Foundry for repair. Reverend Maitland and various church officials posed with fixed expressions behind the bells while Blake took a photograph. As the group dispersed, he managed to delay the Vicar.

"I believe the police have identified the fellow who fell from the tower. Dr Crosbie Sneyd, an historian from Oxford. Have you heard of him?" Blake asked.

"What a terrible business it has been, Mr Blake. None of us can quite believe what has happened. Dr Sneyd? No, I don't think I know the name."

"I met him on Monday evening. He was looking into some matters connected with Dieulacres Abbey and he said he wanted to look at the church records. So, he hadn't contacted you?"

"As I say Mr Blake, I haven't heard of the man. Why he was at St Edward's is as much a mystery to me as it is to everyone else." Reverend Maitland returned to supervise the loading of the bells onto two carts.

Blake was shocked at the Vicar's response. Either the clergyman really didn't know Dr Sneyd and had not invited him to the church, or he was a convincing liar. Whichever was true, there was something suspicious about the note the historian had received and which may have lured him to his death. He decided he must go directly to the *Lion* office to tell Finch what he had learned at the police station.

With only hours to go before the printing press was due to roll, there was an air of fraught urgency, both in the *Lion*'s typesetting department and in the newsroom on the top floor, when Blake arrived. Oliver the reporter was pounding his typewriter keys with greater force than ever whilst FJ Finch was checking proof sheets, muttering to himself as he made rapid corrections with a pencil. The editor, tense and excitable as his deadline approached, looked up as Blake appeared at the top of the stairs and came into the newsroom.

"Something new? Not another death?" he asked quickly.

"It's about our little visit this morning…" Blake paused, his eyes sliding across to the reporter, whose pounding continued unabated, apparently oblivious of the conversation.

"It's all right, you can speak in front of Oliver. He can be trusted, otherwise I'll disown him." Oliver smiled and carried on typing.

"The police went round to Dr Sneyd's room at The George and found…nothing. It looks like the papers had been taken."

"What! Stolen you mean?"

"It certainly appears so."

"A curious affair, indeed! I saw Ramm earlier and he told me he was virtually certain it was Dr Sneyd, but he didn't mention that anything was missing," Finch replied.

"That's just it. Ramm doesn't know there were documents in the room in the first place. I had the greatest difficulty in not letting on that we had been in there. Thankfully your friend Watkins at The George had said that no one had been in the room. He covered up for us, but he might be covering up the theft, too."

"And you didn't tell Ramm about the Abbey papers, then?"

"I thought it was safest not to, at least for the time being," said photographer, rather sheepishly.

"Nathaniel, I'm impressed. We'll make a newsman of you yet."

"So what do we do now?" Blake asked.

"Nothing hasty. I'm not going to mention anything about the Abbey documents or this golden cross in the *Lion* just yet. It's all far too tasty to rush into print until we have the full story. We need to do some more digging. Nathaniel, why don't you go to see your friend Mrs Carter again?"

That was exactly what Blake was planning to do.

It was nearly half past six when Cora Blake arrived outside the roller skating rink in Salisbury Street. Groups of young people were milling around near the entrance, talking excitedly and Cora spotted her friend Polly Pickford. Standing next to Polly were her younger sister Meg, her cousins Ada and Fanny, and a dark-haired girl of about their own age whom she didn't recognise.

Roller skating had become a very popular over the last couple of years and there were now no less than three rinks in the town, but the one in Salisbury Street was the rink that Cora and her friends preferred. For the first hour on Friday evenings the rink was reserved for young folk. Later on the skating would be adults only and the rink had become a popular meeting place for courting couples on Friday and Saturday nights. On either side of the doorway Cora saw posters for some of the special events that were planned at the rink over the coming weeks including a hockey match, several organised dances and even an obstacle race featuring professional competitors.

"Glad you're here Cora. Quick, let's go inside before it gets too busy," said Polly as her friend approached. The girls queued at a hatch just inside the doorway. Cora handed over sixpence – four pence entry and an extra tuppence to hire a pair of skates. Polly and her sister had free entrance tickets because their father allowed the rink's owner to put up a poster in the window of the family's tea room. Further along the crowded corridor they scrabbled through shelves of skates to find ones that would fit, quickly strapped them on over their boots and then went into the main hall. The noise inside the barrel-roofed building was growing by the minute. Young people were shouting to each other as their skates thundered across on the wooden floor. The six girls linked arms and went round and round the rink, managing to dodge other skaters, especially the young lads, most of whom were up to high-speed mischief. After half an hour the girls were breathless and decided to treat themselves to a halfpenny glass of lemonade each in the refreshment room.

"Oh, what excellent fun! By the way, this is Ada's friend Ellen, Ellen Simms. She works with her at the Great Mill," said Polly, introducing the girl whom Cora had not met before.

The six did not linger over their drinks because they wanted to make full use of their skating time and were soon back on the rink. The atmosphere became more frenetic as the "junior hour" wore on, with several groups of youths chasing each other – and the girls – around the rink. The shouting and laughter increased and there were a number of spills. All too soon a whistle announced the end of the session and the friends pushed their way through the crowd of young people who were pouring onto the pavement outside.

"Phew, that's made me hot," said Cora, fanning her face with her hand. "Why don't we sit down and cool off a little," she suggested, pointing to a bench just along the street. Polly's sister decided to go home and the remaining five managed to squeeze onto the bench. After some general chat, Cora took the chance of introducing mill work into their conversation.

"Mr Heathcote showed us around the Great Mill on Tuesday. That place is so large! And it looked really hard work for some of the girls. I think I'm lucky that I only help father in his studio," she said.

"Yes, it's hard, all right. But thank goodness there's only tomorrow morning left and then we've got a whole day and a half off," said Ada. The other cousin, Fanny, nodded vigorously.

"What do you girls think of Mr Heathcote? He seemed a bit odd to me," said Cora.

"What makes you say that?" asked Ada.

"I'm not sure, I just didn't like how he looked at me and the way he was with some of the girls in the mill."

Ellen spoke for the first time. "It's not his eyes you have to worry about."

"When we started at the mill some of the older ones told us to watch out for Handy Heathcote – that's what they called him. We used to think it was a joke," Ada explained. But then her smile disappeared. "I shouldn't have said that! Don't tell your father, will you Cora? Mr Heathcote might find out and then there could be trouble."

"You soon find out it's no joke." Ellen was looking serious now. "But it's something you have to put up with, particularly if you want to keep your job."

"That doesn't seem fair to me," said Cora.

"Lots of things aren't fair, are they? Like you said, you're lucky because you work for your dad. But some of us girls want to better ourselves." Ellen paused, undecided whether to say more. "Old Heathcote's no trouble provided you go along with what he says. Just keep nodding and smiling and laugh about it if he tries to give you a cuddle. Either that or you try to keep your head down and stay out of his way."

Polly looked concerned – she thought Ellen had said enough. "Let's not talk about work any more, especially after we've had such a good time tonight." The little group dispersed soon afterwards and headed home.

Later that evening Blake took the opportunity to tell his wife what had gone on during the day. He knew he had to be honest with

Edith and also felt that talking it through with her might help him get the day's events a little straighter in his own mind. The two youngest children had gone to bed and Cora, now returned from her visit to the skating rink, was reading in her room. Nathaniel and Edith had settled down in the parlour when he launched into his description of what had happened at the Old Church that morning. He knew the conversation was going to be difficult.

"What, another death? And the man you met on Monday? That is awful." Edith was shocked, but her reaction turned to disbelief when Nathaniel told of his visit to Dr Sneyd's hotel room and what he and the editor had found.

"Oh no, Nathaniel! What were you thinking of? Why did you have to get involved?"

"Well, Finch suggested..."

Edith interrupted him before he could say any more. "Finch? Of course Finch would suggest something! All he's interested in is printing another story in the *Lion*. You were probably breaking the law and getting mixed up in something you shouldn't. Isn't this Amos Carter affair enough to be worrying about?" Edith paused for breath, then continued. "Well, at least I suppose you were able to help Inspector Ramm."

"That's the thing...." Blake tailed off as he realised he was getting into even deeper water with his wife. "I didn't actually tell the Inspector about us going to the room or seeing the letters. Well I couldn't, could I? And it turned out someone else went in the room after we did and took all the papers. What do you think about that?"

"What I think is that you should stop. Now. It's the job of the police to investigate such things. You're a photographer, not a detective. What if something strange is going on? You might be putting yourself in danger. And what about Cora? Her name was in last week's newspaper, too. I don't want her involved any more of this."

Edith was adamant. She folded her arms to emphasise the point.

Blake was hardly surprised by his wife's reaction. He knew she was talking sense, but he was equally sure that something suspicious had gone on with Dr Sneyd's papers. Inspector Ramm might be satisfied that Dr Sneyd's death was an accident, but why wasn't the Vicar telling the truth? Why had the papers been taken from The George if not to cover up something? What about the Abbey treasure that the Abbot's letter talked about?

He couldn't help but think about something Ramm had said: "What could Amos Carter have that was worth killing him for?" He intended to visit Mrs Carter the next day in the hope of finding out more, but he knew he had something else to do first. Now the originals had gone missing, he must protect his photographs of the Abbey documents and of Reverend Maitland's letter. He needed to make new prints and bring the negatives back home for safe keeping.

"Edith, you have every right to be concerned and I promise you I will be careful. But it's just something I can't turn my back on. Now though, I need to go back to the studio. I have something urgent I must do."

"Now? It's nearly nine o'clock!"

Saying he would be as back as soon as possible, Blake left the house and entered streets that were still busy. It was pay day in the mills and many provisions shops and public houses stayed open late to serve customers who now had money in their pockets.

Edith heard the front door close. She doubted her opinions would have much effect on her husband. She was used to his sudden enthusiasms – the latest camera, a new bicycle, selling postcards – and his inquisitive nature had been one of the things she had found attractive in the first place. But he would rush into things. She was worried that this dabbling in police matters would get him into trouble, and leave even less time for his family. She decided she would need to keep a closer eye on what he was doing.

In her bedroom, Cora had been trying unsuccessfully to concentrate on the latest book from her literature class at Miss Keates' Academy. Her mind was on other things, especially what the girls had said earlier about working for Enoch Heathcote. She had been uneasy about the man from the start and now she wondered about what Ellen had said about having to give in to him. father was going to take photographs at the trade union event tomorrow and Cora decided that she would go with him to help. That way she might hear for herself if there was any way to help the mill girls.

Chapter Eight

The Leek Lion
SATURDAY, AUGUST 30TH 1902

LOCAL INTELLIGENCE

THE ABBEY GREEN MURDER. – Investigations are continuing into the violent death of farmer Amos Carter at Dieulacres Cottage Farm, Abbey Green, Leek last week. Mr. Carter was found dead from grievous injuries in his barn, having been tied up by an unknown assailant. It is believed he had been beaten about the head and his body mutilated.

The *Leek Lion* understands that the police are trying to identify a man who was seen walking away from the farm on the afternoon of Tuesday August 19th.

Officers were present at Leek Cattle Market on Wednesday this week to gather information from members of the local farming community. However it is understood that no arrest has been made.

Inspector Albert Ramm of Leek Police made an appeal to the public to help solve the heinous crime.

"We are anxious to speak to anyone who was in the vicinity of the farm on the Tuesday afternoon in question," he said. "Mr. Carter was the victim of a most violent attack which, at this time, seems to be without motive. It does not appear that anything was stolen from the farm. There was at least one person near the barn whom we have yet to identify."

A funeral has been arranged to take place at St. Edward's Parish Church on Tuesday, September 2nd at 2 p.m. when a large attendance from the local farming community is expected.

TRAGIC DEATH AT OLD CHURCH. – Arrangements to remove the bells from St. Edward's Parish Church, Leek prior to renovation, were delayed yesterday morning (Friday) after a most tragic event. The body of a man was found on the paving stones within the church precincts.

The discovery was made by the Vicar, the Rev. G.W. Maitland, when he arrived at the church at about seven o'clock to prepare for the bells to be dismantled from the tower. Leek Police were immediately called to be scene and the body was later removed by undertakers. A post mortem examination is to take place.

"It appears that the man may have fallen from the church tower at some point on Thursday evening or during the early hours of Friday morning. We are keeping an open mind as to the cause, but at this time we believe it may have been a tragic accident," said Inspector A. Ramm. As the *Leek Lion* went to press the dead man's identity had not been confirmed officially, but it is believed he was an academic visiting the town from Oxford.

Meanwhile, the St. Edward's peal of six bells was removed later in the day prior to dispatch by train to the Dulwich Bell Foundry, London.

TRADES UNION DEMONSTRATION. – Representatives from the Women's Trade Union League will join members of the Leek Women Workers' Union, the female section of the Braid Workers' Union and unions representing silk and cotton dyers, throwsters, silk pickers, twisters, clerks and warehousemen at a rally in Leek Market Place today (Saturday).

Speeches will commence at 2 p.m. after which there will be a parade through the streets of the town led by the Temperance Band. The event is being organised to persuade more female workers in Leek's silk industry to join an appropriate union and to push for improved working conditions and pay rates compared with their male colleagues.

TALES OF THE OLD ABBEY. – Do you know a legend regarding Dieulacres Abbey? Or you may even have an old artefact that is said to come from the holy place. The *Leek Lion* is planning an interesting series of articles about the Abbey and would be happy to hear from our readers any tales that have been handed down through the generations. Contact F.J. Finch, Editor, The Leek Lion, Market Street.

Enoch and Elizabeth Heathcote were studying the latest edition of the *Lion* on the morning after Crosbie Sneyd's body was discovered. To preserve their accustomed distance either side the breakfast table at Longview, the Heathcotes had two copies of the newspaper delivered first thing on Saturday mornings allowing them both to peruse its pages at the same time. In particular, this arrangement saved Elizabeth the distress of waiting for Enoch to finish his detailed examination of the local cricket reports before she could catch up with the latest instalment of a ladies' novel which was being serialised in the newspaper each week. That day, however, they both had a keen interest in news items contained in the 'Local Intelligence' column.

"It appears Ramm is no further on with the Amos Carter affair, other than trying to find this mystery man. Has he said anything to you about it?" said Elizabeth.

"No, I barely saw him at court on Wednesday. He seemed to be pinning his hopes on speaking to farmers at the livestock market."

"So he still knows nothing about what went on with Carter? And what do you think about this Dr Sneyd affair?"

"Sneyd? According to the *Lion*, it appears that we will not be hearing from Dr Sneyd."

Elizabeth regarded her husband with a calculating expression. "Do you know anything about this...incident... at the Old Church?" she asked.

Enoch seemed surprised by the question. "Me? Nothing at all! A tragic accident, apparently."

"If you say so, dear." Elizabeth replied. Her husband appeared eager to change the subject: "Anyway, today I have something important to attend to."

"The union rally, you mean? The mill women are plotting to squeeze us for more money, less hours and goodness knows what else!"

"No, not that. My motor car is arriving this morning." Enoch could barely contain his excitement at owning the first automobile in the town, outdoing his wealthy friends who talked of buying one of the new-fangled vehicles. Admittedly it had cost a fair sum – as much as one of his skilled men would earn in a lifetime – but think of the convenience, the thrill and the prestige. "As soon as I've finished this kedgeree, I'm going down to the station to collect it. I should be back – driving back, mind – before lunch."

"I wouldn't want the mill workers to spoil your pleasure," said his wife sarcastically. As with other important matters, Elizabeth had already made her own arrangements behind her husband's back. Her "spies" – courtesy of Mrs Gamage – would keep her informed of what went on in the Market Place.

Throwing down his napkin, Enoch went in search of the long leather coat he had bought to wear when driving his new vehicle. He then called for his groom and the two drove to the railway station in the two-wheeled cart. When they arrived, Heathcote looked across to the goods yard where he could see an open-sided railway truck on top of which the motor car was secured with webbing straps. The four-seat Napier 16 horsepower, fresh from the factory in Lambeth, had gleaming green paintwork and deeply-buttoned upholstery in red leather. The bodywork had neither roof nor windscreen and a pair of huge nickel-plated headlamps projected in front of the radiator. The many-spoked wheels were fitted with grey pneumatic tyres and substantial chains connected the rear wheels to large gear cogs on either side of the chassis.

"Magnificent. What a beauty!" said Heathcote, as he strode along the platform, eager to get closer to the Napier. Seeing the stationmaster he seized the opportunity to tell him about the car. "First motor car in Leek, you understand. One of the finest vehicles you can buy. Fastest on the road! Someone's going to drive a Napier around the world, had you heard?" The stationmaster was actually more interested in steam trains, but was courteous enough to the mill owner. "Very nice, Sir, I'm sure," he said.

"Now," Heathcote continued, "can three or four of your men help us to get her off the truck? Perhaps we could use some planks to roll her off the back?"

It took more than an hour to unload the vehicle. Having unfastened the retaining straps, the car was gently manoeuvred down the planks onto open ground beside the tracks. Heathcote enthusiastically climbed into the driving seat and took the wooden steering wheel for the delicate procedure. He and his groom, Simpkins, had visited the Napier factory a couple of weeks earlier to receive instruction on how to drive the vehicle. The car had been supplied with two five-gallon cans of Pratt's motor spirit and so it was ready to take to the road. Once Simpkins had turned the starting handle several times to get the engine running, Heathcote proudly set off from the station forecourt to drive home. He took a circuitous route through the town centre, raising his leather-gloved hand to acknowledge the surprised looks of pedestrians. On reaching Longview, he was rather disappointed that Elizabeth did not immediately come outside to admire the machine, which he parked directly outside the front entrance. Still, he might be able to persuade her to go for an excursion later.

Nathaniel and Cora set off for the Trades Union rally in the Market Place after lunch. To get the best photograph of the crowd, Blake agreed with the licensee of the Red Lion that he could set up his camera in an upstairs room overlooking the cobbled square. By the time father and daughter arrived, the Market Place was a heaving mass of people, women in their best frocks and straw bonnets, men in their Sunday suits with either a cap or bowler hat on their heads. Several large multi-coloured union banners were being held aloft as were placards painted with slogans such as "Rights for all" and "Women deserve more pay". The Temperance Band stood off to one side and was playing with gusto, urged on by their bass drum.

As it was sunny, many of the shop windows which circled the Market Place had white cotton sheets protecting the goods in the windows, men's clothing, pyramids of tinned fruit, huge round cheeses. Outside a butcher's shop, sides of beef were hanging in the open air.

"Good heavens, this crowd is as large as Club Day," said Blake, referring to the town's Sunday Schools Festival which attracted a gathering of several thousand for hymn singing in the Market Place and a street procession. Cora was similarly impressed by the turnout. Women workers' rights was a cause that, until a few days earlier, she had never given a thought to, but she now realised that so many working people took it very seriously.

Blake muttered his apologies as he eased past customers who had gathered in the upstairs room to watch proceedings outside, placed his camera tripod at the open window and disappeared beneath his black cloth hood. Cora stood behind her father and passed him photographic plates as they were needed. Blake took nearly a dozen images as he believed he would be able to sell a series of postcards of an event of this scale.

By the time they had packed up the camera and gone back downstairs, rousing speeches were being made from a platform erected on the far side of the square opposite the Red Lion. The hundreds of spectators fell silent to listen to addresses made by officials of various textile unions, although the crowd couldn't resist raising a cheer when a particularly good point was made. Cora edged around the edge of the throng to get nearer to the speakers' platform and somehow managed to squeeze in front of it by the time the chief guest, North Staffordshire-born Ada Chew, organiser of the Women's Trade Union League, rose to her feet.

"Sisters, I know what it is like to work in a factory. I know how unfair some of the conditions we have to put up with. How we are expected to work for a fraction of a man's wages. But it doesn't have to be like this. Our unions give us a single strong voice, united in a single cause. Together we can make our working lives better, our family lives better." Ada Chew's speech was a rallying call not only for union membership, but for the power of ordinary people. "I know there are already many women union members in the mills of Leek, but there are also many more who could and should join our ranks. Together we can achieve so much more." As she drew to a close with one final call – "One day, we women will even get the vote!" – the crowd erupted in cheers. Placards were waved and the occasional straw hat was thrown into the air.

Cora was thrilled. Before today she had never heard such a passionate speech, never been in the middle of a crowd so energised. She felt buoyed up by the atmosphere, excited by the prospects for women that the union leader had predicted. Even though she didn't work in a mill herself, she wished she could be part of something like this. There was a surge of movement as people began to form into their groups ready to join the procession around the town. Cora managed to push her way out of the square and stand on the pavement. Close by, Ada Chew was being helped down from the platform, but Cora didn't have the courage to shout to her. She was looking around, fascinated by the milling crowd, when someone spoke to her. "That was quite a speech, wasn't it?"

Cora turned round to see a red-headed youth, a couple of years older than herself and at least a foot taller, standing next to her. Still in high spirits after what she had just witnessed, she was glad of the chance to talk to someone. "It was wonderful! I've never quite heard anyone speak like that," she said.

"Me neither. You're Cora Blake, the photographer's daughter, aren't you? I saw your father with his camera leaning out of the Red Lion window. My name's Oliver, Oliver Finch. I'm a reporter on the *Leek Lion*." Holding up his notebook as some sort of proof, young Finch babbled on: "I was writing down as much of the speeches as I could for my report in next week's paper. I want to make a good job of it because something like this is really important, don't you think? But you don't work in a mill, do you?"

Cora hesitated when she heard the newspaper mentioned, remembering her father's disappointment with the *Lion* the previous week. However this lanky young fellow looked friendly enough – rather interesting, in fact – and so she could see no harm in talking to him. "I help my father, but I've got a lot of friends who work in the mills. And I was shown all around the Great Mill the other day. I'm sure things could be better for some of the women and especially the girls."

"I've heard there's a big difference between what they and the men earn. There are so many women working in the mills I don't think they would be in business without them, so the women might be able to get a better deal. But I suppose the mill owners will decide between themselves."

"The mill owners, like Mr Heathcote, you mean? Have you ever met him?"

"I've seen him at council meetings and in court, but I've never actually spoken to him. That's the sort of thing that my father does – he's the editor. He seems to know everyone in town, but that's how he finds stories for the *Lion*."

"I've heard Mr Heathcote's a bit odd. He can be either really nice or really nasty, especially with the young girls who work for him. That's what some people say, anyway."

Oliver had learned from his father that any conversation could prove useful to a reporter. He was on the alert for a story, even when talking to a pleasant young lady like Cora. "What do you mean, he's odd?" he asked.

Cora wondered whether she should say more about Enoch Heathcote, but at the same time she wanted to stay in conversation with the young man. "Well, it's something the girls don't really like talking about, because they're frightened of losing their jobs. I just know that he has his favourites. He makes a fuss of them and they, you might say, have to be nice with him." She was getting embarrassed, not only because of what she was saying, but at how closely Oliver was looking at her. She glanced around and saw Ellen walking past, the girl she had met at the skating rink the previous evening.

Cora called out to her. "Ellen! I didn't know you were coming to see the rally."

"Well it can't do any harm, can it?" said Ellen, looking first at Cora and then at Oliver.

Cora did the introductions. "This is Oliver Finch. Oliver's going to write a piece in the *Lion* about the union rally. Oliver, this is Ellen, she works at the Great Mill."

"Pleased to meet you," said Oliver. "Yes, I'm really interested in what life's like at Heathcote & Co. I'd like to interview one or two of you some time."

"What life's like? What do you expect? We go to the mill, work and get paid. It's not very exciting, is it?" Ellen appeared unimpressed with the idea of a newspaper story.

"And what about Mr Heathcote?" Oliver asked.

Ellen looked warily at the reporter. "Mr Heathcote? Why are you asking about him?"

"Rumours, you know, just rumours." Cora saw how quickly Oliver had spotted a potential story, giving Ellen the impression he knew more than he actually did. She also realised how the reporter might help find out what was going on at the Great Mill.

"It's not something I want to talk about. Anyway, it's time I went home," said Ellen and abruptly turned to leave.

Once Ellen had gone, Oliver turned his attention back to Cora. "Well, it's been nice meeting you, Cora. Let's talk again some time and not just about trade unions! As for this Great Mill thing, if you find out any more get in touch. If I'm not in the office you can always leave a message for me." He walked away towards where the banner-waving procession was about to set off, pulling out his pencil to make more notes. Cora looked around the rapidly-emptying square. The past hour had given her a lot to think about and so had her conversation with Oliver Finch. She would definitely try to see him again.

Blake collected his bicycle from the outhouse at home before heading down to Abbey Green. He decided to walk around the Dieulacres ruins to collect his thoughts and to mull over Abbot Whitney's ancient letter. He tried to imagine the scene at the Abbey that October night when the Abbot had written the document. The monks in fear for their future – perhaps for their lives – heartbroken at the purge of the abbeys, resolute that their precious cross should not fall into the wrong hands.

Wandering around what had been the Abbey precincts he puzzled over where the cross might have been buried all those years ago. What was it the Abbot had written? Within sight of the Abbey, beside the River Churnet, marked by a cross? Blake walked across the field where he and Cora had stood the previous week and reached the riverbank. He followed the Churnet upstream as far as the narrow stone footbridge. For the first time, he looked closely at the pillar which stood at the nearest end of the bridge. Previously he had thought it was a simple stone gatepost, but he now saw it had been crafted with fluted sides like the Abbey's ruined columns. A Latin cross was carved deeply into the mossy side that faced the Abbey. He turned and contemplated the view across the field. His eyes were drawn to a patch of fresh earth a few feet away. It looked like the ground had been disturbed and very recently, too. He was struck by an idea. Was this where the relic had been buried? Surely not. Was the golden cross still down there? He was tempted to fall on his knees and scrabble in the earth with his hands. It was time to speak to Mrs Carter.

The widow looked only slightly less exhausted than the previous week. Life was little better. As well as labouring to look after the farm and its livestock she had her husband's funeral to face in a couple of days. But Blake's arrival gave her the excuse to take a break and share a pot of tea.

"It's getting no easier Mr Blake. I'm worn out from the farm work and the police had been round again asking questions about Amos and that day he died. I've told them, I just don't know any more."

Blake knew he had to be gentle in questioning her. "Tell me, did Amos ever say he had found anything in the fields, belonging to the Abbey? Something very old, perhaps."

Rosa Carter was immediately on her guard. "Well, we got lots of stone, of course. Our whole farm is made of bits from the Abbey and that was something Amos always took very serious. He used to say we were living on holy ground, and that we should respect the memory of the monks who were here all that time ago."

"Yes, I've seen the stones. Did he ever talk about something more valuable? An old relic?"

"Mr Blake, please don't ask me about such things! Years ago Amos made me swear on our family Bible that I'd never talk about it, and I never have. Not once."

"Mrs Carter, it might be important to talk about it now. You see, the fellow who came to visit you last week, Dr Sneyd, was looking for something very precious that had been buried before the Abbey was demolished. But yesterday, Dr Sneyd was found dead."

"Another death? Oh Lord, what's becoming of us?"

"Unfortunately it looks like he fell from the tower at the Old Church. So he won't be visiting you again, but it still might be important to get to the bottom of why he was here."

Rosa Carter sat staring at the kitchen table, lost in thought. Then she decided to break her silence. "It was years ago. Amos had been digging all day, a new ditch to drain the meadow. When he came in for his supper he wasn't only tired, he was in a real state about something. I asked him what was up and he says 'Rosa, I've found something wonderful. But we're not keeping it because it belongs to God.' He was always a churchgoer, you see."

After a sip tea, she continued solemnly. "He said it was sure to be something from the old Abbey. An old cross, it was, wrapped in leather and buried in the ground. He thought the monks must have put it there. And that was where it should stay, he said. So he got our Bible out of the cupboard and we went across the field, near the little stone bridge. At the bottom of a hole he showed me there was an old leather bag of some sort. Looking down at it, I wouldn't have known what it was. We both put a hand on the Bible and Amos said a little prayer. Then he got his spade and filled the hole. And we never spoke about it from that day to this, it was a like a special secret we had between us." There were tears in Rosa's eyes as she relived that memory of her God-fearing husband.

Blake was moved by the story, too, and disturbed by the questions that still remained. Was this what Amos Carter had wanted to talk to the Vicar about? Did he know Dr Sneyd had found out about the cross? Why had both men died within a few days of each other? And who else had been digging near the footbridge?

"So Amos didn't go digging there again? Recently, I mean," he asked.

"He didn't dig up the cross, I'm sure of that. He said it should stay there, and I think he'd keep to his word."

Blake thought it best not to tell Rosa about the ground being disturbed near the bridge – the woman had enough troubles at the moment. The conversation over, he pedalled away, still wondering whether someone else had not only found out about the ancient cross, but had dug it up.

That evening, Isaak Nadin took up his usual place at the bar of the New Inn in Flash and began to read aloud from the *Leek Lion* for the benefit of the villagers gathered around him. The latest item about Amos Carter's death prompted a great deal of head shaking. "Tied up? Mutilated? What's the world coming to?" Several promised to attend Carter's funeral. Caleb Salt, sitting in the corner with his usual friends, apparently ignored what was being said.

There were more mutters of amazement when Nadin read out the story about Crosbie Sneyd's death. "What on earth was 'e doing up the tower?" said one. "Must 'ave threw 'imself off," suggested another. "Rum things goin' on down in Leek. I'm glad we're up 'ere, out of it."

Once the newspaper announcements were over, conversation resumed in the pub, the chief topics being Longnor Wakes and Leek Show, both coming up the following week. One villager strolled over to Salt. "So Caleb, has Mester Heathcote got another shoot coming up?" he asked.

"You'd better ask him yourself."

"I just thought... what with Gamage speakin' to you the other night and you being one of 'is beaters. Was wond'ring if there might be a bit of beatin' work for one or two of us."

"I'm not his gamekeeper, I don't know all his plans," replied Salt, as brusque as ever. The man drifted off and Caleb looked at his pint. He had plenty to think about, other than grouse shooting. There was a boxing match coming up and he had other important things to arrange.

Back in Leek, Enoch Heathcote was potting a few balls in the Longview billiards room while Elizabeth recovered from her first motor car excursion. She had agreed to go out with Enoch in the Napier that afternoon and the journey had been a little longer than she had expected as he had insisted going to Rudyard Lake. He had taken the vehicle as close as possible to the dam head where many people would be able admire it. She had not known quite what to expect from the trip, like the first time she went on a steam train as a girl. The sensation of being propelled along the road without a horse in front of them was rather disconcerting. She felt strangely exposed and there was the noise and fumes to contend with, too. She decided she would sit in the back seat next time. Enoch, by contrast, was in his element as he wrestled with the steering wheel, pulling back the gear and brake levers with gusto.

Once she had calmed down, Elizabeth summoned her companion Margaret Gamage for a report on the day's gossip. Gamage had two of her informers keeping an eye on the rally in the Market Place and watching out for any Great Mill worker likely to be a troublemaker. Several of their mill women were seen prominently at the rally, she reported, as well as the union organisers who, as expected, were shouting loudest. Elizabeth responded with the occasional derisory grunt.

"Martha also spotted something else, Madam," Gamage went on. "There's a girl called Ellen Simms, works in the hand braid room. She was talking to Finch's son from the *Lion*. He was scribbling in his notebook. The photographer's daughter, Cora Blake, she was with them."

"This Ellen, is she one of Enoch's *favourites*?"

"Exactly, Madam. Perhaps we need to keep an eye on her."

"Thank you Gamage, keep me informed of anything else your women see." Elizabeth waved her companion away.

The union rally was also a topic of conversation at the Blake house, where Edith was in Cora's bedroom hoping to gain more than the minimum response from her daughter. Young William and Emily had been the centre of attention at tea so this was her first chance to talk properly to her eldest since she had returned from town.

"Mother, it was so exciting to see all those people in the Market Place, shouting and waving banners and cheering when the union people gave their speeches. It must feel so powerful to be part of something like that," Cora enthused.

Her mother was impressed that she was taking this interest. Her daughter was certainly growing up, Edith thought, but this interest was also a little puzzling, especially as there were no mill workers in the family. "I'm pleased you found it interesting, dear, but why are you so concerned about the mill women?"

Cora's expression became more serious. "It's as if there's a whole side of life that I'd never thought about before. When father and I went around the mill the other day I saw how hard girls of my age, and a lot younger, are working." She paused a beat, wondering how much to share with her mother. "But it's not just that. Some of them say Mr Heathcote can be really odd with the girls. Polly's cousins mentioned it and so did a girl called Ellen Simms. He makes a fuss of them, as long as they play along with him, although I don't really know what they mean by that. I didn't like him from the first time I saw him."

Edith reached for her daughter's hand. She was concerned to see Cora worried like this, but equally Edith was not surprised by what she had heard. There had been gossip about Enoch Heathcote for years. Mothers would warn daughters to be on their guard at the Great Mill. But the subject was never talked about openly. She wondered if she should have spoken to Cora herself before Nathaniel took her to visit the mill. Then again, why plant such suspicions in a young person's mind?

"Cora, you really shouldn't worry yourself about these things. And if you don't like Mr Heathcote, then try keep away from him," said Edith.

Though Cora nodded, at the back of her mind were girls like Polly's cousins and Ellen who didn't seem to have a choice. Edith returned downstairs thinking about the girls Cora had mentioned. She was friendly with Mabel Simms, Ellen's mother. She would ask about her the next time she saw Mabel.

Chapter Nine

Inspector Ramm saw his men exchange some surprised looks when, during their Monday morning meeting, he told them what he planned. "If you have any better ideas of how we can move this Carter enquiry forward, I'll be glad to hear them," he said. No one spoke. And so FJ Finch was in for a surprise when he arrived at the police station an hour later.

"Mr Finch, we are making slow progress with our inquiries into the death of Amos Carter," the Inspector began, once the *Leek Lion* editor was seated in the office. "Until we find the culprit there's a murderer walking amongst us and that is why I need your assistance."

"Certainly Inspector, the *Leek Lion* is at your disposal," Finch replied, relishing the opportunity to revive the shocking story in the next *Lion*, and pleased the officer was asking for his help. Ramm passed him the photograph of the suspect walking away from the barn, the picture first enlarged by Cora Blake and since scrutinised by dozens of puzzled farmers. "I would like this to appear in the next edition of the *Lion*. I take it that is possible?"

Even Finch was lost for words for a moment or two. He had hoped for more gory details and an impassioned plea from the Inspector. But this, a photograph of someone leaving the scene, was altogether more significant. It was what the Yankee newspapers called a scoop. The *Lion* might even help to find the murderer. He tempered his excitement because he wanted to see just how much he could get from Ramm.

"Well, as you know Inspector, the *Lion* has rarely used a photograph before. It's such an expensive process. But it is possible. Tell me more about the photograph."

"Mr Blake took it on the afternoon that Amos Carter was discovered in the barn. We've got young Miss Blake to thank for spotting this person in the picture and bringing it to my attention. However, I think it best we don't mention her name your story, we can't be too careful. The person, whoever it is, appears to be walking away from the farm and that leads us to think that he could have been there when Carter was attacked. On the other hand, it could be a pure coincidence. I know the photograph is a little indistinct, but it may stir your readers to help us."

"Any other photographs, Inspector?"

"There's another which Mr Blake took for police purposes and which I do not want to be published. But in the interests of you gaining a full understanding of this crime, Mr Finch, I've decided you should see it." Ramm handed him the picture taken inside the barn.

"My God, this is awful. No wonder Blake was shaken up. Inspector, you have our full co-operation and I will ensure this matter gets the publicity it deserves."

"Now you can see why we must catch this person," said Ramm.

The Inspector promised to keep him up-to-date with the investigation and Finch hurried from the station. His first priority was to have a printing plate made from the photograph, but as the *Lion* did not own the necessary equipment he went straight to the Moorland Press in Derby Street. The firm printed the books which Finch published as a sideline and he knew they had one of the latest engraving machines which produced printing plates of the highest quality. Finch reasoned that the cost of the plate would be easily outweighed by the kudos – and the extra sales – he would gain from the story.

Back at the police station, Inspector Ramm considered the likely impact of his newspaper appeal. Although it might tip off the suspect about the photograph's existence, it could also improve the chances of identifying the man. His thoughts were interrupted when a telegram boy arrived. The message was from the Cottage Hospital where the Medical Officer, Dr Handbridge, had been due to examine Crosbie Sneyd's body that morning: "Post mortem completed – We need to speak – Handbridge." Ramm left the station with a sense of foreboding. When he arrived at the hospital he was shown into a small office where the Medical Officer was bent over a desk, writing his report.

"Ah, Inspector Ramm, thank you for being so prompt. Come this way," said Dr Handbridge as he led Ramm into the hospital's operating theatre which doubled as the post mortem suite on the rare occasions one was required. Handbridge drew back a white sheet which was draped over the body on the operating table. Ramm was shocked at the devastation to Crosbie Sneyd's face from his fall at the church.

"Multiple injuries, as you would expect. His head was crushed, fractures all over his body, etcetera. It will all be in my report," the Medical Officer continued in a business-like manner. "But there's another reason I called you over ...give me hand if you don't mind." Ramm help the doctor turn Sneyd's body onto its side and immediately saw another injury on the back of the man's head.

"He suffered a substantial impact on the back of the skull, but I cannot for the life of me see how it was caused. From his other injuries it appears he fell face-first from the tower. So how would he hit the back of his head? There are no abrasions, so I don't think he was in contact with the stonework. It's a squarish indention, so it could have been caused by a metal object, perhaps something like a stonemason's hammer."

Ramm peered at the injury. A patch of hair had been shaved off during the examination and the Inspector could indeed see the regularly-shaped depression the Medical Officer had described.

"That is certainly curious, Doctor. I will look into this immediately," said Ramm. This meant more work for the team,

Ramm thought. If Dr Sneyd's death turned out not to be an accident, Leek Police faced not one but two mysterious deaths. And he had already wasted three days since Sneyd had been found.

Walking back from the hospital, the Inspector made a detour via the Old Church. First he stood where the body had been found. There was no longer any sign of the bloodstains on the paving stones. He looked up at the tower to imagine Dr Sneyd's fall. He hoped to spot something protruding from the stonework – an iron support or part of the clock mechanism – which may have struck Sneyd on his descent. Ramm could see no suitable object on the tower wall.

Next he went inside the church and up the staircase to the belfry. Workmen had spent hours dismantling the bell mechanism on Friday and so any evidence of Dr Sneyd's visit would have disappeared. He thought back to Friday morning. He remembered seeing scuff marks in the thick dust in the belfry, but there was no way of knowing how they had been caused. Ramm then slowly made his way up the ladder to the roof. He looked carefully around the lead sheeting, but saw nothing untoward. Neither was there anything on the parapet which would have made a hole in the back of the victim's head.

He left the church and, once back in the station, called a swift meeting with whatever officers were not out on the foot patrols they were expected to make every day.

"Unfortunately, the death of Dr Sneyd may not be as straightforward as we hoped," he told the little gathering. "There's an injury on the back of his head that cannot be explained at the moment. To be on the safe side, we are going to have to speak to whatever witnesses we can find, ask questions, take statements. If it's not an accident and we don't act swiftly, there will be hell to pay." Sgt Reynolds and two constables exchanged glum looks.

Ramm pressed on. "So we need to get cracking on this. Sergeant, Dr Sneyd's sister is coming from Oxford to make the identification, she should arrive at the railway station at two o'clock. It's your job to meet her, take her to the Cottage Hospital and see she's taken care of. A word though, Sneyd looks a hell of a mess, so the sister will have to be forewarned. And mention nothing about his death being suspicious – we must keep this to ourselves at the moment.

"We need to speak to anyone who was at the church on Friday morning who might give us any hint why Sneyd was there. Knowles, I want you to go to the Vicar and Mr Blake. I want to them both down here as soon as possible, so that I can speak to them officially. The Vicar was the first to find the body, I believe, and Blake, strangely enough, seems to be the only person who's had any sort of conversation with the deceased. I want statements from both of them, so I'll want you in my office with your notebook. All right, let's get to it."

Ramm knew that, at times like this, his men expected him to set an example. Despite the tragic circumstances, he was pleased to be doing real investigative work, although anxious not to make a wrong move. A team of detectives had recently been appointed to the headquarters at Stafford and it might be only a matter of time before both cases were taken out of his hands. He was determined to prove he was up to the task.

Nathaniel Blake was on his own at the studio – Cora was attending Miss Keates' Academy – when Constable Knowles arrived. The photographer was developing his pictures from Saturday's trade union rally when he heard the jingle of the front door bell.

"Please hang on," he shouted through the darkroom door as he finished dousing a print in a bath of fixing solution. He hooked his spectacles back on, dashed downstairs and was surprised to see the policeman.

"Need more portraits of your station inmates?" Blake asked.

"I'm afraid not, Mr Blake. I need you to accompany me to the station. Inspector Ramm wants to speak to you." The constable's formal tone indicated this was something more important than a photographic errand.

"Let me turn things off upstairs and I'll be with you," said Blake, returning to the darkroom to extinguish the red lamp. On the bench he saw the photographs of the documents found in Dr Sneyd's room and snatched them up to take with him. He had barely slept for two nights, his mind churning over the deaths of Amos Carter and Crosbie Sneyd and how much he should tell the police. Now he sensed that the Inspector might be going to add to his worries.

Knowles led him into Inspector Ramm's office as soon as they arrived and Blake was concerned to see the constable take a seat and open his notebook. Ramm's attitude confirmed that this was an official interview. "Mr Blake, I would like to talk to you about your conversation with Dr Sneyd last week. Can you tell me again exactly what was said?"

Blake had thought about his conversation with Crosbie Sneyd numerous times over the weekend and had no trouble recounting what was said. Knowles was busy with his pencil.

"So Dr Sneyd said he wanted to visit the church to look at old documents?" asked Ramm.

"Yes, that's right. Do I take it you are investigating his death? You seemed to think it was an accident."

Ramm paused before he responded. "Some new information has come to light which makes it imperative we investigate the matter fully."

"You've seen the letter, then?" Blake had blurted it out before he could stop himself. He knew immediately he had made a mistake.

"The letter? What do you mean, Mr Blake?"

The photographer sighed, realising Ramm was not aware of the letter from Reverend Maitland. "Inspector, I have a confession."

"A confession?" Inspector Ramm and Constable Knowles were both somewhat startled.

"Well, more of an admission." Blake struggled on, opening the envelope which contained his photographs. He handed over the copy of Reverend Maitland's letter. "On Friday I found this letter. Because you seemed to think Dr Sneyd's death was an accident, I presumed it was not important. But now I realise it may be useful to your investigation."

Ramm studied the photograph. "Where did you find this?" he asked.

"In Dr Sneyd's room. FJ Finch and I went there to see if there was anything about Dieulacres Abbey. There was the old document that Sneyd talked about and I also saw this letter. I was surprised when Reverend Maitland didn't seem to know anything about it."

"Dr Sneyd's room?" Ramm looked at Blake sharply. "You and Mr Finch were there before we even had chance to go to the The George? This is highly irregular and very disappointing, Mr Blake. You should have told me about this sooner." Ramm paused as he thought it over. "However, your *detective* work – much as I disagree with it – appears to have uncovered something that someone else did not want to be found. What were the other papers?"

Blake handed him the photographs of Abbot Whitney's Latin document and the translation. "These are the ones about the Abbey which Dr Sneyd referred to when I met him. The other papers appeared to be his notes." Ramm looked quickly at the two photographs. "I'll study these in due course, but Dr Sneyd's visit to the church is what most concerns me at the moment. Thank you for the information...even though it has come rather late in the day."

Seeing the interview was coming to an end, Blake decided not to complicate things by voicing his own theories about what had gone on at Abbey Green.

After Blake had left the Inspector turned to his constable. "Let's see what Reverend Maitland has to say about this letter. And I also want to speak to Mr Watkins from The George."

Ramm was more accustomed to seeing the Vicar in church and was uneasy about summoning him for an official interview. However, in light of the letter Blake had produced, Reverend Maitland suddenly appeared to be a key figure in the inquiry. When Knowles ushered him into the office fifteen minutes later, the clergyman looked suitably puzzled.

"Inspector Ramm, I presume you want to speak to me about the poor fellow who fell from the tower."

"I do indeed, Reverend Maitland. Could you tell me once again how you came to find the body on Friday morning, so that we have it on record?"

"It was just as I said at the time. I went round to the church at about half past seven to meet the verger and prepare for the workmen to arrive. As I went along the path from the vicarage I saw a figure on the ground. At first I thought it was a drunk or a vagrant, but then I saw the blood and realised the man was gravely injured. I knelt beside him and saw he was dead. After that I sent the verger down here to tell your colleagues and I stayed with the poor man. By the time your constable was there, other people were arriving to see the bells moved."

"You didn't know the man?"

"I didn't recognise him, no. Although I must admit he was lying face down."

Ramm pressed on with his questioning. "And what about Thursday night? You didn't see him that evening?"

"See him? Certainly not," the Vicar replied, becoming a little flustered. As Blake had done, out of the corner of his eye he saw Constable Knowles writing down everything he said.

"So if I suggested that you arranged to meet Dr Sneyd at the church on Thursday evening, you would deny that?"

"I most certainly would! What are you getting at, Inspector?"

"This is what I'm getting at," replied Ramm, lifting the photograph from his desk. "This is a copy of a letter, apparently from yourself, inviting Dr Sneyd to the church on Thursday evening to look at some old documents. You suggested meeting him at eight o'clock."

"That is preposterous. I had never heard of any Dr Sneyd and I spent the whole of Thursday evening at the vicarage in the company of my ringers. As there was no bell ringing practice that night, we decided to meet to discuss the removal and return of the bells. We were together from half past seven until nearly ten o'clock." The Vicar's voice was steadily rising. "Ask them! Ask any of them! And let me see that letter." He thrust out his hand for the photograph. The Vicar's eyes opened wider as he studied it. "How dare they! This is a forgery. I never wrote this. That is not my handwriting." He looked up at the Inspector, waving the photograph. "And you thought that I, a man of God, was involved in this? That I invited the man round to the church? Just what do you think I did, Inspector?"

Ramm began to wonder if he had been hasty in questioning the Vicar. He struggled to keep his tone even. "Reverend Maitland, a man has died in tragic circumstances and it is my duty to follow all avenues of enquiry. I apologise if you are offended, but I was led to believe this letter was genuine. Just to put matters straight, I'm sure you will give us a sample of your handwriting. Even if it was not you, someone invited Dr Sneyd to the church on Thursday night and that is where he died. I need to find out who that person was."

The Vicar gave a sample of his handwriting and left, still muttering at the insult he had suffered. Ramm sat thinking how Sneyd's "accident" was becoming more suspicious by the minute. He read through the forged letter again, then looked at the photograph of the ancient Latin document. It meant nothing to him, but the English version was certainly interesting. Did this have anything to do with Sneyd's death, he wondered. Why had someone gone to the trouble of removing the documents from Sneyd's room? Although police officers were not expected to take a break during their shift, Ramm felt the sudden need for half an hour's peace, to think things through. He left the station in search of a sandwich at home.

The afternoon brought little progress. When Ramm had Jacob Watkins brought in from The George, the hotel keeper denied all knowledge of visitors to Dr Sneyd's room on the Friday morning.

"I was busy in the cellar, Inspector, and the girl was cleaning up in the bar. Neither of us saw anything. If there had been a thief about, we would have known," he said.

Ramm pressed on. "It appears that some items were definitely taken, and at least two other people went to Dr Sneyd's room that morning. Mr Blake and Mr Finch saw papers in the room, but they had been removed by the time my man called round."

"Papers, Inspector? I don't know nothing about any papers."

"Mr Watkins, this is an extremely serious matter. It goes beyond a few missing papers. A guest at your hotel died in tragic circumstances and I certainly hope that you are not keeping something back. Should you have a sudden recollection, I want to hear from you." Ramm let the hotel keeper go. He believed Watkins was not being honest with him, but couldn't prove otherwise at the moment. Neither had they found anyone who had seen Dr Sneyd on the fateful evening. In due course, thought Ramm, he would ask Finch to print a new appeal for witnesses.

At Longview, Elizabeth Heathcote was enjoying the afternoon sun in the conservatory, surrounded by ferns. She was growing increasingly worried about the Abbey Green affair. Enoch would be working late at the mill, and besides, she had little confidence in him to do anything. She rose from her wicker chair and pressed the bell to summon the maid. "Fetch me some more tea Eliza and find out if Mr Gamage is in his office. If so, tell him to come." The estate steward appeared in the conservatory shortly afterwards. "It's Carter's funeral on Tuesday afternoon," said Mrs Heathcote.

"Do you want me to attend, Madam?" asked Gamage with barely concealed surprise.

"No, I'm going to send Margaret to represent us in church. I thought that while the service was taking place, it would be an opportunity for you to go to Abbey Green and have a look around the farm. Is there a duplicate key for the farmhouse?" Gamage nodded. "Look for anything Carter might have written down, or his wife for that matter. Anything that mentions us. Mind not to leave any sign that you've been searching the place. We don't want the police called in again."

"Yes, Madam."

"And look if you can see any sign of digging."

"Digging, Madam? I'm sure there has been digging, it is a farm, after all."

Bernard Gamage left the conservatory. He and his wife were becoming increasingly concerned at some of the tasks their employers were giving them. Loyalty was one thing – especially when your livelihood depended on it – but breaking the law was another. Gamage knew that if anything went wrong, he would be the one to get the blame.

Over at the Big Mill, Enoch Heathcote was sitting behind his expansive desk. He reached forward and pressed a brass button to call in his secretary, Mrs Williamson. "I have some errands that need attending to this afternoon. Mrs Heathcote needs a couple of items collecting from shops in the town, there's a small parcel to be delivered, that sort of thing. I thought we could send one of the girls out for half an hour," he said.

"Certainly Sir, shall I ask one of the ladies from the office?"

"No, I'm sure they're all too busy. There's a young woman in the braid room I think we could send, though. This would be a little trial, you might say, because I think she's ready for a more responsible position. Can you have her sent up to see me? Ellen Simms is her name, she's on the hand looms. And make sure she's signed out for the rest of the afternoon."

"As you wish, Mr Enoch." Mrs Williamson left the office. It was not unusual for the mill owner to call on one of his employees – one of the young women – to do his private "errands". They all turned a blind eye to the charade. Similarly when a young woman was given sudden promotion. They were used to Mr Enoch's behaviour.

By the time a junior clerk had been dispatched to speak to the braid room manager, then to find Ellen Simms at her loom and escort her to the owner's office, Enoch Heathcote was pacing backward and forward. He was agitated, a mixture of excitement and dread. He had come up with the idea when he set out for the mill that morning, not in the carriage with Simpkins, but on his own in the new Napier. He had decided he would take Ellen out in the motor car, and if not her, some other young woman who hadn't rejected him yet. They would drive up to the Lodge on the Roaches, an adventure to impress any young lady. Then she was sure to be cooperative, he thought.

Ellen guessed some of what awaited her as she trudged up the oak staircase to Heathcote's office. A few minutes later she was suitably impressed when he collected her in the gleaming motor car, just around the corner from the mill. Admittedly he made her crouch down out of sight in the back until they were out of town, but if this was what it took to get out of the braid room and into a better job, she told herself, then she would play along with the old fool. As it turned out, when they reached the shooting lodge, the mill owner had demanded more than his usual fumbling and Ellen endured the journey back from the Roaches in tears.

Chapter Ten

Isaac Smedley's horse-drawn omnibus was making its laboured way over the hills towards Longnor the following day. Usually the busiest day for Smedley, the Longnor carrier, was a Wednesday. That was when he transported fellow villagers the ten miles to Leek on market day, making the return journey laden not only with passengers but with all manner of goods which rural folk had ordered from shops in the town. Everything from bicycle spares to medicines, groceries to religious texts, would be loaded on the roof and covered with a tarpaulin. This Tuesday morning, however, Smedley had set off unladen from Longnor at dawn. He collected a full complement of passengers outside The Golden Lion Inn in Leek and was bringing them back to his home village in time for the start of one of the major events in the local calendar, Longnor Wakes Sports. Eight people were crammed into the battered four-wheeled coach, sitting close enough to steady each other as the vehicle jolted along the rough road. Passengers had exchanged anxious looks as the two horses struggled to haul the bus up the steep Cat Tor road, but now they were on the top of the moors and there was a sense of relief as they caught a glimpse of Longnor in the distance. The grey limestone village with a square church tower at its centre, stood out amongst the green farmland.

Nathaniel Blake clung to his leather case, fearful his camera would be broken if he left it on the carriage floor, but aware that he was poking his companion, FJ Finch, in the ribs. Blake was planning to photograph the day's competitions and entertainments to produce a set of postcards, while Finch would cover the event in the *Leek Lion*. Although Longnor Wakes didn't necessarily merit the editor's attendance, it did offer a pleasant day out in the country, including lunch at one of the four village pubs. For local people the activities lasted the best part of twelve hours, stretching from the sports in the daytime to a dance in the Market Hall in the evening. During the journey the two had little to say to each other, other than Blake's occasional comment that it may have been quicker, and more comfortable, by bicycle.

Once they had clambered out of the conveyance, Blake and Finch set off for flat fields on the edge of the village where a large crowd was already gathering in the area roped off for spectators. The village school had closed for the day and so whole families had donned their Sunday best to make a day of it. The village constable – 'Bobby' Mellor as he was known – was strolling amongst them, exchanging occasional remarks with the onlookers but chiefly making sure no one strayed into the race area.

Over to one side, a large marquee had been erected for the benefit of officials and the organising committee. Next to the marquee, two smart carriages were drawn up in which well-dressed ladies were seated. They were members of the local gentry who owned not only most of the farms in the area but also most of the houses in Longnor itself.

The smartly uniformed members of Hartington Brass Band were busy sorting out their folding chairs, music stands and sheet music ready to play selections at appropriate intervals during the proceedings. They would stay in the village to provide the music for dancing in the Market Hall much later on.

The first competitions were foot races held on straight and oval tracks marked out on the field with short wooden posts painted white. Cow pats had been removed from the track earlier that morning. More athletic men from Longnor and neighbouring villages were looking forward to showing off their running prowess, while others were simply taking part for fun and the chance of winning a few shillings. Competitors wore substantial boots to cope with the less-than-even grass, vests in various colours including some hooped football shirts, and mix of working trousers and shorts. At the sight of competitors gathering near the starting line, a buzz of eager anticipation passed amongst the crowd and several spectators, especially the young women, shouted encouragement. Several young lads were armed with wooden football rattles which they began to whirl with great vigour producing a din that drowned out most other sounds.

The chief marshal – easily spotted in his straw boater, smart blazer and prominent badge – blew his whistle to call together the runners who had drawn lots to compete in the first of several heats over the first distance, the quarter mile. Having lined up at the start, the runners set off after another blast from the marshal's whistle at which the crowd raised a great cheer. It was a rough and ready race, with some competitors barging into each other and several stumbling as their feet caught in a tussock of grass. With heaving chests the leaders crossed the line to shouts and applause from the spectators, followed at some distance by others who had taken part for fun and the promise a glass of ale from their mates. Results were announced through a tin megaphone and then the whole process was repeated for the next heat and the quarter-mile finals. Those placed first, second and third were led to the officials' tent where the president of the organising committee presented medals and small amounts of cash.

The morning grew steadily warmer, prompting parasols to

appear amongst the spectators and making it increasingly challenging for competitors in the subsequent race over a distance of one mile followed by the hundred yard dash.

A group of young men, under direction from marshals, then busily prepared the course for the obstacle race, dragging hay bales and low wicker hurdles into position. Four hearty lads carried in a galvanised watering trough and hastily filled it using buckets. Then, urged on by the crowd, the dozen competitors set off with enthusiasm, but many were sent sprawling as they negotiated the hazards, either jumping the hurdles or leaping onto the bales. The water trough was too large to jump and required a technique of stepping up onto the nearest edge and striding over to the far edge. Spectators and competitors alike knew it was only a matter of time before someone fell into the water and, on the first circuit, the third-placed runner was greeted with ironic cheers as he missed his footing and plunged into the trough. Soaked through, he clambered out and ran on, but with the edges of the trough now slippery, a succession of competitors fell into the water. It was a bedraggled bunch that finally crossed the finishing line, but the contest had proved a rousing end to the foot races.

Next came the horse riders, mostly wearing white shirts, waistcoats and flat caps, who led their mounts from an adjoining field. With substantial cash prizes on offer – as much as £8 for winners – the two-mile trotting handicap and gallop events attracted serious riders from a wide radius. To give the locals a chance, another two-mile trotting race was reserved purely for riders from the Longnor area.

As with the foot races, there was keen competition in the horse events, the gallop around the oval track seeing the riders urge their mounts to give their all. In the trotting races, competitors piloted fragile two-wheeled carts with all the gusto of Roman charioteers and witnessed some precarious moments when wheels clashed on the bends, neither driver being prepared to give way.

As well as keen competition from the riders, the horse racing saw large amounts of cash changing hands amongst knots of spectators who could not resist placing a quiet bet on the outcome. Constable Mellor, very much a man of the people who lived in a police cottage in the centre of the village, turned a blind eye to the betting. Amongst those handing over and pocketing handfuls of cash was a tall muscular man who some would have recognised as Caleb Salt from Flash.

Roving around the sports ground with his lightweight camera, Blake delighted in taking action shots of the races and the cheering crowd, while Finch was busy outside the judges' tent writing down lists of entrants and results. The two men met up again when the morning's races were over and it was time for refreshment. Foregoing the tea and sandwiches served in the Market Hall, they retired to the nearby Horseshoe Inn. Once seated, each with a pint of ale and a meat pie, both were keen to tell the other latest developments concerning the deaths of Amos Carter and Crosbie Sneyd. Blake spoke first, having not seen Finch since making his revelation to Inspector Ramm the previous day.

"I could see that the Inspector was taking Sneyd's death much more seriously – he told me that he had new information on the case. It seems to me he no longer believes it was an accident. So I had no alternative but to tell him about our visit to The George and those documents we found, especially that letter from the Vicar," he said. "Ramm was obviously surprised to see it. He was bound to call in Reverend Maitland and I'd like to know what the Vicar said about it."

"I will speak to the Inspector before we go to press, so I should find out what's going on with Sneyd. That's quite a shock if it turns out not to be an accident. I presume Ramm wasn't best pleased when he found out we had been to The George," Finch replied.

"Yes and no. He was far from happy at first, then I think he realised we had uncovered something that his own officer hadn't seen. I hope Ramm isn't too frosty when you see him."

"Well, I don't think he will be too bad. The Inspector has asked for my help with the Carter case, you see, so we're working together to some extent. That's what I wanted to tell you. We're going to print one of your photographs in this week's paper."

Blake leaned back in surprise while Finch continued. "Ramm wants us to use your photograph of the suspect near Amos Carter's barn. He hopes someone might identify the man when they see it in the *Lion*. It's unlikely I know, but I'm going to make it as prominent as possible. We've all got something to gain from this, Nathaniel."

The photographer had long hoped to see his work in the *Leek Lion* one day, but never thought it would be under these circumstances. He wasn't sure whether to be excited or concerned. "Please be careful how you word it, FJ. And you're not to mention Cora, you know," he said.

"Yes, yes, of course. Just imagine, if they catch a murderer thanks to the *Lion* – and your picture. Think of the publicity!"

Blake went on to tell Finch of his latest visit to Abbey Green and Mrs Carter's story of how Amos had found the Abbey's cross buried in the field. "I can't help wondering whether what happened to him was connected with that old cross. It might be very valuable, you know. Rosa has already said that Amos was worried about something lately and we know he was going to consult the Vicar. It looks like someone has been digging there recently," said Blake. He paused, then added: "I wonder whether Enoch Heathcote knew anything about it? He seemed awfully interested to know what had happened to Carter, and Rosa said he had talked to her husband quite a few times in past weeks."

"Heathcote? I'd be careful about dragging him into it, he's very powerful in the town, you know," Finch replied. "He's got fingers in a lot of pies, what with the mill, the council, the magistrates and all the property they own. I'm surprised he's not here today, lording it around. It's better to have a person like him on your side, rather against you, Nathaniel. That's why you need to watch what you say. Of course, the money is all down to the wife."

"How do you mean? Mrs Heathcote seems the quiet one," said Blake.

"It's an interesting story from long before you came to Leek," Finch explained. "The mill and all the land and properties belonged to Elizabeth Heathcote's family. Heathcote was her maiden name and she was the last in a long line, they had been an important family for generations. She met Enoch when he joined the mill company as a travelling salesman, somewhat below her status, I would think. When they married, rather than see the family name disappear, Enoch applied for a royal licence to change his surname to Heathcote. Elizabeth probably made him do it, got the idea from another wealthy Leek family who did something similar a few years earlier. So Enoch struck lucky, married into money and has never looked back. He owes it all to her."

"When I took her portrait she barely spoke, but there is obviously a lot more to her than I had realised," Blake replied.

Raising his second glass of ale, Finch continued: "You don't see her around much, at least not compared to her husband. Rarely leaves Longview, I believe. And, of course, she's dead set against the demon drink." He tapped the glass. "Apparently she's threatened to turn The George into a temperance hotel. Cups of tea and coffee only, just like the Coffee Tavern."

Blake knew the Leek Band of Hope, the society that was trying to persuade townsfolk to turn teetotal, was becoming steadily more outspoken. Their alternative to the local inns, the Coffee Tavern, had been going for years, but he was surprised to hear this news about The George. "How on earth could she do that?"

"Well the Heathcotes own the hotel, don't they? Old Watkins has been quaking in his boots, says he'd do anything to hang on to the place and keep pouring the pints."

Having finished their pies and pints, Blake and Finch went back out into the Market Square, where villagers and visitors were milling around stalls selling food and trinkets, groups of children running amongst them. Sitting on one side of the square, his back against the wall of a provisions shop, was an unkempt and bearded figure who Blake recognised as the tramp he had seen around Leek. The photographer suspected he was the person who had tried to talk to Cora and who always seemed to be hanging around in town.

Leaning closer to Finch, Blake said quietly: "FJ, you seem to know everyone around here. What about that man sitting over there, looks like a vagrant?"

"Well, he's certainly a man of the road, but from what I've seen he's not your ordinary tramp. He actually seems quite educated and, stranger still, he's Scottish. That's as much as I know. Now excuse me while I go to see what's happening on the sports field." Finch left and Blake, emboldened by his lunchtime ale, marched over to the tramp. "I say, you fellow, can I have a word?"

"Mr Blake, yes, I think we should talk," came the reply.

Blake was startled by the man's confident attitude. He looked a ruffian, but was obviously no simple-minded beggar.

"Perhaps we could go somewhere a wee bit quieter," the man suggested in a broad Scottish accent, rising to his feet and pointing to narrow a cobbled alley leading out of the square. He walked into the mouth of the alley whereupon he abruptly sat down again and leaned against a wall, using his haversack as a cushion. Blake had little choice but to follow and then peer down at him.

"Well, as you seem to know my name, what is your's, may I ask?" Blake intended to have the upper hand in the exchange, but soon saw that the other man was undaunted.

"Gibb is my name sir, Sgt Major John Gibb, late of the Queen's Own Highlanders. Pleased to make your acquaintance," Gibb replied, thrusting out his grimy hand for Blake to shake. The photographer shook the hand a little awkwardly and said firmly: "I've seen you around Leek. I'm sure you've been watching myself and my daughter. I'd like you to stop."

"Mr Blake, calm y'self. I mean you no harm. In fact, I might be able to tell you something that will help you." Gibb pointed to the cobbles next to him. "Sit ye down here, and hear me out."

Blake had been prepared to dislike the tramp, but found himself intrigued by the man. He glanced at his pocket watch – he had half an hour before Smedley departed for Leek – and then lowered himself next to Gibb. He kept one hand firmly on his leather camera case.

The time had come for Gibb to tell what he knew. His eyes focused on a point across the alley, he began to speak in measured tones. "It seems we've both got involved in the same nasty affair, Mr Blake. A couple o' weeks ago I was down at Abbey Green at the same time as you and your lassie were there.

"I knew Amos Carter, he was a good man. He and his wife have given me many a cup o' tea and even let me sleep in the barn when it was bitter cold. That day I was having a rest in the lane when I saw Rosa come running out, screaming, and you went to help. I stayed there while the police came and took poor Amos away. I read what had happened to him in the *Lion*.

"The thing is, before any of this happened, while you and your lassie were sorting out your camera in the field, I saw a fellow walking away from the farm." Gibb paused, recalling his memory of the fateful afternoon.

"And then, last Thursday night, what do ye think? I was asleep next to the Old Church when that other man lost his life. I'd seen him go into the church and, earlier on, I saw other folk go in there. Now Mr Blake, I'm a man who's faced death before. I fought the Afghans at Kabul and then the Mahdis in the Sudan. I've seen more blood than I ever want to see again. That's why I took to the road when I came out o' the Highlanders and I steer clear of people most of the time. But there's a difference between what I did in the army, serving Queen and Country, and the cowardly murder that's gone on this past week."

Blake was struck by the quiet dignity of this unlikely character. "You saw a man...walking away from the farm?" he asked.

"Oh aye. I might like to keep to myself, but that doesn't stop me from watching what's going on. There was definitely someone at the farm that afternoon and, if I'm not mistaken, I know who it was."

Gibb nodded across the Market Square towards a flight of stone steps that led up to another inn, The Grapes. A group of men were coming down the steps in high spirits, talking loudly, probably having enjoyed some of their horse race winnings. "See the big fellow in the middle. Salt's his name. Caleb Salt. He's Rosa Carter's nephew. I've seen him at the Carters' farm a few times before. I'm sure it was him that day."

Blake saw the powerfully built man Gibb was referring to. It could be the one in the photograph, his battered straw hat looked very much the same, he thought, but there was no way of knowing for certain. "What about at the church? Who did you see there?" asked Blake.

"It was nearly dark and there aren't many gas lamps around, that's why I go there for a bit o'peace. I definitely saw the tall thin fellow with the fancy jacket go into the church," Gibb replied. "Before that another man went in, but, as I said, it was getting dark and I couldn't see precisely who it was. It might have been Salt, but what would he be doing going into church at that time o'night? Unless he was up to no good."

"What does he do, this Salt? A farm worker?" Blake asked.

"People know him round here as a boxer. Not strictly legal, y'know, but it goes on up at Flash, that's where he lives. Bare-knuckle boxing. They say Salt's a man to be feared in the ring."

Gibb kept his voice low now and avoided looking directly over at Salt, who was leaving the square with his arm around the shoulders of one of his companions. Blake decided it best not to stare at the man, either.

"So you didn't see or hear Dr Sneyd again? When he fell from the tower or anything like that?"

"No, I must've been asleep by the time that happened. Heard no scream or anything. I knew nothing about it until next morning when I woke up and there was all the fuss outside the church. I kept out of the way and stayed across the churchyard until folk had gone. Then I saw you and the newspaper fellow come out of The George...."

"What? You saw us there?" Blake interrupted.

"Aye, and just after that I saw Gamage go in."

"Gamage, who's he?"

"Heathcote's man. That hard-faced fellow who runs the estate. He's moved me on a few times in the past, so I keep out of his way. Wouldn't think he's got too many friends round here."

Blake leaned back against the wall, deep in thought, considering what Gibb had told him. This could be vital to the police investigations. He was going to have to pay another visit to Inspector Ramm.

"Nathaniel, look lively! No time for resting, Smedley is going to leave any minute." Finch had appeared out of the crowd and was standing above Blake, amused to see his friend apparently slouched down with a man of the road. The photographer was startled out of his thoughts. He turned to the tramp. "Mr Gibb, I'm sure we will need to speak again. How will I be able to find you?"

"I shall be around and about, Mr Blake. I walk many a mile over these hills and I'm sure I will be down in Leek again before too long."

At that point FJ Finch grasped Blake under the arm, helped him to his feet and hustled him towards where passengers were clambering into Isaac Smedley's vehicle. "I see you have a new friend, Nathaniel," Finch said as the two squeezed in next to each other.

"You don't know the half of it, FJ, but we need to talk about this in private," Blake replied. The horse-drawn bus was no place to discuss what Gibb had said.

When they arrived at the Golden Lion an hour later, Blake decided to accompany Finch to the newspaper office so that he could recount his conversation with John Gibb in privacy.

"It may be important to the investigation," said Blake, after repeating what Gibb told him he had seen at Abbey Green and the Old Church and about Caleb Salt. "This Salt character sounds highly suspicious, even though he's related to Mrs Carter. If he's the culprit I have to tell Inspector Ramm about him as soon as possible."

"Well, no harm in telling the Inspector, but I'm sure he will want to talk to Gibb himself. And let's face it, he may think the word of a tramp is not necessarily the most reliable source. Also you might want to watch your step before tangling with a prize fighter."

"Oddly enough, I was quite impressed by Gibb. Perhaps we shouldn't judge him by the way he looks. And what do you think about this Gamage fellow going into The George? He might be the one who stole the documents from Sneyd's room," Blake replied.

"Well it's hardly surprising he went into The George, is it? The Heathcotes own the place, he might have been collecting the rent. Or sampling an early pint. For all you know, Gibb might have a grudge against Gamage, in fact that's highly likely if the steward had moved him on a few times. Remember what I said earlier Nathaniel, take care of dragging Heathcote into it this affair. He's virtually untouchable in this town."

This wasn't the response Blake had been looking for. He thought

Finch would be as excited as he was about the new clues, however, perhaps it was wise to be guarded. He resolved to think the matter through before going to see the Inspector first thing next morning.

Back at the studio, Cora had spent a long day on her own. Some of the time she had been making postcards from the negatives of the trade union rally pictures. Her father had been impressed with the print she handed to Inspector Ramm the previous week and had told her she could do more work in the darkroom. She served the occasional customer for either pictures or stationery items, then set about making a window display of the union rally postcards. The photographs of the great gathering in the Market Place reminded her of her encounter with Oliver Finch. He was quite different to most of the youths she knew, someone who actually used his brain and was interested in what was going on in the town. Apart from a couple of the really bright boys who had left town to study elsewhere, the young men she had gone to school with were almost all working in the mills now. What's more, the lanky lad seemed to be interested in her and what she had to say, rather than just wanting to lark around. She certainly wouldn't mind seeing him again, especially if they shared an interest in what was happening to the mill girls. She thought how she could engineer another meeting with him. Cora was sure that Ellen could tell them more about life in the mills, but she didn't know how to contact her. She decided to write to her friend.

Dear Polly, When can I see you again? Are you free on Saturday afternoon? I could come round to the tearoom as usual. I had an interesting time at the union rally on Saturday and met Oliver Finch whose father owns the Leek Lion. He's rather unusual! Can you tell me where Ellen lives? I want to talk to her again. I know you will say that I ought not get involved, but we girls should stock together, shouldn't we? Cora.

She put the note in an envelope and, locking the shop door

behind her, took it round the corner to Pickford's tearoom where she left it at the counter. She guessed that her friend would be either in the scullery washing up or in the workroom behind Mrs Pickford's millinery shop next door.

Cora didn't realise that her mother was making her own enquiries about the Great Mill, too. Following her conversation with her daughter on Saturday evening, Edith Blake decided to watch out for Ellen's mother, Mabel Simms, when she was at the local shops. Spotting her outside the greengrocer's on Thursday morning, Edith had made a point of speaking to Mabel. "Our Cora met your Ellen when they were out roller skating the other evening. She said Ellen's working for Heathcote & Company. How is she faring?" she said.

"Well, she didn't like it much at first. She says it's such hard work on the braid looms, her legs were aching as well as her hands. But just recently she's perked up a bit. She seems to think she might get moved to another room. She's got her hopes up that it might be easier work and more money. I just hope she isn't disappointed," Mrs Simms replied.

"That sounds like good news. Do they see much of Mr Heathcote around the mill?" Edith asked.

"Well, right from the start I warned her to steer clear of him, if she could. You know what I'm talking about, don't you? She hasn't complained about anything, thank goodness, although we've all heard tales about him, haven't we?"

"He's no better behaved then?"

"Not according to what some folk say. Our Arthur, that's my brother, says he'll see to Enoch Heathcote good and proper if he touches anybody from our family. But Arthur would probably come out worst – and so would the rest of us."

The two mothers went on their way, Edith relieved that Ellen Simms seemed to be making the best of her job at the Great Mill. Even so, she was glad her own daughter didn't have to work there.

Chapter Eleven

Blake summoned up his confidence as he walked through the rain the following morning. He had thought hard how to approach Inspector Ramm with what he knew and what he suspected. Waiting at the police station front desk, he wiped his spectacles nervously with his handkerchief.

"Now Mr Blake, how can I help you?" said Ramm as the photographer was shown into his office. As it was Magistrates Court day, the Inspector had plenty to do and was slightly puzzled why Blake should be coming to see him again.

"Yesterday I met someone who said that they recognised the man at the Carters' farm on the day Amos died. He believes it's someone called Caleb Salt from Flash. The man is Rosa Carter's nephew apparently."

Ramm sat forward, intrigued. He knew that identifying the mystery man could be vital to finding the farmer's killer. "You are a constant source of surprises, Mr Blake. But first, tell me who this witness is and how he came to speak to you and not to us?"

"It's a man called John Gibb. He's a... a man of the road." Blake's explanation was greeted with raised eyebrows. "I know, I know what you're thinking, Inspector. Can you trust him? Well, I certainly think so after meeting him yesterday."

"Where do we find this John Gibb? Is this *man of the road* with you today?"

"I'm sure some of your men will be familiar with him. He's always around the streets, but yesterday he was up at Longnor Wakes, which is where he told me about what he had seen. He said he wanted to help."

"Mr Blake, I very much appreciate your interest in our investigations. Your enthusiasm, shall we say. But we really need to verify this first." Ramm's mind was on the embarrassment he suffered when he confronted the Vicar.

"It didn't turn out too well after you came here on Monday, I'm afraid. I called Reverend Maitland in and he was highly displeased. The letter to Dr Sneyd wasn't from the Vicar after all and he could prove that he was otherwise occupied that evening. So you will understand my caution before pursuing your latest lead, as you might call it."

Blake took a breath as he digested the news about Reverend Maitland and adjusted his spectacles. Apparently his suspicions about the Vicar were wrong. "Surely if that letter is a forgery it makes the Sneyd affair all the more mysterious. But John Gibb also had something to say about Dr Sneyd."

"What, *more*? Go on, Mr Blake." Ramm leaned back in his office chair to show that, purely out of courtesy, he was prepared to hear the photographer out.

"Gibb was in the churchyard last Thursday night. He goes there sometimes to sleep apparently. He saw Dr Sneyd and before that he says at least one other person went into the church. Gibb reckons that it could have been Salt."

"So your man Gibb has evidence about not one, but two suspicious deaths? Don't you think that in itself is a little strange?"

"Obviously he didn't see exactly what happened. But surely it's worth checking up on this Salt person? I gather he's a rum fellow."

"First we need to find Gibb, question him properly and find out exactly what he did and did not see. It might be a pack of lies, he might even be covering up for something he did himself. Once we have spoken to him then we can move forward."

Undeterred by the officer's sceptical reply, Blake ploughed on with his latest theories. "There's more to it, Inspector. I'm sure that Amos Carter's death is linked with the old cross from the Abbey which Dr Sneyd found out about. That might be the reason Carter was murdered, to steal the cross."

Ramm's response was swift. "But Dr Sneyd wasn't even in town when Amos Carter died. And I gather Sneyd didn't mention the cross when you met him, just an old document."

"Someone else must have found out about it. Amos Carter dug up the cross years ago and then buried it again straight away. He swore his wife to secrecy, but she decided to tell me about it."

Ramm could not disguise his surprise. "Is this something else you haven't been telling us about, Mr Blake? More detective work, is it?"

Blake could tell that beneath Ramm's sarcasm there was a growing curiosity. Blake continued: "I wasn't sure whether to say anything the other day, but now I think I should tell you everything, including one last thing that Gibb said. He also saw Mr Heathcote's steward, Mr Gamage, going into The George last Friday morning, after Finch and I had left."

"And?" Ramm was puzzled what the photographer was getting at.

"Well..." Blake took a deep breath, "...what if Gamage, or perhaps even Enoch Heathcote, is also involved in this affair?"

"No, no, steady on Mr Blake. In the last ten minutes you have managed to produce a new witness, identify a suspect, solve two mysterious deaths and implicate one of Leek's leading townspeople."

"Inspector, I've been thinking about this all night. I'm convinced all these things could be connected."

"I'm sure you are," said Ramm, patronisingly, "but before we go arresting the chairman of the magistrates, let us take this one step at a time. And when I say "us", I mean Leek Police."

"So what are you going to do?" asked Blake.

"First we shall find Gibb and talk to him. Tell me what he looks like. In the meantime, in view of what you have said about this

Caleb Salt, I need to speak to Rosa Carter. Let's see if she can confirm any of this."

Blake give him a description of Gibb, though it sounded like many another man of the road in the moorlands, then he made a last suggestion. "I know this sounds like another one of my fanciful ideas, Inspector, but if you're going down to Abbey Green, perhaps you need to look for the old cross while you are there. Mrs Carter told me that Amos found it near the footbridge over the River Churnet, and when I was at the farm on Saturday I was sure that someone had been digging there."

Ram sighed. "Thank you for the advice, Mr Blake, I will bear that in mind. By the way, could you let me have some more copies of the photograph of the suspect at Abbey Green? I'm sure your friend Mr Finch has told you that it will be printed in this week's *Leek Lion*, so we may need better prints on hand if any more new witnesses come forward. We can but hope."

Blake trudged back to his studio. He had told Ramm everything he knew, but was far from sure what the Inspector would do about it.

Sitting in his office, Inspector Ramm considered that though the photographer's theories might be rather irritating, he could not afford to ignore any new lead. He wasn't actually needed at court today, so perhaps he would give it a miss. Instead he would go down to Abbey Green. He got up to poke the coals that glowed in the office's small cast iron fireplace and, glancing through his window, saw a procession of umbrellas and mackintoshes – it wasn't going to be pleasant at the farm. Before he went there, however, he needed to set his men looking for this Gibb fellow. He called in Sgt Reynolds, gave him the tramp's description and told him to spread the word amongst his officers patrolling the town and especially the constables based in villages across the moorlands. One of them might know the man or where he could usually be found.

It had been only a day since Inspector Ramm had seen Rosa Carter. As a matter of courtesy, he had attended Amos Carter's funeral on the Tuesday afternoon and had been impressed to see St Edward's Church packed. The congregation had been made up largely by the local agricultural community and parishioners from the Old Church, Carter having been a stalwart of both. The street outside had been lined with crowds, and Ramm guessed that most of these people had not known Amos. Instead they had become swept up in the mystery of his death and wanted to catch a glimpse of the coffin arriving and of the grieving widow.

The horror of Carter's death was now the chief topic of conversation in the town, whether across the shop counter or inside the ale house. A veritable whirlwind of gossip had been whipped up when news leaked out that the poor man had been tortured before his death and there were few people in Leek who hadn't settled on one explanation or another. There were tales that Carter had been deeply in debt and was dispatched by moneylenders from Manchester. Others claimed he had fallen foul of a band of gypsies – numerous people said they had seen the caravans passing through that day.

At the funeral Mrs Carter, supported by a small group of relatives, seemed determined to exchange a few words with virtually everyone present. Reverend Maitland had been fulsome in his eulogy, but after the service had ignored the Inspector.

For his renewed visit to Abbey Green, Ramm chose Constable Knowles to accompany him and, as it was still raining, the two men donned waterproof capes before cycling to the farm. They had not been able to forewarn Mrs Carter of their intended visit and, on arriving at the farmstead, found that she was not in the house or the outbuildings.

"Come on Knowles, she'll be around here somewhere," said

Ramm and the two set off across the flat fields in the valley bottom. Squelching through the grass, their boots were soon caked in mud and their trousers soaking wet. Bedraggled cows and sheep turned to watch them march past, the officers thankful their helmets gave at least some protection from the rain. After some minutes they saw Mrs Carter on sloping ground in the distance. She appeared to be tussling with a thorn bush.

"What on earth's she up to?" said Ramm, but as they drew closer he could see Rosa was in fact struggling with a sheep that had become stuck fast in the bush. "Give her a hand Knowles, for goodness sake."

The constable quickened his pace. Mrs Carter was startled when the constable appeared beside her, then gladly accepted his help. Knowles made a clumsy stockman, but between them they managed to free the young sheep, which trotted off towards the rest of the flock. Rosa came down the hillside towards the Inspector, her hair plastered to her head, clothes muddy and clearly out of breath. "Let's get back to the house where we can all dry off. I need a rest," she said.

In the farmhouse, Rosa put the kettle on the stove and turned to Ramm. "Thank you for attending Amos's funeral yesterday, Inspector, it were very good of you. What brings you 'ere today? Is there any news?" she said.

Ramm wanted to be tactful, particularly if it appeared a family member was being implicated. "I can see you've got your hands full here, Mrs Carter, but there are a couple of things I want to ask you about. Firstly, I believe your nephew, Caleb Salt, has spent time at the farm."

Rosa was immediately on her guard. "Caleb? What's our Caleb got to do with anything?"

"Well, it might be useful for us to know the last time Caleb was here. Just so that we can rule him out of any enquiries. Can you remember when you last saw him?"

"Listen Inspector, I admit Caleb's a rough sort. But he couldn't have been involved with what happened to my Amos."

"So when was the last time he was at the farm?"

"Please don't drag Caleb into this," Rosa pleaded. She sighed as she decided to answer the Inspector. "To tell the truth, we hadn't seen a lot of 'im – got plenty of things going on at Flash, so I believe. But just before my dear Amos died, he was down here a couple of times. Don't ask me why, because when he came he spoke mainly with Amos, private like." She added hastily: "But I never saw him that day when I found Amos. And I 'aven't seen 'im since."

"Are you sure it wasn't Caleb in the photograph, the man walking away from the barn?"

"If it was, I didn't recognise 'im. Why on earth would Caleb be 'ere that day. And 'e certainly wouldn't 'arm Amos."

Rosa was shaken by Ramm's questions and the thought of her nephew being involved, but the Inspector pressed on.

"What about anyone else visiting the farm in recent times? Any strangers, anything unusual?"

"No strangers I think, apart from that fellow who Mr Blake said was 'im that fell from the church tower. Other than that, just the usual callers. And Mr Heathcote's been a few times," said Rosa.

"Mr Heathcote? What did he want?"

"I just don't know. Seemed to be private between 'im and Amos."

Ramm looked across to make sure Knowles was getting all this down and then looked earnestly at Rosa.

"Mrs Carter, we've received information about a cross, made of gold, that belonged to the Abbey. Apparently it was hidden hereabouts by the monks. Do you know anything about that?"

Rosa raised her hands in dismay. "Oh Lord forgive me! How do you know about that? Has that photographer been talking to you?" She paused while she thought what to say. "I suppose now Amos is gone, I can do no other than tell the truth. But I don't know why everybody's so interested in it. Yes, Amos found an old cross – it were years ago – and then he buried it again exactly where he found it. It were God's will, he said."

"And Amos never told anyone else about it?"

"No. As far as I know, he buried the cross and he buried the fact that he'd ever found it. Neither of us mentioned it again," Rosa replied.

"Can you show us where the cross was buried?"

Rosa gave a defeated sigh. "Yes I will, but before we go out in that weather again, I need a drink o' tea."

The rain was still coming down as the three set off across the field towards the footbridge. Ramm was determined to get to the bottom of the affair of the Abbey cross, just in case it had a bearing on Amos's murder. Rosa had gone into the barn to find a spade which Knowles was now carrying. When they reached a point near the stone pillar of the bridge, Rosa halted and stared at the ground. "My lord, it looks like somebody's been digging 'ere already," she said.

Ramm looked down at the patch of mud and then glanced across at Knowles who was passing the spade uneasily from one hand to another. Although he was happy to set his constable to work, the Inspector had no intention of a taking up the spade himself if Knowles ran out of steam, and that looked a distinct possibility.

"It's going to be right old job digging in this weather. We'll have to come back another day when the weather's better and the ground isn't so heavy. Then we might find out if there is anything buried here," Ramm announced to Knowles' obvious relief.

As he pedalled slowly back to the station, he was pleased to have been able to confirm at least some of what Blake had said. Judging by Mrs Carter's reaction, they obviously needed to locate this Caleb Salt fellow, as well as the tramp, but it was a pity they had not found the golden cross.

Elizabeth Heathcote felt equally frustrated as she watched the rain stream down the glass of the Longview conservatory that afternoon. Her own search at Abbey Green – via Bernard Gamage – had come up with nothing of interest in the farmhouse, nor any sign of digging, he said. Patience was not one of her virtues and she was growing increasingly anxious about Amos Carter's death.

His mind filled with thoughts of Carter and Sneyd, Blake found it hard to concentrate on his work for the rest of the day. He was on his own in the studio as it was one of Cora's Academy days. As he reprinted the farm picture for Ramm he realised how well his daughter had made the first enlargement. Since their visit to see the Inspector, Cora had said virtually nothing about what had gone on at Abbey Green, he thought. He had been so engrossed with his own theories, he had barely considered how she might be feeling about Amos Carter's death and that of Dr Sneyd whom she had seen only a few days earlier. "I wonder if she's brooding about it all?" he thought. Originally he had thought it best to avoid the subject, but now he felt that may have been wrong. "I've let her down. I must talk to her this evening," he decided.

Unlike many shops which stayed open late because the owners lived on the premises, Blake closed his business in time to be home for the family's evening meal. When he arrived back at Moorside Terrace he handed Cora a note that her friend Polly had brought round to the studio earlier. His daughter read it quickly and smiled to herself.

"Good news, Cora?" asked Nathaniel.

"Yes, I'm going to see Polly at the weekend," she replied.

This might be a good time to see how she was feeling, thought Blake, though he was wary of how to approach her. "I'm glad you're keeping in touch with your friends," he began casually. "The last couple of weeks have been really worrying, haven't they?

Still, perhaps life is getting back to normal now."

"Normal, father? That depends on who you are, doesn't it." Cora seemed as argumentative as ever.

Edith saw the exchange and spoke to her daughter. "Will you be seeing Ellen Simms again? I saw her mother in town yesterday and she said Ellen was happy at the mill. Even hoping she might be promoted. Perhaps you shouldn't worry too much about her and the other girls."

"People don't always tell their mothers everything that goes on," Cora replied.

"Remember dear, you can always tell me about things – you don't have to keep your worries to yourself. I'm proud that you care about other people, really I am. But sometimes there are things you can do nothing about," Edith continued.

"It's still worth trying though, isn't it, mother." With that remark Cora turned from them and went upstairs. Edith looked at her husband. "She seems really worried about girls at the Great Mill. There's been gossip about Enoch Heathcote for years, but I don't suppose you've heard it."

"Heathcote? What do you mean, gossip?" Nathaniel was immediately on the alert. Was there yet another facet to the mill owner's character, he wondered.

"Well..." Edith began, considering how best to word this, "folk have always said he takes a liking to some of young women in the mill. A couple of years ago there was Mary Brassington's daughter who worked there. She left Leek all of a sudden and people said it was because she was with child and Enoch Heathcote... well, he was the father. Poor girl was only fifteen."

Nathaniel's eyes narrowed as he considered Heathcote in a new light. "I know Cora didn't like him from the start, but I thought he seemed sound enough when we saw him at the mill," he said. "Now I'm beginning to wonder whether she was right all along, and there really is something unpleasant about the man."

"Well let's hope she finds something else to think about soon. I don't like her worrying about a character like Heathcote," said Edith.

In her bedroom, Cora read through Polly's note again. They were going to meet at the tearoom on Saturday afternoon and Polly had invited Ellen along too. Undeterred by her mother's advice, she took out notepaper she had received as a birthday present and began to write. Two crumpled efforts later, she put the short letter in an envelope and wrote on the front: *Oliver Finch, c/o The Leek Lion*.

Chapter Twelve

Two days later, well-dressed people queued outside the open front window of a terraced house halfway along Frith Street where a notice reading 'PAY HERE' had been pinned. Keen to be amongst the first spectators at Leek & District Agricultural and Horticultural Society's Annual Show, these were the folk prepared to pay two shillings each for a ticket before making their way along the street to the Belle Vue showground. Nathaniel Blake, who the Agricultural Society had been asked to take official photographs of the event, walked past the ticket window and headed straight to the tented entrance to show his free pass. Cora was by his side, carrying his folding tripod, but as soon as they were on the showground she turned to go back to the studio. As she walked away, she shook the feeling back into her arms to remind her father how heavy the tripod was.

Founded in the 1890's, the Agricultural and Horticultural Show – known by most townspeople simply as Leek Show – had grown into the largest paid-for event in the district. Friday was the first of a two-day programme and by mid-morning the showground was a scene of constant activity. Exhibitors in the numerous classes –

the schedule of entries ran to a hundred pages – had started to arrive at seven o'clock, a melée of farm carts and wagons bringing prize cattle, horses, pigs and sheep. Other competitors came on foot or pushed hand carts carrying their precious exhibits of butter – both plain and ornamental – farmhouse cheeses, bread, eggs, dressed poultry, farm produce, honey and specimen bees. With an array of cash prizes, silver trophies, medals, rosettes and, most importantly, local prestige to be gained, this was a day for serious competition.

After the rain earlier in the week, straw had been liberally spread around to prevent the entrance and pathways from becoming a quagmire. Almost the first person Blake recognised as he looked around the field was Inspector Ramm. He had arrived earlier, not only to have a word with the constable who was on duty at the show, but also to give moral support to his wife Edna, who had entered Class 81, Best Brown Loaf, 2lbs weight. The class was open both to professionals with bakehouses in the district and to home bakers, and Edna, who spent many hours in the kitchen, was proud of the loaf she brought in her wicker basket. She would endure a couple of anxious hours before finding out if she had won a cash prize – ten shillings to the winner – and a certificate of merit.

Ramm was now strolling around the showground, casting a professional eye over the activities. He knew that errant behaviour from the locals was more likely much later in the day when the beer tent had been open for a few hours, however he had been warned of a gang of pickpockets from a nearby town who were targeting events such as this. The showground had been added to the beat of his constable who patrolled that side of the town.

"Good morning Mr Blake. It looks set for a busy day here, I'm sure you will have plenty to photograph," he said.

"Certainly Inspector. I'm making an official record and I am also hoping to sell some postcards as soon as I can," Blake replied, before moving onto his pet subject. "Did you have chance to see

Mrs Carter or perhaps find John Gibb?"

"Mrs Carter confirmed some of what you said. Unfortunately we haven't spoken to Gibb yet, but rest assured, we will find him," Ramm replied. Their conversation was cut short when the Inspector spotted Enoch Heathcote talking animatedly to a judge in the heavy horse ring and decided to steer clear of him. "Now, if you'll excuse me, I need to return to the station," he said.

Blake set to work photographing the bowler-hatted judges who were examining livestock entries, peering at immaculately groomed horses and cattle from every angle and occasionally using a stick to persuade an unwilling bull to stand with its legs apart. Enoch Heathcote, wearing a straw boater, was striding from one judging ring to another. From the lapel of his cream-coloured linen suit dangled a gold-printed badge which marked him out as Vice President of the Agricultural Society. Leek Show was an important occasion for Heathcote as a leading member of the local community. Not only was he on the organising committee, pedigree animals reared on Heathcote-owned farms were competing for various trophies and his head gardener had even brought produce from the Longview vegetable garden to enter in the horticulture tent. But chiefly it was an opportunity to meet and greet fellow landowners and businesspeople and this he did with gusto.

From the edge of the judging ring, the photographer took the chance to observe the man who was increasingly in his thoughts. He could see that Heathcote seemed to look searchingly at everyone he met, just as he had done on his visit to Blake's studio. The mill owner appeared to be in good spirits, mingling, laughing animatedly and shaking hands. However he surmised that Heathcote rarely relaxed completely, he was probably always calculating what business or personal advantage could be gained. "Can he really be involved in not one, but two deaths?" Blake wondered. The man was either innocent or very sure of himself.

Blake moved on from the livestock. The produce and dairy competition tents were closed to the public while visiting judges measured, prodded and sampled the exhibits, so he decided to photograph the early stages of the butter making demonstration. Using dairy equipment and cream provided by town ironmongers Skinner & Co., the competitors were set to spend hours producing butter to be judged later in the day.

The showground was ringed by exhibition stands in tents and open-fronted sheds. Local farmers, many of whom had brought along livestock earlier in the day, clustered around the stands to see what suppliers were offering and to discuss the benefits of products such as Zomo-Sal – "the great blood tonic and corrective for horses and beasts", Cow Drench – "cures costiveness, hidebound, loss of cud" and Errington's Celebrated Pheasant Food. All manner of other livestock medicines and feed were on sale, as well as farm and dairy implements, carts and carriages. In other years, Amos Carter would have been amongst the farmers scrutinising the exhibition stands and livestock rings, but today he was present only in the sombre remarks of those who had known him.

Blake caught a glimpse of FJ Finch and his son Oliver hurrying first from one judging ring to another, and then in and out of competition tents, collecting the day's results. The show's county-wide reputation gave Finch the chance to earn extra income by supplying results to several other local newspapers. Father and son would later spend a frantic hour at their typewriters to ensure the first day's proceedings were reported in tomorrow's *Leek Lion*.

By midday, the breadmaking tent was open to the public and Edna Ramm was delighted to see a certificate alongside her loaf. She would have good news for Albert that evening – a third prize of two shillings and sixpence, and praise from the judges.

Many more visitors passed through the entrance after one o'clock when the ticket price was halved to one shilling, and queues formed at the refreshment marquees. In one, the Old Royal Oak Inn was providing beer, wine, spirits and cigars, while in the other the Victoria Cafe was serving temperance beverages and cold meats. The Leek Temperance Prize Band struck up with their first selections, the strains of 'Pirates of Penzance' floating above the bellowing of cattle. Meanwhile Enoch Heathcote led the judges and officials to the Swan Hotel to enjoy luncheon courtesy of the Agricultural Society.

The wooden grandstand, also used when football matches and military displays were held at Belle Vue, began to fill up with spectators in anticipation of the afternoon's activities. These began with a grand parade of prizewinning animals bearing colourful rosettes and led by white-coated keepers, followed by a horse leaping competition and then a parade of horse-drawn carts and milk floats. The last of the carts were leaving the main ring as Cora returned to help her father carry his equipment back to the studio. As the Blakes left, folk who had been at work during the day were paying sixpence to join in the evening's chief attraction of dancing to the Temperance Band.

"Put your back into it man," Inspector Ramm urged Constable Knowles after the two officers had returned to Abbey Green that afternoon. Having called at the farmhouse to inform Rosa Carter and to collect a spade, they had walked across the field to the spot near the footbridge and Knowles was now digging again. Ramm wanted to lose no time in his search for the Abbey relic.

Though the soil was still heavy from the rain, Knowles made decent progress and the hole was more than a foot deep by the time Mrs Carter came to watch their progress. Ramm himself was familiar with spadework on his council-owned allotment and could tell that, quite recently, the ground had been disturbed to a considerable depth. Knowles, tunic off and sleeves rolled up, paused to wipe sweat from his brow and then returned to his labours. He widened the hole so he could stand in it and dug still deeper. Two feet deep, then two and a half feet, but still no sign of anything in the ground.

"I don't recall Amos burying it this deep," said Mrs Carter, peering downwards.

There was a thud as the spade hit something at the bottom of the hole. Knowles paused and looked back at the Inspector. "Gently now, we don't want to damage anything," said Ramm. The constable scraped around with the spade, but there was no sign of a leather-wrapped treasure – he had hit rock. Ramm stared into the hole and then walked to the nearby riverbank and saw a sandstone shelf jutting out into the Churnet.

"Forget it Knowles, there's rock running all under here. It looks like there's nothing in this hole," he said.

"It's gone then! Somebody's stole that cross, after Amos kept it secret all that time," said Mrs Carter, wringing her hands and looking sadly into the hole.

At Ramm's suggestion, Knowles started to refill the excavation. The Inspector was disappointed not to find the cross. He had a growing suspicion that Carter's murder and the disappearance of the cross were no coincidence, and if so, then neither was the death of Dr Sneyd. Irritating as it might be, perhaps Nathaniel Blake's theories were not as wild as he had originally thought.

FJ Finch often had a sense of anti-climax when the *Leek Lion* was finally on the streets. His highpoint came when the newspaper was rolling off the press on a Friday evening. The following morning he would usually begin to turn his attention to the next edition, but this week was different. Only a handful of people knew the *Lion* was printing the Abbey Green photograph and so Finch was excited to see the public's reaction.

Despite the previous night's late finish, he and Oliver were in the newsroom early that Saturday.

"This is a first for the *Lion*, we're a force to be reckoned with, my boy. Let's see what the readers make of this," said Finch as he admired his work yet again.

Local news coverage on page three was normally a sea of words in the same tiny typeface. This week, however, the photograph of the straw-hatted man walking from the Abbey Green barn was prominent at the top of the page. An appeal for witnesses appeared below and the latest update on Dr Sneyd's death was printed in an adjoining column. Finch could barely believe his good fortune – not one but two murders to write about.

He was particularly pleased with the scoop because Leek's mysterious deaths were now attracting the attention of newspapers from outside the area. The *Manchester Evening News* had carried a particularly sensational account entitled "A Killer on the Loose!". Finch had been concerned at being put in the shade by his bigger rivals, but when they saw this week's *Lion* Leek folk would have even more to talk about.

He left the office, expecting to run across some of his contacts in the town centre – and gauge their reaction to the photograph – before heading to Belle Vue for the second day of Leek Show.

In the Blake household, the family had finished breakfast when Nathaniel, Edith and Cora gathered around the kitchen table to look at the newspaper page containing Blake's first published photograph. His wife and daughter couldn't get close enough to read the story so Nathaniel read it aloud:

> DO YOU KNOW THS MAN?
>
> REMARKABLE DEVELOPMENT IN ABBEY GREEN MURDER CASE. – The continuing investigation into the brutal murder of Abbey Green farmer Amos Carter has witnessed a remarkable development with the release of a photograph of a man Leek Police want to interview. The photograph, reproduced above, was taken on the afternoon of Tuesday August 19th when Mr. Carter's body was discovered in the barn at Dieulacres Cottage Farm. It is an enlargement from a landscape picture by leading Leek photographer Mr. Nathaniel Blake.
>
> Inspector Albert Ramm, Head of Leek Police, said: "There was a man apparently walking away from the farm around the time Mr. Carter was murdered and I am appealing to the readers of the *Leek Lion*: do you recognise him? If so, they should contact Leek Police immediately. Identifying this man is crucial to our investigation of this serious crime. If you are the person in the photograph, but were in no way involved in the incident, I ask you to contact us anyway. Your evidence may be valuable."
>
> *Leek Lion* Editor F.J. Finch commented: "We are delighted to use our position in the community to assist this important investigation. Our readers have been shocked by Mr. Carter's murder and I am sure will want to help find his killer."
>
> Mr. Carter was discovered after being bound and mortally wounded whilst his wife, Mrs. Rosa Carter, was engaged on tasks elsewhere on the farm. There was no apparent motive for the crime. Mr. Carter was a respected member of the local farming community and there was a large attendance at his funeral at St. Edward's Parish Church on Tuesday (see report on page 4).

"Well Cora, you're the one to thank for spotting that man in the photograph. Let's hope this is going to help the police," said Blake, determined to be positive with his daughter. He had not mentioned Caleb Salt to her because he didn't want the girl worrying more than necessary. "The picture isn't quite as clear as I would like, but it may attract some response. If nothing else, it draws attention to Mr Carter's death," he added.

"I just hope they catch this man soon and it will all be over with," said Cora, turning to leave the kitchen. "I'm going to fetch my coat then I've got to pop out for a few minutes. I have something to deliver."

"Oh, what's that?" asked Edith.

"Just a note to a friend. I won't be out long," Cora replied.

Edith, wiping infant Eliza's face with a cloth, gave her husband a knowing look, but by now he was studying the *Lion* again and had come across the item about Dr Sneyd.

INVESTIGATION INTO MYSTERIOUS DEATH AT CHURCH. – The death in Leek of a leading historian is shrouded in mystery. The body of Dr. Crosbie Sneyd, a medieval history scholar at Jesus College, Oxford, was found outside St. Edward's Parish Church on the morning of Friday August 29th. He had apparently fallen from the church tower and his death was initially treated as an accident. But the *Leek Lion* can reveal that Leek Police have now begun an urgent investigation into the incident.

Inspector Albert Ramm of Leek Police told the *Lion*: "We are carrying out a full enquiry into this tragic affair and we are anxious to speak to anyone who may have had contact with Dr. Sneyd whilst he was visiting the Leek area, staying at The George Hotel, or when he was at St. Edward's Church on the evening of Thursday August 28th. We are keen to find why he was at the church, possibly at an unusual hour, who he may have seen there and why he ventured out onto the tower roof. The tower would not normally be accessible to members of the public and he was a stranger in the town. Anyone with information should contact Leek Police without delay."

It is understood that Dr. Sneyd had been staying at The George for more than a week before his death, having come to the town to carry out research into the history of Dieulacres Abbey. Vicar of St. Edward's, the Rev. G.W. Maitland, was not available for comment. An inquest into the death was opened and adjourned on Thursday.

"FJ also has something in here about Dr Sneyd," Blake said to Edith. "The Inspector's still looking for clues about what happened to the poor man." Although he had told his wife what John Gibb had seen, Blake had not mentioned his own theories about the deaths because he knew how she would respond. Neither did Edith encourage him this morning. "Nathaniel, you know I'm not happy about you getting involved in these things. That affair at Abbey Green was bad enough and now you're concerning yourself with how this Dr Sneyd died. Why not leave it to the police?"

"Edith, I have told Inspector Ramm everything I know, so it is in his hands now," Blake reassured her, though secretly he was still puzzling over the deaths. Just then they heard the front door shut as their daughter went out.

Cora walked rapidly, partly because she didn't want to be out long enough to attract her parents' curiosity, and also because she was excited about her errand. From the main street she turned into Market Street and, after a moment's hesitation, opened the green door of the *Leek Lion* office. Like her father a fortnight earlier, the first thing she saw was the black printing press and an ink-spattered lad rubbing it down with a rag. "Er, where are the reporters?" Cora asked, a little uncertainly. "Upstairs," he said, putting upwards to emphasise the direction he meant. In the room above, compositor Alfred looked up from his mound of metal type and, guessing she was not looking for him, said simply "Carry on up."

Cora mounted the next flight of stairs and found herself in the newsroom crammed with papers and books. She didn't know whether to be relieved or embarrassed to find Oliver at one of the two desks, but at least he was on his own. He looked up from his typewriter and smiled when he saw who the visitor was. "Cora, this is a surprise. But a very pleasant one," he said.

Cora held up the slightly crumpled letter. "Hello Oliver, I've written you a note, but as you're here, I suppose I can tell you instead."

"Something interesting? Why don't you sit down?" He pointed to a chair, adding: "Father's out at the moment, looking for compliments about today's paper, I think. I suppose you've seen the photograph?"

"Well, I've seen it before. It was me who printed it and took it to the police in the first place."

"Impressive," said Oliver. Cora, who had remained standing, felt her cheeks redden as she saw the reporter appraising her anew. "I've called round because of what you said last week about wanting to write something about the mill girls," she said.

"Have you seen my report on the union rally? I put a lot of work into that. I think it's turned out rather well, even if I say so myself," enthused Oliver.

To her horror, Cora realised she had not seen Oliver's story, in fact she had read none of the newspaper that morning. This was embarrassing. "Er, I haven't had chance to study it properly yet, father hogs the *Lion* as soon as it arrives. I'll definitely read it when I get back home."

"You must tell me what you think about it."

Cora pressed on. "This afternoon I will be meeting my friend Polly and I think that Ellen Simms – the girl you saw in the Market Place last week – is going to be there, too. We're going to Pickfords tea room. You see, Polly's father owns it." She realised she had been gabbling, but then she started to struggle for the right words. "Anyway, I thought... if you... happened to be around... you could... possibly... see us. You might find out more about Heathcote & Company, or arrange another time to talk about it, or something."

"This afternoon? What time? Father's sending me to report on what's going on at Leek Show. We were there all yesterday, but it will be different today."

Cora was disappointed. Why hadn't she thought he would be going to Leek Show? This was probably what reporters were like, always out and about somewhere, she thought. Her plan to find out more from the mill girls – and see Oliver again – was ruined. It was a crazy idea anyway, she thought. Then Oliver spoke again. "But honestly, give me an idea of the time and I'll try to come round. I'm sure I can slip out of the showground for half an hour without anyone noticing. I can catch up on the results or whatever when I get back," he said.

"We're meeting at three o'clock. But I don't want the others to know I've told you. I thought you could just, well, find us there, as if it was by chance," Cora replied. She was relying on Oliver being as quick-witted as she thought he was. He nodded and smiled, rather liking the idea of a secret plan between the two of them. "I'll do my best, afternoon tea sounds good," he said.

"I have to go now and you must have more...er...typing to do," said Cora. She hurried down the stairs, her stress relieved by screwing up the unwanted letter in her hand.

The latest *Leek Lion* had thoroughly upset the breakfast-time routine at Longview. Elizabeth Heathcote gasped in surprise as she opened her copy and saw the photograph, disturbing Enoch who was studying the front page advertisements. "What is this? Did you know about it, Enoch?" she asked.

He quickly opened his paper to see what the fuss was about, his puzzled expression providing his wife with the answer she had expected. "Certainly not, Elizabeth. Ramm never mentioned anything about publishing a photograph. In fact, I think he's been avoiding me all week," he replied.

"Have you any idea who it might be?" Elizabeth asked.

Enoch found a magnifying glass to scrutinise the photograph. "It's taken from behind and it's not particularly clear. It could be anyone, as far as I'm concerned," he said dismissively.

Elizabeth seemed to be growing more agitated. "You need to keep abreast of matters like these! You're Chairman of the Bench, for heaven's sake!"

Enoch shifted uncomfortably in his seat and glanced down at

his bacon and eggs, now gone cold. "Certainly dear, but I can't do anything about it today because I'm needed at the show again. Perhaps you'd like to come? I shall be using the Napier." His wife considered the idea for a moment and then replied: "The Leek Show could be a distraction, certainly, and Mrs Gamage can accompany me. Ask Simpkins to drive the motor car, will you? It might be safer."

Enoch was about to ring the bell for some fresh breakfast to be brought in when Elizabeth, who was still reading the *Lion*, uttered another gasp. "I take it Ramm hasn't told you about the Sneyd investigation either? The Inspector has certainly been busy this week."

"Now what?" asked Enoch, searching the page.

"According to this, Ramm doesn't think that Sneyd's death was an accident after all," she said.

"Whatever he believes, Ramm has no reason to think Sneyd had any connection with us. So there's no reason for you to be so concerned."

Elizabeth was not reassured. Family reputation was everything to her. Since she was a girl she had known that family interests came first. The Heathcote name, and the fortune that went with it, had to be protected, at all costs.

Cora helped carry her father's equipment to Belle Vue for the second day of Leek Show. No farm animals were on show today, however the tents displaying vegetables, flowers, bread, butter, cheese, eggs and bees were all open and, once again, the butter makers were busy with their churns. The grandstand was packed with spectators, many excited young lads standing in front, ready for the afternoon's entertainment in the main ring. This began with horses leaping over a variety of jumps, followed by obstacle races for both men and youths. One of the highlights was the town's part-time soldiers, the Leek Yeomanry and Volunteers, competing in a series of military tournaments. First, members of the smartly uniformed ranks undertook ten laps of the track in full marching order (first prize £2). Then came a saddling race for the mounted members of the Yeomanry, after which the perspiring troops discarded their brass-buttoned tunics to compete in a tent-pegging competition and eight-a-side tug of war. The riders returned for a novelty contest pushing a giant ball with their horses followed by a gymkhana race.

Blake, his tripod on the edge of the ring, took numerous photographs of the tournament events as well as show officials who stood complimenting Yeomanry officers on the skills of their men. Enoch Heathcote was again prominent in proceedings, frequently stepping forward to congratulate competitors and present the prizes. Earlier Blake had seen the Heathcotes arrive in the green Napier, attracting considerable interest from onlookers. Simpkins – the groom now acting as chauffeur – parked the motor car prominently in one of the unused judging rings and then kept watch to stop lads touching the vehicle. Mrs Heathcote, accompanied by Margaret Gamage, headed straight for the horticulture tent while Enoch had walked off in the other direction.

By the time the troops were sweating it out in the tournament, Cora had met Polly, Ellen and Polly's cousins Ada and Fanny in Pickford's tearoom. The rival attraction of Leek Show meant there were fewer ladies taking tea that afternoon, and so Polly's father had agreed the girl could sit at one of the larger tables. He had even given them a plate of freshly-baked biscuits.

For the first half hour Cora took little notice of what the others were saying because she was concerned whether Oliver Finch might appear or not. The others didn't notice she was repeatedly looking towards the door. She did her best to hide her relief when the tall reporter finally arrived and looked casually around the room. He immediately walked towards them and said: "Cora, nice to see you! And it's Ellen isn't it?"

Oliver may have been putting on an act, but there was genuine surprise amongst the young ladies. As her friends stared up at Oliver, Cora responded hastily: "Oliver, I didn't know you came here." She introduced him to Polly and her cousins and asked if he would like to join them.

Oliver drew up a chair, asked the waitress for tea and took one of the biscuits, while Polly and her cousins appraised the confident newcomer. Ellen avoided looking at Oliver and appeared uncomfortable when he turned and said: "So Ellen, how are things at the Great Mill?"

Ellen tensed. "Perhaps you should ask Ada and Fanny," she replied, nodding across at the two girls, "they work there too, you know."

"Oh, excellent," said Oliver, turning to Polly's cousins. "I want to write something about what life's like for young people in the mills. It would be so much help if I could talk to you about it some time."

The two exchanged nervous looks and shook their heads. "We'd have to ask permission first. I don't think we would be allowed," said Ada, the elder of the sisters.

Cora feared her scheme might fail, so she joined in. "What about you, Ellen? I'm sure Oliver wouldn't use any names or anything. I bet there are plenty of people who might be interested to know what it's like in the Great Mill." Not wanting to scare Ellen off, she avoided mentioning what she was actually interested in: Enoch Heathcote.

"Cora's absolutely right. I'm sure there would be interest in it, and, of course, anything said would be anonymous," added Oliver. In his enthusiasm he chose to forget that his father decided what appeared in the *Lion*. Ellen looked down at her empty teacup as she considered the idea. She suspected what they actually wanted to find out about. Like the rest of her workmates, she avoided talking about Heathcote, but what had happened with the mill owner earlier in the week had made her think again.

"If I talk it's not going to be in here and not today," said Ellen.

"I'll arrange something, then. I'll send you a note," said Cora.

"Please can we talk about something else?" pleaded Polly.

Oliver finished his tea and gave his apologies as he had to dash back to his duties at Leek Show. As he left, Polly and her cousins exchanged smiles and the friends moved on to new topics.

The three mill girls hadn't noticed that Martha Robinson, who also worked at Heathcote & Co, happened to be sitting at a table behind Ellen. The woman earned the occasional shilling by feeding gossip to Margaret Gamage. Although apparently talking to her companion, she was watching what went on at the girls' table and doing her best to listen in to their conversation when Oliver Finch arrived. Martha had been the one who reported seeing him talking to Cora and Ellen the previous week – now she would have something else to tell Mrs Gamage.

Weeks later Cora would think back to the tearoom that day and wonder at how naive she had been. What had she and Oliver believed they could achieve on their own? She had given no thought to the risks of stirring up trouble with Heathcote & Co, to the harm it could cause.

After a hard day in the quarry near Buxton, Caleb Salt was looking forward to his first pint – and then a few more – when he walked into the New Inn in Flash that evening. He had barely taken a mouthful of ale when Isaak Nadin began his weekly reading from the *Leek Lion*. Usually some people carried on talking during the weekly news announcements, but this Saturday the room was struck silent when Nadin almost shouted the headline *"Do you know this man?"* He read out the item in suitably dramatic fashion and then held the newspaper aloft to display the photograph. There was a surge towards Nadin with ale spilled as drinkers elbowed each other out of the way to take a closer look.

Amos Carter's death had attracted much speculation in Flash. The murdered farmer was well known and his widow – who many folk referred to by her maiden name, Rosa Salt – still had family in the village. Several men glanced towards her nephew sitting in the corner and muttered amongst themselves after examining the photograph of the man in what appeared to be a familiar straw hat.

Caleb Salt stared at his glass. He knew people were looking at him, but didn't intend to show any reaction in a pub full of gossips. He hadn't particularly liked his uncle Amos, anyway. Deep in thought, Salt barely noticed Isaak Nadin had moved on to another item until he heard St Edward's Church mentioned. Folk from Flash were less interested in the demise of an outsider from Oxford and there was little reaction to latest news on Dr Sneyd. Suddenly Salt didn't feel like finishing his ale. He got to his feet, nodded to his two companions and walked out. The village shop would still be open and he had decided to buy his own copy of the *Lion*.

The two-room cottage he shared with his widowed mother was at the end of a rough track leading up the side of Axe Edge, one of the highest and bleakest points thereabouts. Mrs Salt was already in her tiny bedroom, so Salt quietly lit an oil lamp in the half of the cottage which served as kitchen, living room and the place he slept. The lamp gave just enough light for him to read the newspaper, in particular the stories about Amos Carter and Dr Sneyd. He took a close look at the photograph. This Blake fellow had been at Abbey Green that day, and, according to last week's *Lion*, so had his daughter. He wondered just how much these Blakes had really seen. The police said they were looking for witnesses. He threw the newspaper down. It wouldn't be long before he had more than enough money to start a new life, far away from this damned place, he thought. The sooner he was gone, the better.

Chapter Thirteen

When Albert and Edna Ramm attended morning worship at St Edward's Church, the Inspector had hoped for a respite from work, however this Sunday it proved otherwise. Not only had the Old Church come to represent a crime scene for him, but he was preoccupied throughout Reverend Maitland's sermon with how the Vicar would react to him. As it turned out, after the service the Vicar chose not to refer to either his police interview or Dr Sneyd's death, but there was no warmth in his greeting in the church porch. Ramm had never particularly liked Reverend Maitland, he was a little too superior in his ways, he thought. Walking out of church, the Inspector had failed to avoid Enoch Heathcote who questioned him closely about both the Carter and the Sneyd cases. A few yards away, Mrs Heathcote and the Vicar were standing in private conversation – probably discussing some finer point of his sermon, thought Ramm, grudgingly.

Enoch Heathcote voiced his disappointment that the Inspector had failed to keep him, as Chairman of the Magistrates, informed about what was going on and particularly the publication of the photograph. Previously Ramm had been simply irritated by Enoch

Heathcote's inquisitiveness. Now, following the wild ideas that Nathaniel Blake had suggested, he wondered if there might be something more sinister behind the man's persistent questions. Until he was sure of his facts, he resolved to be as guarded as possible in his dealings with Mr Heathcote.

Inspector Ramm was glad to hear some good news when he arrived at the police station on the Monday morning. "Good morning sir. We've found Gibb and he's in the cells," announced Sgt Reynolds at the front counter. "Constable Mellor up at Longnor knows Gibb and some of his haunts, and he found him in an old building near the Reapsmoor cheese factory yesterday. Mellor thought of putting him in the village lock-up, but decided to bring him down here last night – used his initiative and hired a cart."

"We kept Gibb in the cells just so he didn't wander off again. He's even had tea and toast this morning," the sergeant continued. "We looked through his knapsack. In his purse there were a few coins and a medal – it looks like a DCM. No ribbon, but his name's on it."

"Distinguished Conduct Medal, eh?" said Ramm with raised eyebrows. Like many police officers, he and Reynolds had served in the army before joining the force and both knew the medal was a significant honour. "And there was this," Reynolds added as he reached below the counter and produced Gibb's dirk, the pointed dagger-like knife with a stag's head on the handle.

"Did you indeed. That's a handy weapon," said Ramm, picking up the knife and drawing the gleaming blade from its sheath. "Bring him up to my office. Send Knowles in to take notes – and get me a mug of tea."

Though it wasn't usual for a potential witness to be detained in the cells, he thought that the tramp was in no position to complain, particularly if he'd had a free breakfast. When John Gibb was ushered into his office, the Inspector wondered whether their hospitality should have also included a bath. Gibb's face was as grimy as his collarless shirt and he brought a distinctive aroma into the room.

"Mr Gibb, I gather you have some important things to tell us regarding Mr Carter and Dr Sneyd's deaths. But first, for our records, can we have some details about yourself and how you come to be living here in the moorlands?" Believing that Gibb could be a suspect as much as a witness, Ramm intended to leave no stone unturned. Like others who had met Gibb for the first time, he was struck by the bearded tramp's measured tones, his serious attitude.

"I will do that, Inspector, I have nothing to hide. As you can tell, I'm not from these parts," Gibb replied before recounting his earlier life. The son of a Church of Scotland minister, he had received a good education but rebelled against a strict father who had hoped his son would follow in his footsteps. Instead he had joined the Queen's Own Highlanders Regiment and risen to the rank of Sergeant Major.

"The army life suited me, at least at first, and I had the wits to get ahead," Gibb went on, looking past Ramm and into the memories of his past. "It was a tough life and got much harder when we were sent to fight the Afghans. I was out there three years and our lads had a hell of a time with those tribesmen in the mountains. Thankfully we had Indian troops by our side and we won more battles than we lost. But a lot of our lads died – one or two of them even got medals for their trouble." Gibb paused before continuing.

"No sooner were we home than we shipped out to Sudan. The Mahdi tribesmen were the enemy this time and they were even more savage than the Afghans. After General Gordon and his men were lost at Khartoum, we were sent home. And that's when I started to wonder what was the point of it all. I decided I'd seen enough killing, I'd done enough myself, and thank God I'd served long enough to come out of the regiment with honour.

"But I hadn't known a normal life, you might say, for twenty-odd years and I couldn't settle. I came to see an old comrade who'd taken over a pub down here and stayed with him for a while. Then one day I just walked out and carried on walking." Gibb opened empty hands to show he had come to the end of his story.

Ramm looked across to Constable Knowles, wondering how much of that he had managed to write down, and then puffed out his cheeks. He had some sympathy with what Gibb had said, although in his own time in the army he had seen none of the horrors the tramp described. However they needed to focus on the investigation. "Well Mr Gibb, that's quite a story. But let's come to the present and what you know about Mr Carter's death."

"It's just as I told Mr Blake. The Carters have been good to me for years. I was having a rest in the road by their farm that day. A few minutes before Mrs Carter came across the field, screaming, I'd seen a man walking away towards the footbridge. It looked very much like Rosa's nephew, Caleb Salt – I've seen him before, at the farm and other places."

Ramm reached for a copy of Blake's photograph and showed it to Gibb. "So you say this man is Salt?"

"Yes," Gibb answered firmly.

"Did you go into the barn that afternoon and have an argument with Amos Carter?"

"No."

"Were you trying to steal something from the Carters?"

"Certainly not. I did nothing, I simply saw what I've told you."

"If that is the case, why didn't you come forward earlier? Why tell Mr Blake rather than us?"

"At first I didn't want to get involved. For some reason, Inspector, people don't always understand the sort of person I am, they don't believe what I say." Gibb stared at Ramm from beneath bushy eyebrows.

Ramm opened his desk drawer and placed Gibb's knife between

them. "What about this? It's a fearsome blade, probably deadly in the wrong hands. Are you sure you don't use this when people *don't understand* you, as you put it. As you said, you know all about killing."

"I'm a peaceable man, Inspector."

"So why have you got the knife?"

"Living a life like mine, on your own in the countryside, you need a knife for all sorts of things. Skinning a rabbit, peeling a turnip. And that one's precious to me. It's from my time in the Highlanders – that stag's head is our badge. When I hold that dirk I think of some of the brave men I served with, I think of the ones that never came back."

"Are you sure you didn't whip this out in a fit of rage and attack poor Mr Carter? And then decide to pin the blame on someone else?"

"I've already told you I had nothing to do with his death. I was fond of Mr Carter and I'm trying to help you find out who did kill him. I could have kept my information to myself and surely that's what I would have done if I'd been involved?"

"All right, let's move on to the following week and what you saw at St Edward's Church."

Gibb repeated what he had seen at the church that evening and outside The George the following day.

"And you think that Salt may have gone into the church that night?" asked Ramm.

"It might have been him, but I'm not certain. As I said, it was going dark."

"What about Dr Sneyd? Had you met him before?"

"When I saw him on the ground, I recognised his jacket from the night before. But I had no idea who he was."

"And Mr Gamage going into The George. Surely there was nothing suspicious in that, was there? Aren't you dragging him into this simply because he's crossed you in the past? Someone else who doesn't *understand* you."

"I admit that I don't like the man, but I did see him that morning. It's for you to decide if it's important or not."

"It's also for me to decide if we can believe what you say, Mr Gibb. Isn't it rather a coincidence that you were in the vicinity when both these deaths occurred? But you say you did nothing other than watch what was going on."

John Gibb shrugged: "I've told you all I can."

Inspector Ramm gave an exasperated sigh. There was no evidence against the tramp, other than he was on the scene and he possessed a knife which could have caused Amos Carter's injuries. But if Gibb was responsible, why tell Blake, knowing the photographer would come to the police? Ramm realised he could not charge Gibb with anything, not yet at least, but neither could he detain him indefinitely. On the other hand Gibb had given them a first-hand identification of Caleb Salt.

"Mr Gibb, as you are of no fixed abode and we will need to speak to you again, I will have to keep you in the cells until tomorrow while our enquiries continue. Constable, escort our guest back downstairs."

Gibb nodded resignedly. "Keep me here if you like, Inspector, but be careful you don't let the real culprit get away," he said as Constable Knowles took his arm. The comment stung Ramm into action. He went back to Sgt Reynolds at the reception counter.

"Any news from our rural colleagues on this Caleb Salt?" Ramm's tone left no doubt he was looking for results.

"Apparently he lives in a cottage with his old mother up at Flash, but unfortunately it's over the border in Derbyshire which makes it awkward if we want to arrest him there. He works in a quarry out Buxton way," Reynolds replied.

Ramm began to fire instructions. "Telephone Buxton police and tell them we need their help with a murder enquiry. Ask them to send someone round to this quarry and, if Salt's there, detain him until we can question him. We should get someone up to Flash to speak to the mother – send a telegram to Constable Mellor at Longnor and ask him to do it. Oh, and if one of you is free this afternoon, take Gibb around to the baths to clean him up – I don't know how long I can stand that aroma. Tuppence should cover it." A visit to the individual 'slipper' baths was routine for the many townsfolk who had no bathroom of their own, but Ramm guessed that Gibb was unlikely to be a customer there.

"Yes, Inspector. And what about these, Sir?" Reynolds pointed to a ledger that lay open on the counter, its foolscap page filled with writing.

Ramm slid the ledger around to look at a list names. "What's this about?" he asked.

"It's names, Sir, from people who say they recognise the man in the Abbey Green photograph. We've made a note of each person who's contacted us and who they reckon it is. There's been about twenty since the *Lion* came out, all different," Reynolds explained.

Ramm had no idea what response the photograph would bring, but had not expected this. Nor had he considered the time now needed to follow up the suggestions. And it could all be a waste of time, he thought bitterly. "Power of the press, eh Sergeant? Eventually we may have to bring these in for questioning and that's no small job. But first we need to concentrate on Salt."

Before Reynolds could respond, the telephone on the reception counter began a strident jangle. He lifted the handset from its brass-spindled cradle, exchanged a few words with an operator and then passed it to Ramm, saying "It's Headquarters, Sir."

The telephone was one of only a handful in the town and Ramm had to admit he found it disconcerting to speak to a disembodied voice at the other end of the line, which was why he let Sgt Reynolds make most of the station's calls. This particular conversation turned out to be even more awkward, however, as the tinny voice in the earpiece was that of his Superintendent in

Stafford asking why Ramm had not consulted police headquarters before publishing the photograph in the *Leek Lion*.

"I felt we had to attract the public's attention. It may help secure a conviction, Sir," Ramm responded. He was surprised that the Stafford office had found out about the photograph so quickly.

"It certainly attracted attention. We've had a call from the Chairman of the Magistrates this morning, Mr Heathcote, complaining that he hasn't been kept abreast of developments," said the Superintendent. Ramm put his hand over the mouthpiece and cursed. Heathcote – he might have guessed!

"That's not quite correct, Sir. I know Mr Heathcote is very... curious... about the case, but we've got two suspicious deaths on our hands now. I'm not prepared to divulge too much outside the station – you know what small towns are like, stories can spread like wildfire," Ramm replied.

"Well, make sure you keep Heathcote off our backs."

"I will try, Sir."

"Are you quite sure you can handle this, Inspector? We may have to send a detective up to take over the investigation – especially if the Magistrates are not happy."

"Sir, the good news is that we have information from a witness, a list of suspects to get our teeth into and we're in pursuit of one man in particular."

This seemed to satisfy the Superintendent, although before ringing off, he warned Ramm not to take any more unusual steps without consulting Headquarters first. Ramm sighed deeply as he replaced the handset. Despite his confidence on the telephone, he knew that solving both cases – and keeping his superiors happy – was getting no easier.

Nathaniel and Cora Blake were fully occupied at the studio that day. Working side by side in the cramped darkroom, they were developing and printing the many images he had taken at Leek Show, both for the Agricultural Society and as postcards. Blake wanted to have the cards on sale as soon as possible, in his own window and at other shops in the town. These were likely to be the only images of the event many local people would see.

In the intimate setting of the dimly-lit darkroom, Blake felt more comfortable talking to Cora and, because they were concentrating on their work, they could avoid looking at each other. It was important to talk with his daughter after recent events, particularly as he had begun to share her unease about Enoch Heathcote. He started casually enough: "You didn't have much to say about meeting your friends at the tea room. What are they up to?"

Cora was wary of revealing too much to her father, particularly after her mother's warning about getting involved with Heathcote & Co. "Oh, they all seem fine," she said.

"Some of them work at the Great Mill, don't they? I suppose they know Mr Heathcote, then?"

Cora seemed in no mood to be drawn into a conversation about the mill owner. "Father, you know I didn't like him from the start, but you seem to think there's nothing wrong with the gentleman. Mother has told me to keep away from Mr Heathcote, so perhaps we shouldn't talk about him either."

"Actually, I'm beginning to wonder if you were right about him," Blake replied. In the darkroom's red glow Cora shot him a questioning look, surprised by this change of heart. "But the more I hear about Heathcote, the more I agree with your mother that you shouldn't have anything to do with his mill or concern yourself with his workers," he continued.

"What if he is doing something wrong, and we do nothing about it?" said Cora, exasperated that her views were being ignored.

"I didn't say that nothing should be done. I'm sure the truth will come out eventually, but I want you to stay safe. A young lady like you shouldn't get involved in such things at the mill."

Blake was trying hard to give fatherly advice rather than an order, but Cora seemed undeterred. "Even when it's my friends? What if I could help them?" she asked.

Blake felt he was not going to win this argument – he could hardly persuade her not to help her friends. "Please be careful, dear. And if someone says anything about Mr Heathcote, tell me about it, too," he said.

Later, while Cora was printing more postcards, Blake went downstairs to do some paperwork. As he looked through the orders for his portrait photographs he spotted a distinctive piece of cream notepaper, embossed with *"Longview, Leek"* at the top. Using business-like language, Enoch Heathcote had ordered a substantial number of reprints of his wife's portrait and signed the note simply *"E Heathcote"*.

Although Blake had dispatched the photographs, he had yet to send an invoice. He began to write one out but stopped, troubled by a memory he couldn't quite bring to mind. He opened a drawer and took out large envelope which contained his secret detective work – notes he was keeping on the Carter and Sneyd murders. There were also the photographs taken at Abbey Green, the Old Church and in Dr Sneyd's room. Leafing through them he found what had triggered his recollection – the photograph of the letter supposedly written by Reverend Maitland. The handwriting looked to be the same as the photograph order from Heathcote.

"Surely not!" he gasped. He placed the two letters side by side on his desk. With shaking hands he polished his spectacles and peered first at one and then the other. He was sure they were both in the same hand. The sweeps of some of characters appeared identical. Studying the photograph of the letter to Dr Sneyd, he spotted something else – the top edge of the paper was not completely straight, as if a strip had been scissored off. The forged letter was on blue paper, not cream, he recalled, but could it have been a piece of Longview stationery?

Blake sat back to think. If he was right – and he grew more confident by the minute – this meant that Enoch Heathcote was responsible for luring Dr Sneyd to his death at the Old Church. And the following day he had sent Gamage to steal Sneyd's papers to protect himself. Now it all made sense, but who would believe him? Finch had warned him against the Heathcotes and Inspector Ramm was openly skeptical of his theories. He would need more proof. Blake was in for another sleepless night.

Cora came out of the darkroom a little while later and told her father she would not walk home with him because she wanted to leave a note at a friend's house. Blake guessed it was for Polly.

After hearing her father's new doubts about Enoch Heathcote, Cora was determined to press on with her own investigation, especially now that she had Oliver Finch to turn to. While Nathaniel was downstairs, she quickly wrote a note to Ellen Simms:

"Ellen, I will be outside the mill when you finish work on Wednesday. Look out for me. Tell your mum you are meeting a friend. Cora."

Then she wrote another to Oliver.

"Can we meet outside your office at six o'clock on Wednesday? I have asked Ellen to come. Cora."

Ellen was still at the mill when Cora called at the family's terraced cottage later, so she handed the note to Mrs Simms. At the *Lion* office she went straight to the top floor. She hadn't thought what she would say if FJ Finch had been there, but was relieved to find the newsroom empty and left Oliver's message on his desk.

At the police station, Sgt Reynolds brought disappointing news to the Inspector. Buxton Police had called to say they had visited the quarry where Caleb Salt worked, but he had not shown up that day. "Let's hope Constable Mellor has better luck," said Ramm.

Mellor cycled from his police cottage at Longnor to Flash at the end of the day and, after asking directions at Flash Bar Stores, made his way to the modest house where Salt lived with his mother, a quarter mile out of the village. "Am I in Staffordshire or Derbyshire?" he wondered as he pushed his bicycle along the rough track to the cottage.

When Mrs Salt – Rosa Carter's sister-in-law – finally answered the door she kept the constable on the doorstep and said little, except to confirm she hadn't seen Caleb since the previous day.

"Weren't you worried when he didn't come home?" Mellor asked.

"Why should I? 'E can look after 'imself," Mrs Salt replied. The constable could see the widow had no intention of helping him further.

After cycling back into the village, Mellor tried a different approach. Conversation fell silent as he entered the New Inn and went to the bar. "Good evening Mrs Sheldon, perhaps you can help me? I'm looking for Caleb Salt. Has he been in recently?"

"Here on Saturday night, but I ain't seen 'im since," the landlady replied.

"He's not at his mother's. Any idea where he might be?"

Mrs Sheldon shrugged. "Expect 'e's at work. If not, I've no idea."

Mellor was aware that everyone in the inn was watching him. He raised his voice to address the small gathering. "We'd very much like to talk to Mr Salt about an important matter. If anyone knows where he might be, I would like to hear from them." Silence, other than the scrape of a chair. "If anyone should see him or hear where he is, they should contact either me at Longnor or Leek police as soon as possible. A telegram will be quickest." Mellor looked around the room at blank expressions and decided to leave. Next he called at the village post office where he interrupted the postmaster's evening meal to send his own telegram to colleagues at Leek. Not that he had much to report.

Once the constable had left the inn, Mrs Sheldon busied herself behind the bar to avoid getting drawn into conversation about Caleb Salt, while several drinkers exchanged knowing looks.

"Salt's in trouble, by the looks of it," said one. "I'd think twice about letting on where 'e was, even if I knowed," commented another. "Well, one or two of us know where he'll be this Friday – not that we're likely to tell the bobby about it," his companion replied with a smile.

Barely had the regulars resumed their pints when someone else arrived in search of Salt – Bernard Gamage. However the Heathcote estate steward learned no more than the policeman had.

Enoch Heathcote was at the wheel of the Napier when he set off for the Great Mill the next morning. After his excursion to the Roaches with Ellen Simms the previous week he had decided to try something similar that afternoon. His groom-cum-chauffeur Simpkins had topped up the tank and packed spare cans of motor spirit. Enoch simply had to think of an excuse to have a young woman called to his office and then they could enjoy a pleasant couple of hours together in the country. Not Ellen Simms though. After their little outing last week it was perhaps time he moved on to someone else.

At Leek Police Station, Tuesday had brought Inspector Ramm no nearer to finding Salt, but closer to having to release John Gibb. Suspicions alone were not enough to keep the tramp in custody. However it was important Gibb did not wander off until the cases were solved. Ramm was about to have the tramp brought up from the cells when Sgt Reynolds came in, bearing the ledger of names prompted by the newspaper appeal.

"Another half dozen, Sir. It strikes me some folk are settling a few grudges," said the Sergeant.

"And wasting police time," said Ramm wearily.

"But at least we've had something new. A fellow came in to say he was near the Old Church on the night Dr Sneyd was there. Apparently he was tending to a cart outside The George and saw comings and goings at the church."

Ramm sat up, alert. "You've got his details? Right, have the man brought in so that we can take a proper statement. We need as much information we can lay our hands on."

"What about Gibb, Sir?"

"Let's leave him downstairs until we hear what this new person has to say. In the meantime, I'm going out for half an hour."

Energised by the prospect of a new witness – and by his superior's veiled threat to send in a "proper" detective to take the cases off his hands – Ramm decided to check out what Reverend Maitland had said about the meeting at the vicarage on the fateful evening.

Ernest Corbishley, captain of the St Edward's bell-ringers, welcomed the Inspector with a friendly handshake when the officer walked into the family's grocery shop in the Market Place. Corbishley, dressed in his habitual white apron, was surrounded by provisions of every sort. The wall behind him had wooden shelving from floor to ceiling, containing tins of Californian apricots, jars of Bovril, packets of Lyons tea, Pears soap, Johnson & Co black lead, Reckitt's Blue Bag starch, all arranged in meticulous pyramids. On the floor in front of the polished counter were open sacks bulging with potatoes, dried beans and oats, an aluminium serving scoop resting on the top of each one.

Seeing there were no customers in the shop, Ramm wasted no time. "Could I have a private word Ernest?" The two men knew each other not only through the church but also watched the occasional match at Leek Cricket Club's pitch at Beggars Lane.

"Certainly Albert, come into the back room, if you will," the grocer replied, telling his assistant, a girl of about 14 wearing white apron and mop cap, to look after the shop.

"It's about this sad affair of the fellow who fell from the church tower. I'm just going over a few things to make sure we have a correct record of what was going on that evening," Ramm began conversationally, wanting Corbishley to be as candid as possible.

"It was shocking, absolutely shocking. How can I help?"

"The Vicar tells me there was a meeting at the vicarage that night to discuss the bells. I presume you were there?"

"Yes, most of the bell-ringers were, along with Reverend Maitland and the verger."

"Did you notice anything going on at the church? Did anyone go outside at any point?"

"I didn't see anything at the church and once we were settled into the vicarage parlour no one went outside. In fact the Vicar told us it wouldn't be necessary."

"What do you mean by that, Ernest?"

"Well, I for one felt we should have a final inspection in the belfry before they bell frames were dismantled the following day. Just so that we were all in agreement on the work that was needed. It seemed a good idea to me."

"But the Vicar said not?"

"That's correct. He was quite adamant. 'We've been over all this before, so there's no the point of looking at them again. We should sit and plan for when the bells are returned,' he said. I thought he was a little abrupt, I don't mind telling you, but Reverend Maitland always knows best, doesn't he?"

It was obvious to Ramm that his own feelings about the Vicar's air of superiority were shared by Corbishley.

"So Reverend Maitland didn't go out at all?"

"Only to go and make us all a cup of tea. It was his housekeeper's evening off and I must say it took him some time to sort it out. I don't think he's used to being in a kitchen."

"What time did you have the tea?"

"It was around eight o'clock. I remember the church clock striking eight and thinking that folk wouldn't be hearing the bells for quite a while once they had been taken down the next day," said the shopkeeper.

"And after the meeting. You didn't see anything suspicious?"

"As far as I know, everyone went straight home from the vicarage – there was no reason to go near the church. It was dark by then. I saw nothing unusual, but then, I wasn't looking for anything."

Inspector Ramm thanked Ernest Corbishley for his help and left the shop, pausing at the counter to hand over a shilling for a packet of his wife's favourite Peek Frean lunch biscuits. Walking back to the station he mulled over what the shopkeeper had just told him. "Does the Vicar know more about that night than he's admitting," he wondered, "or am I grasping at straws?"

Half an hour later the new witness was escorted into Ramm's office. Joseph Tanner, a thin man in his forties, drove a cart delivering coal from Leek Wharf and, on the evening of Dr Sneyd's death, had been unhitching his horse before stabling the animal behind The George.

"It was getting on for eight o'clock, so I wanted to crack on and get back home. Another cart pulled up along Church Street, a fella got down from it, but it was nobody I knew. He went up the steps an' into th' Old Church," Tanner explained.

"Go on," urged Inspector Ramm, glancing to make sure Knowles was scribbling his notes.

"I took notice, you see, because I thought it were a bit funny going to church at that time o' night. A big fella with dust all over 'im, like 'e'd come from a stone hole or something. He was wearing some sort of straw hat. It looked like there was a 'ammer poking out of his pocket, so I wondered if 'e was doing some work in the church."

"Did you see anything else?"

"Well I was just going to lead Jonty – that's the 'orse – into the yard and I was right by the door of The George when this tall man comes bounding out and goes straight across the street and into the church."

"Do you recall anything about him?"

"Striped jacket, that's why I noticed him, apart from the fact 'e nearly walked into me and never said so much as 'Excuse me'. Seemed to be in a real hurry. When my lady told me what was in this week's paper I wondered whether that might be 'im that fell. So I thought I'd better tell somebody… just in case there's a reward or something." Tanner looked hopefully at the Inspector.

"No reward, I'm afraid, other than my sincere thanks Mr Tanner," said Ramm. "What about after you stabled the horse, did you see or hear anything else at the church?" Tanner shook his head, disappointed he was to get no money. Then the Inspector reached into his desk for a copy of the photograph taken at Amos Carter's farm. "We're also looking for this man. Do you recognise him? Do you think he was the one you saw at the church?"

Tanner peered at the photograph. "This is taken from the back and I saw 'is back as 'e walked up the steps to church. I can't be certain, but it might be 'im," he said.

After Tanner left, Ramm sat back and considered the evidence he had gathered. Like pieces of a jigsaw, elements were coming together to make a compelling picture of Dr Sneyd's death. A letter lured him to the church where his attacker waited inside. The man was hit from behind with a hammer, then hauled up the tower. Though tall, Sneyd was lightly built and Ramm believed a fit man could have lifted him to the roof and thrown him over the parapet. Meanwhile the gathering at the vicarage was told not to venture out to the church.

It was a convincing train of events, thought Ramm, but what

was the motive? What did Sneyd either know or do that would make someone murder him? Did the Vicar know something about it? Whoever was responsible, it had been planned with care. And if Salt was the attacker, it could be another link between the deaths of Sneyd and Carter.

Though they had still to find Caleb Salt, Tanner's story seemed to confirm what John Gibb said he had seen. Ramm called for him to be brought up from the cells and was taken aback when he was led into the office. He no longer looked, or smelled, like the tramp of the previous day. His face and hands were free of their ground-in dirt, his hair was shorter, so was his beard, and even his clothes looked cleaner.

Seeing the Inspector's surprise, Sgt Reynolds explained. "When some of the lads heard about Sergeant Major Gibbs' service record, being ex-army themselves, they decided to make a bit of an effort. We paid for two sessions in the slipper baths, then took him to the barber's for a bit of a trim, and one of the lads brought him a fresh shirt."

"I thank ye all very much," said Gibb, nodding at the Sergeant appreciatively.

"Mr Gibb we have another witness who seems to bear out your own observations at the Old Church. However, we have made no arrest regarding either Dr Sneyd or Mr Carter's death," said Ramm, realising that the cleaned-up Gibb now looked less of a suspect.

"No sign of Salt then?"

"Not as yet," Ramm admitted, "and because we are still investigating, I want to be able to speak to you when I need to. I am prepared to release you only on two conditions. Firstly, you must report to this station once a day. If you don't, there will be a warrant for your arrest and you will be back in the cells. Secondly, I intend to hold onto your knife – your dirk, as you call it – until these matters are cleared up. Do you agree?"

Gibb was not happy to be deprived of his dirk, but had been

heartened by the officers' generosity – they reminded him of some of his old army pals – and so accepted Ramm's terms. Shouldering his pack, he walked into the street, glad to be in the fresh air again.

Ramm barely had time to collect his thoughts before Sgt Reynolds was back in the office to inform him that Nathaniel Blake was in reception. After hours of consideration, Blake had decided it was his duty to tell the Inspector about Heathcote's handwriting – even if the officer didn't believe him. As soon as Blake sat down, it was obvious Ramm wanted to keep the exchange as brief as possible.

"Mr Blake, I know you are fascinated by our enquiries, so let me tell you we found John Gibb and he has told us what he saw at Abbey Green and the Old Church. We also have another witness in the Sneyd case. We are still looking for Caleb Salt, but rest assured we will track him down."

Blake took a deep breath and explained his latest theory about Enoch Heathcote, then leaned forward to place the Longview note and the photograph of the forged letter on the Inspector's desk. Ramm took out his magnifying glass to study the handwriting. He fixed the photographer with a serious expression. This may be a new lead, but he knew it could also land him in a heap of trouble.

"So you are still doing your *detective* work, Mr Blake? I agree that discovering the author of this letter could help us find out what happened to Dr Sneyd. But," he paused, "you are making a very serious allegation."

"Yes Inspector, but you must see..." Blake was cut short by Ramm's raised hand.

"Yes I can see there are similarities, however I am no expert and neither are you. It was embarrassing enough when I tackled the Vicar about this letter, so I will proceed only when I am absolutely certain of the facts."

Blake was sure Enoch Heathcote's powerful position was the reason for the Inspector's reluctance. "So you will speak to him about it?" he asked, trying to put Ramm on the spot.

"When and if I am sure of the evidence. But we have two murder enquiries going on and I will do nothing to jeopardise them," Ramm replied.

"Surely this could help?" Blake persisted.

"Only if we tread carefully."

Ramm brought the conversation to an end, asking Blake, with some irony, to keep him informed if he made any more discoveries. After the photographer had left, he looked again at the two letters. Although he hadn't admitted as much to Blake, they did appear to be by the same hand. But how was he to proceed? If he accused the magistrate of being involved in the mysterious death, and he was proved wrong, it could destroy his police career. But if he did not act, was there a risk that a murderer could escape justice?

Chapter Fourteen

It was Wednesday morning and at the photographic studio Nathaniel Blake looked out on a street busy with market day shoppers, but his mind was elsewhere. His meeting with Inspector Ramm had left him uncertain if he would be able to help the police bring justice for Dr Sneyd or Amos Carter. This morning, Enoch Heathcote, who he suspected could be involved in both deaths, would be at the Magistrates Court. Passing judgment on folk who had a lot less to answer for, Blake thought.

The shop door bell sounded. Blake paid no attention because he had asked Cora to remain downstairs to deal with customers. The Leek Show postcards were selling particularly well. A few seconds later, his daughter came to the foot of the staircase and shouted, rather nervously, that there was someone to see him. Blake went down at his usual brisk pace and saw a familiar figure standing by the front door. Except that John Gibb looked subtly different, certainly less dishevelled than he had remembered.

"Mr Gibb, I'm glad you're out and about. You were able to help the police, I take it?"

"I gave the Inspector something to think about, although at first he seemed to suspect I was mixed up in it all. He wants me to stay around Leek for a wee while, but my conscience is clear." Gibb glanced at Cora and lowered his voice conspiratorially. "Some of the lads have been talking in the Market Place, Mr Blake, and I've heard a whisper that there's boxing at Flash on Friday. I wouldn't be surprised if Caleb Salt was there."

"Shouldn't you tell Inspector Ramm?"

"I don't think there would be much point. They're far too crafty up at Flash to let the bobbies anywhere near those fights. They'd recognise them a mile off, probably finish up in chaos and Salt would be gone. But you," Gibb prodded towards Blake, "on your own, you might sneak a wee bit closer."

Blake was excited and slightly frightened by the idea. He had been intrigued when Gibb first told him about the bare knuckle contests at Flash. Now this might be the chance for him to take a closer look at the man who could be responsible for Amos Carter's death, and perhaps even take a photograph of Salt.

"How should I go about it?" Blake asked cautiously.

"Get y'self into the village towards the end of the afternoon. There'll be plenty of men about and the pub will be heaving. Keep a sharp eye out and see where they're all making for – they choose a different barn each time there's a boxing meeting. Then it's up to you. But don't let on you're snooping, or it could turn nasty."

Gibb's warning reminded Blake that he would be venturing into a world he knew nothing about. He would have to take care, but this might be his chance to find out where Salt was hiding and help the police to track him down.

There was little to report at Leek Police Station that morning. Buxton Police, as well as constables based in villages across the moorlands, had been warned to watch out for Caleb Salt. If they didn't find him soon, Ramm intended to make a public appeal. Distributing a mugshot might have made all the difference, he thought. The Inspector had also given two of his team the task – a thankless one, perhaps – of following up the leads from the *Leek Lion* photograph. The job could take days because the men had to fit in these extra enquiries with their compulsory patrols around the streets of Leek.

Ramm knew that there was a growing tide of gossip in the town about not only the mysterious deaths but the lack of arrests. He was determined to make progress of some sort and was in no mood to shilly-shally when Jacob Watkins from The George was brought in once more. "So Mr Watkins, have you had any further recollections from the night your guest Dr Sneyd died or the following morning?"

Looking around the room as if searching for inspiration, Watkins began to stumble over a few non-committal words but was immediately interrupted. "Let me make this clear. I know that you allowed Messrs Finch and Blake into Dr Sneyd's room," said Ramm.

Watkins' eyes widened. "Oh yes, I think the gentlemen were on some sort of errand. But it had nothing to do with this horrible death, surely?" he replied.

"After that, I gather Bernard Gamage called at The George. What did he want?"

Watkins looked uncomfortable. "Mr Gamage, yes, I do believe he came in. What with sorting out in the cellar and such, I clean forgot about that. He's Mr Heathcote's man, so we see him quite regular like."

"That morning, what did he want? And before you answer, let me point out there's a Licensing Committee next month. Such a pity if there was an objection to your licence at The George," Ramm said, fixing the hotel keeper with an uncompromising look.

Watkins realised that if he co-operated with Ramm he might risk being thrown out of The George on some excuse by Gamage. But if he didn't help the Inspector, he could lose his licence and be barred from hotel-keeping anywhere else.

Watkins swung his head swung from side to side as if trying to raise some memory. Then his shoulders sank. "All right, Mr Gamage asked to see the bunch of spare room keys, said he wanted to check we didn't need any more cutting, or something like that. I gave him the keys and he told me to carry on in the cellar. What was I supposed to do, Inspector? He's Mr Heathcote's man, and

Mr Heathcote owns the place."

"And?"

"I didn't see him again. When I come back up from the cellar he'd hung up the keys and gone. If he took something, I never saw it. I never saw nothing." Watkins was trying to salvage some of his earlier innocence.

Ramm dismissed the hotel keeper and sent a constable to Longview to bring in Bernard Gamage.

When the steward arrived he added little to Ramm's knowledge. Though clearly surprised that the officer knew he had been to The George, he gave a hard-eyed response to every question. He denied being anywhere near the church on the fateful night or having ever met Dr Sneyd. However he did agree that he had asked for the room keys. It was a matter of maintaining the security of Heathcote properties, he said.

The battle of wits drained Ramm's patience and he went on the offensive. "I suggest that you used the key to enter Dr Sneyd's room – one of this bunch of keys which you say is so important – and then removed the dead man's papers. You sent Mr Watkins to the cellar so he wouldn't know what you were up to or what you were taking away."

Gamage had faced down dozens of tenants in his time and had no intention of giving way to the Inspector. He replied impassively: "This is pure speculation without the slightest shred of evidence. Now if you've finished with me, Inspector, I have work to do for Mr Heathcote."

"I may have finished for today, Mr Gamage, but I will doubtless need to speak to you again." With that the interview was over. Ramm could see Gamage was a shrewd negotiator. He had stonewalled the questions, choosing his words carefully, but neither had he flatly denied going to Dr Sneyd's room.

Bernard Gamage had mixed feelings as he climbed into his pony trap to return to his office at Longview. Although he was confident

Inspector Ramm could prove nothing against him, he was not happy being called in for questioning. He wasn't prepared to lie to the police – unless his influential employer could protect him from the consequences.

Cora Blake stood across the street from the Great Mill as the whistle sounded at half past five, marking the end of the working day. She had told her father that she was seeing a friend. Crowds of mill workers streamed through the main door. Young lads jostling each other, men pulling on their caps, women hurrying home to start the evening meal. Cora looked anxiously amongst the crowd, fearing she would miss Ellen Simms, but as the flow of people started to subside she spotted the young woman and waved. Ellen approached her with an uncertain expression. "I'm not sure whether I should be doing this," she said.

"Don't worry, no one will know that you've been talking to us. Anyway, we're trying to improve things, aren't we?" reassured Cora, taking Ellen's arm. Amongst the crowd leaving the Great Mill was Martha Robinson, one of Margaret Gamage's informants. Neither Ellen nor Cora noticed Martha follow them as they walked towards the middle of town, past the cattle market where men were sweeping out livestock pens after the day's market. When they reached the *Leek Lion* office, Cora was unsure what to do. She had heard nothing from Oliver since leaving the note for him and was nervous of going up to the newsroom in case his father was there and asked what was going on. She and Ellen waited outside for what seemed like ages and Cora could see that Ellen was thinking of leaving when, to her relief, Oliver appeared at the green door.

"Hello you two. I'm afraid we won't be able to talk inside because my father's in there," he said, looking up and down the street wondering where they might go. Then his eyes fixed on the Methodist Church across the street where the door stood open.

"I know, we'll go in the church for some peace and quiet. I think there's a service tonight, but there won't be anyone around for ages yet." Oliver checked there was no one inside and then the other two followed him in and sat down. Standing at the end of the street, Martha Robinson decided she had seen enough.

Prompted by Oliver, Ellen began to tell of her working life at the Great Mill, which she started as a twelve-year-old half-timer. Her pride in handing over precious shillings to her mother. Her friendship with girls in the same work room. Her uncles and cousins who also worked at the mill. And her determination to better herself.

"That's why I agreed to play along with old Heathcote. I thought it would be worth it. He made a fuss of me and said he'd move me to a better job," Ellen continued, "but now I'm starting to think it was all talk. He just uses people." Oliver and Cora fell quiet as they let Ellen to tell the story at her own pace.

"Long before he chose me, I'd noticed girls being called out of the workroom, especially on a Tuesday afternoon. It happens in other departments, so folk say. Some girls laugh about it, they think he's a funny character."

Ellen grew serious as her thoughts went back to her last trip to the Lodge with the mill owner. "After last week – he went too far, he did things to me he shouldn't have done. I won't be going with him again and he knows it. Another girl was called to the office yesterday. From now on I'm going to get my head down and do my work like everyone else." Cora could see Ellen was on the verge of tears and reached for her hand.

"How does he get away with it?" asked Oliver.

"Because he can," Ellen replied. "He's high and mighty and we need the work."

Hearing her worst suspicions confirmed, Cora was angry for those Heathcote took advantage of. "Where's this place that he takes people to?" she asked.

Ellen had been up to the shooting lodge on the Roaches often enough to be able to describe the way to it. "It's a stone place built almost into the rocks. I found it really scary when I first saw it a couple of years ago, it's like a little castle, but old Heathcote has nice things inside." There was a fearful look in her eyes as she thought about the secret trips there. Then she snapped back to reality. "I won't be going again," she said.

At that moment the church minister walked in and they realised their private meeting was over. "Oh, do we have some new recruits?" asked the clergyman with a hopeful smile.

"We were just going actually, Sir," said Oliver as the three stood up and made for the door. Once outside, Ellen turned to Oliver. "You're not going to mention me in the paper, are you? I've been talking tonight because I'm upset, but I can't afford any trouble at work – and neither can the rest of us."

"I'm going to have to think about the whole thing and I certainly wouldn't want to make it worse for any of you," Oliver replied. Cora and Ellen headed off in different directions and he went up to the newsroom. Sitting at his desk he had a sinking feeling that Ellen's story, shocking as it was, might be too big for him to handle. How could he write something against one of the most powerful men in town? And would his father dare to print it?

As Cora walked home she didn't share Oliver's misgivings. If anything, Ellen's story had stoked her anger at the unfairness of it all. She was more determined than ever to try to change things – on her own, if necessary. She had nearly reached Moorside Terrace before it dawned on her what she could do.

"What the hell's Ramm up to?"

An exasperated Enoch Heathcote threw down his napkin at breakfast the next morning. The previous evening Bernard Gamage had told him about his visit to the police station but had assured his employer there was nothing to be concerned about. Heathcote was still fuming, however. The Inspector was wasting time interviewing one of his trusted employees when there was a murder to be solved.

"I just can't understand what he's playing at. If he wanted to speak to Gamage he should have approached me first. Obviously Gamage had nothing to do with Dr Sneyd."

Elizabeth Heathcote was more shaken than angry when she heard Gamage had been summoned by the Inspector. Gamage and his wife both owed them their loyalty, but ultimately Elizabeth trusted no one. And the estate steward was just one step away from the Heathcotes themselves.

"I'm going to speak to Ramm about this today. In fact I might even telephone police headquarters again," Enoch blustered on.

"Perhaps it would be best not to antagonise the officer," his wife suggested quietly.

Enoch looked at her across the table. This was surprising. Usually it was Elizabeth sounding forth and telling him to 'sort things out'. "Do you honestly think so?" he asked.

"I know it was bad form by Ramm, but if Gamage says the interview was routine then perhaps we shouldn't become involved. Let Ramm waste his time if he wants to." It was best not to make a fuss at the moment, she thought, rather than attract unwanted attention from the Inspector.

"Well, I'll think about it," Enoch replied grudgingly, "but I'm not going to forget this."

Before he left for the mill, Enoch reminded his wife that he would be going out on the Friday afternoon and would not be home until late. He had been invited on a "gentleman's jaunt" by one of the land-owning families from up at Warslow. A spot of shooting on the moor, drinks and then supper. "It's Algy's birthday, so I think there will be some high jinks. Goodness knows what, but it should be capital fun," he went on.

After Enoch left, Margaret Gamage came into the breakfast room to report her informants' latest observations. "On Tuesday Mr Enoch went on one of his usual excursions ...with a young friend," she said.

"That Simms girl again?" asked Elizabeth.

"No, Madam. A new one this week. But I have some other news about Simms."

"Why, what's she been up to?"

"After work last night she met Cora Blake, the photographer's daughter, and the two of them went to see young Finch from the *Lion*. They hid themselves in Brunswick Church, so I don't know what was said."

"That's at least three times they have been seen together. Why is a reporter so interested in girls from our mill, and that girl in particular?"

Mrs Gamage was silent. They were both thinking of the repercussions of a reporter delving into life at the Great Mill.

"And you say Mr Heathcote didn't see her this week?

"Apparently not, Madam."

"This situation may be more serious than we thought. Something must be done about it."

Mrs Gamage stood patiently while her employer sat deep in thought before she gave her instructions. "Find Simpkins and tell him I need to go into town. And I also want one of your mill women to do me a little service. I will give you the details later."

Within the hour the groom was helping Mrs Heathcote out of the carriage in front of an imposing Georgian building in Derby Street. She marched straight in and told the office clerk she wanted to see her lawyer, immediately.

At the police station, Inspector Ramm was finding it difficult to concentrate that morning. At the back of his mind he expected to hear the station telephone ring at any moment. It would be Enoch Heathcote calling to complain about why he had questioned

Bernard Gamage. Or worse, his superintendent in Stafford, smarting from another Heathcote complaint direct to Headquarters. But to Ramm's relief the call never came. No indignant blustering from the magistrate, which surprised him. Thanks in part to the imaginative Mr Blake, Ramm found himself pondering Enoch Heathcote's motives, innocent or otherwise. Did this mean Heathcote was leaving the police to their inquiries at last, or had he decided to lie low? If they could find Caleb Salt, the Inspector thought bitterly, he might have something definite to work on.

After lunch, FJ Finch was finishing a story on extensions to the North Staffordshire Railway while Oliver was typing prices from the previous day's livestock market when a young messenger burst into the newsroom breathlessly. "Mr Finch? It's urgent," he said as he handed the editor a letter and sped out again.

Finch opened the envelope excitedly, hoping it was hot news, but his face clouded as he read the sheet inside, which bore the name of the town's leading solicitors' practice. Scratching his thinning hair, Finch read it a second time and then stared across at his son who was pounding his green Imperial.

"Oliver? What in heaven's name have you been up to?"

The youth's fingers stopped in mid-key and his head shot round. From his tone he knew his father wasn't being his usual jokey self.

"This," said Finch, waving the letter, "is a request, no actually it's an order, stating that you should desist the harassment of employees of Heathcote & Co; that you should not undertake any enquiry into the company or its owners; that any material gained from employees should first be referred to the company's representatives; and that any subsequent reportage would be subject to legal scrutiny with the likelihood of court action and a claim for damages."

Oliver's mouth dropped open and his cheeks reddened. "Er..."

was all he could say as he thought desperately of a convincing excuse to pacify his father.

"*Please* tell me that you haven't gone behind my back, pursuing an exclusive all on your own, your sights set on Leek's biggest employer owned by a family that could wipe out the *Lion* in the blink of an eye. And probably send us to jail!" Finch fumed.

"Hang on, father! You know I wouldn't do anything to damage the *Lion*," his son replied, trying to muster the confidence to sound indignant.

"Well, what have you been doing then, to bring the wrath of the Heathcotes on our heads?"

"Nothing...yet. Just talking, to a young woman, well two, actually. Cora Blake and another girl called Ellen."

Oliver proceeded to explain his chance meeting with Cora at the union rally, the conversations that followed and the growing suspicions about Enoch Heathcote and his dealings with some of his young workers. "But, to be honest, I'd started to realise that we may not be able to do anything about it."

Finch was secretly impressed that Oliver was showing his initiative in chasing a story, but appalled that he had chosen a subject he couldn't hope to write about. After the initial shock of the solicitor's letter, he was becoming a little more conciliatory towards his son. In fact, he thought, as a young reporter he would have probably tried something like this himself. Neither did he like being told what to do by either a mill owner or a lawyer.

"Look Oliver, even if Enoch Heathcote was taking advantage of the young ladies, there's no way we could print a story without cast iron proof, and plenty of it. And if we did print, Heathcote would be bound to sue for defamation, just to save face. Your informants wouldn't testify, we would lose, Heathcote would walk away with our money and we would probably have to close the *Lion*."

"What puzzles me," Finch went on, "is how they knew what

you were doing. These people must have spies all over the place. Next time you have a brainwave, Oliver, speak to me first."

His son blinked at his typewriter and said nothing. He hadn't admitted that he had only got involved in the story as an excuse to see Cora Blake again. Now he was imagining her reaction when he told her there would be no more investigation, no story in the newspaper. It was going to be a difficult conversation.

His father read through the lawyer's letter again. The more he thought about it, the less he liked it. Exactly who did they think they were, trying to gag the free Press? He was already disappointed at having so little new material on Leek's biggest story, the mysterious deaths. Everyone was talking about it and they would expect something in this week's *Lion*. He was irked that rival newspapers were starting to send wily reporters to the town to rake up juicy and usually fanciful details about Amos Carter and Crosbie Sneyd. And now he was being bullied by Heathcote & Co.

It was time to do something about it. Finch picked up a pencil and jotted down the outline for an editorial in this week's edition. Usually the editor's leading article tended to poke fun at the local council and the town MP. This one would be different. He already had the headline: *The Evil in Our Town.*

Chapter Fifteen

Nathaniel Blake had not been completely honest when he told his wife he was going out to take landscape photographs with his new portable camera. It was Friday and he had gone home for lunch with Edith, leaving Cora to look after the studio for the rest of the day.

"You haven't mentioned Inspector Ramm for a couple of days. Has all that quietened down?" Edith asked as they sat in the kitchen.

Blake pretended to concentrate on chewing his sandwich before responding. He had become uneasy about discussing the Carter and Sneyd cases at home. Partly because he did not want to worry Edith, but also he was embarrassed at how important his detective work had become to him. Whether his theories were taken seriously or not, he felt compelled to carry on digging for evidence until the killers were run to ground.

"The Inspector has told me to leave it to them. I haven't heard anything for a day or two," he replied.

"Perhaps you will return to your Sherlock Holmes stories then? Reading a detective novel is a lot safer than trying to do it yourself, you know," said Edith, relieved enough to poke fun at her husband. Not wishing to deceive his wife any further, he changed the subject.

After lunch Nathaniel wheeled his Sunbeam bicycle from the outhouse with a mixture of dread and excitement. He knew the climb to the highest village in England would be challenging and, no matter which route he took, he would have to push up some painfully steep hills. The journey was going to take the best part of two hours, especially if he paused to capture some countryside views – and catch his breath. And once he got to Flash, he was far from sure what would he would find.

He secured his leather camera case to the handlebars, packed the folding camera and two rolls of the new-style celluloid film. Lighter than his usual glass plates, the film was also much less likely to be damaged on the ride along rough roads.

Once out of the town, his spirits lifted as he began to enjoy this rural excursion on a pleasant late summer afternoon. The views towards the high hills, the gritstone bluffs of the Roaches facing west and the jagged Ramshaw Rocks to the east, were inspiring. Stopping frequently to take pictures and admire the moorlands, Blake began to forget the real purpose of his journey. He was in even better spirits after a glass of bitter at the inn in Upperhulme, halfway up the steepest climb. When he reached the top of the hill, the road levelled out somewhat as it crossed the open moor and Blake could see for many miles towards Cheshire where rain clouds were forming on the horizon. A landscape of tough grass and heather was dotted with poor farmsteads, some with small newly-built hay ricks in their fields, others with not enough grass to make hay.

As he entered Flash from the Buxton road, Blake passed white-smocked girls at play outside the village school, unaware that the handbell which sounded the end of their lessons would soon be heard in a boxing ring. The village itself consisted of a couple narrow lanes lined with small cottages, some lime-washed, and at its far side rose the three-storey bulk of the Methodist Chapel. The last time Nathaniel was in Flash it had been virtually deserted apart from the occasional chicken pecking at the roadside. Today, numerous carts were drawn up in the lanes and groups of men were strolling around, talking animatedly. Some crammed into the doorway of the New Inn which, judging by the noise from within, was already packed.

He had been worried about being spotted as a stranger, but soon realised that most of those in the village today were visitors like himself. Seeking somewhere unobtrusive to sort out his equipment, he wheeled his bicycle through the gate of St Paul's Parish Church. The building had been transformed the previous year with an extension paid for by a local land-owning family. With his bicycle propped against the churchyard wall, he was crouching down to load a new film into the camera when three open carriages came along the lane. Each driven by a liveried groom, they carried a party of well-dressed gentlemen, laughing and talking loudly. As Blake watched, the carriages came to a halt and the grooms extracted wine from wicker hampers. Bottles were handed to the passengers, each of whom took a hearty draught before passing it on.

The well-to-do are joining the ruffians for the evening's entertainment, he thought. Then he froze – sitting in one of the carriages was Enoch Heathcote. His cheeks bright red and grinning at something one of his companions was saying, the mill owner was obviously enjoying himself.

Blake still did not know where the boxing was going to take place but, as Gibb had suggested, he would wait to see which direction the crowds headed and tag along behind. After some minutes he saw that the inn was emptying and knots of men were coalescing into a ragged procession that made its way towards the other end of the village. The gentlemen got down from the three carriages and started to walk away, too. Blake couldn't resist following Heathcote, especially as he seemed to be too occupied with his friends to notice anyone else. Blake pulled down his cap to try to hide much of his face and hung back at a safe distance, concealing his camera inside his tweed coat.

Fuelled by alcohol and excitement about the sport to come, the atmosphere was becoming more raucous. Blake realised that the police, hampered by the county boundaries, must turn a blind eye to such events. Certainly the group of gentry seemed to have no fear of a police raid and Blake followed them through a roadside gate and across a field, seeing the occasional flash of silver when a hip flask was produced.

The path descended a slope towards a hollow containing a huge wooden barn, previously hidden from view. Men were milling about around the building, some joining a queue to go inside, as did the group that Blake was following. All except Enoch Heathcote, who detached himself from his companions and walked purposefully towards the far side of the barn. Blake managed to make his way through the crowd in time to see Heathcote hammer on small door cut into the barn wall. A cloth-capped man poked his head out, exchanged a few words with Heathcote and disappeared back inside while the mill owner waited, looking around frequently and taking another swig from his flask. Blake, worried that Heathcote might see him, considered retreating but then saw a sheep fold some yards away. He left the crowd – as had others who were relieving themselves against stone walls – and walked quickly to the sheep fold. He darted inside and crouched behind its low wall, stealing a glance back to the barn to check that Heathcote was still there.

As he watched, the door opened again and a new figure appeared, stripped to the waist. It was Caleb Salt. As Heathcote began to speak, Blake took his camera out and rested it on the top the wall. His hands were shaking and there was little time to focus, but he knew he must take a photograph of the two men together.

Hunched behind the camera, while trying to hide at the same time, Blake took a series of pictures, hoping at least one would turn out. He looked up to see Heathcote reach into his pocket and produce a wad of banknotes which he handed to Salt. Blake wound on his film frantically and pressed the shutter as the boxer riffled through the cash, folded it and stuffed it into the top of his tight-fitting black breeches. Salt nodded to Heathcote who slapped him on the shoulder before walking off. The boxer went back inside. Blake could only guess at what he had just seen. Why was Heathcote handing Salt the money? He was sure it was proof that Enoch Heathcote and the wanted man were involved in something shady. This was more evidence against the mill owner, he thought.

The photographer realised the crowds outside the barn were dwindling while sounds from within the wooden building were growing louder. There was talking, laughing, shouting and Blake guessed the boxing would start soon. He walked around to the main door where a tough-looking man, his face bearing the scars of his own boxing days, barred the way and held out his hand for a shilling entrance money. Blake handed him a coin and edged into the barn which was packed with men standing shoulder to shoulder. As one of the last ones in, he was at the back of the crowd and glanced around to see that betting was under way, cash and slips of paper being exchanged in dark corners. In the centre of the building, on a platform standing about four feet high, was the makeshift boxing ring, a rope around its edge supported by posts. Immediately above, corrugated iron sheets had been removed from the roof so that natural light cascaded down into the shadowy interior, illuminating the ring.

Blake was almost physically knocked back by the atmosphere inside the barn – hot, sweaty, dusty, filled with tobacco smoke and, above all, noisy. The hubbub of dozens of shouted exchanges turned into a cacophony of cheers as a group of men, sleeves rolled up and towels around their necks emerged from the far end of the barn which had been curtained off with sheets. They forged a path through the crowd towards the ring, followed by the first two boxers. As they climbed into ring and into full view of the crowd, Blake saw that one of the fighters was Caleb Salt. The local hero was greeted with a roar of encouragement that reached a crescendo as he turned and raised a hand to acknowledge his supporters.

As the fighters paced back and forth impatiently the referee managed to make himself heard above the noise enough to announce that the contestants were Caleb Salt of Flash and Jacob Whitethorn of Bakewell. Blake was aware that bare-knuckle boxing was brutal, but had never seen a fight for himself. The next twenty minutes was to be a demonstration of one man's relentless determination to pound another into submission, unconsciousness, perhaps near-death.

As soon as the bell rang, Salt strode across the ring and landed a blow to his opponent's face before the other man had time to gather himself. From the start it was destined to be an unequal contest. Whitethorn was shorter than Salt and, even to Blake's inexperienced eye, his muscles were far less well-defined. Neither did he have the sheer menace that saw Salt deliver blow after blow to his opponent's head and body. After each volley Whitethorn staggered back then bravely came at Salt but managed to land few significant punches.

When a cut opened up above Whitethorn's eye the bout descended into a gory spectacle, blood covering not only the man's face but smeared across his torso and spattered onto Salt's hands, arms and chest. As the man's energy ebbed away and his vision clouded, he grew less able to respond to the battering from Salt. At one point he slipped on a patch of blood on the floorboards and fell to one knee before getting up again. The crowd was baying louder than ever. Blake thought "Someone should stop this. The man needs to be saved," but bare-knuckle bouts like this continued until one man was knocked down and didn't get up.

Blake had edged towards the back of the barn where he clambered onto a bale of hay to improve his view. Everyone around him was transfixed by the fight and so he risked pulling his camera from beneath his coat. At that moment Whitethorn fell face down on the wooden floor and lay there apparently unconscious. The barn erupted in cheers for the winner and Blake took a surreptitious image as Salt looked out across the crowd, arm raised in victory. Blake could not stop himself taking the picture even though, in that light, there was little chance it would come out. Unfortunately, a burly fellow standing near to Blake thought something more sinister was going on.

"What's that bloke up to? And what's that he's holding?" the man shouted, pointing towards Blake.

It attracted the attention of others nearby who turned to stare at the photographer still clutching his camera.

"Is that a camera? Who's 'e taking pictures of?" said another man aggressively, loud enough to be heard clearly now that the fight had finished. More of the crowd looked in Blake's direction and a shout went up "He's from the coppers!"

Just as Gibb had predicted, things were turning nasty. These men thought that only a troublemaker or a police officer would be taking photographs at an illegal event like this. He fumbled to hide his camera again, jumped from the hay bale and made a desperate lurch towards the exit. Someone grabbed hold of him, Blake stumbled forward but managed to wriggle free and his assailant only succeeded in wrenching his jacket off. Blake didn't hesitate, he was more concerned to protect his camera and its precious photographs. His cap was knocked from his head and men cursed as he barged his way past them to the reach the doorway and out into the daylight. By now there were a dozen in pursuit, surging out of the barn, men shouting wildly, seeing Blake's flight as proof of his guilt. More turned to see what was going on and from the ring Caleb Salt looked down at the commotion.

"Looks like somebody's been taking photographs," said his trainer, handing him a towel. Salt scowled at the escaping photographer. "Find out who it is," he said.

Blake was several yards ahead as he ran up the slope from the barn and across the field towards the village. One by one his pursuers were dropping away, shouting the bloody consequences should he show his face in Flash again, but the more determined ones carried on. Now gasping for breath, he ran past the pub, not daring to look back. Once through the church gate he snatched up his bicycle and frantically pushed it out into the lane. Only when he was in the saddle and pedalling madly was he more confident he could stay ahead. Seeing the bicycle pull away, the last of those in pursuit came to a halt, one shouting and shaking a fist in Blake's direction.

The camera was swinging wildly from the strap around his neck, so, before reaching the main road, he stopped to stow it safely in the handlebar bag. Looking up, he could see dark rain clouds being driven towards him across the moors, but his mind was filled with his escape from the barn. Would some of these ruffians follow him? Did Enoch Heathcote or Caleb Salt see him chased away? As he turned towards Leek, the first heavy raindrops struck his shirt and he realised he was going to get very wet.

Back in the barn, someone had picked up Blake's tweed jacket and was beginning to search through the pockets when Salt's trainer elbowed his way through the crowd. "Give that here," he called, making a grab for the jacket. The other man knew better than to argue and handed it over to the trainer who walked back to the other end of the barn. Inside the curtained-off section Salt and his dazed opponent were sitting on stools, the latter with his head tilted back while someone tended to his cuts.

"This belongs to him that was taking photographs," said the trainer, handing the jacket to Salt. The boxer felt in all the pockets and found nothing except a couple of handwritten notes and a slim wooden case. He expected it to contain cigarettes, but instead there were business cards, printed in elegant script: *Nathaniel Blake, Photographic Artist*. Salt cursed as he screwed up the card in his fist.

Down in Leek, workers were pouring out of the town's mills and the shops and public houses were getting ready for their busiest evening of the week. Although it wasn't the end of the working week, Friday was pay day and so men, women, boys and girls had been queueing to collect their wages before leaving the mills. Out in the town, provisions shops and public houses would stay open late to serve customers who now had money in their pockets to settle their debts and start spending again, women buying food for their families, most men more interested in a pint or two of ale.

Ellen Simms was as anxious as anyone to get her weekly pay, although six of her seven shillings would be handed over to her mother. After grabbing her cotton lunch bag from beside her chair in the braid room, she headed for the wages office and joined the jostling line outside the hatch to be handed her wage packet by a harassed cashier. She opened the small brown envelope immediately and was surprised to find that, as well as the seven shilling coins, there was a note. *"Miss Simms, please report to Mr Heathcote's office before you leave this evening."*

Her feelings were in a turmoil. Did Enoch Heathcote want something more from her? Or was she finally going to be rewarded with a better job? She pushed her way through the tide of people heading along the main corridor and, instead of heading out of the main door like everyone else, she turned and climbed the grand staircase that led to the offices on the first floor. Ellen found Heathcote's secretary was nowhere to be seen and stood wondering what to do next. She stepped forward and tapped hesitantly on the frosted glass of the door into the owner's office.

"Come!" The confident voice was not what she had expected – it was a woman.

Ellen opened the door and stepped inside to see Elizabeth Heathcote sitting behind the impressive desk. Standing beside her was one of the women overseers, an unsmiling woman whom Ellen had never spoken to before. The only times Ellen had seen Mrs Heathcote before she had been riding in a carriage with her husband. Now, standing just a few feet away from the owner's wife, Ellen felt the full force of the woman's steely gaze.

"Are you Simms?" Elizabeth asked, appraising her from head to foot. "What on earth does he see in these...children?" she wondered.

"Yes, Mrs, er.. Madam." Ellen stumbled over her words because she had sensed immediately that this conversation was not going to go well.

"I have a serious matter to ask you about," Elizabeth continued, seeing no need to ask Ellen to sit. "In recent weeks a number items have gone missing in the mill. Some senior employees have apparently had items stolen. Do you know anything about it?"

Ellen simply gaped at her inquisitor, any response knocked from her by the shock of the question. "Er.... no, Madam," she managed to utter.

"There is good reason to believe that you are the culprit, young woman. Several people have expressed their suspicions."

"It's not me, I don't know what you're talking about," said Ellen, her hands shaking.

"Then you won't mind us looking in your bag, will you? Mrs Dampier, can you see to that?" Elizabeth continued, turning to the overseer, who stepped around the desk and put out her hand for Ellen's cotton bag.

Ellen handed it over and Mrs Dampier brusquely emptied its contents onto the desk – a flimsy bonnet, a tiny leather purse and then, to the girl's dismay, a small fob watch clattered onto the desktop. The overseer snatched it up, glanced accusingly at Ellen and then said earnestly to Elizabeth Heathcote: "Yes Madam, that's the one."

"I've never seen that before. Whose is it? Who put it there?" said Ellen, her voice rising in panic.

"Shut up girl," Elizabeth ordered. "We know exactly who put it there, you did. This watch went missing from Mrs Dampier's bag this morning. She thought you were to blame, and obviously you are."

"But, but... I've never stolen anything." Ellen was on the verge of tears now.

"I don't want to hear any more from you. Either we call the police and have you prosecuted for theft," Elizabeth paused to add emphasis to the threat, "or you can leave our employment forthwith. I think the latter is preferable. Your employment is terminated!"

"But this is wrong. I've not done anything!" gasped Ellen.

"Silence!" shouted Elizabeth, slamming her thin, bejewelled fist on the desk. "Leave immediately!"

Ellen snatched her belongings off the desk and, tears running down her cheeks, turned and ran from the room.

Elizabeth Heathcote, her performance over, sagged into her husband's leather office chair. "That's got rid of her," she said with satisfaction.

In the crowded barn at Flash, where three more boxing bouts were to take place that evening, the failing light made the interior even more claustrophobic. When the rain began, the roof panels above the ring were rapidly replaced and, with oil lamps lit, there was an air of anticipation inside the building. The shouting spectators, many of them as aggressive as the boxers, shared the blood and sweat of the ring, the pain and the exhaustion of the contestants.

Enoch Heathcote and his companions did not stay until the end. They had enjoyed their time celebrating Algy's birthday – a spot of shooting, some hearty food, plenty of alcohol and now the fisticuffs. But after the excitement of the first bout, the brutality of it all was becoming a little monotonous. Heathcote's man, Salt, had done them proud and several of them had made a few sovereigns on the fight. Perhaps it was the effects of the last bottle of brandy, but the gentlemen were rather worse for wear as they settled into their seats to leave, the carriage hoods raised against the weather.

Caleb Salt stayed to watch the other bouts – he had a financial interest as well as a sporting one. He handled bets on the fights, although as a boxer he shouldn't have done. However, strictly speaking, all of the betting was illegal, as was the fighting. He refused an offer of a celebratory drink at the New Inn, collected the bag containing his winnings and headed for his mother's home. He had been lying low for the best part of a week, bedding down at a friend's farm miles away, but tonight he would stay at the family place.

He had been unsettled by that damned photographer showing up again. Blake had been responsible for that photograph at Abbey Green the day Carter died, and now he had come to Flash trying to take pictures of him. What did the man want? "I'll have to teach him a lesson if he comes near me again," Salt thought. But there were other things he needed to do, and quickly.

After walking back to the cottage he found a scrap of paper and a pencil. He would leave the village at dawn and, on the way, post an important letter. And within days he would be gone from Flash, forever.

Nathaniel Blake was dozing in an armchair at Moorside Terrace. His ride from Flash had been hellish. Battered by rain and wind, he had soon become soaking wet and was near exhausted by the time he had plunged from his bicycle while riding down Cat Tor hill. Thankfully his camera and the films had survived, but when he finally arrived home he had struggled to explain to Edith what had happened to him at Flash – and how he had lost his jacket.

She despaired that once again he had landed himself in a pickle that risked putting all of them in peril. The only consolation was that there was nothing of value in the jacket, he kept his watch and a few coins in his waistcoat and he had forgotten to take his door keys with him that afternoon.

Edith went upstairs to check that William and Eliza had not been disturbed by their father's return. Nathaniel sat on his own in the parlour, thinking what he should do next and wondering if he should have ever become mixed up in this complicated affair. His first priority would be to develop the photographs he had taken that day and see if he had captured the scene of Heathcote and Salt together. If the picture was clear enough, he would need to go to Inspector Ramm as soon as possible. Surely this time the officer would take his theories seriously.

Blake was jolted from his thoughts by the sound of the front door knocker. Frowning, he glanced at the mantelpiece clock to see that it was now after nine o'clock and then went to open the door. It was a young woman he didn't recognise. Her clothes were soaking wet from the rain and her long dark hair was straggled across her face. She was obviously distressed.

"Is this where Cora Blake lives? I need to speak to her!"

Cora came downstairs. She took one look at the distraught Ellen Simms in the hallway and ushered her into the kitchen, closing the door firmly behind them. Nathaniel knew better than to try to find out what was going on, and although he heard raised voices in the kitchen, he could not make out what the two were saying.

It was Ellen who spoke first as soon as the two were alone together.

"Who did you tell? Come on Cora, I know it must have been you. Who did you tell about me and Heathcote?" Ellen was no longer upset. Her tears had flowed easily enough when she had got home from the mill that afternoon. Now she was angry.

"I didn't tell anyone! Why, what's going on?" Cora replied. She reached out for Ellen's hand, but was brushed away.

"What's going on? I've been given the sack, that's what! By Mrs High-and-mighty Heathcote."

Cora gasped in surprise. "You've lost your job at the mill? Why?"

"They say I've been pinching – but that's just rubbish. Mrs Heathcote said it was either the sack or they would call the police. But we all know it's nothing to do with things going missing. She's just getting rid of me in case I say anything," said Ellen.

Her distress had turned into a furious need to blame someone. When she had got home she had sat on her bed thinking about it for a couple hours. She knew that someone had planted the watch in her bag – it was probably Mrs Dampier herself – and then they had pinned the blame on her. She was equally sure that it was because someone had found out she had spoken to Cora and Oliver Finch about Enoch Heathcote. She knew she wouldn't be able to rest until she had been to the Blakes' house to have it out with Cora.

"I should have kept my mouth shut," she said, bitterly.

"It wasn't me. I've said nothing to anyone," said Cora, though at the back of her mind she remembered mentioning Ellen's name to her mother a couple of weeks ago. Both her parents knew she suspected Enoch Heathcote of something – and had told her not to get involved – but they knew nothing of what Ellen had said to her and Oliver. "Surely they can't just sack you?" Cora went on.

"The Heathcotes can do what they like, can't they? Especially with this invented story about me stealing things," Ellen replied. "Anyway, I won't be talking to either you or Oliver again. Just stay out of my life!" With that Ellen turned, snatched the kitchen door open and ran down the hallway and out into the night.

Nathaniel and Edith had been waiting patiently in the parlour. On hearing Ellen leave, they got to their feet, anxious to speak to Cora. Their daughter was sitting at the kitchen table, head in hands, sobbing.

"Cora my dear, what on earth's going on?" asked Edith, placing her hands gently on her daughter's shoulders.

"Ellen's lost her job...at the mill ... and she thinks ...I'm to blame for it," Cora replied haltingly, her voice muffled by her hands still held across her face.

"How can that be?" said her mother.

"It's that awful Mr Heathcote, isn't it? He's to blame," said Cora, standing up, avoiding looking at her parents. "But I don't want to talk about it now – I'm going to bed." She shrugged off her mother's attempted embrace, went out of the room and stamped up the stairs.

Chapter Sixteen

The Leek Lion

SATURDAY, SEPTEMBER 13TH 1902

THE EVIL IN OUR TOWN The shocking deaths of two highly respectable men have plunged our town into a pit of fear, suspicion and bewilderment.

Mr. Amos Carter was a hardworking farmer known to many in the Leek moorlands. A dedicated member of the St. Edward's Parish Church choir, his voice brought pleasure and solace to countless congregations. Yet he was brutally murdered, mindlessly tortured in his last moments. The reason unknown. The culprit not found.

Dr. Crosbie Sneyd was a peaceful and cultured historian, visiting Leek to further his interest in matters of antiquity. An honest man of learning who was dedicated to uncovering the past. His life ended horrifically as he was hurled from the Old Church tower. The reason unknown. The culprit not found.

Were these heinous crimes linked? Will there be more deaths before those involved are brought to justice? Are murderers being shielded in our midst? Can our town Constabulary cope with the menace? How long will the uncertainty continue? These are the questions we are all considering as we lock our doors at night.

But the evil in our town runs deeper than these two alarming events that have grabbed our attention. Evil that sadly cannot appear in our pages because witnesses, and even victims, fear the retribution they might suffer; because the perpetrators – sometimes powerful people in our community – will coerce and bully to achieve their aims; because we may all be prepared to turn a blind eye rather than face the uncomfortable truth.

Those who seek to subvert the truth, who plan to avoid justice, who wish to gag free speech, be warned. The *Leek Lion* will not be swayed from its pursuit of the facts. When we have that information, that precious truth, we shall publish it for the good of our readers, for the good of our town.

Finch's angry editorial created a stir in many Leek households that Saturday morning. His reference to a hidden evil struck a chord with townsfolk who knew the powerful figures who thought they controlled life in the town, figures who would take advantage of others – especially if those others were lowly workers in a silk mill. For readers with family at Heathcote & Company, it brought to mind one mill owner in particular. Some even wondered if they might now dare to speak out.

However Finch's piece went unnoticed in the Blake household where breakfast was a subdued affair. Nathaniel and Edith drew little from Cora about what had gone on with Ellen Simms the previous evening. "I told you I thought Mr Heathcote was a bad man, now Ellen's lost her job and I'm sure it's because of him," Cora said defiantly.

"Please be careful what you're saying about Mr Heathcote. And what you're doing. Leave it to the proper authorities," Nathaniel told her before she left the kitchen.

Blake couldn't help feeling rather false in warning his daughter against something in which he himself was deeply involved. With every new day he became more consumed by his suspicions – his pursuit – of the mill owner. Cora was just a girl, she needed to be protected, he thought, whereas he was getting closer to solving something that the police had not.

Edith was wringing a tea towel with worry. "Even if these Heathcotes are a bad lot, there's nothing we can do about it," she said. "We must keep Cora out of it and you, Nathaniel Blake, must stop this detective palaver. Look what's happened to the Simmses? If it gets spread around that their Ellen's been stealing – whether it's true or not – they'll all suffer for it."

Nathaniel tried to reassure her. "It will be all over soon, and then life can get back to normal," he said.

His mind was still filled with the previous day's drama at Flash. He was eager to get to his darkroom and see if his photographs had been worth the risk. Leaving that morning's *Leek Lion* unopened, he hurried from the house.

When Cora came downstairs shortly afterwards she offered to go on an errand to the shops for her mother, "to get a breath of fresh air," she said. Partly she wanted to avoid any more questions from mother, but mainly she was desperate to see Oliver Finch and tell him about Ellen. When she reached the top floor of the *Leek Lion* offices she found Oliver's father was also there.

As Cora walked into the newsroom, the young reporter swivelled round to look at her, obviously embarrassed, while FJ Finch looked up from his papers and gave a knowing smile. "Miss Blake, how nice to see you. What can we do for you?"

"I need to speak to Oliver," Cora replied bluntly, looking sharply at the reporter who was already out of his seat ready to usher her back out of the office.

"Well, I'm sure he's got one or two things to tell you," FJ went on, rather enjoying the young people's discomfort "How is your father, by the way?"

"He's his usual self, thank you. I think he's in the studio this morning, developing some photographs he took at Flash yesterday," Cora replied.

"Flash, eh?" Inquisitive as ever, Finch was wondering if he had missed something.

"Let's go outside," said Oliver.

They went to sit on a bench outside the Methodist Church on the opposite side of the street. In contrast to his usual easy manner, Oliver was tense and didn't seem to know where to begin. But before he could speak, Cora launched into her speech.

"Ellen's lost her job at the mill. They said it was something to do with stealing, but she's sure it's because of Enoch Heathcote. And she's blaming us!"

After the fuss with his father over the lawyers' letter, Oliver had been dreading telling Cora about it. Now her news about Ellen made things even worse. "Poor Ellen, that's awful. I'm really sorry to hear that," he said, pausing to think how to broach his own bad news. "She might be right, though. I think someone has been spying on us. They must have seen you, me and Ellen together."

"Then we've got to do something about it!" Cora's voice rose almost to a shout.

"It's not going to be as easy as that. Heathcote & Co's lawyers have ordered the *Lion* not to talk to their workers. Father's not happy about it but he says they will sue if I write anything they don't like and he can't risk it. It looks like I ...er... won't be able to write anything about this business with Enoch Heathcote." Oliver knitted his fingers together and looked into Cora's face in the vain hope she would understand.

She frowned at him, bitterly disappointed that he had given in to Heathcote's bullying. But instead of being deflated by the setback, she seemed re-energised.

"That might be the end of it for you, Oliver. But they can't stop me, can they?" she declared. Determined not to show him how upset she was, Cora stood up and hurried away.

When Oliver returned to the office his father could tell from his son's expression that the conversation had not gone well. "Did Cora understand the situation?" Finch asked sympathetically.

"She understood, although that doesn't mean she's finished with it," said Oliver. He was worried what she might do next, but Oliver couldn't help being impressed by Cora's determination.

On his usual Saturday morning stroll around the town, a copy of the latest *Leek Lion* under his arm, FJ Finch called at Nathaniel Blake's studio on the off-chance of hearing something new about the murders. He was also curious to find out what Blake had been up to at Flash.

No one was in the showroom when Finch entered. There was a

muffled "Please wait a moment" from upstairs before the photographer eventually appeared on the stairs.

"FJ! What can I do for you?"

"I was wondering if you had any more theories about these murders. Have you read my latest piece?" said Finch, waving his folded copy of the newspaper.

"Sit down FJ. I've not had chance to look at the *Lion* yet, but I have some important things to tell you," said Blake. So much had gone on over the past few days and Blake was glad of the chance to talk to Finch, hoping for a sympathetic ear.

First he explained how John Gibb had been found and had given his account to the police. Then Blake said he was sure Enoch Heathcote had invited Dr Sneyd to the Old Church. Blake produced his copies of the notes so that Finch could compare the handwriting for himself.

"This is a serious allegation indeed, Nathaniel. It's shocking if you are correct," said Finch. He could already imagine the lurid headlines.

To Finch's growing amazement, Blake went on to tell of his experiences at Flash: Salt and Heathcote together, the bare-knuckle boxing, his escape from the mob.

"Heathcote's involved with Salt, no doubt about it. I've got the proof!" said Blake excitedly. He dashed up to the darkroom and came back down with one of the photographs he had developed that morning.

"Here, look at this!" he said as he handed over a picture clearly showing Enoch Heathcote talking to the bare-chested Salt.

"So that's what Salt looks like. And are those banknotes in Heathcote's hand?" asked Finch. Blake nodded.

"It's powerful stuff," Finch continued, already thinking how his newspaper could expose a gruesome plot. Then he added with a smile: "I'd like to see the Inspector's face when you show him this."

"I shall take it to him on Monday and then surely he must do something," Blake replied.

"Just be careful with Heathcote, Nathaniel. I've seen it for myself this week. I don't know if you knew, but your Cora and my son Oliver have been talking to young people about the man's behaviour, shall we call it, with some of his workers at the Great Mill. And Heathcote & Co are far from happy about it."

"I've warned Cora about this, but I didn't know she had got Oliver involved."

"He isn't any more. Heathcote's solicitors have told us not to talk to their workers."

"Can they do that?"

"Well, I'm not happy about it, at all, but there's a big difference between gossip and making a story stand up in court. No doubt Inspector Ramm thinks the same about your theories."

Blake realised that this could explain why Ellen Simms had lost her job, poor girl. But he wasn't prepared to be deflected from his own enquiries. "Don't let them dare threaten my daughter, or me for that matter," he declared.

"Quite right, old chap. I've had a rant of my own in today's edition," said Finch, opening his newspaper and pointing to the editorial.

Blake studied the paper and was impressed. "Strong words, FJ. It looks like you are preparing to do battle."

"It might stir up one or two people. Best of luck with the Inspector – and keep me informed," Finch said before leaving.

Blake returned to his darkroom to look through the photographs he had taken at Flash. He printed a selection showing Caleb Salt and Enoch Heathcote together and then turned his attention to the image of the victorious Salt in the ring. Much of the picture was dark except for the figure of Salt illuminated by light streaming through the roof. Blake was pleased with a photograph that had cost him his jacket.

Looking at the photographs he realised his meeting with Inspector Ramm could not wait until Monday. Aside from Enoch Heathcote, the fact that he had seen Caleb Salt in Flash the previous day might help the police find him sooner. He decided to go to the police station as soon as the prints were dry.

Albert Ramm arrived at Leek Police Station that Saturday morning to be handed a telegram delivered from the town's general post office an hour earlier.

"Attention of Inspector Ramm – Amos Carter, Crosbie Sneyd cases – Full progress report required Monday at latest – Headquarters Detective to be assigned – Fraser, Detective Superintendent"

Ramm knew exactly what was happening. His superiors, unhappy with the apparent lack of progress, were going to take the cases out of his hands and he would have to kowtow to some self-important plain clothes sleuth. No phone call to discuss it, just this blunt message.

Ramm felt the investigation had actually moved forward in the last week, although he was still no nearer a motive for either murder, let alone an arrest. Neither was he confident to approach Enoch Heathcote yet. Perhaps he should talk to the Vicar again, he wondered. Try to rattle the clergyman's resolve, just in case he knew more about Dr Sneyd than he was letting on. Or he could have another crack at Heathcote's steward, Bernard Gamage. Ramm knew he was clutching at straws. Arresting Caleb Salt was the key. He would send another order to the rural constables to keep their eyes peeled while on their beats around the villages.

Walking into his office, Ramm noticed cold ashes in the fireplace. "Knowles," he shouted down the corridor, "get this fire lit!" As a bachelor, Constable Knowles slept in the small upstairs dormitory reserved for officers who were single. This brought additional duties including answering the station's doorbell during the night while colleagues were on their beat, and lighting the office fires in the morning. He hurried into the Inspector's office carrying a zinc bucket of coal, sticks and rolled newspaper. His next priority would be to make his boss a mug of tea.

Ramm meanwhile settled behind his desk and began to sift through the growing pile of documents relating to the deaths of Amos Carter and Crosbie Sneyd. In addition to witness statements and medical reports he had pages of notes, including a list of Nathaniel Blake's theories. And, of course, there were the photographs Blake had taken: the pathetic figure of Amos Carter's body in the ransacked barn, Dr Sneyd spreadeagled outside the church, copies of the letters... He was going to have to distill all this into a convincing report for his superiors. He would write it out by hand and then Constable Moulton – the only officer who could type – would transcribe it on the station's typewriter, using carbon paper to make a second copy. The whole process could take most of the day.

He was on his second mug of tea and halfway through drafting his report when Blake arrived. Inspector Ramm sighed as he laid down his fountain pen and looked up at the photographer. "I hope this is important Mr Blake."

"I believe so, Inspector. I certainly do," said Blake who, though excited at his latest discoveries, was nervous about the Inspector's reaction.

"Well, what have you got for me?" asked Ramm, guessing that the brown envelope in Blake's hand contained more photographs.

"Yesterday I went to Flash where there was a bare-knuckle boxing contest taking place," Blake began.

Ramm grimaced to be reminded of the boxing. He was aware that such things went on "up in the hills", but he and his colleagues from neighbouring forces agreed it was more trouble than it was worth to try and police them.

"Caleb Salt was there – boxing – and Enoch Heathcote was one of the spectators. I saw the two of them having a private conversation and Heathcote handed Salt a wad of banknotes. Here, I photographed them," Blake continued, thrusting the picture at the Inspector.

Ramm virtually snatched the photograph from Blake's hand and studied it carefully, reaching for his magnifying glass to take a closer look.

"So this is Salt and he was back in Flash last night? Excuse me a moment," said Ramm, rising from his chair. At the front desk he spoke rapidly to Sgt Reynolds. "Send a telegram to Mellor at Longnor. Get him up to Flash as soon as he can. Salt was in a boxing match there last night and he might still be around. Even if he's gone, Mellor might get a lead on him."

Back in his office, Ramm looked at the photograph again and then returned his attention to Blake. "I presume it was no coincidence that you happened to be in Flash, but we won't go into that now. Have you any other photographs?"

Blake handed him an enlargement of the photograph of Heathcote and Salt, focused on what was in Enoch Heathcote's hand. It certainly looked like cash. He also gave the Inspector a print of Salt in the boxing ring after the fight.

The Inspector realised that the photograph of Salt's face could be valuable in trying to find the man and asked Blake to produce more prints showing only the suspect, as sharp as he could manage and as quickly as possible. Apart from the sighting of Salt, the latest revelation about Enoch Heathcote had shaken Ramm.

"Whatever was Mr Heathcote doing at an event like that, I wonder. Tell me more about what you saw of him," Ramm said to Blake.

The photographer explained how he had seen Heathcote arrive with a party of friends and then observed the mill owner make contact with Caleb Salt. "Unfortunately I was too far away to hear what they were saying, I was hiding behind a wall," he added, "but there certainly appeared to be some sort of transaction going on."

"Hiding behind a wall? As resourceful as ever, Mr Blake. Thank you once again. I might need a written statement, but at the moment I must press on with my investigation."

"So you are going to speak to Mr Heathcote?"

"You can rest assured of that."

Blake left, promising to return with the extra prints within the hour. He had said nothing to the officer of other suspicions about Enoch Heathcote's behaviour at the mill, nor how Cora's friend had been dismissed and the *Leek Lion* gagged. It might disrupt the search for the murderer, he thought.

Ramm stared into space, stroking his moustache. A confrontation with Enoch Heathcote was inevitable. The search for Salt had not been made public, so he expected Heathcote to claim he was unaware the man was wanted by the police. But there were now so many questions for Heathcote to answer and Ramm realised that, with a headquarters detective expected any day, he could not put off the interview any longer. He would marshal his evidence and on Monday morning he would tackle Heathcote.

The mill owner himself was enjoying a worry-free day's grouse shooting with a group of business associates. He and his wife had spoken only briefly at breakfast because he was in a hurry to go up to the Lodge to welcome the shooting party. He had given her only a sketchy account of Algy's party because he knew Elizabeth wasn't interested. Neither would she approve.

For her part, Elizabeth Heathcote saw no reason to inform her husband what had gone on with Ellen Simms the previous day. She had dismissed young women in the past and Enoch, having already moved on to other things and other people, seemed not to have noticed. With that little problem out of the way, Elizabeth could apply her mind to the more important matter of Amos Carter.

Sitting on her own at Longview, she perused the *Lion*. Her

attention was drawn to the headline on Finch's editorial. A worried expression came across her face as she read it. How much did this fellow know, she wondered. What was he planning to do about it?

Finally she threw the newspaper down with a look of disdain. "Pursuing the truth?" she muttered. "Just let them try."

Chapter Seventeen

By eight o'clock on Monday morning, Enoch Heathcote was at his desk drafting a letter for his secretary to type when his telephone gave a metallic jangle. He picked up the heavy handset.

The office woman responsible for answering incoming calls spoke timidly. "Sir? Leek Police have just rung."

"What did they want?"

"I don't know. They just asked if you were in the office today."

Puzzled, Heathcote dropped the handset into its brass cradle. Ten minutes later the phone rang again. "Inspector Ramm is on his way up, Sir."

Ramm had avoided the mill owner by not accompanying Edna to church the previous day. Instead he had spent most of Sunday morning planning how to tackle Enoch Heathcote. He needed to take the upper hand from the start, refusing to be intimidated – even if Heathcote threatened to contact Headquarters again.

Heathcote looked up as his secretary tapped on the door and opened it to admit the policeman. To his surprise, the Inspector was followed into the room by a constable. Although Ramm looked confident, his colleague glanced around the office nervously.

Inspector Ramm ignored the handshake Heathcote offered and stood stiffly in front of a desk that was at least twice the size of his own back at the station. "Mr Heathcote, there have been significant developments in the Carter and Sneyd investigations. I need your assistance with a number of points and Constable Knowles here will take a note of what is said. If you are not happy with that arrangement, you are welcome to accompany me to the police station."

"This is all rather unusual, Inspector," Heathcote huffed," but, as Chairman of the Bench, I have a duty to assist the Constabulary whenever I can. We are all on the same side, are we not?"

The two officers sat down and Knowles extracted his notebook as Ramm began. "Let's start with the incident at Dieulacres Cottage Farm, if we may. I gather you went to speak to Amos Carter a number times before his death. Why was that?"

"Oh, it was on matters concerning the farm, his tenancy and such," Heathcote replied with his usual assurance, waving his hand vaguely.

"Surely your steward, Mr Gamage, would deal with that?"

"Well, Amos was a very long-standing tenant. Excellent fellow, excellent fellow." Heathcote was employing his customary bluster, but was halted by Ramm's next question.

"Your visits did not concern an ancient cross thought to be buried on the farm?"

There was an awkward silence as the mill owner's staring eyes moved from Ramm to Knowles and back again. "Ancient cross? I'm afraid I don't know what you are talking about," he said finally, forcing a smile to show he was mystified by such a bizarre suggestion.

"Did Dr Sneyd contact you about a cross belonging to the Abbey?"

Heathcote acted as if he was mulling over the question, checking his memory, before responding. "No, I have no recollection of that at all."

Ramm kept up the pressure. "What about when Dr Sneyd came to Leek? Did you write to him at The George?"

"Certainly not! Where are you getting these ideas from, Inspector?"

"So this is not your handwriting, Mr Heathcote?" asked Ramm, handing over the copy of the forged letter to Sneyd.

Heathcote looked at the photograph and peered at the writing, his expression changing from self-confidence to puzzlement to genuine concern. Seeing the look on the mill owner's face, the Inspector was sure he did know something about the letter.

"No, it is not my writing," Heathcote said at last, his voice solemn. "And before you make any more wild allegations, Inspector, here is a sample of my handwriting. There are plenty more to be had." He passed over the document he had been drafting before the officers arrived. Ramm could see that the writing bore no resemblance to either of the two notes which Blake had copied. It looked like the photographer's theory was embarrassingly wrong.

Heathcote was equally forthright when questioned about Bernard Gamage: "I'm afraid I do not know all of my steward's movements, but he certainly did not visit The George on my orders."

Ramm had kept his trump card to the last. He produced the photograph Blake had taken at Flash.

"Finally, Sir, can you tell me why you were talking to this man on Friday last?"

Heathcote's eyes widened as he looked at the photograph. "Where on earth is this from? Who took it? Do you have spies watching me, Inspector?" he asked indignantly.

"How the photograph was taken is of no concern. What interests me is the man you were seen with, Caleb Salt. It appears you were handing him a sum of money. Salt is wanted for questioning in connection the deaths of both Amos Carter and Crosbie Sneyd."

"The deaths?" Heathcote said incredulously. He paused while he considered what to say next. "But this has nothing to do with me. Salt is a… a casual worker. He works as a beater at my shoots, that's all."

"And the money?"

"Wages, of course!" said Heathcote, but with decidedly less confidence because he himself realised that the bundle of banknotes far exceeded a beater's earnings.

Inspector Ramm could see that the photograph had rattled Enoch Heathcote. He was now certain something suspicious was going on between the mill owner and the boxer, but he had no chance to press the matter further because Heathcote suddenly became angry.

"Inspector Ramm, I object strongly to your insinuations. This interview is entirely unwarranted – it may even be illegal – and I am not prepared to answer any more questions. If you wish to speak to me further it will have to be in the presence of my solicitor." With that, Enoch Heathcote stood up, strode to the office door and opened it. "I bid you both good day."

Once the officers had left, Heathcote sat down again, head in hands, his mind racing. He was furious at the policeman's audacity. "How dare Ramm question me like that?" he muttered to himself. But the interview had left him deeply worried. He was shocked how much the Inspector knew, although a lot of it could be deflected and denied, especially once his lawyer was involved. But where on earth had that letter come from? And who had been at Flash taking photographs of him with Salt? Talking to a murder suspect – he wasn't so sure he could explain that away.

When FJ Finch arrived at Leek Police Station for his usual Monday morning check on developments over the weekend he was horrified to find three more reporters waiting to question the Inspector on the murders. Perhaps he should not have been surprised. Recent events in Leek were gaining wider notoriety as newspaper readers of all classes seemed to have an unhealthy interest in gruesome murders and mysterious deaths.

The four men stood uneasily by the reception desk to wait for Ramm. "With all this *evil* going on in Leek, we've got to keep our readers informed," said one of the newcomers, looking slyly at the *Leek Lion* editor. Finch said nothing about his editorial. He knew it had caused a stir in the town over the weekend and was secretly pleased that other newspapers had noticed it, too.

At that moment the Inspector marched in from his clash with Enoch Heathcote and saw that he would now have to face the Press. He nodded to the journalists and said "Gentlemen, give me a moment" before heading to his office.

He had known the risks of tackling someone as powerful as Heathcote and had expected him to bluff and bully his way out of anything awkward. His failure with the handwriting had been disappointing, but there was no question that the mill owner was disturbed to see the letter. And the man was clearly shaken by the mention of the Abbey's cross and positively stumped when he saw the photograph of himself with Caleb Salt.

Overall Ramm was feeling rather pleased with himself – he had finally faced down Heathcote. There might be consequences, but he would worry about those later. Now it was important not to lose momentum, he thought. Perhaps he should speak to Blake again? It went against his natural inclination, but Ramm accepted that the photographer had uncovered several important clues. What's more, some of Blake's extravagant theories – the theft of the Abbey cross, Gamage's involvement, even that of Enoch Heathcote – were beginning to look distinctly plausible.

Before seeing Blake, the Inspector would first have to face his tormentors and so called the newspapermen into his office. The three newcomers sat down and looked earnestly at Ramm, while FJ Finch chose to stand behind them and lean casually against a wooden filing cabinet. Several minutes of the usual back-and-forth followed, Ramm managing to deflect any awkward questions, and Finch saw that they were going to learn nothing new.

However the editor had come up with an idea how he might turn the impromptu press conference to his own advantage. Invigorated by his hard-hitting editorial, he saw an opportunity to stir up trouble for the bullies at Heathcote & Co – and avoid any blame.

"Is it true, Inspector," he asked, "that your enquiries have been widened to include a prominent family in the town?"

His rivals turned to look at Finch in surprise and then focused back on the Inspector, eager to hear his response.

"Is this some sort of gossip, Mr Finch?"

"No, Inspector. I have it on good authority that one of the town's mill owners, one of the leading townspeople in fact, was seen with your chief suspect, the man you are currently scouring the moorlands to find."

As Finch expected, the other journalists' were racing shorthand across their notebooks. Heathcote & Co might try to gag the *Lion*, he thought, but let's see what they could do when lurid suspicions started to spread across the rest of the Press.

Ramm guessed that Finch had seen the photograph his friend Nathaniel Blake had taken at Flash. Normally this would have upset him, but in his current ebullient mood, he decided he would play along with the editor. He too would seize the opportunity.

"It is correct that I have new information which is leading me ever closer to the man we want to speak to concerning both deaths. His name is Caleb Salt, he comes from the village of Flash, and today I am issuing a photograph of the man which I would like circulated as widely as possible," said Ramm, fishing in his desk drawer for copies of the head and shoulders picture of Salt that Blake had produced.

One of the reporters posed the obvious question: "What about this prominent family? Who are they?"

Ramm paused, both thinking what to say and adding a certain weight to his reply. "I am anxious to speak to all contacts that Salt has had in Leek and the moorlands. As Mr Finch suggests, these do indeed include a prominent Leek family. An individual has been questioned this morning. Our enquiries continue. As yet, no charges have been brought, but I am convinced we can bring these two most distressing cases to a conclusion as soon as possible."

"No names, Inspector?"

"It would be inappropriate for me to divulge any names at present, other than that of the man we are seeking, Caleb Salt."

After flurry of follow-up questions, the journalists departed, pleased with this new angle on the deaths. Ramm blew out his cheeks, relieved the grilling was over. He knew there were risks in telling the Press so much, but certain prominent people were not being honest with him and he had to try to flush out the real culprits.

For much of the weekend, Nathaniel Blake had been preoccupied with his inner world of speculation and suspicion. On several occasions Edith found him sitting staring into space, going over how Enoch Heathcote could be involved in the deaths of Carter and Sneyd and whether Cora had put herself at risk from the man.

Therefore Blake was pleased when Inspector Ramm called at the studio later that Monday morning. This was a chance, he thought, to find out what was going on with police investigations, and, more importantly, if his own detective work was correct. It turned out, however, that there was a new puzzle to solve.

"Have you spoken to him? Enoch Heathcote, I mean. What did the fellow say?" Blake began before the Inspector had chance to speak.

"It wouldn't be in order for me to tell you precisely what Mr Heathcote said," Ramm replied. He looked round to see if Cora was listening and was relieved to see that she was going upstairs. "But you will not be surprised to hear he was somewhat disconcerted to see your photograph. He particularly wants to know who took it, so I would stay quiet about that, if I were you."

Blake could tell from Ramm's tone that their relationship was changing. There seemed to be a new respect in his attitude. Perhaps the officer was starting to take his theories seriously.

"I must thank you once again for your efforts at Flash. Those photographs may become valuable evidence," the Inspector continued. "Unfortunately we still have some things to clear up, which is why I wanted to speak to you."

Ramm produced the copy of the fateful letter to Dr Sneyd. "This is not Mr Heathcote's handwriting," he said.

Blake couldn't hide his dismay. "What? But it must be! The hand looks precisely the same as the order I received from him."

"I agree, it does look the same and that, Mr Blake, is the conundrum. If Enoch Heathcote did not write the letter, then who did? Tell me, when did you receive the order for his photographs?"

"It was the last week in August. But the order wasn't for his photographs, as such. It was for prints from a portrait session I had with Mrs Heathcote," Blake explained.

"Mrs Heathcote? You didn't mention this before," said Ramm sharply.

"Er, perhaps not. I suppose I was so sure it was him..." Blake's voice trailed off as he realised his mistake. "Perhaps the 'E Heathcote' who sent me the order wasn't Enoch...."

"It was Elizabeth Heathcote," Ramm finished the sentence for him.

Ramm stared at the letters, his mind spinning. Elizabeth Heathcote! Dragging that woman into the investigation could create as many problems as it solved. He had already accused – wrongly, as it turned out – first Reverend Maitland and then Enoch Heathcote of writing the letter to Dr Sneyd. Now he would have to try a third suspect. And after his heated exchanges with the mill owner, he knew any false step with Heathcote's wife would not only be embarrassing. It could be the end of his police career.

His first reaction was to go to Longview immediately, but he decided to pause and think through a confrontation that could be just as bitter as the one he had that morning. Mindful that Blake seemed to be sharing all his discoveries with FJ Finch, Ramm asked the photographer to tell no one of what they had discussed and then hurried out.

Blake, too, was stunned by the revelation about the handwriting. "How could I have made such an error?" he thought. Did this mean the Heathcotes were in the foul business together? He wondered what his daughter would make of this, for he had little doubt she had heard what had been said.

In fact, Cora had been unable to curb her curiosity and had listened in to the conversation from the top of the stairs. She was hardly surprised to hear her father and the policeman discussing Mrs Heathcote. After the way Ellen Simms had been sacked on Friday, Cora was growing to suspect that Elizabeth Heathcote was just as evil as her husband.

Returning to the station, the Inspector gave instructions that the constable who patrolled the west side of town should extend his beat to Longivew that afternoon. It would be a courtesy call on the pretext of checking that no suspicious characters had been seen around the mansion, but the main aim was to ascertain Elizabeth Heathcote's whereabouts. Ramm had no intention of making a wasted journey to Longview only to find that Mrs Heathcote was not in or, worse still, her argumentative husband was there too.

As the afternoon wore on, Ramm's ruminations about the two murders were interrupted several times. A message came from Constable Mellor at Longnor: Caleb Salt was indeed in Flash on Friday evening, but had not been sighted since. A telephone call was received from Headquarters: Ramm was to expect a detective to arrive on Tuesday to "assist" with investigations. Finally, there was a report from the Leek beat officer: Elizabeth Heathcote would not be at Longview for the rest of the day. She was meeting fellow members of the Temperance Movement to plan a rally in the town, a servant had said.

Enoch Heathcote had already arranged to see his lawyer at the mill that afternoon to discuss an important business meeting he was due to attend in Manchester the next day. A secret conference had been called by textile magnates from across the North West, owners of both cotton and silk mills, to discuss an alliance to combat the growing power of the unions. The owners realised they needed to form a united front – just as their workers were. It proved a timely opportunity for Heathcote to consult his lawyer on rather more sensitive matters.

Following Inspector Ramm's aggressive questioning that morning, Enoch was sure that the officer would want to speak to him again and, at that point, he would need legal support. He had considered complaining to Police Headquarters about Ramm again, but feared that it might draw further attention to the questions the Inspector had raised. At which point he would need convincing answers. The Chief Constable might be an acquaintance, but even he might draw the line at condoning illegal betting on a bare-knuckle fight, if not worse.

After talking to his solicitor, Heathcote felt slightly more assured when he returned home to face Elizabeth. Of course, he had not been completely candid with the lawyer. After all, he was paying the man to take his side, whether or not he divulged the whole truth. Things rapidly became rather more fraught when he got back to Longview, however.

Seeing Elizabeth in the drawing room, Enoch went in immediately and closed the door firmly behind him. "Elizabeth, we must talk," he said with some urgency. "Inspector Ramm gave me a grilling this morning. The man thinks he's on to something. Thankfully I gave him no satisfaction. In fact, I sent him away with a flea in his ear."

Elizabeth's eyes narrowed. "Why was he questioning you?"

"Ramm knew that I had seen Salt – he's the chief suspect apparently. The Inspector was putting two and two together."

"Salt? When did you see Salt?" asked his wife sharply, leaning forward in her armchair.

"Didn't I mention it? It was on Friday evening, when I was out with Algy and the chaps. Salt was in a boxing match up at Flash – he's a dreadful ruffian, you know – and I..." Enoch's confidence in facing Elizabeth was draining away and he was now having difficulty finding the right words. "Well, the fellows wanted to place a bet on the fight and I handed him some money. And some damned spy took a photograph of me with Salt! Dashed underhand behaviour, I call it. I wonder if it was that fellow Blake?"

"You absolute fool, Enoch! I presume alcohol had something to do with this?"

Enoch ignored the reference to his penchant for whisky. "How dare you call me a fool? What about yourself? Did you write to that fellow Sneyd? I'm sure it was your handwriting on the letter. Thank God I had the presence of mind not to give anything away when Ramm showed it to me."

"Letter to Sneyd? Now what are you talking about?" Elizabeth barked.

"Ramm has a picture of some letter that Sneyd received. Goodness knows where he got it from."

This time Elizabeth gave no reply. She was deep in thought, her mind going over the train of events.

Her husband went on excitedly: "It's all part of Ramm's grand theory. A cross buried at the Abbey, me going to see Carter, Carter being killed, Sneyd being killed, me talking with Salt... I tell you, my dear, the fellow thinks he's got me dangling on a hook! Or in a noose!"

"Calm down, Enoch." Elizabeth was regaining her composure and there was the familiar steel in her tone. "Ramm has been investigating for a month now and has barely got anywhere. I doubt he's going to solve anything and he certainly will not to be able to implicate us."

Out in the hallway, Margaret Gamage had begun listening in to the conversation as soon as she heard raised voices. Walking softly to the drawing room door, she leaned one ear towards it. She was used to bending the rules for her devious mistress, but she was alarmed to hear that the police were taking a closer interest in her employers. It was worrying enough when Bernard had been called to the police station the previous week, even though he had tried to reassure her that Enoch Heathcote would sort it all out. Now, she was even more concerned to hear that Mr Enoch himself had been questioned.

She returned to the modest sitting room-cum-bedroom that the Gamages occupied at the back of the house and told Bernard what she had heard. Her husband listened with a serious expression. For years he had helped to enforce the wishes of wealthy employers, but he also had a strong instinct for self-preservation. He hadn't liked what Margaret had told him.

"Neither of us is going to take the blame for something the Heathcotes might or might not have done," he told his wife. "If anyone asks about anything, we say that we were simply taking orders."

"But what if we lose our positions?" Margaret asked.

"Then we start again somewhere else. Better that than go to prison."

The Blake household was discussing arrangements for the following day when Nathaniel was due to take a set of photographs at Alton Towers, the stately home a dozen miles from Leek. It was a prestigious and profitable commission from the Earl of Shrewsbury and he had decided to catch the train for the journey to Alton Station where the Earl's carriage would collect him. He planned on taking his full-size field camera, tripod and a substantial number of glass plates.

"I shall leave first thing in the morning and take the omnibus to the station as soon as I have collected my equipment from the studio. The photography could take all day, but it should be worth it," said Nathaniel, relieved to have a decent project to take his mind off the suspicious goings-on in Leek.

Although it should have been one of Cora's days at Miss Keates' Academy, she agreed to go into work as normal, but only for the morning. "Miss Keates has asked some of us to help her plan the entertainment for the harvest festival at the church in Meerbrook. So I must be there in the afternoon," said Cora.

"So you're going Meerbook?" asked her mother, rather puzzled. This was the first time she had heard that Cora's teacher was involved in the village church, four miles out of town.

"Yes, I think Miss Keates has been attending there for a little while," Cora replied matter-of-factly, with a shrug of the shoulders. "Several of us older girls have decided to go on our bicycles. And don't worry if I'm late coming home because Miss Keates says it might take all afternoon."

Later that evening, Nathaniel and Edith agreed it was a relief their daughter was involved a something fresh, even if this new-found enthusiasm for a church event was a little surprising. A ride out with some friends was probably the attraction, Edith thought. And if there was a group of them, Cora should be safe enough.

Up in her room, Cora was relieved too. She had achieved the first part of her plan, but she knew the hard part was still to come.

Chapter Eighteen

Caleb Salt had spent the Monday night at his mother's cottage. Having arrived from his hideout near Buxton after dark, he had resisted the temptation to call at the New Inn – a friend had warned him that the police had been looking for him in the village again.

It was daylight the following morning when he peered out cautiously through the small front window of the cottage to check if anyone was about, then darted through the door and around the back of the humble dwelling. Glancing to either side and seeing no one, he strode across the rough grass until he reached a tumbledown animal shelter about fifty yards away. Here and there on the moorland were rotting planks of wood that covered old mine workings and Salt watched his step because he knew there were some shafts that had no covering at all.

He ducked through what remained of the ruined building's entrance, went inside and began to dismantle a pile of stones stacked against the back wall. The sizeable blocks presented no problem to a man of Salt's physique. Finally he pulled out a sack which had been hidden underneath. Slinging it over his shoulder he returned to the cottage.

He knew he had hours to spare, but he wanted to leave nothing to chance. He would cut across the bare moor, avoiding lanes and paths where he might be seen by someone he knew, and then he would find a hiding place amongst the rocks of the Roaches. From there he would keep watch until it was time to act.

As Cora Blake wheeled her bicycle out of the backyard on Tuesday morning she saw the familiar shape of the huge chimney that towered above the Great Mill. Its smoking hulk filled her with foreboding for what lay ahead. She had decided to take her bicycle to the studio to save time later, but when she arrived, she struggled to haul it up the two stone steps in front of the shop door. She was slightly built and found the heavy machine difficult to manhandle, although it bowled along nicely when she was perched in the saddle.

Once inside, she leaned the bicycle gingerly against the whitewashed wall. Her father would not have approved – he was a stickler for keeping the showroom neat and tidy – but he had already caught the train to Alton and would be out all day.

Cora was happy enough to tend the shop on her own for the morning, but first she had more important things to do. She immediately ran upstairs, opened the door to the darkroom and was relieved to see that her father had taken only his large camera for the day's photography. His new lightweight camera, which folded into a handy leather case, was still on the work bench. She picked up the camera and unfolded it, then went to the window and practiced focusing on various buildings across the street, depressing the shutter and checking adjustments although she knew there was no film inside.

She went back into the darkroom and opened the cupboard where the supply of photographic plates and films was stored. Cora planned to use the new-style flexible celluloid film today, just as her father had done on his trip to Flash the previous week. The time she had spent watching him at work was now put to good use. After lighting the red-shaded lamp, she loaded a roll of film into the camera, making sure that it wound forward smoothly and that the back of the camera was closed firmly.

Then she returned the camera to its leather case and went downstairs to attach it to her bicycle. It was harder than expected to stretch the stiff leather straps around the handlebars and fasten the brass buckles tightly, but she was determined the camera should be as secure as possible. She didn't want to risk damaging her father's latest gadget. Sighing with relief once it was attached, she looked across at the wall clock and began to count the minutes until midday.

Inspector Ramm's Tuesday morning did not go quite as planned as he had barely sat down behind his desk when he was called to the telephone. It was another barbed enquiry from his Superintendent at Stafford. That day's *Birmingham Daily Post* had already been seen at Police Headquarters. It carried a lurid piece about the "mysterious market town murders" which included quotes from Ramm that a prominent family was involved. Apparently one of the reporters in Leek the previous day was a stringer for several large newspapers and the Inspector's revelations were now being read in cities far beyond Staffordshire and its moorlands.

"You have surprised us yet again, Inspector. I hope you have the facts to back up these latest pronouncements," said the Superintendent sarcastically.

Ramm was not going to admit that his statement to the Press had been entirely unplanned. Instead he gave an impression of confidence as he explained he was on the verge of a breakthrough and his comment had been an attempt to flush out the culprit. It sounded plausible, Ramm thought, but his superior was unconvinced.

"We are sending you some expert assistance. Detective Inspector Sutcliffe is on his way to Leek this afternoon. Please give him your complete support," came the reply.

Ramm put down the handset. His resolve to tackle Elizabeth Heathcote while he was still in charge, was stronger than ever. He was considering what he was going to say at Longview when he was interrupted by news that a telegram had arrived from PC Mellor at Longnor. One of the constable's contacts had told him that Caleb Salt had been seen in Flash the previous evening.

After breaking off to charge two men following a brawl in Leek the previous night, Ramm next asked Sergeant Reynolds to call the Great Mill and find out Enoch Heathcote's whereabouts. A secretary explained that Mr Heathcote would be away all day,

"Reynolds, order a trap from Hammersley's stables. You and I need to go down to Longview as soon as possible," Ramm told his Sergeant. Although Reynolds usually looked after the station when the Inspector was out, Ramm had decided he needed a show of force to shake Elizabeth Heathcote into some sort of co-operation. It was after midday when the horse and trap arrived and the two officers climbed in. "Longview, and waste no time," Ramm told the driver.

The clock showed quarter past twelve and Cora could wait no longer. She locked the shop door from the inside and headed upstairs to take off her skirt and put on a pair of cycling bloomers she had brought in her bag. Women wearing bloomers when riding had been a hot topic in the *Cycling Notes* of various newspapers – usually written by men – and Cora's parents didn't particularly approve of the practice. However she had secretly made herself a pair in sewing class at Miss Keates's and thought they would be ideal for today's adventure.

Cora was determined to find proof of what the evil Mr Heathcote was up to. And as she could no longer rely on help from either Ellen Simms or Oliver Finch, she realised she would have to do it on her own. She had invented the story of the trip to Meerbrook Church with Miss Keates. Ellen had said that it was usually on Tuesday afternoons when Mr Heathcote took his young friends to his country retreat, so Cora had decided she would go there too. She would cycle up to the Roaches, the rocky crags on the moors outside Leek where the Heathcote shooting lodge stood, and see what was going on. See who Enoch Heathcote was taking there. And just like her father had done at Flash, she would take a camera to photograph anything she saw.

Rather than cycle along the main Buxton Road out of town, Cora decided to take some of the quieter lanes. Whichever way she went there would be hills that would mean getting off and pushing, so she knew she had to allow plenty of time for a ride of five miles or more. Having locked up the shop, she set off first along cobbled lanes and past mills and dyeworks before reaching the edge of town at Abbey Green. Cycling past the track that led to the Abbey ruins her memories came crowding back. Tragic deaths, police questions, the suspicious Heathcotes, secrets from her parents, the upset with Ellen, meeting Oliver Finch… So much had gone on since she had come here with father that day, she felt she was almost a different person now.

The route she was taking had, centuries before, been walked by monks and the folk who lived and worked the Abbey estate. Today the lanes were deserted except for a teenage girl on a bicycle. The sun came out and Cora grew hot, realising the folly of setting out without a drink in the bag that was slung over her shoulder. Half an hour later, after much pushing followed by the relief of a downhill, she reached the village of Meerbrook and was glad to see a cast iron water pump near the Methodist Chapel. Working the stiff handle with one hand, she managed to scoop a pitifully small amount of water in the palm of her other hand. This was hopeless, she thought. Glancing round to see that no one was watching, she bent down and worked the pump to slosh water over her head and face and into her mouth. She was soaked but refreshed. Next she unwrapped the cheese sandwich her mother had given her that morning and made short work of it.

An ancient fellow sitting on a bench outside the village pub watched with interest as she pedalled past, branching right at the village school and into a lane which snaked higher towards the Roaches. In the distance, the green fields rose up to a moorland skyline of bare rocks dotted with pine trees. Cora knew her destination lay somewhere near that forbidding crest and turned her pedals as hard as she could. A new incline, steeper than ever, brought her to a complete halt and from then on she pushed, her boots turning grey with dust from the limestone surface of the lane.

Leaning forward on the handlebars, Cora forced the bicycle up the final steepest section before stumbling to a halt as she reached a junction with a lane which ran parallel with the rocky ridge. Putting the bicycle down while she caught her breath she spotted a stone trough by the roadside, filled to the brim with water dribbling from a spring hidden amongst the heather. Fronds of green algae floating beneath the surface made her think twice about drinking any, so she plunged her handkerchief into the trough and used it to cool her face. Looking back over where she had come Cora now appreciated how high she had climbed, a green panorama of fields and trees sweeping towards Leek, where church spires and mill chimneys looked tiny in the distance. The long thin shape of Tittesworth – the reservoir that provided Leek with much of its water – shone silver like a spill of mercury in the valley bottom.

Although Ellen had described where Enoch Heathcote had

driven her to reach his shooting lodge, Cora did not know precisely where the building was. She pedalled on, spotting a couple of farmsteads on the hillside, but neither fitted Ellen's description. Then she came upon what she was sure must be the Lodge. Built from the same purple-grey stone as the Roaches which loomed behind it, the Lodge seemed to have almost grown out of the rockface. The windows had pointed arches, as did the door, and along the roof the stonework was shaped like battlements. It was a miniature castle looking out over a kingdom, the Heathcote kingdom. A few yards further on she saw that a track led up to the unusual building. The stone gateposts, at least six feet high, were helpfully carved with the name "Heathcote Lodge". Cora had arrived.

She could see no carriage outside the Lodge, nor the motor car Mr Heathcote had been showing off around town, so Cora hastily pushed her bicycle onto the heather-covered hillside. She laid it on the ground and wrenched out handfuls of fern fronds to cover it. After taking the camera out of its case on the handlebars she made sure the bicycle was hidden and then ran over to a huge rounded rock on the hillside. It was big enough to hide behind and close enough to the Lodge for her to watch who arrived. She sat down by the rock and prepared to wait.

The maid looked suitably surprised when she opened the heavy front door at Longview and saw two police officers.

"Mrs Heathcote, please. Tell her Inspector Ramm wants to speak to her," the Inspector announced.

"I'm sorry, Sir, but Madam has gone out," the maid replied.

"Did she say when she would return?"

"No, I don't think so. If it's important I could ask Mrs Gamage, she might know."

"Let me speak to Mrs Gamage," said Ramm, determined that

his visit to the Heathcote mansion should not be a total waste. He could see fear in Margaret Gamage's eyes when came into the hallway. The maid was still hovering in the background, so Ramm took a step over the threshold and suggested they talked in private.

Without a word, Mrs Gamage turned and led the policemen into the drawing room where they all remained standing. The very fact that she had not asked what was wrong told Ramm she was not surprised to see them. "Do you know where Mrs Heathcote is?" he asked.

"She asked Simpkins to take her out in the carriage. I don't know where to or how long she will be."

"What about Mr Heathcote. Is he with her?"

"He's out for the day, I believe."

"Perhaps you can help me then," Ramm continued. He opened a document case and took out the copy of the order for Blake's portrait photographs. "Is this Mrs Heathcote's handwriting?"

Margaret Gamage gave it a cursory glance. "Yes, it is."

"What about this one?" the Inspector asked, showing her the copy of the forged letter to Dr Sneyd.

"Er... Madam couldn't have written that because it says it's from Reverend Maitland," she answered with little conviction.

"Do you have something else that Mrs Heathcote has written, so we could compare them?"

Margaret Gamage knew this would be the moment of truth. She and her husband had decided the previous night that they had covered up for their employers for long enough. Perhaps it was time for them to move on.

"Come this way," she said, turning abruptly and leading Ramm and Reynolds into another room off the main hallway, this one much smaller and more intimately furnished. In the corner stood an antique French secretaire, decorated with intricate marquetry. Margaret Gamage produced a bunch of keys from her skirt pocket and selected a suitably ornate one. Elizabeth Heathcote had no idea that her companion had a key to her private writing desk, but Mrs Gamage had long ago realised it was in her own interests to keep an eye on her mistress's affairs. And she had been well schooled in secrecy.

She inserted the key and lowered the cabinet's hinged front to reveal numerous letters and documents, either in pigeonholes or stacked in neat piles. She selected a piece of paper and handed it to Ramm saying "This is Madam's handwriting." Although her expression revealed nothing she knew this was exactly the evidence the policeman wanted to see.

Ramm looked at the new document intently. It was a private letter that had no bearing on his investigation, but the handwriting was a perfect match with the copies he held. Clear proof that Elizabeth Heathcote was involved in Sneyd's death.

His cast an eye over the rest of the desk's contents. Amongst the notepaper he saw an ancient scroll of parchment which he guessed was the Abbot Whitney document, removed from Dr Sneyd's room. Then something else caught his attention – a dirty envelope addressed to Mrs Heathcote in a crude almost child-like hand. Curious, he picked it up and inside found a crumpled receipt from an ironmonger's in Buxton. He flipped it over and saw a message had been scrawled in pencil on the other side. "Meet me at the lodge, 2 o'clock Tuesday. The price is £500. Come alone." It was unsigned.

"Look at this, Reynolds," he said, handing the scruffy note to his Sergeant. Ramm turned to the Mrs Gamage and asked if she knew when the note had arrived. She confirmed it had been the previous morning.

"So this must be where she's gone now. 'Meet me at the lodge', where is that?"

"It's Heathcote Lodge up on the Roaches. Madam doesn't usually go there, it's where Mr Enoch takes his friends…er… when they're shooting," Mrs Gamage replied.

Ramm glanced at a brass carriage clock on the mantelpiece. It was already well past one o'clock. "We need to get up there straight away! Do you know where it is?" Mrs Gamage nodded. "Then you must come with us."

He dashed into hallway and then stopped abruptly as it dawned on him that their horse and trap would struggle to carry four people up the steep hills to the Roaches. He looked around wildly and, through a glazed door to the rear courtyard, caught a glimpse of green-painted coachwork. Ramm flung open the door to see a stable boy polishing Enoch Heathcote's Napier 16 HP motor car.

He turned to the Sergeant who had come up behind him. "Reynolds, you know how to drive one of these contraptions, don't you?" Ramm asked. The Sergeant had been sent to Headquarters to learn how to operate one of the force's newly-acquired Star trucks, but hesitated before replying. The trucks, intended for transporting prisoners, were a completely different beast than the high-powered saloon standing in the cobbled yard.

"Well, Sir…. I know the basics, steering, gears, brakes and such. But every vehicle's different and…"

"Excellent!" Ramm cut Reynolds off before he could say any more. There was no time to prevaricate, they needed to leave as soon as possible. Pointing at the motor car, he continued: "Go on, give it the once-over, man. Check the controls or whatever you need to do, and then we must go."

The lad swung the starting handle to spark the engine into life and Reynolds hesitantly drove the Napier across the yard. There was a grinding noise from the gears and he stalled it after a couple of yards, but once it was started again he managed to pilot the car onto the gravel drive and almost as far as the front gate. He pulled on the brake and, to be safe, left the engine running whilst Inspector Ramm and Margaret Gamage hurried down the drive to the car. Ramm climbed into the front beside Reynolds and Mrs Gamage sat in the back. The car jerked forward and Reynolds turned left onto the main road, heading for town, the hills and Heathcote Lodge.

Cora was sitting in the heather leaning back against the boulder. It seemed ages since she had taken up her hiding place and she began to wonder if it had all been a waste of time. At last she heard the sound of a horse-drawn vehicle coming along the lane. She edged around the rock to stay hidden as the carriage turned up the track and stopped outside the shooting lodge. Now on her hands and knees, she peeped out to see who the mill owner had brought with him today. But it wasn't Enoch Heathcote she saw climbing out of the carriage, it was Elizabeth his wife.

Cora watched as Simpkins, the groom, offered his hand to help Mrs Heathcote from the carriage then returned to his seat as she walked purposefully to the Lodge, unlocked the door and went inside. Minutes went by and nothing seemed to happen, then Cora saw movement amongst the fir trees high up behind the Lodge. She flattened herself on the ground and peered out through a clump of ferns to see a man drop down from the rocks and approach the Lodge from the opposite side to where the carriage was waiting. The man, who had a sack over his shoulder, strode quickly to the door and went inside. Simpkins was offering the two horses a nosebag of hay and seemed to have noticed nothing.

Cora was annoyed that Enoch Heathcote had not turned up, but still she sensed that something suspicious was going on and decided to get a closer look. She crawled through the bracken, clutching the camera in one hand. The knees of her bloomers were stained blue from bilberries she squashed in the heather and soaked from sodden clumps of moss. She reached another boulder, smaller than her original hiding place but within yards of the Lodge. She unfolded the camera and pointed it towards the door. She should be able to take a photograph of someone coming out of the Lodge, she thought, but it was going to be difficult to stay hidden while she did so.

Inside the Lodge, which was cool and dark thanks to the thick stone walls and small windows, Elizabeth Heathcote had waited impatiently for the person who had summoned her there. She was not surprised when the door swung open and Caleb Salt walked in.

"I thought it would be you. So you decided to take things into your own hands, did you? Thought you could cheat me?" she said angrily.

"I've got what you wanted," Salt replied, holding up the sack.

"I only wanted you to find out where it was buried! I didn't pay you to do away with Carter and steal it yourself."

"How was I to know the stubborn old fool would take so long to talk? I didn't know he would snuff it. Anyway I got rid of Sneyd for you, just like you ordered."

"Yes, but when I paid you for Sneyd I didn't know you had already hoodwinked me and stolen the cross," Elizabeth said bitterly. She nodded at the sack. "Come on, show it to me, then."

Salt placed the sack on a table and took out what looked to be a roll of leather, stained and cracked with age. He unrolled it to reveal a cross nearly two feet long, cast in solid gold and decorated with rubies and emeralds. The gold shone despite the gloom, facets of the precious stones reflecting light from the window. The cross had come a long way since it was created by craftsmen in the Holy Land nearly a thousand years before. First a focus of worship in Jerusalem, then carried across Europe by victorious Crusaders before being cherished by monks in the moorlands of Staffordshire. And in the last month it had cost two lives.

Elizabeth Heathcote snatched up the cross and ran her fingers over its richly engraved surface. She clutched it to her chest and a rare look of joy, almost ecstasy, came across her face. "At last," she gasped, her eyes closed. "A gift from God. The Heathcote family has waited more than three hundred years for this day."

"Where's the money?" Salt asked curtly. He wanted the transaction over and to leave as quickly as possible.

Mrs Heathcote was roused from her reverie and put the cross down. She reached into her handbag and produced an envelope which she thrust at Salt. "Here, you devil. Take your money and get out of my sight."

Salt looked in the envelope and ran his thumb over a wad of £10 notes. He was used to counting his betting returns and this looked about the right amount. He flung the door open and marched towards the carriage, startling Simpkins who had been dozing on his bench seat. Salt reached up, wrenched the groom to the ground and knocked him out with a fierce blow to the head.

He seized the reins and was about to make off in the carriage when he saw a figure appear from behind a boulder a few yards away. It was a young woman, peering at something in her hands. Was that a camera? In a flash he guessed that Elizabeth Heathcote had set some kind of trap – more photographs taken, more proof against him.

"Hey, you!" Salt shouted and jumped from the carriage. He started towards the girl.

Cora turned and began to run across the hillside as fast as she could. She was young and nimble enough to jump between the tussocks of rough grass, but her legs were tired after the bicycle ride and she was nowhere near as powerful as the six-foot-plus fighter who was pursuing her. She was driven on by the sudden thought that this could be Amos Carter's murderer, the man responsible for the horror in the barn. She wanted to scream, but was panting too hard.

Salt was getting closer, Cora could hear him breathing and the sound of his boots in the bracken. She tried to run faster, but her legs felt like lead. She found herself scrambling wildly over boulders, then she fell forward. Everything went black.

Chapter Nineteen

Sergeant Reynolds was beginning to enjoy the raw power at his disposal under the long bonnet of the Napier. By the time they were a couple of miles out of the town he had got used to the gears and they were now making good speed along the flat straight road at Blackshaw Moor, dust flying up behind the car. They were halfway to the Roaches. Inspector Ramm held on to his cap with one hand and gripped a handle with the other, praying they could reach Heathcote Lodge in time and in one piece. He was sure they must be exceeding the 14 mph speed limit but he neither cared, nor dared look across at the speedometer.

Approaching the Three Horseshoes Inn Reynolds saw a carriage coming in the opposite direction and slowed so as not to frighten the horses. As the carriage passed, Mrs Gamage called out from the rear seat. "That's Mrs Heathcote's!"

Ramm swivelled round to see that the carriage had a single occupant, a man whipping the pair of thoroughbreds as it sped towards Leek. It looked to be the burly character he had seen in Blake's photographs. Caleb Salt.

"Stop the car!" the Inspector ordered and the Sergeant pulled on the brake. Ramm thought fast. "I'm going to get out and follow that carriage. You and Mrs Gamage go up to the Lodge and see what's gone on. I have a bad feeling about this." Without further ado Ramm jumped down from the car and ran back towards the Three Horseshoes, about fifty yards away, where he had seen a battered cart drawn up outside.

He burst through the door of the inn, found out who owned the cart and pulled the man away from his pint. "Police business. I need you to take me to Leek. Now!"

The man stirred his nag into life and the cart trundled off towards Leek, Inspector Ramm leaning forward and peering into the distance, even though he expected that Caleb Salt was long gone. He just hoped Salt would halt at some point. Ramm wondered why the suspect was heading away from his usual haunts on the moors. Perhaps he had a hiding place in Leek or perhaps he had other plans. An idea came to Ramm – Salt might be making for the railway station.

A strange scene greeted Reynolds and Mrs Gamage when they reached Heathcote Lodge. Simpkins, the groom, had a black eye and was kneeling at the doorway dabbing Elizabeth Heathcote's forehead with a wet cloth. She was lying on the ground semi-conscious and also showing every sign of having been hit about the head. She was clinging to what looked like a bundle of old leather and groaning incoherently.

Margaret Gamage crouched to attend to her mistress while Reynolds addressed the groom. "What's gone on here, my man?"

"I was sitting waiting for Madam to come out of the Lodge when some fellow ran up and gave me such a clout he knocked me out," said Simpkins, still a little dazed. "It must have been a robber because by the time I woke up the carriage was gone and Madam was lying here looking like he had belted her as well."

Simpkins sat down on the ground groggily and Reynolds went to check on Mrs Heathcote.

"Who did this, Madam?" the Sergeant asked. Mrs Heathcote mumbled something and shook her head. Either she could not or would not reply.

"This lady needs some attention. We should take her back to the station and send for a doctor," Reynolds said to Mrs Gamage.

Taking an arm each, they lifted Elizabeth Heathcote to her feet and guided her to the car. It was slow progress, her unsteady gait further impeded by the heavy package which she refused to let go. They helped her into the rear seats, Mrs Gamage held her upright and Simpkins got in the front, somewhat bemused to see the officer behind the steering wheel.

The motor car rumbled off down the track from the Lodge and onto the lane which would carry them towards Leek. No one noticed Cora's bicycle hidden in the ferns.

Urging his new companion to coax extra speed from the aged horse, Ramm told the man to drive the cart directly to Leek Railway Station. Ideally he would have liked to have stopped at the police station and summoned help, but he dared not waste a minute in his pursuit of Caleb Salt. When they reached the railway station he saw the Heathcote carriage standing in a corner of the cobbled forecourt. There was no sign of the wanted man.

The Inspector jumped from the cart and dashed through the station entrance. He ran along the platform, looking urgently from side to side, scanning groups of passengers to see if any resembled the man whom Blake had photographed at Flash.

Turning back he saw a plume of smoke as a train neared the station from the south. He looked across to the opposite platform where travellers were now moving forward ready to board the approaching train, bound for Macclesfield. Amongst them he spotted a tall figure who he was sure was Salt.

Ramm gave a mighty shout and pointed to where Salt was standing: "Stop that man!"

He glanced back to see that the train would be in the station any second and realised that he was about to lose sight of the suspect. He leapt from the platform and clambered across the tracks, barely feet from the front of the approaching locomotive. The driver sounded the train's whistle furiously.

On the other side of the track Ramm struggled to haul himself up onto the platform. "Want a hand Inspector?" Two men who Ramm vaguely recognised reached down, grabbed a wrist each and pulled him to safety. Breathless, he got to his feet in time to see Salt turn and start to run away. "After him!" he shouted to the startled onlookers.

Nathaniel Blake had been standing at the carriage door as his train returned from Alton and pulled into Leek. Lowering the window, he put his head out and looked towards the station – and saw the extraordinary sight of Inspector Ramm being lifted from the path of the train. The policeman was shouting and pointing, and then Blake saw why. Was that Caleb Salt disappearing into the crowd? Folk didn't seem to understand what was going on, but Blake did – and he knew he had to help.

With his heavy camera case slung over his shoulder and his tripod in one hand Blake opened the carriage door and stepped unsteadily onto the platform almost before the train had come to a halt. He looked around, spotted a station porter and called "Young man! Take these – I'll be right back." He handed his equipment to the surprised youth and started to run towards Ramm, who was by now pushing his way through a melée of passengers who were either leaving the train or trying to get on it.

As Blake caught up with the Inspector he saw Salt jump down from the back of the platform and head towards the station sidings. "Mr Blake, on the scene as usual, I see," said a breathless Ramm.

No one else had joined the chase, so it was the two of them versus Salt. Side by side, they jumped down from the platform and began to cross the tracks of the sidings. They lost sight of Salt behind a line of stationary coal trucks. Blake hauled himself onto the coupling between two trucks and then jumped down on the other side. Ramm managed to do the same but twisted his ankle as he landed.

"Damn and blast. Where is the man?" said Ramm, exasperated by his own lack of fitness as much as the elusive Caleb Salt.

Blake's gaze searched the scene ahead. More railway trucks were lined up at the coal wharf which adjoined the canal basin. In the background loomed the town gas works, a collection of tall, windowless buildings, smoking chimneys and metal gas holders. Then he glimpsed Salt trying to hide on the far side of a coal truck. "There! Behind that wagon," said Blake, pointing at the spot.

Salt was on the move again. He looked about wildly, considering which way offered his best escape. The canal was only yards away, but he would be easy to see on the towpath. The main Newcastle Road was close too, but he would have to scale a steep embankment to reach it. Then he spotted a small tunnel sunk into the side of the embankment. A conveyor climbed into it at an angle from the coal wharf, a chain of metal buckets inching forward as two workmen laboriously filled them with coal.

Salt ran to the conveyor and, ignoring protests from the workmen, jumped onto it and began to scramble towards the tunnel. Grabbing the edge of buckets to steady himself on the moving conveyor, he bent low as he reached the mouth of the tunnel. It had not been built to take a man and Salt threw himself almost flat on the coal containers to fit below the tunnel roof.

Blake and Ramm reached the coal wharf just in time to see Salt disappear into the dark opening in the embankment.

"What now?" asked the photographer.

"We have to follow," replied Ramm. Turning to the two workers he shouted: "You men! Stop this contraption. We're getting on it."

The conveyor ground to a halt and Inspector Ramm, still limping from his injured ankle, stepped onto it with his decent foot. He swung his other leg up and began to climb slowly but tenaciously along the buckets. Blake looked around uncertainly and realised he had no alternative but to follow.

When they reached the tunnel, both men were forced to scramble along on their hands and knees. It was dark and dirty in the sloping shaft that led beneath the road. Their trousers were soon filthy, their hands covered in coal dust and bleeding from cuts and torn fingernails.

Emerging on the other side they tumbled from the conveyor as it abruptly slanted steeper to enter the gas works buildings. They gulped for air, but there was little relief in an atmosphere thick with sulphurous fumes, smoke and steam.

Blake looked up at the towering building in the middle of the site. *"Ex fumo dare lucem"* was picked out in light coloured brickwork seventy feet above him. "To give light from smoke", the words of a Roman poet was now used as a gas company slogan. Ramm, who was standing beside him, began to cough partly from the fumes and partly the exertion. He spotted Salt across the yard and managed to find enough breath to blow his whistle and shout "Stop!"

Salt turned around to look menacingly at his pursuers, then snatched open a door in the great building behind him and ran inside.

"You go first Mr Blake and I'll follow. I can't keep up, not with this ankle," said Ramm. "Quick man!" he added as he sensed Blake hesitate.

Blake threw down his jacket and ran across the cobbled yard, pulling open the door that Salt had gone through. He was knocked back by the heat and fumes of the hellish interior. This was where mountains of coal were heated to release the gas that fed street lights, wall lamps and cookers across the town. He stared up at a mass of iron vessels and pipework rising perhaps six storeys high. He could hear the roar of flames and the hiss of steam.

He peered around to see where Salt might be hiding and was about to check behind a bank of vertical pipes, creaking ominously with the heat, when he heard the sound of footsteps from above. He looked up to see Salt, some twenty feet above him, making his way along a fragile-looking iron gantry that circled the inside of the building. Blake had a fear of heights. Normally he would have gone nowhere near a gangway like that, but today he had no choice. He dashed to a metal staircase and climbed the steep open treads as fast as he could.

By the time he reached the next level his legs were shaking. He dared not look down through the open grating beneath his feet. Grasping a feeble handrail he leaned out cautiously to see where Salt might be, then staggered back as the handle of a shovel struck him on the shoulder. Salt had thrown it from above. Blake cried out as much in shock as in pain, then cowered with his hands over his head as a heavy spanner and a wrench bounced off the walkway. Pain was knifing into his neck and shoulder, although he knew it would have been much worse if one of Salt's missiles had hit him on the head.

"Give up, man! The police are waiting in the yard. You can't escape." Blake tried to sound confident as he shouted upwards to where he thought Salt was standing. Inspector Ramm was still the only policeman below them, but he had now ordered the yard gates to be locked and was assisted by the works foreman who was keeping watch on the door.

Blake made his way around the walkway and went up another flight of steps. He neared the top in time to see Salt at the bottom of a vertical metal ladder leading ever higher. Blake hated ladders, but adrenaline drove him on and he too made for the ladder. The higher he climbed, the hotter he became. He was gasping for breath and his shirt was soaked with sweat as he hauled himself upwards, blanking out his fear by focusing on the pencil-thin rungs. Above him, Salt ran along a gangway, barging past a man shovelling coal into a hopper and another who was turning an iron valve wheel. Stripped to the waist and streaked with sweat and dirt, both turned in amazement at an intruder in their domain.

The air was baking hot and clouded with smoke and steam as Blake climbed on to the highest gantry. He paused to wipe his steamed-up spectacles on a corner of his shirt. Looping them back on his ears he saw that Salt had halted at the end of the walkway and had turned to confront him, fists clenched.

"Get out of my way you fool!" he snarled.

"Give yourself up. There's no way out," Blake replied, surprised at his own fortitude with a man who he had last seen battering an opponent in the boxing ring.

"Who the hell are you to tell me what to do?"

"My name's Blake. I want to know what happened with Carter and Sneyd."

"So you're Blake! The one that's caused all the trouble," said Salt angrily. "Let me pass or you'll finish up down there," he added, pointing over the handrail.

Blake was determined to keep him talking. This might be his only chance to speak to Salt. "Why did you do it? Was Heathcote behind it all?" he asked.

"That Heathcote witch you mean. She's the one you should be chasing." Salt glanced downwards and saw movement below. Inspector Ramm and two men were blocking the doorway, peering up to see what was going on.

Salt turned and tried the handle of a low wooden door, some kind of inspection hatch, set into the wall. He wrenched it open and looked out, daylight slanting into the darkened interior.

Blake realised that the man was going to jump through the hatch – to what he was sure would be certain death sixty feet below.

Blake lunged forward and grabbed hold of Salt who toppled backwards dragging the photographer with him. Both plunged through the opening and out into the daylight.

A terrifying blur of sky, rooftops and tangled metal flashed before Blake. Then his breath was punched from his chest as he sprawled onto a sheet of corrugated iron just feet below the opening. They had landed on the narrow roof covering a conveyor which carried coke out of the gas-making plant before cascading it onto a conical heap below.

Blake clung facedown, trying not to panic. The metal framework was shaking as the conveyor rattled along beneath them. He raised his head to see Salt crawling towards a metal tower that supported the far end of the structure.

Salt stood up and began to walk precariously towards the tower and his escape. He never made it. His foot slipped and he fell sideways, the rusted corrugated iron tearing into his hand as he made a desperate grab for its edge. He lost his grip and pitched off the roof, through the air and onto the pile of coke far below. He screamed out in pain as the skin of his back, arms and legs was seared off when he plummeted down the steaming hot coke. As he came to rest at the bottom of the pile, Inspector Ramm and the two workmen took hold of him and pulled him onto the cobbled yard.

While the workmen stood over the groaning Salt, Ramm ordered a yard lad to run to the railway station and tell the stationmaster a cart was needed straight away. "We need to get this man to the Cottage Hospital – before he goes to the cells," he said.

The Inspector looked up to see that Blake was still on the metal roofing above the conveyor, holding on for dear life. As he watched, a workman reached out through the hatch to persuade Blake to his feet and pull him to safety.

It was some minutes before Blake could face going back down the metal ladders and stairs. He simply sat hunched on the gangway, spectacles on his forehead, hands around his knees, trying to come to terms with what had gone on in the last hour. His shoulder hurt, his legs and arms ached, his hands were scratched and blistered, his clothes were filthy. But Salt had been captured.

A semi-conscious Caleb Salt was lying in the yard when Inspector Ramm formally arrested him on suspicion of two murders. The fugitive managed to groan only a few words: "The Heathcote woman's to blame."

As Salt was lifted into the back of a cart, an envelope slipped from the pocket of his breeches. Ramm picked it up, saw the wad of banknotes and confiscated the evidence. He and Blake climbed onto the bench beside the driver. Their first stop was the railway station where Ramm used the stationmaster's telephone to call the police station and the photographer collected his equipment from the left luggage office. He ordered two constables be sent to the hospital to guard the prisoner when he arrived.

At Leek Police Station, Ramm's colleagues had known nothing of the drama at the gas works. When Sergeant Reynolds had arrived in the Napier car, his first thought had been to place Elizabeth Heathcote in Inspector Ramm's office, but was shocked to find a stranger sitting behind the desk. Before Reynolds could say anything, the man stood up and spoke. "Sutcliffe's the name, Detective Inspector. Perhaps you can tell me what's going on."

To the detective's growing surprise, Reynolds gave a brief but colourful account of events at Longview and the Lodge. He was relieved when Sutcliffe agreed that Mrs Heathcote should be detained until they were sure what exactly had happened. Simpkins was allowed to leave.

Elizabeth Heathcote, leaning on Margaret Gamage, was ushered into a spare office. She was still clinging to the package. The Heathcote family doctor was summoned to attend to her bruised face and he said he would send a sedative dose to calm her nerves.

In the meantime she sipped a cup of tea, declaring the awful fate that awaited the Inspector for the way she was being treated.

Inspector Ramm eventually arrived limping, uniform coated in coal dust, trousers torn and a bloody handkerchief wrapped around his hand. A similarly battered Nathaniel Blake was at his side. Reynolds, shocked at their appearance, kept his voice low as he warned Ramm that both a Detective Inspector and Mrs Heathcote awaited.

Ramm turned to the photographer. "Mr Blake, you have done us a great service. Go home and rest." With heavy steps, Blake set off towards Moorside Terrace with his camera case in one hand and his tripod in the other.

Ramm was walking just as slowly as he went to his office. Finding his desk occupied by the newcomer, he slumped in the spare chair.

"Inspector Ramm, it appears you have been fully occupied today," said the detective.

Ramm was too tired to bristle at the inference he was not normally this busy. "The main suspect arrested, another detained, vital evidence secured. Yes, I think we have been done enough," he said with some satisfaction.

At that moment a constable tapped on the door and announced: "Mr Heathcote's in the front office, Sir."

When Enoch Heathcote had alighted at Leek railway station from his meeting in Manchester he had been puzzled to find not only Simpkins waiting for him in the Napier, but also the family's carriage in the corner of the courtyard. From the groom's garbled account, Enoch learned that Elizabeth was at the police station and so made haste to her rescue. Striding into the front office he had demanded to see Inspector Ramm.

"What precisely is going on, Inspector? Have you gone mad, man?" he shouted, his bulging eyes fixed on the officer across the counter.

"We need to speak to Mrs Heathcote on a number of very serious matters, Sir."

"Then I insist on being present when you do so. By the sound of it, Elizabeth has had an horrific experience – robbed, assaulted, detained by the police – and she must have my support and be out of here as soon as possible."

Grudgingly Ramm agreed and so, shortly afterwards, six people crammed into his office. Ramm, Detective Inspector Sutcliffe and a note-taking constable on one side of the desk; Elizabeth Heathcote, her husband and Margaret Gamage on the other. Ramm thought it was an unsatisfactory arrangement, but he was determined to wring some sort of admission from at least one of the Heathcotes.

Elizabeth had regained some of her usual combative attitude and was looking around the room agitatedly. Enoch focused his attention on Sutcliffe, spying an opportunity to impress and inveigle the newcomer with his position in society. It was to no avail. Sutcliffe, who had barely caught up with the rapid turn of events, agreed that Ramm should lead the questioning and settled down to observe proceedings with the detached air of a school examiner. Margaret Gamage looked decidedly uncomfortable about what might be revealed.

"Mrs Heathcote, let's start with today's distressing events. Why did you go to Heathcote Lodge?" asked Ramm.

"Why shouldn't I visit our own property?" she shot back.

"Were you not meeting Caleb Salt there?" Ramm continued. Enoch Heathcote, who had been looking solicitously at his wife, suddenly stared at the Inspector.

"Caleb Salt? Is that the man who robbed me?" Elizabeth replied.

"It was he, I believe, who wrote to you asking you to meet him." Ramm flourished Salt's tattered note he taken from Mrs Heathcote's writing desk. She snatched the paper off him and stared at it.

"Where did you get this from?" she asked sharply, her voice rising.

"Calm down, dear," said Enoch, patting his wife's arm. She pushed him away.

"It was in your bureau and addressed to you. I suggest you went to Heathcote Lodge and gave Salt the £500 he demanded. The money was found in his possession."

"My bureau?" said Elizabeth, swivelling to glare at Margaret Gamage. The reality of her predicament was beginning to sink in.

"Was that payment for the object you are so keen to keep hold of?" Ramm continued, prompting Mrs Heathcote grip the leather package even tighter. "Perhaps we could see what it is?"

"No, no," she wailed, her face becoming a mask of manic determination. An unholy scuffle broke out as Ramm reached forward for the package, Elizabeth reared backwards, Margaret Gamage tried to stop her falling, while Enoch got to his feet and began to protest. The precious item clattered to the floor. Sutcliffe was forced to intervene. "Please Mr and Mrs Heathcote, can we have some co-operation?"

Ramm came around the desk and snatched up the package as Elizabeth shouted "No, give that back! It belongs to the Heathcote family!"

The room fell silent as Ramm unwrapped the leather bindings to reveal the golden cross in all its glory. It was the first time he had seen the jewel-encrusted cross and he had a flash of understanding how such a treasure could drive people to do awful things. He placed it on the desk and looked at Mrs Heathcote. There were tears running down her face.

"Glorious isn't it? The Heathcotes have waited centuries for this day," she said with wavering voice, a distant look in her eyes. Then she became aggressive again. "My ancestors were granted the Abbey and everything that went with it. Everything! The land, the buildings, the stock! Except what that devious abbot stole. He took what was rightfully ours. But now," she pointed triumphantly at the cross, "now, we have it at last!"

This woman is mad, thought Ramm. He glanced across at Enoch who was looking aghast at his wife's outburst.

"So Caleb Salt stole it for you?" asked Ramm, but before she could answer Enoch interrupted. "Elizabeth my dear, you don't have to say any more." She ignored her husband.

"I sent Salt to question that numskull Carter, when *he*," she pointed at Enoch, "couldn't find out anything from the man. Useless, once again. But I never told Salt to kill Carter. That was all his doing and then he stole the cross for himself."

"How did you know about the cross? When Dr Sneyd wrote to you?"

"My family had known for many years that there was a missing treasure, but we didn't know where to look. Thanks to Dr Sneyd we knew it had been buried. But then Sneyd himself turned up and started to sniff around," she replied.

"And that's when you decided Dr Sneyd had to killed. You couldn't allow the man to get in your way." Ramm's statement struck Elizabeth silent and her expression hardened. Her confessions had come to an end.

Ramm pulled the copy of the letter to Sneyd from his pocket and held it towards her.

"You wrote this letter to Dr Sneyd, did you not? Pretending to be the Vicar to lure the poor man to the church where Caleb Salt was waiting for him. And Salt did the dirty work you paid him for."

Elizabeth pushed the letter away. "I do not know what you are talking about," she said imperiously.

"You cannot deny that this is your writing. I'm sure your husband recognised your hand when I showed him the letter yesterday, and certainly Mrs Gamage did."

At this new betrayal Elizabeth glared at her companion.

"After the deed was done, you sent Bernard Gamage to remove

the evidence from Dr Sneyd's room. But you did not know that someone else had already seen those letters and copied them."

Elizabeth still looked impassive. Ramm rose to his feet and addressed her solemnly.

"Caleb Salt is under arrest and has already implicated you in the crimes. We have witnesses, we have the evidence and now, Mrs Heathcote, we have you. I hereby arrest you for conspiring to murder Mr Amos Carter and soliciting the murder of Dr Crosbie Sneyd. Additional charges, including theft and forgery, may be placed in due course."

Elizabeth said nothing and stared at the cross on Ramm's desk. Enoch Heathcote leapt to his feet. "Inspector! This farce must stop!" he ordered.

Emboldened, Ramm turned to the mill owner. "Actually Mr Heathcote, I would like to ask how you were involved in these tragic affairs. You visited Amos Carter several times before his death, no doubt to quiz him about the cross. What more did you know about your wife's plotting?"

"Nothing," Heathcote replied, shaking his head as he looked at Elizabeth sadly. "I never knew that things had come to this, my dear. That you had become so... obsessed." His wife sighed irritably as if trying to ignore his concern.

Ramm pressed on. "Can you explain why you secretly gave Caleb Salt a large sum of money some days ago?"

Enoch Heathcote's usual bravado was draining away. He looked defeated.

"It was a bet. Ask the others if you like. We were betting on Salt winning his fight. I know it was against the law, but I swear to God it was nothing to do with this other... business." He looked across at Elizabeth and started to shake his head again.

Regaining some of his composure he addressed Ramm. "Inspector, permit me to summon my lawyer. Elizabeth and myself need to be properly represented before this... process... can go any further." He was struggling with what had happened in the interview. He needed time to think if there was any way out for them both.

The three police officers got up to leave. Margaret Gamage hesitated until Mrs Heathcote told her to get out. Ramm picked up the cross – "This is now police evidence," he said – and Elizabeth's gaze followed it out of the room.

"Well Inspector, it appears you may not need my assistance after all," said Sutcliffe. Ramm didn't reply. After a day like this, he felt neither triumph nor relief – he was too exhausted.

As Nathaniel Blake neared his front door he could not decide which he needed most – food, a bath or his bed. However he knew that first he would have to explain to Edith how he had got into this state. It was only days since he had arrived home bedraggled after his escape from Flash. This evening he looked even worse.

He opened the door to be greeted by the glow of gas lamps and the blessed smell of supper cooking. Suddenly he felt quite emotional to be amongst home comforts again and had to steady himself before going into the kitchen. His ravaged state would be shock enough for Edith without him bursting into tears. As he put down his camera equipment on the hallway tiles Edith came to greet him.

"Nathaniel! Whatever has become of you? Have you been in an accident?" she said, grasping his arm and looking into his filthy face.

"It is another long story, my dear. I went to help Inspector Ramm and finished up falling from the gas works. The good news is that the mystery of murders may soon be solved."

"Murders? Is that all you can think about?"

Edith was more agitated that he had expected. In fact she seemed on the verge of tears. A moment later he knew why.

"Cora's not home yet," she said.

After the events of the past couple of hours Nathaniel had completely forgotten that Cora was cycling to Meerbrook that afternoon with her school chums. But now it was nearly dark and she should have been home long ago.

Chapter Twenty

Gas lamps cast pools of light on the dark streets of Leek as Nathaniel and Edith Blake set out to find out what had happened to Cora. Although Nathaniel would have preferred to go on his own, his wife was too anxious to stay at home.

"But what if Cora turns up?" Nathaniel had asked her.

"I can't just sit here. I must do something," she had replied before going to ask a neighbour to keep an eye on William and Emily, who were both asleep upstairs.

The Blakes' first call was at the studio in case something had befallen Cora whilst she was there that morning. Nothing appeared amiss downstairs, but when Nathaniel went upstairs to check in the darkroom he spotted his new portable camera was missing from the work bench. Had Cora taken it with her, he wondered.

They hurried to the house which Cora's teacher Miss Keates shared with her unmarried sisters. She had seen nothing of Cora that day and, strangely, she said there had been no plan to go to Meerbrook Church either.

"I can't believe Cora would lie to us," said Edith, shaking her head sadly. "What on earth is the girl up to?"

"Wherever she went, she took her bicycle," replied Nathaniel.

Next the Blakes tried Cora's friend Polly Pickford, but she had not heard from her in days. Nathaniel and Edith looked at each other, feeling increasingly helpless.

"Who else can we try?" Nathaniel asked. Then he recalled FJ Finch telling him that Cora and Oliver had been become friends. They had been investigating the Great Mill together, he had said.

"Finch might know something," Nathaniel announced, taking

Edith's hand and heading towards the newspaper editor's house in Bath Street.

"Nathaniel, Edith, do come in. This is most troubling," said FJ after Blake had explained the reason for their late visit. Showing them into the parlour, he continued. "Oliver may have an idea where she is – he and Cora certainly seemed to be close. He's reporting on a council meeting tonight, but he should be back soon."

The Blakes decided to wait, glad of the chance to sit down. Mrs Finch poured tea and tried to reassure Edith while Nathaniel told FJ of his pursuit of Caleb Salt that afternoon. "But none of that matters now. We simply want to know that Cora is safe," said Blake with an exhausted sigh.

When Oliver arrived he was clearly alarmed to hear about Cora. "I hope she hasn't got into any trouble. You know how... er, headstrong she can be," he said.

"Why do you think she might be in trouble?" Edith asked, more worried than ever.

"Well, she was so determined to find out what Enoch Heathcote was up to. Especially after I said I couldn't help any longer," Oliver replied uneasily. Now more than ever he felt he had let Cora down.

"You mean she might have gone to the mill on her own?" asked Nathaniel. He was feeling guilty too, concerned that his own obsession with the murders and the Heathcotes may have fuelled his daughter's suspicions.

"Not the Great Mill. Ellen Simms told us Mr Heathcote usually takes his… young ladies… to the country on a Tuesday afternoon. They go up to Heathcote Lodge, so perhaps Cora went there."

Heathcote Lodge. The words struck fear into Blake. Inspector Ramm had told him earlier that Salt had been at the Lodge that afternoon. What if Cora had gone there with the camera? What if the murderer had come upon her?

The mention of Heathcote's name also upset Edith. "I said

nothing good would come of concerning ourselves with those people. Now look what's happened," she said.

Blake realised the situation could be even more serious than they had feared. He got to his feet. "We must go to the police!"

"I'm coming with you," said Finch, pulling on his coat.

Nathaniel and Edith almost ran to the police station with FJ and Oliver following. They arrived to find the blue lamp over the entrance glowing, but the door locked. A brass bell-push bore a small sign stating "Press for assistance". Nathaniel did so, waited a few seconds, then impatiently pressed it again for much longer.

They heard the sound of the door being unlocked and Constable Knowles, roused from his room on the first floor, peered out. He shone a bull's eye lamp into the faces of the four people outside.

Without waiting for Knowles to speak, Nathaniel launched into their story, explaining that Cora was missing and she may have somehow become involved with Caleb Salt at Heathcote Lodge. "We need to go and look for her," he said forcefully.

"There are two men on town patrol, Mr Blake. In half an hour they'll report in and I'll tell them to look out for your daughter," said Knowles.

"I'm not talking about the town!" Blake replied, exasperated. "She's probably up on the Roaches, injured or goodness knows what."

Edith gasped as Nathaniel put into words exactly what she feared herself.

"We must see Inspector Ramm about this," said Blake, becoming more agitated.

Finch intervened. "Perhaps, Constable, we can speak to the Inspector? He lives in Queen Street doesn't he? I'm sure he will understand how urgent this is."

"The Inspector might be in bed already, he's had a long day," Knowles replied.

"Haven't we all!" said Blake as the four turned away from the police station and started to hurry towards Queen Street.

Inspector Ramm, wearing a dressing gown over a collarless shirt, was clearly ready to retire for the night and somewhat startled to see the group on his doorstep. But he soon grasped the seriousness of the situation.

"A pity we can't question Salt, but he's unconscious. They've sedated him because of his burns," he said, before telling Finch: "Find a carriage or something big enough to take us all up to the Roaches. Tell them it's police business. Then meet us at the police station." Finch hurried off to call in a favour from one of his contacts.

"I wonder if Mrs Heathcote might know something?" suggested Nathaniel.

"I'll speak to her when we get to the station. I've got her tucked up in the cells, but only after her husband insisted on sending over a few home comforts," Ramm replied sourly.

Roused from her cell, a disgruntled Elizabeth Heathcote claimed to have seen nothing of Cora and was of no help.

Edith, now feeling worn out with worry, realised she could not face the journey to the moors and agreed it was best she returned home. "Just bring her back safe, Nathaniel," she said, squeezing her husband's hand.

It was eleven o'clock by the time the search party set off. Finch had used the missing girl's plight to good advantage and managed to borrow a wagonette pulled by two horses. Inspector Ramm sat beside the driver while the others – now including Constable Knowles on Ramm's orders – faced each other on the two benches in the rear. They started the jolting journey in near silence – all had their minds on what might lie ahead.

Blake's emotions were conflicted: he was afraid Cora was lying injured somewhere, he was disappointed she hadn't told them the truth, but also he had a touch of pride at his daughter's determination. Oliver was wracked with regret for not helping the lively young woman he had known only a month. FJ was concerned for the Blakes, of course, and yet couldn't help being excited by the unfolding drama. Only Ramm truly appreciated the difficulty of their task on a rock-strewn moorland in the pitch dark. He and Blake also shared another reason to be fearful – they had both seen the result of Salt's violence before.

The wagonette was on the edge of town when Ramm spotted a familiar figure walking at the roadside and asked the driver to rein in the horses.

"Where are you bound for, Mr Gibb?" the Inspector shouted.

"Tonight it's a barn just along the road, Inspector," replied John Gibb, looking up at the policeman before casting a quizzical eye over the serious expressions of the passengers. "What's to do? It looks like some serious business is afoot."

"Cora's gone missing, Mr Gibb, and we're going to look for her," Blake explained.

"Well, if you don't mind, I'll join you," said Gibb. He unslung his pack and climbed into the cart.

They trundled on towards the high ground above Leek, Ramm and Blake taking it in turns to tell the tramp what had gone on over the last few days. As he recounted Salt's capture Blake was reminded how important John Gibb had been to the investigation. There was much to thank him for, he thought. In fact Blake felt a kind of bond had grown between them and was glad to have Gibb along tonight.

Ramm saw a lamp glowing in the window of the Three Horseshoes on Blackshaw Moor as he passed it for the second time that day. Up ahead, he could make out the jagged silhouette of Ramshaw Rocks in occasional gleams of moonlight. Laden with seven people, the wagonette made slow progress as it climbed towards the moors, splashing through the ford at Upperhulme and past the village dye works before climbing again to the rocky slopes of the Roaches. There was little sign of life, apart from the occasional bark of a farmyard dog or the screech of an owl.

"It's not far now, watch out for the gateposts on the right," said Finch, who liked to think he knew every nook and cranny of his newspaper's patch. He was familiar with the curiously-designed lodge, and so too was John Gibb who regularly tramped these moors.

Minutes later the cart turned onto the track which led to Heathcote Lodge. The men got down and Constable Knowles unloaded a crate containing half a dozen bull's eye lamps, which he proceeded to light and hand out. There was a smell of burning oil in the night air as smoke started to filter from the lamps' chimneys.

"Where do we start?" asked Blake, clearly at a loss as he peered around in the dark. The hillside's covering of ferns, heather, bilberry bushes and tufts of coarse grass was occasionally illuminated silvery grey when the moon appeared from behind clouds, but for most of the time little could be seen in the blackness.

"Cora! Cora are you here my dear?" Blake shouted and then the others joined in, calling her name as they looked in different directions across the moorland.

Ramm took charge. "First we should check around the Lodge, although I'm sure Sergeant Reynolds would have seen Cora this afternoon if she had been close by," he said. The group searched in front and on either side of the Lodge and even shone their lamps up the sheer rock face at the rear. The door was still unlocked, but there was no sign of Cora inside.

Next Ramm told the men to form a line and to walk slowly across the piece of moorland that fronted the Lodge. "Keep spaced out and in a straight line. If we do this higgledy-piggledy we might miss something. If anyone finds anything, call out and I'll come to take a look. The rest of you hold your positions."

Oliver, nearest the gateway, was the first one to call out as he nearly tripped over Cora's bicycle hidden in the undergrowth. "Inspector! Here! I think it's her bike."

The others halted, but despite Ramm's orders Blake couldn't stop himself charging through the heather towards where Oliver stood waving his lamp.

"Yes, it belongs to Cora," said Blake, his voice breaking with emotion. He stooped to shine the lamp closer and saw the leather case fastened to the handlebars. "Well, look at that. She did bring the camera with her!" he exclaimed. Now he was sure what his daughter had been up to – trying to take photographs to use as evidence, just as he himself had done at Flash.

"This means she definitely came to the Lodge – and she might still be here, somewhere," said Ramm. "Back to the search!"

By the light of their lamps they resumed their steady progress. Gibb, more used to walking on rough moorland at night than the others, strode purposefully forward. He looked from side to side, using a broken stick to poke around in the heather. Then he stopped and peered at a patch which seemed blacker than the ground around it.

"Men! Watch your step!" he called out, his tone recalling those long-ago days when he was a Sergeant Major. "There are old mine shafts around here. I've nearly stepped in one."

He was just about to walk around the mouth of the treacherous shaft when he halted again and then leaned forward in concentration. He thought he had heard something, but then the sound was lost in the noise of the others moving through the undergrowth.

"Men, be still! I need to listen, if you please," Gibb shouted.

It was an unlikely situation, a tramp telling a police inspector and a newspaper editor what to do. But like a well-drilled platoon, the search party stood stock still, hardly daring to breath in case the Scotsman was on to something.

Gibb listened, focusing all his attention on the black hole in the heather. There it was again, a faint whimper like an injured animal – or a person. He flattened himself on the ground and crawled forward until his face was over the mouth of the hole. "Is that you Cora?" he called into the shaft.

"Help me, please!" came the faint reply, a desperate plea from the darkness below.

Gibb scrambled to his feet and shouted triumphantly to the others. "She's here! She's down below!"

Patches of yellow light converged on Gibb until all the lamps were aimed at a ragged hole in the ground, wide enough to take a man.

"Cora! My dear, are you hurt?" Blake shouted into the shaft.

"Father? I'm….." Cora's voice tailed off.

"We need a ladder and some rope," said Inspector Ramm. "Knowles, use the cart and find the nearest farm. Quickly man!"

"I'm going down there," said Gibb, throwing off his customary overcoat and rolling up his sleeves. He didn't intend to discuss the matter. "I've been in one or two of these holes in the past and there's usually footholds or some such. I'll climb down and see where the girl is… and what condition she's in."

Blake began to protest, "No, Mr Gibb, it should be me…," but before he could say any more Gibb was lowering himself over the lip of the mine. Oliver darted forward to give the Scotsman a hand until he had a firm footing, then the others moved closer to the edge and shone their lamps downwards. They saw Gibb's head and shoulders gradually recede into the hole.

Gibb was soon in the total darkness, feeling the sides of the roughly hewn shaft for ledges for his feet and something to hold onto. Thankfully, when the shaft had been sunk years ago, iron stakes had been driven into the rock at regular intervals. He moved slowly, in fear of dislodging debris onto the girl below, or worse still, losing his grip and falling down himself.

Finally he reached the bottom and felt around him to find Cora crumpled on the ground. He crouched down beside her and said gently "It's all right, my dear. We'll soon have you out of here, don't worry," although he was not sure how that was going to be accomplished.

"What's happening Mr Gibb?" came a muffled shout from above.

"We're at the bottom of the hole. It's not too deep, thank God," Gibb shouted upwards before asking Cora, "Where does it hurt?"

Cora was exhausted and barely able to speak because her throat was so dry. She had been drifting in and out of consciousness and had no idea how long she had been in the hole. But now she rallied a little, thinking her ordeal might be coming to an end.

"Everything hurts!" she sobbed. "My ankle and wrist are the worst and my chest hurts, too." She put her hand out and recoiled when she touched Gibb's bushy beard, but was reassured that at least she wasn't imagining her rescuer. "I thought I was going to die," she said.

"Can we do anything, Mr Gibb? How is Cora?" This time it was Blake shouting from the surface.

"When you've got the rope, send a lamp down first. It's as black as hell in here," Gibb replied.

He had an overwhelming sense of responsibility for the brave young woman. He'd helped countless young recruits when he was in the Highlanders, but had never had children of his own and nowadays led a solitary life. Now he felt a sudden rush of emotion – he had to get Cora out of there.

Blake was growing increasingly impatient as they waited for Knowles to return and had started to pace around, peering into the dark. "Where on earth has your man got to? This is taking far too long. Cora's in pain down there," he said to Inspector Ramm.

FJ Finch reached into his pocket and produced a hip flask, which he uncapped and handed to Blake. "Nathaniel, a swig of this might calm your nerves. And have one yourself, Inspector," said Finch.

Minutes passed in silence other than for the distant yelp of a fox across the moors. Then all four of them turned as they heard the sound of the cart on the lane. It had barely come to rest at the Lodge when Knowles leapt down and started to dash towards where they stood, stumbling on unseen rocks as he carried a substantial coil of rope.

"Sorry Inspector, the farmer took some waking. I hope this is long enough," said Knowles as he held out the rope to Ramm.

Ramm tried to fasten one of the lamps onto the rope, but cursed when he found it was too thick to pass through the handle of the lamp. Oliver whipped off his tie, threaded it through the handle and then knotted both ends securely to the rope. With a nod of thanks to Oliver, Ramm started to lower the lamp slowly into the hole, taking care the oil didn't spill or the flame go out.

Gibb could see the glow from the lamp grow stronger as it dangled closer and finally he reached up and untied it. He cast its beam around and for the first time saw Cora. Startled by the sudden brightness, she raised a hand in front of her eyes. Blood had dried from a gash on her forehead and her face was streaked where tears had run in rivulets through the dirt on her cheeks. One wrist was twisted at an unnatural angle and her legs were doubled up underneath her. Seeing her bloomers torn he quickly turned the lamp away.

A substantial wooden ladder was brought from the cart and lowered cautiously into the hole. Once Gibb had manoeuvred it into the base of the shaft, the top of the ladder was a couple of feet short of the surface.

"Now, let's get you out of here," Gibb said to Cora, then pulled on the rope. "Give me as much slack as you can," he shouted up.

He lifted Cora up and supported her as she stood unsteadily on one foot. Then he gently looped the rope under her arms and secured it around her body. She cried out as she caught her broken wrist against the rock wall and pain shot through legs which had been crushed awkwardly underneath her for nearly twelve hours.

Gibb glanced down to where he had placed the lamp and saw a metallic object glinting amongst the sticks and leaves. Cora saw it too. "Father's camera, I mustn't lose it," she said urgently. He picked it up and stuffed it inside his shirt.

Cora's twisted ankle meant she would not be able to climb the ladder herself, so he planned to climb with her astride his shoulders. Her weight would be no problem and he hoped she could use her good hand to grasp each rung as they moved up. The rope, kept taught from above, would help to steady her. But no matter how careful he was, Gibb knew it was sure to be a painful experience for Cora.

He called up to the surface to explain what he intended, then turned to Cora. "Don't worry, I'm going to take it very slowly and the rope will stop you from falling." She nodded, but by now her whole body was shaking with fear as well as cold.

Gibb crouched down and managed to lift Cora onto his shoulders. She gave another cry of pain and grabbed for the ladder with her good hand to steady herself.

"We're ready to go," Gibb shouted. "Keep the rope tight, but don't pull too hard."

And so he began the painfully slow climb up the ladder, halting on each rung to make sure Cora was safe on his shoulders. On the surface Finch and Blake held the rope taut to support Cora's weight, pulling it as smoothly as they could each time they felt her move upwards.

It seemed to take an agonisingly long time but at last the light of Ramm's lamp picked up movement in the dark shaft and they could see Cora begin to draw closer. Once she neared the top of the ladder, Finch and Blake reached forward into the shaft to seize her under the arms and lift her out. They laid her gently on the heather while Ramm and Knowles hauled Gibb into the open.

"There was a man. He chased me. I thought I was going to die," Cora gasped.

Blake fought back tears of relief as he brushed his daughter's hair from her face. "Hush Cora, you're safe now. It's over."

TWO CHARGED IN CONNECTION WITH LEEK MURDERS. – A quarry worker has been charged with the murders of Leek farmer Mr. Amos Carter and Oxford historian Dr. Crosbie Sneyd. The mysterious deaths had been the focus of a police investigation and widespread speculation for more than a month.

The arrest of Caleb Salt of Axe Edge Cottage, Flash, on Tuesday followed a remarkable chain of events in which the wanted man was chased across Leek Railway Station and into the town's Gas Works. Inspector Albert Ramm, Head of Leek Police, detained Salt with the assistance of Leek photographer Mr. Nathaniel Blake. Salt apparently fell from the top of the Gas Works' Retort House while being pursued by Mr. Blake and is being treated for extensive burns at Leek Memorial Hospital.

In a further startling development, a member of one of the town's most prominent families, Mrs. Elizabeth Heathcote of Longview, Macclesfield Road, has been charged with conspiracy to murder. Mrs. Heathcote is a leading member of the Leek Temperance Society and the wife of Mr. Enoch Heathcote, Managing Director of Heathcote & Company, silk dyers, spinners and weavers. She has been detained in custody at Leek Police Station.

Yet another twist to the investigation has been the discovery this week of a valuable medieval gold cross, believed to have belonged to Dieulacres Abbey. Inspector Ramm said that the existence of the cross was thought to be a factor in the murder of both men.

"We believe that both crimes arose from a desire to possess this ancient artefact. Our investigations are continuing but we are satisfied we have detained the chief suspects involved in this sorry affair," Inspector Ramm told the *Leek Lion*.

Mr. Heathcote was not available for comment as the *Lion* went to press.

DARING RESCUE ON THE ROACHES. – A retired Sergeant Major performed the brave rescue of a Leek teenager who was trapped in a disused lead mine on the Roaches.

The rescue was carried out at dead of night by Sgt. Major John Gibb and followed the disappearance of Miss Cora Blake, of 6 Moorside Terrace, which provoked a frantic search in the late hours on Tuesday.

A search party, which included *Leek Lion* Editor Mr. F.J. Finch and reporter Mr. Oliver Finch, made haste to the Roaches in the belief that Miss Blake, aged 15 years, had cycled there earlier in the day. An inch-by-inch search of an area of moorland near to Heathcote Lodge first revealed Miss Blake's bicycle, and then the unfortunate young woman herself was found in the disused shaft.

While equipment was being found, Sgt. Major Gibb, aged 50 years, sprang into action and descended the mine and gave comfort to Miss Blake who was lying injured some 20 feet below the surface. He then enacted a remarkable rescue by carrying her on his shoulders up a ladder to safety.

Miss Blake's father, photographer Mr. Nathaniel Blake, was present to tend to his daughter until she was transported to Leek Memorial Hospital where she was treated for concussion and fractures to an ankle and wrist. Mr. Blake afterwards praised Sgt. Major Gibb for his quick thinking. "Without him we may never have found Cora or got her out of that hole. We shall be forever in his debt," Mr. Blake told the *Lion*.

Scottish-born Sgt. Major Gibb is no stranger to bravery. He saw active service with the Queen's Own Highlanders in the Afghanistan and Sudan campaigns and was awarded the Distinguished Conduct Medal following the Seige of Khartoum. He has lived at various locations in the Leek and moorlands district for a number of years.

A fund has been launched to pressent the intrepid rescuer with a suitable reward. Donations should be addressed to the *Lion* office in Market Street, Leek.

Epilogue

Four weeks later

Nathaniel Blake looked around the congregation as he sat in St Edward's Church on a bright autumn Sunday morning. The Old Church was full for this special service.

The Blake family were not regular church-goers, but today they were all there. Edith held Eliza in her arms and young William sat between his mother and Cora. Nathaniel had helped Cora along the church path – her foot and wrist were still encased in plaster of Paris– but once they were inside the porch, she had declined his help and reached the pew on her crutches. Heads turned and comments whispered as people saw her enter.

Looking across at her now, Nathaniel thought with pride how Cora was so determined to recover from her injuries and start her life anew – typical of his feisty daughter. The distress of the incident on the Roaches was in the past, but he would always remember how she had been prepared to risk herself for something she cared about. She would be back in the studio soon and from now on he planned to let her take some photographs herself.

Nathaniel saw Inspector Ramm and his wife Edna take their seats. Ramm had kept him up to date with the investigations, so Blake knew that Caleb Salt was due to appear at Stafford Assizes the following week. The murderer was fit enough to stand trial... and face the hangman.

Next Nathaniel spotted John Gibb, smart, straight-backed and barely recognisable as the tramp of a few weeks ago. Folk had been generous to Gibb when they learned of his bravery in rescuing

Cora. The Scotsman had decided to quit his wanderings for a while and was helping Mrs Carter with a few jobs on the farm. He was even wearing his Distinguished Conduct Medal, freshly polished and hanging from a new ribbon that had been donated by one of the town's silk mills. "It's thanks to him that Cora is with us today," thought Blake.

With the organ playing discreetly in the background, there was a murmur of conversation as the congregation waited for the service to begin. Nathaniel guessed that many would be talking about two people who were absent from their usual pew – Enoch and Elizabeth Heathcote.

Although Salt had been captured, Nathaniel couldn't help feeling bitter that the woman who had snared the boxer with her murderous obsession would never stand trial. At a closed hearing, a judge who was an old pal of Enoch Heathcote according to Ramm, had ruled that Elizabeth Heathcote was mentally unfit to be tried. Instead she had been committed to an institution for the rest of her life, not the County Asylum at nearby Cheddleton, but one buried in the North Wales countryside where her husband hoped no one would recognise her.

And despite all Blake's suspicions and pursuit of Enoch Heathcote, the mill owner had not been charged either. Heathcote claimed he knew nothing of what his wife was up to and the police could not prove otherwise.

At least Nathaniel – and Cora – had the satisfaction of seeing Enoch Heathcote disgraced. He had been forced to resign from the Magistrates and the Council, and had disappeared from the district. Longview was shuttered and the Great Mill sold to a Manchester rival who had given Ellen Simms her job back.

"He won't be preying on his young workers again," Nathaniel reflected. "Perhaps I should make this is an end to my detective work."

His thoughts were interrupted when Reverend Maitland stood

to address the gathering. Behind the Vicar, in pride of place on the altar, was the golden cross, its gemstones sparkling as a shaft of sunlight burst through the chancel window.

"We are gathered here to re-consecrate this holy treasure," he began, turning to look at the altar. "A beautiful cross kept by the Christian brothers of Dieulacres Abbey for centuries before they hid it for its own safekeeping. From this day onwards we will cherish it on our own altar. Please stand while we pray...."

As Nathaniel glanced across the aisle he saw Rosa Carter wipe a tear from her eye. Amos Carter's buried secret had been restored to its rightful place.

Historical Note

Although this is a work of fiction, many of the scenes reflect what life was like in Leek and the moorlands in Edwardian times.

Descriptions of the town's markets, the railway station, the gas works and a silk mill are based on contemporary accounts. Some timescales have been amended. Although Leek Agricultural & Horticultural Show was held in early September 1902, the first Longnor Sports did not take place until later in the decade, as did a Trades Union rally in Leek at which Ada Chew spoke.

The ruins of Dieulacres Abbey still stand on the edge of Leek, but nowadays are not accessible to the public. Abbot Whitney did try to retain some of the Abbey treasures after Dissolution, although it's not known if there was a golden cross!

Many of the public houses mentioned are still in business, including the New Inn at Flash and the Three Horseshoes at Blackshaw Moor. The George, where Dr Crosbie Sneyd stayed, was demolished for the widening of Church Street in 1972, as was the nearby Golden Lion where Blake and Finch caught the cart to Longnor (Isaac Smedley did operate such a service in 1902).

Photographs used in the chapter headings were mostly taken in the Edwardian era.

Research sources included:
In the Highlands of Staffordshire by WH Nithsdale
Images of Edwardian Leek by Paul Anderton
Dieulacres Abbey by Michael J Fisher
A History of Trade Unionism in the North Staffordshire Textile Industry by Frank Burchill and Jim Sweeney
The Leek Times edited by MH Miller